HEART

FIRST DANCE

Di Anne Sandvik

Cover Designed by Tiffany Huegele for Tiffany's Designs.

Formatted by Brenda Wright, Formatting Done Wright

Table of Contents

Always remember...
You will live
You will love
You will dance again
- Jennifer Lopez

Steps of the Heart

When I awake some mornings, I have to remind myself that all this is real.

I mean my life now, where I am, and who I have become. Yes, it's all real. I know exactly who I am because I have worked hard to become this "me". But believe me I paid a huge price along the way. My sore aching body reminds me of that fact every morning. I am the reigning World Latin Dance Champion, Victoria Moore. If you had told me five years ago that I would be a Latin dance champion living in a loft apartment in New York City, and owning my own dance studio, I would have told you that you were absolutely crazy.

To this day, mornings are hardest. It's been five years since the day my world turned upside down. The morning when I felt like I lost everything. I can still hear the pounding at my front door.

Opening it to find my husband's boss Scott standing there with such a look on his face. A look that I will never forget. He was there to deliver the news that the love of my life, my amazing husband Blake, had been killed on a job site. The devastating shock and sadness that followed those first few days is still too painful for me to even think about. In that one moment, my life had tragically ended.

One year before Blake's death I had to deal with the tragic loss of my parents. They were killed in a terrible car accident, and as an only child, I had to handle everything: funeral arrangements, selling the home I grew up in and settling their affairs. My husband Blake was there to help me through what I thought was the hardest thing I'd ever had to do. We always had each other's back. Little did I know one year later I would face the unthinkable. Only this time, I had no one. I was alone with nothing but grief, loss and utter emptiness.

I've struggled everyday since Blake's death. Reliving all the memories of our life together. It hurts so much to remember. But I fear more that the memories will fade and become just that, memories. God, how I miss him. He had the most amazing turquoise eyes that changed with his moods. Blake had ruggedly handsome features that were accented by his perfectly bronzed skin. It came from years of working outside in the Florida sun. We shared a love that I know I will never experience again. How do I know this? Because I've chosen to close my heart off. Oh, I've tried dating these past five years but when you compare every man you meet to the one that captured your heart and soul so perfectly you eventually just give up. He was more than just my husband. Blake was my best friend. He was my everything. Why chase perfection

8

when you've already had it? A love like ours only happens once. That's why I have put everything into my career. It's my way to escape the reality of it all. I hide within the comfortable routine of my life. I bet you're wondering how I can consider my life routine. It just happens. You shut yourself off from love, close your heart and then life becomes routine.

Selfish as this will sound, I miss his touch the most. Waking to mornings like this with his memory fresh on my mind reminds me how I loved to wake to his hands and lips all over my body. The site of his perfectly tanned, muscular body draped over mine was my favorite "Good Morning". Blake always referred to himself as my personal alarm clock. Like I said, he was perfection. To remember Blake's touch is painful. But what's worse is to live with that fact that I will never feel it again. There were so many amazing things about him, but the loss of his touch is what I mourn most.

We were in our late twenties when we married. It seemed we were always working so hard just to make ends meet. There was no time and even less money, in those early years of marriage, for children. I learned that day when everything changed, that we had run out of time. All the things we hoped for were never going to happen.

It was a long, emotion filled road that led me to where I am today. I can still remember the day I received the call from my husband's insurance company. They gave me the "we're so sorry for your loss", and told me that had a check ready for me. When I received it, I had no idea he had taken out a million dollar life insurance policy. A letter was enclosed. It was written in Blake's own handwriting and addressed to me. He had taken the time to write me a letter that was to be delivered with the check if anything ever happened to him. The letter is stained with my tears but his words brought me great comfort. I still carry that letter with me to every dance competition as a reminder. A reminder not to give up, to keep going, to move forward in life, and to be happy. He wrote that he never wanted me to have to return to work. He wanted me to enjoy life and do something I always wanted to do.

In Blake's letter he said, "Maybe you should take those dance classes you always wanted us to take, but I was never interested." Ever since I was a young child I have always loved dancing. My mother sent me to the local dance studio and I took ballet, tap and jazz like every other young girl wanting to dance. I've always had this need and desire to not only dance but to perform and be the center of attention. But just like everything in life, we change, we grow, we mature. Real life begins to take over and our dreams are forgotten.

It was just like Blake to think that a million dollars would send me straight to easy street. Yes, the money has made it less difficult, but I still had to work hard to get here. I have learned money is not everything. For me it just helps fill a void for the things that are taken from you. I will be forever grateful to my husband for making sure he provided for me, even after his death.

Financial security did make life more comfortable, but it wasn't until I received an unexpected call from Scott a few months later that made it possible for me to go after my dreams. Blake worked as a technician for Scott's utility company. He was their lead man. It seems my husband was killed due to a piece of machinery that malfunctioned. Scott sued the manufacturer. They sued on behalf of the company, and on Blake's behalf as well. I knew his boss had felt responsible for his death, but I had no idea he would go after the company that built the faulty machinery. He called and told me that there could never be any amount of money that would ease my pain, but that he wanted to do what he could for me. Apparently the manufacturer did not want any bad publicity. They were eager to settle both lawsuits out of court. When he told me the amount they settled for on behalf of my husband, I was shocked. Not only was the settlement for five million dollars, but the manufacturer had also agreed to pay all the attorney fees.

So I was rich as far as money goes, but what I really needed was time to heal. Life had lost all meaning. It was as though I had no purpose. No reason to get out of bed in the morning. My days were empty and I felt there was nothing to look forward to anymore. The real healing didn't take place until a friend of mine stepped in to lend me a much needed helping hand. He was a wonderful man that I had met through work. I call him Dr. R. He was a customer who shopped at the department store where I worked. We became fast friends. Dr. R was a psychiatrist who practiced in the Central Florida area where I was living. He also had an estate in his hometown of Cartageña, Colombia. When he heard about Blake's death he invited me to his casa in Cartageña to help me with the whole healing process. It was my first trip to South America. I knew his intentions were nothing but professional. He has an outstanding reputation in the community helping sexually abused children. Over the years he has become a great friend.

I was not sure exactly how the trip to Cartageña was going to help me, but Dr. R. insisted I needed to step away from everything to begin to heal. I had resigned myself to to a life of sitting on the couch every day and crying. I figured I had nothing else to lose so I took him up on his offer. I had to do something. I was getting so good at picking the "Baby Daddy" before the results were revealed on Maury Povich that I was even starting to worry about myself. No matter how many close friends you have to help you get through something like this, their lives return to normal after a few weeks. But yours doesn't. That is when the reality of everything sets in place. Dr. R. knew this, of course, and stepped in at the right time. If it wasn't for him, I'm not sure what would have happened to me.

My first few days there he left me to myself. He owned a beautiful home on the coast. As cliché as it may sound, I took countless walks on the beach and spent time just thinking and remembering what I had and what I had lost. Once I adjusted to my new surroundings and felt ready to open up and talk, Dr. R and I would meet every afternoon for one on one counseling. During those first sessions we didn't talk much -- instead, he just listened to me cry. Trust me, I cried a lot. It was as though my tears were speaking for me. They represented my pain in a way I just couldn't put into words. At least not yet. Sometimes I wondered how he could do it -- just sit there and let me cry, saying nothing at all about what I was going through. But looking back, I can see now that this was the only way to get to the heart of what I was truly feeling. I was finally grieving. I cried until there were simply no more tears and my tear banks were empty. Eventually, he started doing the talking and pointed out all the wonderful memories I had with Blake. He showed me how, once I began verbalizing those memories, I could feel good about them. How to cherish them and keep them with me forever. It was only then that I was able to step away from the pain and focus on the fact that I had a beautiful marriage with an incredible man. Dr. R reminded me that some people never get the chance to love. Even though Blake was gone, and we shared a short time together, we were among the lucky ones. We had that chance. *We loved.*

Cartageña not only was a place of healing for me, it was my impetus. It was here where I took my first steps toward a completely new life. My new life. A life I could never have predicted.

We spent most evenings going out to dinner to some of the lively neighborhood cafés. The selection of entrée's were a mix of flavors from Spanish to Afro-Caribbean. My favorite was the ceviche: a raw fish marinated in thyme and citrus. A new tantalizing flavor. The hearty empanadas and the stiff margaritas had also become a favorite. It has been said when a person cooks for you they are speaking to you. If that's true, then Cartageña speaks many languages. After dinner was served, they would clear away the tables. The music was turned up and suddenly the atmosphere was filled with electricity. I loved to watch the locals dance. Dancing like I had never seen before. Latin dancing. And I mean REAL Latin dancing. Not the ballroom shit you see on TV. I'm talking about couples moving together with such passion and energy, it would make you blush. As though you were watching something intensely intimate. It was hot. It was exciting. It was sexy.

Dr. R. noticed my fascination and one evening he dared me to accept an invitation to dance with one of the locals. I took his dare. I had no idea what I was doing, but the minute I stepped onto the dance floor I knew it was where I wanted to be. When the young dancer first took me in his arms, I was scared to death. It made me feel so uncomfortable. Their style of dancing was so raw and heated. I almost felt I was doing something unacceptable for a woman who was supposed to be grieving the loss of her husband. But it was also, so liberating to let go. To not worry and just get lost in the dancing. No one here knew anything about me and my suffering. So no one judged me. No one looked at me with those pity filled expressions.

By the end of my stay in Cartageña I had become a regular. There were nights I danced way into the early mornings to the point where my feet ached. Sleep came easily from the sheer exhaustion. At first the dancing was a way to help me forget my pain, and a way to sleep. But as time went on the pain disappeared and I was left with a feeling of joy and contentment. I had discovered that the counseling sessions with Dr. R. weren't the only thing that healed me during my stay. There was no denying it. It was the dancing.

Now I was ready. It was time. Time to put my big girl panties on and go home. I no longer wanted to sit around and feel sorry for myself. I wanted to take that feeling back home with me. I wanted to dance. Crazy as it seemed, I wanted to dance.

When I returned I started looking for a dance studio. A place where I could recapture that time in Cartageña. I found a great studio in the Orlando area that taught all styles of traditional as well as the new Latin dances. After the first few lessons I felt like I was born again into the thing I was meant to be from the very beginning. After that, I never looked back.

Even though my life usually is so full, there is always that tugging feeling at my heart that something is lacking. But not today. Today I have no time. Only for what needs to be done. Planning this season of dance competitions and workshops. Training with my partner, costume fittings, rehearsals, and let us not forget the countless spray tans. I plan on being on the road nonstop for the next six months.

Staying busy keeps my mind from wandering. Dance is what saved me from those dark days in the beginning, when I wasn't sure where I'd be, and what my life would become without my husband, my soul mate. Dance has filled the holes in my life with such joy and accomplishment, and most of all, excitement. It was the way for me to heal from my loss, and keep my mind and body busy. I had the funds to buy the best training available in the Central Florida area. I quickly learned that having the top trainer didn't make it easy. It was easy because I was good. No, I was very good, and I excelled quickly. The first time I was invited to dance competitively, I laughed. Then I thought, "What do I have to lose?" I took first place in that competition, and I was hooked. Addicted was more like it, from then on I never looked back.

In this world at this level competing was not cheap. But I had money that enabled me to buy the best partners. Early on in my career, I made some really bad partner choices. It seemed whoever my partner was at the time, we became romantically involved. What I should really say is that we were sexually involved.

I loved none of these men. Becoming top in the Latin dance world became my obsession. I had no time for love.

I met my current dance partner Mateo Chavez while I was romantically involved with my then-partner, whose name, not surprisingly, escapes me. We were competing for the first time in the World Latin Dance Championships, and it was the first round of preliminaries. On the night before competition was to begin, I caught him in bed with another woman in our hotel room. There was so much tension and hatred between us on the dance floor, we did not make it past the preliminaries. After we lost, I decided to stay and enjoy the rest of the competition. When the final night of competing ended, I joined some of the other dancers to celebrate their win at the hotel bar. Among the winners was Mateo Chavez. It was there he approached me, handing me a business card. As he pressed the card into my hand, he confidently said to me, "When you want to become the next World Latin Dance Champion, call me." Then he simply walked away.

Hell, when the reigning champion offers you an open invitation like Mateo did, you call. Because that is exactly what I wanted. The first thing Mateo told me was that I needed to move to New York City if I wanted to train with him and become his new partner. He said that I had outgrown the talent and training that Central Florida had to offer, and I needed to be in NYC if I wanted to become a champion. I certainly had the money, and no longer had any emotional ties to Florida, so I packed up and said goodbye to my friends and the place I had spent my entire married life.

Like I said, I learned early on being involved with my partner did not work for me. Mateo is an incredibly handsome man. But with Mateo I have no worries. He has no interest in what I have to offer, he plays for the other team. I have used this to my advantage, training and dancing without any distractions. Our style of dancing is so intimate, so with a partner you want to make sure that sexual energy shows. Mateo and I push those limits. We give the audience the illusion of what they want to see but our personal feelings never come in to play. It works for us.

Beside the good looks, Mateo has the body of a Greek Adonis. Women adore him. I tell him all the time he doesn't know what he is missing. But he likes to remind me, he likes dick. He is so strikingly handsome both men and women alike stare at him. Mateo is what I call a head turner. You know what I mean, his drop dead gorgeous looks constantly turn heads. I have seen some women give themselves whiplash staring at him. Ashley, my assistant, thinks he looks like Ricky Martin and I laugh because women have actually stopped Mateo in airports asking for a autograph.

I think I'm not so bad in the looks department myself. You can't compete at the level I do and not have a dancer's body. I'm not only known for the heels I wear dancing but also for my legs. They are flawless because of the time I spend dancing and in the gym. Now Mateo has the Latino good looks but you wouldn't mistake me for a Latin girl. Trust me, I would love to have Jennifer Lopez's looks but I'll have to settle for more of a Jennifer Aniston, All-american girl next door. But I do have a bit of a JLo ass on me. Yep, I got some junk in my trunk.

It's hard for me to say I'm attractive, after all I am a woman with my own insecurities. But Mateo reminds that I am the hottest female on the circuit. Thanks to him I have learned to embrace my looks and use them to our advantage. Not only does the audience love us but the judges do as well. So Mateo and I aren't just the couple to beat, we are the hottest looking ticket on the Professional Latin Dance Circuit. Together, we turn heads!

My move to New York City was a major culture shock. Living in Central Florida was so laid back and quiet compared to New York City. People in Florida are in no hurry and I had to learn that was not the case in the Big Apple. First thing I did was sell my car. No one owns one here. Thankfully Mateo was a big help during those first few months. He taught me everything about NYC. How to hail a cab, ride the subway, where to eat and where to shop. OK, I can hail a cab like a real New Yorker, but to this day I avoid the subway. Most importantly he taught me how to protect myself and be safe. Some days I so miss the Florida weather and the laid back lifestyle. But I knew if I wanted to be a champion Latin dancer I had to give NYC a real chance. I threw myself into the city life and I adjusted very quickly. I was eager to learn everything and wanted my moment at the top. I wanted that title. It was my drug and I craved it.

I spent most of my time dancing and training with Mateo in the studio that I now own. The original owner was a wonderful elderly gentleman named Archie Reynolds. He had spent his whole life devoted to ballroom dancing. He loved us both, myself and Mateo, and he said he knew that one day we would be World Champions. I just wish Archie would have lived a few more years and had the opportunity to see his vision of our success come to fruition. Before his death he had to go into a nursing facility and offered to sell me the studio and attached loft apartment. The crazy thing is that he sold me the studio and loft for $50,000.00. He told me he knew the studio was going to someone that would continue his dream, and he was right. The loft had to be gutted and completely remodeled, and that turned out to be costly. I had invested my settlement money, and was doing very well. My accountant had long been encouraging me to invest my money and was very happy that I was buying this place.

I have always been careful with my money, even before I was awarded the settlement. I am pretty modest about my wealth, especially how I attained it. I never wanted anyone to think that I bought myself a World Latin Dance Champion title. Even those closest to me don't know how financially secure I really am. The money thing is an ongoing issue for me. It's been so hard to accept how I got it. At times I even feel guilty about it. Always remembering that I would trade it all just to have my Blake back. I get insulted when people try to use it as a way to sway me. It's something I have been working on but it's hard to forget that you lost everything you loved.

The annoying ringing of my cell phone brings me back to my senses, and stops my mind from drifting to my past once again. I immediately recognize the assigned ringtone of my manager, Ken Ortega. Whenever Ken calls, I hear Donna Summer singing "She Works Hard for the Money." I am sure he is calling to add something to my already overloaded schedule. Before I can even say hello Ken starts yapping, even though I cannot understand a word he is saying. I can feel the excitement in the tone of his voice. Before he finishes rambling his unrecognizable sentences, I stop him.

"Slow down Ken." I demand. It was still early in the morning, and I wasn't fully awake. "Calm the fuck down and repeat to me slowly what you just said."

Ken took an audibly deep breath and said, "You need to cancel everything you have planned for next week and be in Los Angeles by Monday to shoot a music video."

A music video? Is he for real?

"Ken, did you say a music video?" I have to be sure I heard him right.

"Yes, Victoria, a music video," he says in a matter-of-fact tone.

"By Monday? It's Friday already. Talk about last minute Ken," I scold.

"I know it is last minute Victoria, but it is a great opportunity for you. They are willing to pay you very well for this last minute trip," Ken says in an almost begging tone.

"Ken I don't have the time to choreograph a music video right now," I tell him. I am not saying that I don't choreograph dances and I have nothing against music videos. But I am leaving in a week to travel the workshop circuit for two months. Then when I return we start practice for the up coming competition season. I just really don't have time. Also, to be perfectly honest, dealing with artists from the music world is sometimes not always fun. They have huge egos.

"Actually, they want you to dance in the video, with Sonny. Sonny de la Cruz," he tells me, as if I am supposed to know exactly who this artist is. "The Sonny de la Cruz."

Ken has to repeat his name and then proceeds to recites what sounds like a five minute resume of this man's career. Seems he is the one of biggest stars in Latin music with an almost cult like following. His music is poetic, dark and moving, a bit underground. All of this is according to Ken, who still seems a bit too excited for some reason. Ken finishes by telling me he has always stayed true to his Latin roots, and has never been considered a sellout. After processing Ken's lengthy description of this guy's career I have a question for him.

"Ken, why does he want ME to be in his music video?"

Ken explains the Latin Superstar did not request me but his wife did, who is also his manager. She says I am the best in Latin dance world. I am perfect for the dance sequence of the video. They want me because I am the real deal. I am laughing in my head thinking, "I bet they think I am Latin." His wife actually found me on YouTube.

Yes, YouTube. I am thankful for it. Mateo and I have become popular all over the world because of it. Some of our dance competition videos have several million hits. We also have Twitter and Facebook pages with thousands of followers. Social networking has catapulted both of us to a celebrity-like status.

"I really don't have the time for a music video that I will waste God knows how many days shooting. Then I am sure most of my hard work will be left on the cutting room floor after they edit it. We both know it's not about the money, so you can lose that angle." I tell Ken.

"Victoria, do you really think I'd let you waste your time on something that wasn't going to benefit you in some way? You will not end up on the cutting room floor. I can assure you. Besides, I have already addressed that in your contract."

I remind Ken that I choreograph for videos, not perform in them. Not to pat myself on the back and brag a bit, but I am beyond the music video dance sequence she thinks I am perfect for. Ken insists, and tells me it is just the perfect vehicle and the timing is right for my career. It will get me the exposure I need. I hate to admit it, but Ken is right. I can't compete for the rest of my life. I need to think about where my future is headed. Remember, I started very late in this dance world, and have not stopped or slowed down for five years straight. So against my better judgement I finally agree to do the video.

"Since I am agreeing to do this, I will need you to clear my calendar for next week, and make the arrangements for all the travel and lodging," I ramble off quickly to him.

"Victoria, do I need to remind you that is what you pay your assistant, Ashley, for?" Ken fires back.

Before I can answer his question, he tells me he is sending Ashley all the information she will need in an email. He is also having the contract messengered over. I will need to sign it this morning and send it back so he can get it overnighted to Sonny's management team in LA.

I don't need to be reminded by Ken about my personal assistant and office manager, Ashley Jones. She came to me when I first bought the NYC dance studio. I was looking for someone to help me manage my dance studio and my personal affairs. From the moment she arrived for the interview, I knew she was the right choice for the job. She'd arrived early, and witnessed me losing control as I juggled multiple phone calls while trying to make myself a cup of coffee. Without a word, Ashley grabbed the phone right out of my hand and effortlessly handled the onslaught of calls so that I could get my head together with a much-needed jolt of caffeine.

From that moment forward, she has been my assistant. She's my right hand, and takes care of everything for me. Ashley is like the sister I never had. Not only is she an amazing assistant she is also a great friend. My shopping buddy, my dinner date and my shoulder to cry on. Yep, I still cry and she is always there for me and even though Ashley is efficient and great at her job she has her insecurities just like me. You know the usual stuff all of us women suffer. That's where I come in. Religiously I drag her kicking and screaming to the salon every month. I know deep down she enjoys some of the beauty rituals I make her experience. She's into the facials, mani's and pedi's but draws the line for spray tans and waxing. Even though she doesn't share my obsession with beauty products and makeup, the girl can apply a wing liner with perfection. I know underneath those jeans and t-shirts she wears to work everyday is a smoking hot body. One day I'll get her to discover her inner goddess. Mark my words.

When I walk into my studio office, I can tell by the phone conversation Ashley is involved in that she is already busy booking my flight and hotel for the trip to Los Angeles. When she finishes the call I am waiting for her comments, because she has an opinion for just about everything I do.

"So you are going to LA to do a music video?" she quizzes me.

I can tell by her tone she does not think this is a good idea, so I head for the door to enter the dance studio.

"Don't run off anywhere! I need you to sign this contract before you start your day," she yells after me, waving papers in the air.

"Yes, Ashley, I am going to LA to shoot a music video. It's too early in the morning; I've already had to deal with Ken's ass." I scribble my signature on the contract.

I know I don't have to read any of it. Ken takes good care of me, and he has never given me any bad career advice. He was another benefit of moving to NYC. I met him through Mateo. Mateo told me he could be trusted, and has become a close friend as well. Mateo and I are an amazing dance couple, but without Ken and his great skills as a publicist we would never have become such a household name in the dance world.

"Who is this Latin Superstar called Sonny de la Cruz? If I don't know who this guy is, *you* certainly have no idea who he is. Do they know you don't speak Spanish?" Ashley asks.

I don't need to answer her because she can tell by the look I just gave her that I don't care if they know this or not. This language issue seems to come up quite a bit. Since I am a Latin dancer, people assume I speak Spanish. Mateo is always traveling with me and takes care of translating when I need to know something. I just have had no time or really any interest in learning.

"I can't wait to hear about this venture when you return from shooting your little music video with an artist you know nothing about, Victoria," Ashley sarcastically remarks as I walk out the office, ignoring her and slamming the door behind me.

I have just one day to pack and get ready for LA. By now, I am wishing I had said no. I can't believe I'm going to be dancing in a music video that I will probably never even see. The guy sings in Spanish. Come to think of it I won't even understand one single thing he is singing about. What was I thinking? Something about this just doesn't feel right. I keep thinking this is going to be a complete waste of my time.

Ashley has me arriving in LA late Sunday morning. The weather is beautiful this time of year and it's probably the only thing about this trip I am excited about. I really should have had her come with me. At least she would be here to keep me company. She has arranged for a limo to pick me up, and got the best accommodations that she could negotiate. I am staying at the Chateau Marmont in West Hollywood. The Marmont is an infamous West Hollywood icon. James Dean supposedly jumped through a window here to audition for *Rebel Without a Cause*. My suite is so beautiful I feel like I just arrived in a eloquent residence in France, certainly not what you think you would find in West Hollywood. It's one of LA's hidden treasures. The staff member that checked me in said, "If you must get in trouble, do it at the Chateau Marmont". I had to giggle to myself thinking what kind of trouble could I possibly get into here in this place.

I am sure Sonny's people would only spring for a regular room, and yet I have this beautiful suite. Trust me, there is no telling Ashley no about anything. You might as well agree with her and give her what she wants because she is relentless and going to get it anyway! She thought it was best for me to arrive a day early so I could rest. Then I planned to have an early dinner with my cousin Wayne and his wife Cathie, who live in West Hills. Ashley provided me with countless hours of reading material on this Latin superstar. She also took the liberty of downloading my iPod with several of his songs. She is so way beyond efficient. Another thing that is so Ashley, she googles or wikipedia's everything and everyone. I did take some time on the long flight to read about him and listen to some of his music. If I got anything out of Ashley's research, I did feel a definite connection to his music. It was pure, it was raw and surprisingly, it was seducing in some way -- considering I don't speak a lick of Spanish!

Dinner with Wayne and Cathie is just what I need to help me relax before I have to be on the set tomorrow. I am starting to feel a little nervous. It's not like me to be nervous and certainly not about dancing. Spending time with my family will help take my mind off of tomorrow. Ashley was the one that suggested I call

Wayne and let him know I was going to be in town for a few days. Again that is so her, always thinking, always planning ahead. She knows how I hate traveling alone so I was thrilled when she suggested I call Wayne.

Wayne and Cathie are a wonderful couple. Just watching them together makes it easy to see how much they love each other. It reminds me of Blake and I. Love like that is the best and everyone should have it at least once in their life. We spend the evening outside on their beautiful patio catching up on all that has been going on in our lives. The time is filled with great conversation, delicious food and some amazing wines. One thing about California is the outdoor living, something I've missed about Florida and don't get much of in NYC. Blake and I spent many evenings outside grilling dinner and relaxing after a long day at work. Thanks to Blake being so handy and talented, we had a gorgeous patio that was our very own private oasis. Wow, I haven't thought about missing Florida in a really long time. Come to think of it I haven't thought about relaxing and enjoying life since I threw myself into this world of competition dance.

Wayne is curious about this Latin Superstar Sonny de la Cruz, and says he's not sure he has heard of him. Cathie quickly chimes in and tells me she has heard of him and that he is very popular and well known in the LA area. Wayne asks me the question that everyone seems to ask, "Do they know you don't speak Spanish?" I laugh and tell him, "They are about to find out." We finish the evening with some impromptu dancing. Wayne and Cathie have been taking ballroom dance lessons and they wanted to share what they have learned. For just a moment, I reflect on Blake again. Taking ballroom dance lessons was the one thing we never got to do. I love their enthusiasm, and teach them some Latin dance steps. They are thrilled to learn and can't wait to show it off at their next class. There is nothing better than seeing two people that are in love with each other dance together.

Early the next morning I arrive on set after a beautiful drive in the limo. I am feeling refreshed from a great night's sleep. I think all the wine we had at dinner had something to do with it. Wayne and Cathie had just returned from their annual trip to Italy with some amazing wines. I also have to admit it might have been the hauntingly seductive music from the Latin Superstar playing in my Bose headphones that provided me with such a sound sleep.

I am wearing my usual practice dance attire. Black Capezio dance capris, black camisole and a black zip front hoodie. It's what we call our uniform in the professional dance world. I have brought my practice dance heels which are a bronze metallic color and a few other pairs of competition shoes as well. My shoes are the most treasured part of my uniform. All of mine are custom made. I'm also infamous for dancing in the highest heels made. It's one of the things that separates me from all the rest.

I am not quite sure why but for some reason I am feeling excited about meeting this man and his wife. She that thinks I am perfect for the dance sequence in his video. Ashley's research material on this man was very insightful. I learned that this Latin Superstar has been married to his manager/wife since they were in their late teens. They came from Puerto Rico, where they met in high school, and have been inseparable ever since. She appears to have been the driving force behind making him the Superstar he is today. Their love story sounds like something out of a fairytale. One article in Vanity Fair quotes him as saying, "Without her I would still be back in Puerto Rico playing in bars." The photo shoot for this article also depicted a man who seems to really be into men's fashion. The photos were several over stylized shots of him in beautiful suits from Gucci and Armani. Maybe it is just the Superstar in him, but he seemed to outshine the wife. He certainly is handsome. Don't get me wrong, she is beautiful -- but in a plain, and understated way.

Walking on the set for the first time can be intimidating even for someone like me and especially since I am traveling alone on this trip without my trusted assistant, manager, or dance partner. I am immediately greeted by the Latin Superstar's wife, Maria. She greets me promptly with a gracious hand shake.

"Bienvenida, Victoria, I am Maria de la Cruz. Thank you so much for changing your busy schedule to be here. I know it was short notice, but we want the dance sequence of this video to be very realistic. So when I saw you and your partner on YouTube, I knew you would be perfect."

She is just as the photos depicted her. Beautiful but plain. Her style is what I would call classic. She is wearing khaki capris, a crisp white cotton blouse and ballet flats. No makeup but she really doesn't need it. She is tall, slender build like a ballerina but it's her hair that catches my attention. It's a beautiful mane of thick jet black curls that trail down her back almost to the her waist. Before introducing me to the director she tells me she will not see me again until tomorrow and that she will have some wardrobe choices for me in the morning during hair and makeup. After the introductions to the director she says her goodbyes. He then takes me through a picture board of his idea for the video. This dance sequence has me dancing with the Latin Superstar in a smoke filled nightclub. The director asks if I can choreograph a salsa to be performed to the song-- the new song from his upcoming album. They want to release the video early to raise interest in his long awaited and overdue album. He must think I speak Spanish because he keeps talking in English but slips into Spanish from time to time. I'm having a hard time understanding exactly what it is he wants. Though I do understand some Spanish. Just a few basics and some dirty words that I have picked up from Mateo. But I just can't understand all of what this director is asking of me.

"I am sorry but I don't speak Spanish. Could you please repeat everything you just said, but in English this time?" I ask the director.

He looks at me in shock and even a bit appalled. This is something I have learned to become accustomed to. Not easy being the Queen of Latin dancing and not being able to speak Spanish. The director then makes an announcement to everyone on the set in Spanish. I think he has just told them. I am thinking this because they are all now staring at me. This has no effect; it's nothing compared to being stared down by a group of couples getting ready to compete for a world title in Latin dance.

I make a mental note to bitch Ken out for not telling them. Maybe it's Ashley I should bitch out. Well, someone is going to hear about this when I get back. I spent most of the day in the studio with a stand-in dance partner, working out a dance sequence for the song. My talented dance partner almost passed out when he saw who he would be working with. The best part, he spoke english. This made me feel a little better. At this point, I'm really missing having Mateo with me and beginning to think I may have gotten myself in over my head.

Four hours into the day, there's still no sign of the Latin Superstar. I'm hungry and I'm starting to get bitchy. Time for a break. A buffet lunch of all types of salads has been set up for everyone on the set. I can't figure out how I am going to teach this singer how to dance. My break was spent getting to know my dance partner who's name is Randy. He lives here in LA and teaches dance at a local studio but doesn't compete. I encouraged him to look into competing. He's actually a good dancer. After a short lunch break we finish laying out the steps to the dance sequence. Since I have no idea what type of dancer, or what level of dance Sonny can handle, I keep the steps simple.

Finally the director arrives and explains that they have been shooting the other scenes of the video in a studio next door. Really? What the hell! Someone could not have told me that at the beginning of the day.

"Are you ready to show us the dance sequence?" he asks.

"Yes, we are ready," I tell him.

Finally I get to meet the Latin Superstar Sonny de la Cruz. I have to admit my interest is piqued. It's time I meet the man that Ken was so excited about.

As the door opens to the studio, my heart begins to race a bit. What the hell is going on with me? I am never star struck over anyone. The director enters first, blocking my view of the Latin Superstar. As the director approaches, I finally get my first glance!

Then everything changes and it all becomes very surreal. Everything seems to be in slow motion as I am watching him walk toward me. There he is, the Latin Superstar Sonny de la Cruz. Why am I so nervous? Why is my heart racing? What the hell is going on with me?

One of my first thoughts is, he is as good looking, if not better, in person. So much better than the photos Ashley provided me in my research material. I don't know too many Latin men other than Mateo but this man is hot. I would never tell Mateo this but this Sonny de la Cruz is hotter than even him. My entire body feels as though it's coming alive. I'm feeling things in parts of my body I haven't felt in years. All this Latin Superstar has done is walk into the room. Fuck me! I mean,oh fuck! Hell I'm so mesmerized by just his looks I don't know what the fuck I mean. Get a grip Victoria!

Gone is the slick down hair and designer suits. His hair is much longer in a more relaxed style. He is wearing baggy khaki cargo pants, a black V-neck T-shirt and boots. Casual, but definitely all designer. He wears the clothes well. He walks with great confidence, but not arrogance. The director introduces us, and before I have a chance to put my hand out to greet him, he moves toward me with grace and ease, grabs my hand, and pulls me to him to kiss each of my cheeks. I hope the flushed feeling I am experiencing is not visible to him.

Before I can say anything, he speaks.

"Let's see what the reigning Queen of Latin dance has prepared for us," he says almost mockingly.

In person his voice is rough, raw and enticing, just like the songs he writes. I ask them to cue music, and my starstruck stand-in and I begin. This is one time I am not nervous. I know what I am doing, and I am the best at it. The director explained to me earlier that the song's title translates to Object of Desire, so I have choreographed a seductive, slow-moving dance filled with salsa, samba and some tango steps that build with the music.

When we finish the dance Sonny is the first to speak.

"You're good," he confirms with an almost surprised tone to his voice.

"The routine is perfect for the video. It's just the style of dance we were looking for. Maria was right, she can dance." The director adds.

Good? What the fuck? Did he really just say good? I am not really sure what the director just said but I think he was trying to compensate for Sonny's "good" comment. The only thing I can think about right now is his flippant assessment of my performance and I am pissed. This man just called me good. Good? Really? I was considered *good* years ago when I started out dancing. I'm number one in the Latin dance world and all he has to say is "you're good." I guess he has no clue who I am. I can feel my blood pressure rising. I can tell even my dance partner Randy was insulted. The director spoke with Sonny for a few seconds. But I can't understand what they are saying because they are, naturally, speaking in Spanish.

Sonny walks over to me with what seems to be more swagger and attitude than when he first walked in. I wonder if he senses my unhappiness.

"So you're good. But let's see just how good you are. Now you need to teach me this dance," he says.

The director informs my stand-in that he is no longer needed, and thanks him. I also want to thank Randy and say goodbye but the Latin Superstar is standing in front of me. I can't seem to take my eyes off of him. His deep, dark eyes are spellbinding.

The director then tells us that he is going to let us work on the dance for a few hours. We will meet again at 9 am for hair and makeup and will start shooting at 10:30. My mind is racing with thoughts. Can this man even dance? I don't remember reading anything about him being a dancer in the research. How am I going to teach this man to dance in only a few hours?

Before we begin, I need to put him in his place about the "good" comment. He just insulted me.

So I look the Latin Superstar squarely in the eyes and say with plenty of attitude: "You say I'm merely good. I'm better than good. I am at the top in my field. So I'm insulted if you think that performance was just good. My performance was great. The actual dance routine is good because you couldn't handle the difficulty level of a routine that I would dance in competition."

He seems to be unfazed by the ass chewing I just handed him. He is so damned good looking I am having trouble remaining angry, and I think he knows it. Suddenly, a huge grin stretches across his face.

Laughing he says, "I see you don't lack confidence."

"I have earned my rank in the dance world. So, no, I don't lack confidence," I snap back to him.

He seems surprised that I came back at him so quickly.

"Now that you have made yourself clear about just how *good* you are, let's see if you are *good* enough to teach me this *good* routine," he says. He accentuates good every time he says it. If he wasn't so damned bewitching, I would walk out of here.

I am so captivated by his eyes I didn't even see the director leave. It is just the two of us now, and I began to feel nervous again. A different kind of nervous. A feeling I haven't had in so long that I barely recognize it. I have no idea what is going on with me. Why I am having trouble focusing? I hope it is not obvious to him. For some reason, I am extremely attracted to this man! I tell myself to stop and focus. This is what I do best. So do it. Damn those eyes!

"It's been several years since I have danced. I am sure it is like riding a bike or having sex. You never forget," he says to me with a smirk on his face.

Did he just compare dancing to sex and riding a bike? He thinks this is a joke.

"So you know how to dance?" I ask, with a surprising tone.

"Yes, my mother loved salsa dancing. She sent me to dance classes and I studied for several years. Then one day I discovered a guitar class down the hall from the dance studio and I was hooked. Dance unfortunately took a backseat to my love for music," he explains.

"Well, I am surprised and happy to hear you have experience. Like you said, it's just like having sex so let's just see how much you remember and if you are any good. They say good dancing engages the brain and that great dancing engages the heart. So let's see Mr. de la Cruz what you are made of."

"Oh, I am good. No, actually, I'm great. You don't have to worry about that," he replies mocking my words.

"I am sure you were referring to the dance part, right?" I say with a quick comeback. Just when I think he has met his match he comes back at me again.

"OK, enough of this flirting with me, Victoria. Let's get started on this dance lesson."

I just stand there and roll my eyes because I can't think of any thing to say back to him. I am speechless, which is quite unusual for me.

I begin to explain some steps to him and he approaches me to take me in a standard dance hold. This is where everything gets weird. This man, this Latin Superstar, puts his arm around the small of my back and takes my other hand in his and raises it. I have no other way of describing it other than to say it was a feeling of pure passion. When he drew me to him I was able to smell him and feel the heat of his body and it was intoxicating. It was a seductive enchantment. Listen, I have danced with hundreds of men over the past five years and nothing, and I mean nothing, up to this point ever felt like this. I am suddenly not so focused and can't seem to gain control of my thoughts. I know this is crazy. My mind starts racing and thinking about Ashley's research material. How in every article I read described how this Latin Superstar and his wife had weathered the test of time in their relationship, and were so in love. I need to stop this silliness and do the job I was hired for.

"So are we going to dance or are you going to stare into my eyes all day?" he asks.

I blink and am embarrassed by his comment. I think he is amused, and seems to enjoy bringing this to my attention.

So I refocus, and we begin. I am pleasantly surprised at just how good he is, and how quickly he learns the steps. It certainly shows that he had some formal training. He is patient, listens to me, and follows my direction. At times he seems overwhelmed, but continues over and over until he gets it. I can tell he realizes this is not as easy as he thought. But he pushes me to make him get the steps down.

"If you need to take a break we can," I tell him.

"No, I don't need a break. Do you need a break Miss World Latin Dance Champion?" he says to me, as he is trying his hardest not to sound winded.

"No, I am used to eight hour practice sessions, so I am fine. I was just worried because you seem to be breathing heavily," I say politely.

"Eight hours. Really? Maybe you are as good as you claim," he jokes.

"You are referring to my dancing skills?"

"Look if you can do this for eight hours a day, I am quite certain you are good at everything you do."

I laugh, and it seems to put both of us at ease. He continues to push himself, and listens for direction. He tells me when he can't get a step down, and we go over it, again and again, until he gets it. At times he gets mad at himself. There are times he pulls me to him so he can lean on me and catch his breath. We both find this amusing, but he keeps pushing. We are becoming very comfortable and friendly. Something I also share with my dance partner Mateo but this is different. The contact with Sonny has my mind on overload. I forgot what it was like to feel the touch of a man. A touch that has parts of my body awakening to feel things I haven't felt in a long time.

After about 3 hours of practice he finally has the dance down. We are ready to perform to his song.

"Let me drink some water and then let's do it to the music," he says.

"We can take a break if you like," I tell him again.

He shoots me a look and we both start laughing as he chugs down a bottle of water.

When the music starts and we begin to dance, a different side of this man emerges. I see exactly who he is and what he is about. Not only is he doing an amazing job with my steps, but this man dances with *feeling* to his own music.

There are people that dance great and go through the technical steps flawlessly, but lack the passion and emotion. When you get to see that real human side of a dancer, you know that person is in tune with both the music AND the dance. It's so rare to find someone like that. To be able to share that with someone is a very special thing.

I have always been one of those people. Early on in my career some judges even marked my score sheets with comments that said I had the emotion and passion, but I lacked the technical skills. The technical stuff can be taught. You can't teach someone passion.

The feelings I have been experiencing throughout the day become even more intense. We both get caught up in the dance and his music. I am sure it's just me but this feels crazy. I guess it's just been a really long time since anyone has made me feel this way. I keep reminding myself that it doesn't matter, he is a married man. I tell myself to just enjoy the moment, and to remain the professional. This is only a job. When we finish, he holds me close after the dance sequence has ended and the song keeps playing. I can feel his breath against my neck, and the pounding of his heart. His hand still around my waist, there is a spark of heat between our bodies. We are jolted back to reality by the ringing of his vibrating cell phone in the front pocket of his pants. We both pull away abruptly, and for a moment I am sure I saw something in those dark, intense eyes of his -- something that told me he was feeling the same way. The way he has to pull himself together just to answer the phone does not go unnoticed by myself or him. He quickly takes the call and speaks only in Spanish. Hmmm...still wondering if the director told him about me not understanding Spanish.

"I need to go. I think we are ready for tomorrow. I am sorry I insulted you earlier with my "good" comment. I can't imagine what you go through practicing eight hours a day with a much more difficult routine," he says.

There is a tangible change in his mood after taking the call. He is no longer relaxed and playful. He says goodbye the same way he greeted me, a kiss on each cheek. He doesn't release me, instead he pulls me closer and whispers in my ear.

"Pasar una tarde maravillosa Victoria. Eres una mujer muy talentosa y hermosa. Fue difícil concentrarse porque su belleza me había efectuada. Estoy deseando bailar contigo en la mañana."

Really? What the fuck did he just say? I have no idea what he has just said! I feel myself blush and turned on by his whispering.

"Thank you. Have a great evening," I say. I know before the words left my mouth they sounded stupid, but I didn't know what else to say.

It must have taken me 15 minutes to regain my composure and pull myself together to exit the studio where the limo is waiting. The ride back to hotel gives me time to rerun the day in my mind. I try hard to remember what he whispered. Maybe if I can remember Ashley can translate it for me. As I am trying to process and shake these feelings, that familiar ringtone is blasting from my cell. It's Ken and the excited tone is again in his voice.

"Are you still on the set? What did you think about the Sonny? Is he as handsome in person? I bet he was sexy. Can he dance? What was his wife like? What did you think of his music?" Ken rattles on and on to me.

"Hello Ken. I have just spent ten hours choreographing and teaching a dance routine. I have to be back on the set at 9 am for hair and makeup. I'm hungry and exhausted. Thank you for asking," I rudely say.

"I am sorry, Victoria. I am just excited for you. This is a great opportunity," Ken apologizes.

I answer all of his questions on the ride back to the hotel, which keeps my mind on work and off of the Latin Superstar. For the moment.

"Good luck tomorrow, Victoria. Go and get some dinner and some rest. I am looking forward to hearing about the shoot," he says before hanging up.

I know I told Sonny I was used to eight hour sessions but I have to admit I am dog tired. And not just physically tired. I'm mentally drained from today. Something about this Sonny de la Cruz has my mind going in a hundred different directions. I am experiencing feelings I haven't felt in a long time. But I need to put all that on hold for now because my body is begging for a hot shower and some food. Food always makes everything better.

The room service at the Chateau Marmont is nothing short of deliciousness. After filling my tummy with spaghetti bolognese and hot fudge cake smothered in caramel and chocolate sauce I am ready to crawl into this enormous bed with it's thousand count sheets. With my appetite sated and my body relaxed I let my mind drift to thoughts of Sonny de la Cruz's hand wrapped around the small of my back. I feel warm and tingly in places on my body that I wasn't even sure still worked. I fall asleep reading through Ashley's research material with a renewed interest in the Latin Superstar. Not sure what I am searching for, but the more I read about him, the more intrigued I become.

Chapter 4

I arrive back on set at 9 am and the director takes me straight over to hair, makeup and wardrobe. There is an army assembled to take care of everything. Which is great because it is going to take an army to get me looking good. I woke up at 2am and struggled the rest of the night trying to get back to sleep. I just couldn't get Sonny de la Cruz out of my mind. The warmth of his body against mine and the feel of his hand on the small of my back. They brought up feelings, or maybe it's just jet lag. Yeah, keep telling yourself that. This is just silly thinking this way. Damn, I guess it's been a while since I've had a booty call. Yeah, that's all this is, I'm horny. Great, I just choose to lust after a married man. Get a grip girl, be the trained professional here.

I keep my eye open for the Latin Superstar. I'm starting to feel like a girl in high school waiting to get a glimpse of the hot boy, her current...latest...crush. Oh, Victoria you really need to start dating. Finally, about an hour into hair and makeup, Maria de la Cruz arrives carrying a garment bag. She unzips the bag and starts to pull out several dresses. There must be at least four or five of them. She hangs them on a rolling rack and walks over to greet me.

"I have some dresses I would like you to try on so I can see which one will work best," she announces.

The hair and makeup team excuse themselves and close the curtain in the dressing room area. By the way everyone has cleared the room, I am assuming she must want me to try them on in front of her. No biggie, I have changed costumes in front of Mateo and a room full of other dancers. I know what kind of shape my body is in because of dance. I begin to strip down and try on her wardrobe selections. I think I have caught her off guard when I start to undress. She quickly turns away and occupies herself by straightening the dresses on the rack. I believe she may even be blushing. Her first choice is a crepe charmeuse black dress. It is beautiful and perfect for dancing. It has a long sweeping train on one side. Very revealing and body hugging. It's simple but sexy. Definitely designer, and not flashy like most of my costumes I wear for competition. She seems not to like it and hands me the next one. This goes on for 4 more dresses. I can tell by her attitude she does not want my opinion so I keep my thoughts to myself.

"You will wear this one" she says as she pulls the first dress I tried on and hands it to me. Then she goes to a large black duffle bag she has also brought in with her and starts pulling out shoes.

"I wear my own dance shoes. I am sorry but those shoes you brought are nothing a real salsa dancer would ever wear," I tell her as politely as I can.

"Whatever. That's fine. Just make sure they are black and not some tacky metallic color like I have seen so many dancers wear," she rudely says.

She's referring to my practice dance shoes that I had on yesterday. Does she really think I was going to wear those today for the video shoot? I can't believe she just made such a rude comment to me. I'll bet she would be shocked to know how much I pay for a pair of my custom made dance heels. She needs an ass chewing just like I gave her husband. I can't let her comment go. I need to set her straight.

"All of my dance shoes are custom made for me. The tacky bronze metallic shoes your referred to are a standard in competition Latin dancing. The neutral color extends the look of the leg and doesn't call attention to the feet. " By the look on her face I don't think she enjoyed the schooling I just gave her. "I have several pairs of black ones. Would you like to see what I have brought with me?" I ask politely trying to understand her mood.

"No, as long as they are black and have a high heel," she snaps back.

Wait a minute. Did she just fucking snap at me? I am not sure if she is pissed because I won't wear the shoes she brought, or what the hell is wrong with her, but she is not going to be allowed to be rude and snap and talk to me in that tone. She has no idea who she is dealing with. I have had to learn to stand my ground over the years. When I first started out, I let people walk all over me. Mateo taught me how to handle myself and be more confident. Now I don't let anyone or anything challenge my confidence. I have learned to play the bitch game better than anyone.

"Well, lucky for me I've been told my legs go on for days. So black it is! How tall is your husband?" I ask her. This time not so politely. The change in the tone of my voice is quite noticeable.

"Why?" she turns on her heel and glares at me.

"It will determine what height of heel I choose. I don't want to be taller than your husband in my dance shoes," I explain to her.

"Oh, he is five foot eleven. I will see you on the set," she replies to me as she quickly walks out of the dressing room.

The hair and makeup team return to finish working on me. I decide I will now wear the tallest dance heels I have brought with me. Remember, I am good, so I am about to show this woman just how right she was choosing me for the video.

I step on to the set, and the response I get from the crew means I must look pretty damned hot. My hair has been styled into a classic chignon knotted bun and my makeup features a smokey, seductive eye and a dramatic red lip. The dress is a perfect fit and hugs all my curves. The hair, the makeup, the dress...everything is perfect. The set has been transformed into a dark, sexy Latin club complete with a dance floor in the center. Suddenly I hear his rough, raw, seducing voice and know he has arrived on the set. He also looks amazing. He is wearing black trousers that are very trendy. They look like a men's riding pant. The pants are tucked into beautiful designer black knee-high boots. He is wearing a black shirt and vest with leather detailing. His hair is styled to look messy, and goes well with his facial hair. He looks like he hasn't shaved for several days. It all looks very GQ. Here I go again. Those feelings are returning again. Damn it. Not *now!* I have to focus and show everyone on this set why I am called the Queen of Latin dance. Once they see me dance they will all forget I don't speak Spanish.

The director has cleared the set, so that the Latin Superstar and I are alone. We are standing face to face and he looks amazing. He even smells amazing. He scans my body and returns his gaze to me. My heart is pounding. I cannot turn away from those dark, seducing eyes.

"Usted es absolutamente magnífico. Quiero que relajarse y disfrutar. Se trata de un momento mágico entre nosotros," he whispers.

"You do realize I don't speak Spanish," I whisper, my eyes locked on his.

"I know. You really should learn," he says with a huge smile on his face. He then has the nerve to wink at me.

Really! Omg! I can't believe this guy. Then before I can respond, the director says, "Action, roll music," and with a smirk on his face we begin to dance. I can't believe he has remembered every step. Again the emotion and passion in his expressions and dancing encourage me to forget about the director, the crew and everyone assembled to work on the shoot, including his wife, who is watching. As I dance and watch his face and feel and smell this man as he leads me through the steps. I completely lose myself in him and the choreography. It is the first time I have ever felt this connected to the dance. I don't want this to end for fear I will never get to feel this way again. As the sequence ends, everyone on the set starts applauding and whistling. This goes on for several minutes and I realize we just danced the entire routine, and it was perfect. The director comes over and says, "It was amazing. Perfection! I don't think we need to shoot it again. We will need some still shots of certain moves and also some photos for promotional use." All through this, I am trying hard to focus, and trying even harder to conceal how and what I am feeling. But I cannot take my eyes off of him.

"It's a wrap," the director announces two hours later. Everyone bursts into cheers and applause. Then, when the crew starts packing up equipment, a feeling of sadness comes over me. I don't want this day to end. I know when it ends it will be the last time I see Sonny de la Cruz. I go to the dressing room, change, and as I am coming out carrying my bag, I am approached by Sonny and his wife. He has also changed and is wearing jeans, a T-shirt, and a leather jacket. I don't really notice Maria because I am, once again, hypnotized by this man.

"Thank you again for changing your busy schedule on such a short notice. After seeing you dance, I know I made the right decision by choosing you for the video," she says in a fake, sugary-sweet voice.

"Victoria. You are an amazing dancer. Thank you for making me look good," he says.

"Thank you both for this opportunity. It was a great experience for me. Good luck with the new album and the video," I tell them both.

They both extend their hand for a goodbye handshake. No kiss on the cheek, this time from the Latin Superstar.

That's it. It's over. I head out of the studio to get into the limo. Just as I close the door, it is pulled open again and the Latin Superstar leans into the limo. He is holding something. I am confused because I made certain I did not leave anything behind. So I am not sure what he is handing me. And then I see it -- it is the dress from the video.

"Victoria, I want you to have this as a gift from me," he says as he hands it to me.

"No hay ninguna mujer que podría ser tan hermosa como usted en este vestido. Espero que la próxima vez que nos reunimos. Sé que nos reuniremos otra vez," he says to me.

"I have no idea what you just said to me, but thank you for the dress," I say.

"You really should learn to speak Spanish," he says with a big smile.

"Gracias," I say to him. He smiles and laughs as he closes the limo door.

The flight home from LA was long and I am exhausted. I spent most of the flight thinking about the Latin Superstar and his eyes. *Those eyes...I just can't get them out of my mind.* I am sure I saw something in them. Some kind of connection between the two of us. Maybe it's just wishful thinking. He certainly is hot. Everything about him is so mysterious and seducing. I need to stop all this silliness and get back to reality. He has been the first man to spark my interest in such a long time. Just my luck he is married!

As I deplane, I am happy to see Ashley and Ken waiting for me. Ken is holding a beautiful bouquet of flowers, and Ashley is holding a welcome home sign written in Spanish. If she only knew how ironic that was. It just reminded me of him whispering Spanish in my ear. Damn I wish I knew what he said!

They are both smiling, and bombard me with questions about the trip. Trust me, I have no intentions of revealing what I am really feeling. I'm cautious about what I tell them. I can only imagine what they would say if I told them how I am lusting after this man. Ashley would lecture me about him being married. Although I think Ken might have enjoyed hearing about it.

Fortunately, I have no time to dwell on the trip to LA and my time with the Latin Superstar. I only have one day off to regroup and repack my bag, then it's off to the airport for a flight that will take me to Miami for my first round of dance workshops. I will be spending the next two months traveling nonstop to Miami, Orlando, three cities in Texas, Toronto and then Puerto Rico. Workshops give me the chance to work with some of the best dancers in the Latin world. I get to spend two months touring with other dancers, doing workshops on salsa, bachata and the latest dance rage, kizomba. It also gives me time to slow down a little before the hectic schedule of competition season begins. In about four months, Mateo and I will be defending our title.

For the next few months, no matter how busy I stay, I can't seem to keep my mind from thinking about Sonny de la Cruz. If I could only remember what he whispered to me, I could ask some of the Spanish speaking dancers what it meant. There were a few that asked me about the video shoot. Since it has been released there are several million views of it on Youtube and Vevo. The single is also getting quite a bit of air time on the Latin music stations. His fans are waiting anxiously for the album to be released. Secretly I have been following all this. Reading all the reviews I can find online. Everyone wanted to know what I thought about the Latin Superstar, Sonny de la Cruz. I am very vague about telling them how I'm feeling, but listen closely to hear what they know about him. They all speak of his wife and how important she has been to his career. How their love has endured over all these years. They also talk about the struggle the two have had because she has not been able to have a child. She had suffered several miscarriages. I spend my spare time searching the Internet for any information on the him. I am secretly obsessed with this man. His music has taken over my world as well. I have downloaded several more of his songs and translated the lyrics to English. This man's lyrics are so alluring and sensual. I swear they are haunting me. At night my dreams are filled with visions of him. I know all of this is just a stupid, crazy phase. I really need to start dating.

At the end of our two month workshop in Puerto Rico, and much to my surprise, I began to be recognized as the dancer in Sonny's video. People are stopping me and asking for my autograph. I hate to admit it, but Ken was right to insist I do the video. It is exactly the boost my career needed. I make a mental note to myself to thank him when I return to the states next week. Damn, that's gonna hurt.

When I arrive back in NYC I am so happy to see Ashley at the airport. But I am surprised when I see Ken. I was not expecting for him to be here. He seems to be in a great mood and very happy to see me. Before I get a chance to tell them about all the attention I have been experiencing, and thank him, he announces, "I received a call from Sonny de la Cruz's management team and they would like you to call them tomorrow."

As I navigate the words around the lump that's formed in my throat, I ask Ken, "Do you know what they are calling about?" I try not to show my excitement, but inside, I am dying. Could I really get another chance to see him again?

"No, Victoria, you need to talk to them to find out what they want." Ken replies.

"Don't give me that look. I have no idea why they called." Ashley snaps when I look to her for answers.

I am not sure, but I think Ken is hiding something. I am desperate to know why they called. Great, now I will never sleep tonight.

The next morning I am really feeling the effects of the long flight home and a very restless night. My mind has been racing ever since Ken told me about the call. Sonny's people are on the West Coast I will have to wonder a little longer. I try to wait patiently, but I am starting to feel anxious. Ashley has been watching me all morning like she knows something is up. I try to play it cool, but I don't know how long I can keep it together. I decide they must open his office by 9 am, so at 12:01 PM my time, I pick up the phone in my office and call Ashley. "Please get me Sonny de la Cruz's office on the line."

A few seconds later my phones buzzes. "Sonny de la Cruz is on line two for you." Wait! It's HIM? I thought I would be talking to his people, not the Latin Superstar himself! I am in a panic, but I don't want Ashley to catch on, so I tell her I'll take the call. I get up and close the door to my office for privacy. I am sure she finds this extremely weird, but I want to be alone when I talk to him. No distractions.

I take a deep breath and pick up the phone. I do my best to sound normal asI say hello.

"Buenos días, señorita." he says in that velvety-smooth voice of his.

Then he laughs and asks with that smart ass tone. "Did you take my advice and learn to speak Spanish since the video shoot in LA?"

"No, I have been too busy working and traveling to play around with Spanish lessons," I shoot back at him, slightly amused by his sarcasm.

His tone quickly changes from playful to serious. He begins by thanking me for coming to LA to shoot the video, and tells me that the video is doing well and the song is a hit on iTunes and Amazon. Of course I pretend I am completely unaware of the single's success. If he only knew how much time I've dedicated to following anything and everything that has to do with Sonny de la Cruz. I'm a little hesitant to tell him about the recognition I'd received in Puerto Rico. But I decide to go ahead and tell him about being asked to sign autographs. The change in the tone of his voice tells me he is very excited to hear this.

"Victoria, that is exactly why I am calling you. The album is ready to launch in a few weeks, but we still need to do the cover. Since there has been such a great response on the release of the video, my team has decided you should be on the cover." Then he pauses and I can hear him take in a deep breath before he continues. "I am calling to see if you would do the cover shoot."

The thoughts start to fly through my head. Will I be doing the photo shoot myself? Will we be on the album cover together? Will I be able to handle seeing him again? I'm so caught up in all my thoughts, that I almost miss what he is saying.

"The new album is called "Despojado" which translates to "Stripped" in english." I am thankful he has translated this for me and was very polite about it. Gone is the smart ass tone and I am just about to learn why his tone has changed.

"Since the album is named "Despojado" they would like to feature the two of us in a dance pose." He says. Then, a few beats later, he adds, "Naked."

My breath catches and I am sure it is audible. "I am sorry, did you just say naked? As in no clothes?"

"Yes, Victoria. Naked.As in no clothes."

There's the smart ass I remember.

"Do you have an issue with getting naked?" he asks. "It would be artistic, of course."

My mind is reeling. Naked! Naked! Naked! Oh my God, he DID say naked! Trust me, it is not easy trying to sound calm when the man who I have not stopped obsessing over for weeks has just asked me to get naked with him. For artistic purposes.

"No, actually, I am very comfortable with my body." I brag.

"Yes, I know. Maria mentioned you were very comfortable stripping down in front of her."

I can't believe she told him about that. Wonder what she said about my body? While I am relishing in the thoughts of her talking about me stripping naked I am wondering if I really can do this. Naked.

"Why me?" I push him.

"What do you mean?"

"Why not just pick a model and use them?"

"Because of the music video. Everyone loves the video. It has over five million hits already. People will put the connection together when they see the album cover. It seems you have a following as well and this too has helped the video." He says as though he is trying to sell me on this.

Oh, he doesn't have to sell me on anything. I already know about the five million hits. 5,299,436 last time I checked. I just realized I could very well be arrested for stalking this man.

"Victoria, would you please consider doing this?" It sounds almost like he is begging me. My complete silence must have him worried, because he quickly adds that the photographer will shoot us naked but nothing will really be exposed. "He will make sure that we look naked but our bodies will cover each others private areas."

Did he just say private areas? Oh my God MY naked body against HIS naked body. Is he crazy? Am I crazy for even considering this? Though I am very comfortable with my body, I am not sure I could make it through a photo shoot with this man, Naked, touching each other. Naked. Without hesitation or thinking clearly I blurt out "I really need to speak to my manager Ken about this and see what he thinks."

"I understand, Victoria. But I will need your answer by the end of the day."

"I'll call you back with my answer by 5 PM my time."

He ends the call by saying he hopes I will do the photo shoot, and promises it will be beautiful and tasteful. He also adds that the photo shoot will need to take place no later than the end of the week.

I am nervous about calling Ken. I am not sure what he will think of this. When he answers, he doesn't even give me time to ask.

"So are you going to do it? I mean the album cover." Ken asks with that familiar excited tone to his voice.

"I can't believe you already knew what they wanted and did not tell me when you met me at the airport. You made me wait all night to find out." I scold.

"Victoria, I wouldn't be a good manager if I didn't already know up front what they wanted. I always have your best interest in mind, and would never lead you down the wrong path in your career. I just thought it would be best if you heard it from his people first."

I guess I zoned out. I can't get the thought of being naked around him out of my head.

"Victoria, you aren't saying anything. Are you okay? Is this something you think you would consider doing?

"I think it will be another great way to advance my career and get me noticed, but I'd be lying if I said I wasn't nervous about shooting a cover naked. There were so many people on the set in LA for the music video. As comfortable as I am with my body, Ken, I am not sure I can do that in front of all those people. Let alone in front of his wife."

"Then let's set the rules for this shoot. We will put everything into a contract for his people. They will have to agree to your stipulations or you won't do it."

"What do you mean set the rules? Can I really request certain things?" I had heard of celebrities having riders on their contracts, but I never imagined being on that level myself.

"Yes, rules. Conditions you are willing to work under. If they want you naked we need to set some rules, and they are going to have to do it your way. I would never let you do this any other way."

So Ken and I map out a rider for my contract.

Rule #1: I get a copy of all the photos taken. Photos can be used for the album cover design. Photos can also be used for a promotional tool. The photographer will have no photo rights and cannot use the photos.

Rule #2: A completely closed set. The only people present on the set during the photo shoot will be myself, Sonny, the photographer and one assistant for the photographer. Makeup and hair will be done in a separate room.

Rule #3: The photo shoot will take place in NYC not LA. It will not begin before 3 pm. I don't feel I can get naked at 9 am!

Rule #4: I want a bottle of Crown Royal, ice and ginger ale. I will need something to get me a little relaxed.

Rule #5: His wife is not to be at the photo shoot. I do not feel comfortable being photographed nude with a man who's wife in the next room.

"This is fun." I say to Ken.

"No, not fun, but it is a way to protect you and your career." Ken says. He also adds in a few more legal rules, and emails a copy to Sonny's management for their approval. A few hours later Ken receives a response, and they have agreed to all the terms. They also say they will be in touch with all the details for the photo shoot.

I feel I need to call the Latin Superstar to let him know my decision. It's also another chance to hear that voice. He seems surprised when he realizes it's me calling.

"I just want to let you know I've decided to do it." I announce.

"Naked?" He questions with a seductive tone.

"Yes, Naked." I say with confidence.

"Well, I guess you *are* comfortable with your body."

Damn he sounds so sexy.

"I have worked hard to get where I am. That includes my body." I make my voice a little breathy, hoping I don't sound stupid.

"I'm confused, Victoria. Are you saying you have worked hard with your body to get where you are or your body is the result of your hard work?" He teases.

"I am going to let that comment slide and hope that you just think you are being funny. Like I told you, I take my career very seriously, just as you do."

"I love your request for alcohol, and for my wife not to be present." He laughs.

"Sonny, I requested that out of respect for her. Also it would be very uncomfortable for me to do this with her watching. And yes I admit, the alcohol is to help me relax."

"Why, do I make you nervous, Victoria?"

"Let's just say that you have a way of making me feel something I haven't felt in a long time." I can't believe I just said that to him.

"Realmente tiene el mismo efecto sobre mí. Me pregunto si se siente lo que estoy sintiendo en mi corazón.

"That is SO not fair. I have no idea what you just said, and you know it."

"Victoria, you really should have requested a no speaking Spanish clause in your contract."

That smart ass! And the worst part of it is *he's right*!

"Is it too late to have that added?" I put on my sexiest voice, which I'm certain must sound ridiculous.

Laughing he says, "Yes, I'm afraid it is too late. Victoria, I do enjoy tormenting you this way."

He tells me he's looking forward to seeing and working with me in New York, and we say our goodbyes. After he hangs up, I sit, frozen for what seems like ages, with the phone still up to my ear. Did I really just agree to what I think I agreed to? What the fuck am I thinking? How the hell am I going to get Naked with this man?

There is so much I need to do before the photo shoot. Ken called and said he received all the logistics and had the contract. He needs my signature right away so it can be Fed Ex'd back to the Latin Superstar's office. He is messengering it right over. The shoot will take place at the photographer's studio. The photographer is well known in the entertainment industry and has worked with many musicians. I am not well-versed in this world and have no idea who he is, which is probably all the better. I'd rather not know this man at all. The shoot is in two days and I need a fresh spray tan to even out my skin tone. I also need some time with a professional for some serious groom time. Ashley has been busy setting up appointments for these things as well as rearranging my practice schedule. I'm just hoping all this is going to be worth my time and effort. If it advances my career, then it will all be worth it.

"Victoria I can't believe we have spent two hours debating over how you should have your vagina waxed. I hope you know what the hell it is you're doing here." Ashley says with concern and a little sarcasm.

This pisses me off. "Ashley why don't you just fucking say it? You think this is a bad idea."

Ashley worries too much. Even though she's the same age as I am, you'd think she was twice as old with all her nagging.

"I am not in charge of your career. Ken is and if he thinks it's a good idea, then my opinion shouldn't matter. It's just that you couldn't pay me enough to strip down to nothing and be photographed with a man I barely know," she explains.

"This is by no means easy for me. I am stepping well outside of my comfort zone here. I'm scared to death to do this. But I do trust Ken and I think it will pay off for my career." I say, wondering who it is I'm really trying to convince -- Ashley, or myself?

"Please. If there's one thing you don't have to worry about, it's your body. You look amazing." Then she gets in that one last jab, true to form, just as I'm heading out the door to the spa. "Probably best you do this now, though, because you're not getting any younger. Besides, I don't even remember the last time you had a date. Might as well let *somebody* see that perfect body of yours."

But I have the last word this time just as I reach the door knob. "Really? As I as recall you have not been on a date in years, many more than me. I am sure your vagina could use time at the spa as well."

No need for me to turn around because I know Ashley is staring at me with her mouth wide open and cannot believe what she just heard. I can't help feeling smug and triumphant. Without thinking I throw my fist up in the air knowing I have beat her at her own game. Just let me have my moment. Because trust me it's rare you beat Ashley at anything.

I am off to the spa for a spray tan and some grooming! And honestly, this is just what I needed: a spa day. When I arrive, I realize Ashley not only set up appointments for tanning and grooming, but also a day of pampering. Nails, toes, facial and a full body massage. Before the spray tan I get a complete body scrub which is amazing. Although it's weird having someone scrub certain parts of your body. Speaking of weird, next up is grooming. OK, let's just say I am waxing my vagina. There's really no sophisticated way to put it.

Once I get home, or should I say float home, I spend most of the evening in front of a mirror examining myself at every angle. Even a few maneuvers that were a bit impossible, making sure everything looks good. I need to stop, because although I do have a great dancer's physique, I have begun to pick myself apart. I've convinced myself I need a boob job and a butt-lift. I guess I'm just like every other woman in the world -- my insecurities get the better of me. Well, it's too late to back out now. I have signed the contract and the shoot is tomorrow. I have got to get some sleep.

It's shoot day and I am a complete mess. Thank God I don't have to be in hair and makeup until 3pm. I spent 30 minutes showering making sure my skin was smooth and flawless as I could get it using my the body brush attachment on my new Clarisonic

Smart Profile. I keep a running dialogue in my head, chattering on about how I'm going to handle seeing this man naked. Better yet, HIM seeing ME Naked! I remind myself to remain professional and to stare into his eyes and nowhere else. Really? Like *that's* going to happen! I need a drink now!

We arrive at the studio for the shoot, Ashley and Ken are with me. Ken thought it was best for me to have my team with me so I wouldn't feel intimidated by everyone. He also wants to ensure that everything runs as requested in my contract. Besides, Ken thinks it makes me look more important to have people with me. He introduces me but my mind is elsewhere. I'm just scanning the studio for any sign of the Latin Superstar. The shoot coordinator directs me to a room and hands me a white robe and ask me to undress. She tells me they're sending in a body makeup artist to see if I will need any touchups or corrections prior to the shoot. Before I head to the dressing room Ken asks me if I'd like the bartender to make me something to drink. Bartender? YES! A bartender! They've hired one and set up a complete bar for the photo shoot. And I plan to take full advantage of that. There's no way I'm getting through this without a little - okay a LOT - of alcohol.

"I would love a drink. Crown and ginger ale on the rocks, please."

Wow, 3pm and I am drinking! I am hoping it will help me relax. My nerves are starting to really take over.

I head into the dressing room with my drink in hand. I undress and change into the robe and wait for the makeup artist to join me. While I am waiting, I use the time to enjoy my drink and try to relax. But my nerves are starting to get the best of me. I need more alcohol. Yes, please.

When the makeup artist arrives I drop my robe, and she scans my skin for flaws, marks, and imperfections. She is a striking blonde, probably 10 years younger than me and gorgeous, so I am a little more than merely intimidated as she scrutinizes every inch of my body.

"Your color looks really good and natural. Very even and smooth." She says.

The only thing she does is brush my chest, shoulders and arms with a bronzer. When she's done she stands back again to make sure everything looks good.

"Your body is smoking hot!" she says to me as she stands surveying my body.

"Really? Are you sure? You're not just being nice, are you?" I was never was good at taking compliments.

"Trust me," she says matter-of-factly. "I see a lot of skin in my line of work. Yours is one of the best bodies I've seen in a long time."

I don't know why it is, but her comment about my body seems to make me feel a lot more confident. Or maybe it's the liquor. I grab my drink and throw back the rest of it. She tells me I am ready for hair and makeup.

Sitting in hair and makeup, I am handed my second drink. Or is it the third? Hell, I don't know. I'm not counting. I think Ken ordered it for me. I just keep thinking how I'm going to be naked in front of the man I have been obsessing on for two months. Not sure if it is the alcohol starting to take effect but this is all starting to feel strange. Trying to focus; trying to relax. I need to breathe. Just as I am about to lose it, in walks Sonny de la Cruz! Holy shit, here we go!

"Hola, Papi." I sing out without even thinking how stupid that must have sounded. Really? It must be the alcohol. Everyone in the room turns and stares in my direction so I know this comment sounded out of place. But I really don't care what they think. Another few more sips of my drink and I won't even remember their stares.

Laughing, he says, "I see you have started your Spanish lessons Victoria!"

His people then introduce him to Ken and they all chat for a few minutes. It's obvious from Ken's beaming smile he is very excited about meeting the Latin Superstar.

Ashley, who has been working on her iPad since we arrived, immediately comes over and whispers in my ear, "Victoria! You failed to mention how hot he is."

"Really? I never noticed. I guess he's just not my type." I slur, trying to sound uninterested.

"Oh my God, Victoria, you're drunk! What was with that "Hello Papi" comment? Do you even know what that meant? And you need to get your dance shoes on." Ashley chastises. I ignore Ashely's questions and sip more of my drink.

I almost forget their request that I wear a pair of black dance shoes. I wanted to bring my bronze metallic competition shoes and wear them just to get back at his wife Maria for the rude comment she made in LA. While they continue to work on my hair and makeup, Ashley helps me with my shoes, since I clearly cannot do it by myself at this point.

Sonny is taken through the same routine as they hand him a white robe and offer him a drink. He declines and heads off to the dressing room. They're not in there long so I am assuming he doesn't need any body makeup either. I find myself wondering if he did any grooming.Yes, men worry about that area as well. I'm not sure he is that type. I guess I'll know soon enough. I hear an electric razor running so I think they are trimming his facial hair. My hair and makeup have been restyled to mimic my look from the video shoot. The only difference is I won't be putting on a dress. I'm NAKED! When we're both ready to go, the photographer walks in to announce he is ready as well.

Sonny stands and says, "All right, let's do this." I am afraid to move and quickly finish my second drink. Wait, third? Oh hell, I don't know and I don't really care. Ashley comes over to help me out of the chair.

In a very concerned voice she whispers, "Are you all right?"

As I make a bold attempt to stand, I tell her, "I am *fine*." But quickly realize I am not exactly fine. For the first time in my dance career I have trouble balancing myself on my heels. I don't know if I'm nervous or drunk, or both. I take another sip of the fresh drink Ken just brought me and ponder the thought.

Sonny introduces me to the photographer and the three of us head into the closed set. I am so nervous I have forgotten his name already. He looks like a photographer. He has that 90's rocker look and I would say he is in his late 40's. When I say 90's rocker look I mean it in a good way. White tee, ripped up jeans, boots. He is very good looking, which only adds to my uneasiness.

When we enter the studio I notice there is a guy setting up lights. He is young and good looking. What the hell are they trying to do, make me a nervous wreck? So it's just me and three hot men? Great, now I am screwed.

There is music playing in the background and I recognize it immediately -- it's Sonny's song from our video. The photographer (what the hell is his *name*?) explains his vision for the shoot, and asks me for my take on authentic Latin dance poses.

I go for another sip of my drink and hear the words I've been dreading all day long: "Let's get the robes off and start this shoot," the photographer orders.

"Just relax and keep your eyes on mine Victoria and we will get through this." Sonny says in a calming voice.

He assures me it will be fine. He tells me to pretend it's just the two of us. His eyes are so captivating his suggestion won't be difficult to follow. Why does his voice have to be so sexy? I almost feel like I am in a trance. Our eyes locked and as I take a deep breath and I let my robe fall to the floor. He drops his gaze and his eyes wander down my entire body. I clear my throat to get his attention back to my face. He grins, and without hesitation he takes off his robe and turns to throw it to the side.That's when I notice he is wearing some sort of flesh-colored sock to cover his penis. I have heard of these being used during explicit movie scenes. I just can't help it. I feel like this is cheating! I'm completely naked, and he gets a cock sock? How is that fair? Oh well, even with the sock thing on I can see everything this man's body has to offer and it is amazing. He has such a great ass, his abs are perfection and his strong, muscular arms are covered in tattoos. I struggle keep my eyes on his but it's impossible not to stare at this man's body. At one point, I am sure he catches me, so I guess we're even. I keep thinking what the makeup artist said about my "smoking hot" body and hope the Latin Superstar is thinking the same thing.

The photographer asks me to select a dance pose. I take Sonny's hand in mine, and he places his other hand on the small of my back, and Bam! that feeling is back. The one when we first danced on set for the video. It is a feeling like no other. He draws me towards him and I breathe him in...he smells delicious. I've tried to figure out what he is wearing. After all my years working in a department store you would think I would know his fragrance. The heat of his naked body against mine is overwhelming. I just want to melt into him. Concentrate, Victoria! I guide him into our first pose. The photographer, whom I almost forgot was there, asks if I could tilt my head a little to the right and tells Sonny to move his hand lower on my back. His hand is now resting on the top of my ass. Just as we are what seems as close as we can possibly get, the photographer directs us to move even *closer*. Now we are so close we can feel each other's heartbeats. The photographer (what the hell is his name?) says, "It's still not enough. I can't get the shot I want. Sonny spread your legs apart." Sonny does and then he says, "Good. Now Victoria you can move closer in and position yourself between Sonny's legs." Sonny looks at me and grins as he pulls me in closer and places me right between his legs. The photographer then says, "Perfect. Hold this position for me while I get some test shots." Test shots? It's freezing in this studio and my nipples are so hard I could cut glass with them! That sock thing is pointless, I can feel his penis resting right above my knee. I don't need to see Sonny's face. I just know he is loving this. I cannot believe I am standing here flesh against flesh with this man. My breathing has increased and I hope it is not noticeable. He asks us to hold this pose for what seems like an eternity. Sonny murmurs in my ear, "Relax, you look amazing. Just enjoy the moment." Relax *how*? Instead of relaxing I'm starting to feel turned on. I can't believe this man is whispering in my ear.

We go into the next pose and I'm asked to bring my right leg over Sonny's and lean into his body. The best way to describe this is to say I am now leaning on Sonny with my crotch resting on the side of his hip. Let's just say leaning against him at this angle is feeling really good. Again, he whispers, "Relax, I've got you, Baby. Just relax and enjoy."

Did he just call me Baby? Relax and enjoy?

I'm feeling these drinks and I have begun to relax. So I decide to do a little whispering of my own. What the hell? It's just the two of us. It's weird how alcohol can take you from that giddy feeling and into a seductive, sexy mood. The photographer and his assistant cannot hear what we are saying to each other with the music playing. What's a little flirting going to hurt?

"You seem to like whispering in my ear. Is this a turn on for you?" I purr in his ear.

"Why do you ask, Victoria? Does it turn you on?" He quips. "I think it does. I can tell by your breathing. You *are* turned on."

"I think you are the one that is turned on. You're just afraid to admit it!" I coo, playfully. I have no idea where my boldness has come from.

Just when I think I have gotten to him, he comes back with, "I am not afraid to admit anything, Victoria. Yes, I am turned on by you. How could I not be? You are gorgeous."

Every time he whispers in my ear I can feel the moist warmth of his breath against my neck. At this point I am so turned on that if Sonny were to move his hip I might just explode.

The photographer has me take us through several more poses. He makes adjustments on each pose to get the best shot without exposing too much. Sonny's music continues to play in the background and the photographer seems excited, so he must be getting some great photos. We become pretty comfortable touching each others bodies as we move through the poses. Sonny continues to whisper in my ear throughout the photo shoot and he seems to be enjoying what it does to me. Sometimes he even whispers in Spanish. Fully aware I don't understand a word of it, which frustrates me all the more. I tell him it's rude to speak in a language he knows I don't understand. He whispers back, "Then it's a shame you will never know what you are missing." Not sure if he is just trying to make me feel comfortable or flirting with me. Whatever is going on here I am certainly in no hurry for it to end.

The photographer asks for one more pose and I guide Sonny into a pose where he is standing with his feet spread apart, his arms down in front of him and he has me back in a dropped position where I am almost touching the floor but looking straight up at Sonny. The photographer loves this pose and thinks it will make the perfect album cover shot. He makes just a few final adjustments. Just when I think I can no longer hold this position the photographer announces he is done. He says he has gotten some amazing shots.

Sonny pulls me up from the pose, draws me close to his chest. Wrapping his arms around me, he kisses me softly on the cheek and tells me "You did a beautiful job." Oh my, I was not prepared for this. My naked breasts are touching his chest. OK, everything is touching him right now. Right before he releases me, he whispers in my ear "Eres una mujer hermosa. Fue un placer conseguir desnudo con usted." Really? again with the Spanish? Just when I am about to ask him what he said, the photographer invites us over to view the photos on a monitor. Excitedly, we rush over to see the photos and are shocked by how stunning they are, even before they undergo any editing. The photographer is right about using the last pose for the album cover. It is perfect. It shows off Sonny's body, stripped and seductive. The way he shot this position shows my naked body but not one private part is exposed. It is tasteful. This photographer is amazing. I look like a fucking supermodel! Victoria won't be a "secret" for long!

When we are done viewing the photos, I am shocked when I realize we're both still naked. Suddenly I feel very exposed and I think Sonny has noticed this, because he quickly retrieves my robe and helps me into it. He also puts his on as well. The photographer and his assistant begin packing up their gear. Before we exit the studio, I grab his hands and stand in front of him. I have caught him off guard. I tell him I have say something to him before we leave. I want to do this because I feel it may be the last I time I will see the Latin Superstar.

"Thank you for these opportunities -- this photo shoot and the music video. This has been a great chapter added to my life. Your music is beautiful. If it wasn't for this I would never have known your music existed. This experience has changed my life and taught me so much about Latin music. Music that I had danced to but never really understood."

When I am done he says, "Victoria you are a very talented and beautiful dancer. I know during the music video rehearsals I gave you a hard time. I do recognize and appreciate your amazing talent." He then pauses taking in a deep breath and says, "I am also sure your husband would be very proud of your accomplishments."

Before I can ask how he knows about my husband he says, "You were not chosen for your dance ability alone, but also for who you are and how your journey brought you to this point in your life. After meeting you in LA I did a little research on this beautiful dancer that can go for eight hours straight without a break. I needed to know more about you, Victoria."

Then it happens. I feel tears welling up in my eyes. As one spills down from my eye, Sonny gently reaches out to me and runs his thumb across my cheek. He pulls me in close and wraps his arms around me. This is the first time in a long time that I have cried and relived the sentiment of losing Blake. After a short while, we both pull away but our eyes seem to be saying more to each other. Uncharacteristically, Sonny quickly looks away from my eyes. He seems to be a bit rattled by this moment we just shared.

We both shake hands with the photographer and thank him for his breathtaking work. "My job was made easy, because my subjects were so connected and in tune with each other. So thank you both," he said.

As we both exit the studio, hair and makeup are packing up their gear. Ken and Ashley are waiting as well as Sonny's team of people. I had no idea we were in there for several hours. We both head to the dressing room to get dressed. He offers to let me go in first. But then we both just laugh and go in together, realizing that by now we have seen every inch of one another. I can only imagine how this shocks everyone.

We are alone again, and probably for the last time. As we change, I feel a heat rise up inside me. I *want* this man. I don't see anything wrong with a little harmless

flirting. After all I just spent the last two hours completely naked with him. What do I have to lose? I'm not going to pass up my last chance to play with my Latin Superstar.

As we both take off our robes and begin to dress, I keep my eyes locked on his. Noticing this he says, "Victoria, what are you doing?"

"I am keeping my eyes focused on yours just like you instructed me to do in the photo shoot."

He laughs and tells me, "We're done working and your eyes can focus on what ever they like." But I'm still feeling flirty and drunk. "Don't tempt me...there's plenty I would like to look at."

Laughing, he picks up his jeans and begins to pull them on. Looks like he is going commando. No underwear! As he pulls them up (and trust me I am watching his every move) I realize he is going to have to remove the sock thing that has been covering his penis.

As smooth as he is, he turns away from me at the last minute so I can't get even a glimpse of it. When he turns back around he has the biggest smart ass grin on his face. My breathing hitches and I am entranced. He sits down to put his boots on and I use this time to put on my own little show for him. I am so thankful I bought a matching La Perla bra and panty set just for today. I read in an article online that he likes buying his wife expensive lingerie. He finds it very sexy when a woman considers what she wears underneath her clothes important. The set I am wearing is a very beautiful 50's inspired black and powder blue lace set. The panties are not the everyday thong panty. They are similar to a full cut panty but completely sheer lace. You can see everything. The bra is an underwire demi cup so my tits look great. While he puts on his boots he sits across from me staring at me while I get dressed. He seems to be enjoying himself and never takes his eyes off me. I purposely take my time pulling on the panties and then after I hook the bra I lean forward, filling the cups completely as I pull the straps up on my shoulders. I should win an Oscar for the performance I just gave. He surprises me when he ask if my lingerie is La Perla. I can't believe he knows who makes it. He does know his lingerie. I finish dressing by putting on my black DKNY dress and pull on my black knee high platform boots.

Smiling, Sonny looks at me and says, "Now that you are done with that little show you just put on for me, I think we better get back out there before everyone wonders what we are up to."

I can't help myself and respond with, "Well, you certainly seemed to enjoy it." He holds the door open for me and I make sure I brush up against him as I walk by.

Drawing in deep breath I set to my memory the notes that makeup the intoxicating fragrance he wears. I need to smell him one more time before this moment between us becomes nothing more than memory.

When we exit, everyone is staring in our direction. They seem to be curious about our trip to the dressing room together. We join the group to say our goodbyes.

I get one final hug from the Latin Superstar and yes, he whispers one last time in my ear.

"Hasta que nos encontramos de nuevo a mi hermosa reina de la Salsa. Y nos reuniremos otra vez. Prometo esto."

I have no idea what he has said to me, but I bet he has that smart ass grin on his face. I am not going to let him get the last word, or in this case, the last whisper. Before he releases me I pull him back for one more exchange, "You not only use Spanish to torment me but also to hide what you are really feeling."When I let go and pull away, I see in his eyes something is different. It's as though I have read his thoughts and I am not sure he wanted me to.

When we are all back in the car Ashley and Ken start firing questions at me.

"I saw him whisper in your ear. What did he say? But more importantly, what did you whisper back?" Ashely quizzes me excitedly.

"I don't know, it was in Spanish." I tell her as though I really didn't care. "I was just thanking him for the opportunity to work with him again."

"What does he look like naked?" Ken probes.

"How do you *think* he looks, Ken, and why are you so curious about that anyway?"

Their questions are beginning to make me feel uncomfortable. After all, this man is married. Something I keep having to reminding myself.

As we ride back to the studio the inquisition continues. They want to know everything. I feel like a 6th grader being drilled by my friends after a round of "seven minutes in heaven" with the hottest boy in class! In a futile effort to redirect their schoolgirl-like curiosity I tell them about the cock sock. The both stare at me in disbelief. They agree it was weird, and although they've heard about it in the film industry. They find it odd that Sonny was covered and I was vulnerably not. As for their question about why we changed together after the shoot, I shrugged it off. I explained there was nothing left to hide after we had pretty much exposed everything that afternoon. Still, I couldn't seem to get Ken off the subject. He wanted to know if I saw Sonny's penis when he got dressed. I told him Sonny was a gentleman and turned away from me, but that he clearly enjoys going commando. Ken's question puzzled me though, considering he is a straight man.

"Ken, what's with your fascination with the size of Sonny's package, anyway?" I asked.

"Well, rumor has it he is quite well-endowed."

"Oh, really! Where do you get this information?

"Um, how about the same place you have been getting yours." Ashley chimes in.

Before I can say a word, she whispers, "You really should delete your google searches."

When we arrive back at the studio Ken rushes off to finish up at his office.

Sometimes I forget that I am not Ken's only client.

Ashley and I go over next week's practice schedule. I am exhausted so I send her home for the day. Before she walks out, she turns to me and asks, "Are you all right? Your mind seems to be elsewhere since we left the shoot."

"I'm fine. It's been a long day and I have a lot on my mind with competition season ahead of me. It's time for me to get back to reality. I don't know, I just think I need some sleep." I don't think I was very convincing at all.

That night I still can't stop thinking about him. I replay every single minute over and over again in my mind. Wondering if he was feeling what I was feeling. I guess I'll never know. Like I told Ashley, it's time to get back to reality. I need to be real here. I will never hear from this man again. He is married and I am not a part of his life. It was just some stupid flirting, anyway. Besides, the Latin Superstar probably flirts with every attractive woman that crosses his path. I put on my Bose headphones and let his voice sing me to sleep.

7 o'clock Monday morning my alarm clock jolts me back to my real life. Mateo and I will start practicing today for the competition season that begins in two months. We will practice five days a week for about 6 to 8 hours a day. I turn thirty-seven the day of the finals this year. These next few months will be really hard on my body. I am in excellent shape. I don't smoke or do drugs. But I'm not so foolish to think I can dance competitively forever. Truth is, I only have a few years of competition left in me. The body can only

take so much. Every year there seems to be younger and younger couples competing.

But this year Mateo and I are THE couple to beat. We are the reigning champions, and I am not ready to give up my title just yet. Not without a fight.

Mateo arrives promptly at 9 am for a full day of practice. I have been dancing with him for about 2 years now, Mateo is about 5 years younger than me. But there are some days that I feel 10 years older. I have not seen Mateo for a few months. He owns a successful dance studio in Brooklyn that keeps him busy during the off season. We will be working on a new dance routine. He has chosen a song from a new up and coming Latin singer. I always let him pick the music for our routines because I really don't listen to Latin music. Well, until now. It seems I can't get enough of listening to Sonny de la Cruz's music. He has become my own personal lullaby.

I like to give my body about a half hour head start on warming up before Mateo arrives. I need it to keep up with him. My body and my mind are telling me it's time for competition season. It's like it has it's own built in alarm clock alerting me it needs the adrenaline of competing. I crave it. I just hope when it's time to retire and give it up my life will have some new meaning. Maybe a new adventure. Maybe even a man. Hey, a girl can dream.

My thoughts are interrupted by a very familiar voice that instantly brings a smile to my face. There is no mistaking that Mateo has arrived. "Baby Girl, I have missed you these past few months. But I see you have been busy. A music video with a Latin singer? Did you even know who this Sonny de la Cruz was?" He teases me.

I laugh as Mateo greets me with his questions along with a big hug and kiss.

"Oh, Mateo, I've really missed you too! Of course I had no idea who he was. Ken said it was a great opportunity for me and it went really well. You would have loved the look on the directors face when I told him I did not speak Spanish."

"I know that look. I would have loved seeing that. His song is great but the music video is what seems to be getting all the attention. There are millions of views of it on Vevo. What surprised me was that Sonny de la Cruz could dance! That man is *muy caliente*, Victoria! What was it like working with him?"

"You know, I was surprised he could dance, too. He took direction really well, and we actually had a lot of fun. Sonny's a good sport and very charming."

"Charming? That's it? You spend all that time with THE Sonny de la Cruz and you call him charming? Prince William is charming, Victoria. Sonny de la Cruz is sex on a stick, baby girl!"

He makes me laugh. "Boy," I giggle, "your mind is *always* on sex. But this time I will have to agree with you. He may be sexy, but he is also very married."

"You really love to suck the fun out of things, don't you? Who cares if he is married? You got to dance with him in a video! Do you know how many women and men for that matter would kill for that chance? I mean really, girl!"

"Well, for your information, I can be fun. How about this for fun? I just returned from doing the cover shoot for his soon-to-be-dropped album!" I waited a moment before revealing the best part. "Oh, did I forget to mention? I was Naked!...and so was he!" I taunted.

"Ok hold on, hold on...Naked? Wait! The first year we competed together you wouldn't even change clothes in front of me -- ME! and I'm gay! Now you expect me to believe you got naked with the sexiest singer in the Latin music world? YOU?? Get the fuck out of here with that noise!"

"Yes, Me, boring little me. I got completely naked with Sonny de la Cruz and pressed my naked body against his naked body. NAKED! Skin on skin."

"Okay, okay, I get it! Naked! ¡Ay dios mio! How long were you going to hold this information back from me? I want details. What did he look like without his shirt on? Wait, no...without his pants on! You saw his dick! Oh my God! I want to know how big it is, and you better not leave one single thing out. Start talking, baby girl! Give it up!" Mateo gestures like a madman and sits down, waiting for me to spill it.

Mateo makes me laugh. I appease him with my own version of the inside scoop, and tell him everything. Well, maybe not *everything*. I have not revealed to anyone how I have been thinking and dreaming about this man since working with him. I can't seem to get Sonny out of my head. Why, am I so attracted to him? I feel like a lovesick teenager. I have not thought about a man in this way in such a long time. It has been five years now. There hasn't been one man come into my life since Blake's death that has that has this kind of effect on me. Yet, here I am, obsessing over a man who isn't even remotely close to available. Once I satisfy Mateo's demand for information, we get down to work.

Mateo and I spend the next several weeks working out our routine. I am also coaching two other couples in the evenings and weekends. One couple is just starting the dance competition circuit and will compete in Bachata, a dance originating from the Dominican Republic where the music also was born. In partnering, the lead can decide whether to perform in open, semi-closed or closed position. Unlike salsa, bachata dance does not usually include many turn patterns.They are so young but very talented. If they stick to it and work hard they will be champions in the next few years. Competition is very tough in Bachata. The other couple is Rafael and Lily. They compete in Kizomba, which I refer to as the dance for lovers. Kizomba is the new Latin dance rage and they are the couple to beat. They are a YouTube sensation, and you can tell the couples who are lovers from the ones that are not. Rafael and Lily are surely lovers. That's what makes them so amazing. When they dance you see the passion ignite and burn between them.

The weeks are flying by and it feels good to be busy. It keeps my mind off wondering what the Latin Superstar is up to and when the new album will be released. Sonny de la Cruz is way too cool for a Twitter or Facebook account so finding anything on him is next to impossible. My best information comes from the Latin entertainment networks. I often have to use the Bing translator just to figure out what they are saying. I think I might even be picking up a little Spanish from all my research. There is talk on several sites about the album. It looks like it is going to launch very soon. I keep asking Ken if he knows what photo they have chosen for the cover. He says he has not heard a thing. I can't help but wonder what his wife thought of our photos. Did it bother her that her husband got nude with me? I'm sure she hated the fact that I asked for her to not be present during the shoot. I need to remind

Ken that I would like a copy of the photos. I believe that was in my contract.

Ashley greets me with an uncharacteristically cheerful hello this morning when I enter the office. The one thing I love about my place is that my loft is right above my studio. I spend so much time traveling during the year, it is great to have everything in one building when I am at home. As I sit down to my Mac to check my email, her cheerfulness fades. She becomes almost panicky, pushing me away from my desk and escorting me toward the studio.

"What is wrong with you, Ashley?" I ask her as she ushers me out of my own office.

"Mateo is waiting for you in the studio. You can look at your email later. You know how he hates to wait." She seems nervous. I don't like it.

"Why do I have this feeling you are trying to get rid of me? Mateo can wait one minute while I check something online." I say as I turn back toward my desk, ignoring her.

"No, I am not trying to get rid of you. It's just rude to leave him waiting." She is completely unconvincing.

I defiantly sit down and pull up my email. There is a message from iTunes notifying me that Sonny's album is available for advance ordering. I immediately click on the link and there it is. The album. The album with our photo on the cover! My heart races as I look closer to see which photo they've selected. Not to my surprise, I see they have chosen a photo from the last dance pose. That was an intense shot. Then I look closer, and my excitement is replaced with shock. You cannot even see my face in this photo! I can't believe it! They used one where my head is turned in toward Sonny's leg and you can't tell it's me at all. The woman in this photo could be anyone. It's a great pose; my body looks gorgeous, but what the fuck? You can't tell that it's Me! Out loud and with anger in my voice I yell out, "Fuck, Fuck, Fuck!"

"Oh, Jesus." I can hear Ashley sigh from the other room.

I yell out to her from my office, "Yes, Ashley, did you really think you could keep this from me? I'd have seen it eventually. Fuck!"

"I'm sorry. I was hoping Ken would have called by now to let you know about this." She apologizes.

"Ken fucking knew about this?" My shock has just turned to rage.

Ashley is frantic, "Yes, but I'm not sure how long he has known about it." She is hiding something. I have known her too long.

"Cancel practice with Mateo and get Ken on the phone Now!" I demand as I get up and slam the door shut. Again I yell out, "Fuck, fuck, fuck." I bet it was his wife's idea to use this fucking photo.

The longer it takes for Ashley to get Ken on the phone, the more pissed off I become. All the while I keep staring at the album cover.

I don't take my eyes of the computer screen until Ashley buzzes my phone and says, "Ken is on the line for you. Victoria, please think before you say anything to him. He may not have had any control over this."

Before she can continue I cut her off and pick up the line Ken is waiting on. "What the fuck, Ken? They pick the one photo where you can't see my face. It's my body, but who is going to know that? How the hell did this happen?"

Ken is prepared for me because I am sure Ashley filled him in on how upset I was, "Victoria, you need to calm down."

Slamming my hand down hard on my desk I scream out to him. "I will NOT calm down! I am pissed and want to know how long you knew about this?"

"I just found out." I know he is lying. "We own the rights to the photos they took, but we do not have authority over the photo selected for the cover. This is Sonny de la Cruz's album and, unfortunately, it is about him."

"Well, then they could have used any damn model for that fucking photo! It was a complete waste of my time. I lost practice days for this shit! This was to be a vehicle to help my career. So much for that!" I am shaking I am so damn mad.

"They are going to use some of the other photos for promotional tools and on the inside sleeve of the CD. People will know it is you when they see those photos. You were paid very well for the shoot." He says trying to reassure me that this was still a good career move.

"Like that is supposed to make me feel better? Stop with the money thing. You know it's not about that for me." I slam down the phone as hard as I can. I tell Ashley to clear my schedule for the rest of day. I grab my handbag throwing it over my shoulder and walk right by her without a word. I make sure to slam the door behind me.

I spent the rest of the day shopping. I need some retail therapy to forget about this shit. I feel used. Stupid. All that preparing and worrying for nothing! I can't believe I got naked for that man! I guess I was wrong about him. There was no connection between us. If he felt anything even close to what I did, he would have made damned sure to choose a photo where my face was at least visible!I guess I have been so out of touch with my feelings that I can't even recognize something real from something I have created in my mind.

Four pair of designer shoes, a pizza, a bottle of wine and a carton Ben and Jerry's strawberry cheesecake ice-cream and I still feel dispirited. Oh yeah and I dropped bank in the cosmetic department at Neiman's on every skin care product that the beauty consultant introduced me to. She probably made her sales quota for the month just off of me. I spent the rest of the evening with a detox mask on my face hoping it would also erase my mind of all memories of Sonny de la Cruz. Stepping into a hot shower I wash not only this mask off, but also the disappointment from today. As I lean my back against the cool tiles and let the hot water wash over my body I close my eyes and say a silent prayer asking for the strength to move past this.

After crawling into bed with my Macbook I must have looked at the photo of the album on iTunes at least 20 times. I will admit the man looks hot and it really is a beautiful photo. But as for me -- I was just a body. An amazing body, but just a nameless body. I am not even sure I will ever listen to his music again. I need to move on and forget about all of this. I have no time for this. Tonight, instead of Sonny de la Cruz singing me to sleep, I will fall asleep to nothing but the sound of the city outside my window.

Ashley is surprised to see me the next morning when I walk into the office.

"Has Mateo arrived for practice?" I am all business.

"Yes, he is the studio waiting for you. Are you all right?"

"I am fine. It's over and I don't want to hear anything more about Sonny de la Cruz. Got it?" I don't give her a chance to respond.

As soon as I step into the studio, I notice Mateo seems concerned. "Baby Girl, is everything OK? It's not like you to cancel practice."

"Yes. I am sorry I walked out on you yesterday."

"Look, you know you don't have to apologize to me. But you know you're my Baby Girl, and I am here if you need to talk about anything." He gives me a supportive hug and a kiss.

That's the thing about Mateo. Not only is he an amazing dance partner but also a great friend. He is the one man in my life that I can talk to about anything and when I don't feel like talking he gives me room. I just can't seem to bring myself to tell him about my silly, pointless feelings for the Latin Superstar.

We worked a full day on our routine. It felt great to concentrate on nothing but dancing. Dancing is the thing I do best. It's the one thing that never confuses me.

90

Never frustrates me. Never abandons me or makes me feel stupid. Over the next few days everything starts returning to normal for me. Ken has even called and apologized several times. I told him I didn't want to talk about it and I never want to hear from Sonny de la Cruz again.

The weeks of practice are flying by and we have less than a month before the start of the competition season. Mateo and I now have our new dance routine down and it's perfect with the music. We meet with our costume designer and work out the final details. Every season I design new costumes for the finals. My simple life has returned to normal and memories of Sonny de la Cruz are fading.

It's been a full day already and I still have Rafael and Lily coming in for a coaching session later this evening. Before they arrive I have time for a quick shower and something to eat. As I'm getting dressed, I open my drawer filled with all my bra and panty sets. I pull out the La Perla set I wore the day of the photo shoot. My first reaction is to throw it back in the drawer and choose another set. But I realize I am well past that and slip into the sexy beautiful set. I don't even think about the last time I put them on. I am done with that. I pull out my favorite black dance pants, camisole, hooded sweat shirt and of course my tacky bronze metallic practice shoes.

Before entering the studio I stop and ask Ashley to take care of a few things. She says she will let me know when she is leaving. Before I walk out she says, "You seem to be back to your old self again. I'm happy to see it."

I slam the door behind me because I really don't want to hear what she has to say. I know what she is referring to and just don't want to think about it.

Rafael and Lily are already stretching and warming up. I love watching them dance. Kizomba is one hot sexy dance. Lily's body and movements are mesmerizing to watch. Combine that with both of their hot looks and they are pure sex to watch while dancing. This style is the most sensuous form of all the Latin dances. Kizomba has become so popular there are groups that make music solely for that style of dance. The song they've selected for their routine is perfect: Mika Mendes' "Mágico."

Ashley is buzzing the studio phone. She must be going home. I pick up the phone and before I can tell her to have a good evening, she blurts out, "There is someone here to see you and they have a package for you."

I don't why she is bothering me with this. She knows I am busy teaching. "Just sign for the package."

She whispers in the phone to me, "It's him! He is here and he has a package with him!" I can tell by her tone she is excited about whoever he is.

My mind flashes and I tell myself she can't be talking about Sonny de la Cruz. Still confused I demand from her, "Ashley, stop whispering and tell me who is here to see me."

"Sonny de la Cruz is here to see you," she announces.

My heart immediately feels like it is going to pound right out of my chest. I am pissed at this man about the album cover but also deliriously excited about him being here at my studio. I have to get control of myself. I take a deep breath and I calmly tell her, "Explain to him that I am in a private lesson. If he would like to come in and wait I will be done in about 20 minutes. If not he can just leave the package with you."

I hear her speaking to him and she comes back on the phone and tells me, "He would like to come in and wait until you are finished. He wants to speak with you."

"That would be fine." Fuck! Why did I give him the option? I should have told

Ashley to tell him to leave the package and go. What the hell was I thinking? Why is he here?

"Do you need anything else from me before I leave?"

"No, I am fine," I lie. "See you tomorrow."

She buzzes the door open to the studio and in walks the Latin Superstar Sonny de la Cruz. It's one of those crazy, almost surreal moments. I am standing here watching him walk into the studio and again it seems to be happening in slow motion. Like the time he first walked in to the video shoot. Why am I sweating him? This is the same man who apparently did not feel my face was cover worthy. I am supposed to be furious with him but instead I am thinking how damned hot he looks. He is carrying a large flat package wrapped in brown paper. Wearing baggy cargo pants, boots and a leather jacket. This man is, as Mateo so eloquently puts it, Sex on a Stick! He has on shades so I can't see those eyes. It's a good thing too because it's his eyes that get me every damn time!

He walks over to where I am standing and smiles. "Buenas noches, Victoria." No kiss on each cheek this time. I think he can tell by my body language that I am not happy with him.

"I will be done in about 20 minutes." I say flatly.

If he only knew what I was really feeling. My heart and stomach could win a gold medal in gymnastics for their performance.

"I will be happy to wait, Victoria."

I think he loves saying my name, it is laced with flirtation. He can flirt all he wants. I am pissed and I am not giving into this man. He must be here because he wants something. But I am done with him. No more videos or photos for him…ever!

Rafael and Lily stop dancing and are whispering to each other. They must recognize him. They look to me as if they want to say something. I shake my head, no, so they continue with their dance.

Sonny asks, "What style of dance is this?"

"It's called Kizomba." I reply with no emotion.

"I have never heard of it or even seen it danced."

"It is the newest form of dance in the Latin dance world. It's becoming very popular."

"Victoria, do you dance Kizomba?"

"No. It is the dance for lovers and I don't have a lover. I have a dance partner and we dance all the traditional Latin dances." I decide the best way to handle his questions is to give him back rude answers. Hoping he will get it. He needs to shut the hell up.

"You and your partner are not lovers? Kizomba is a very sensual dance to watch."

"That's really none of your business. But since you asked, no, we are not lovers. He is gay. I prefer not to be romantically involved with my dance partner. My career has me traveling several months out of the year and I really don't have the time for a relationship."

Damn him! What the hell is wrong with me! He is fishing for information and I just handed it to him. He knows full well what he's doing to me! He's trying to break me and no matter how hard I try I still can't resist this man. I need to hold my ground with him. I am not giving into his game.

I wish this lesson would never end because I am in no mood to talk to him. I even try to extend the lesson a little longer, but Rafael keeps checking his watch and seems to be ready to leave. I walk Rafael and Lily out and tell them I will see them in Miami for our first competition. Before they leave, Rafael whispers to me, "Is that Sonny de la Cruz?" I nod yes to them. Now I have to face him alone.

I lock the studio doors and head back in to face Sonny and find out why he is here. I'm also curious about the package he is carrying. When I come back in, I notice he's removed his sunglasses. I make sure I do not look into those eyes, I ask him directly and with absolutely no warmth to my voice, "Why are you here?"

"Is there a place we can sit down and talk, Victoria?" Sonny says in his soft, seductive voice.

See? There he goes again with my name! He loves using my name. "We can sit down and talk in my apartment, which is upstairs." I regret the words as soon as they come out of my mouth. I have no idea what he could possibly be here to talk about. At least I get to show off my huge loft apartment. I want him to see just how successful I am. I don't need his stupid album cover to make my career.

"That would be perfect, Victoria."

He uses my name again!. He even rolls the "r" in it to make it sound so damn sexy. He is so good at trying to break me down. I am not going to let him win though. Yeah, keep telling yourself that Victoria.

The walk upstairs to my apartment is in complete silence. But I am sure he enjoyed it. He was behind me as we walked up the long flight of stairs. I'm sure he just loved staring at my ass on the way up. Oh, don't worry, I gave him a show.

As we enter he comments immediately on my loft. "Wow! This place is beautiful. Your view of the city is amazing. This place had to cost you a small fortune." I clearly have made my own way, as he can see. I love it. It's my home. It has no walls to speak of, just a complete open space. With a clean modern decor. The only space closed off is the hallway that leads to my bedroom, which is the back of the apartment. People are usually shocked when they see how large my bedroom space is. But my bedroom is not included in his tour of my loft.

Instead I direct him over to the kitchen area and he takes a seat at my granite covered island. I ask if he'd like a drink. He only requests water, I offer him some wine, as I open a bottle and pour some for myself, to calm my rattled nerves. He declines, so I hand him a glass of water and join him at the island with my wine. I sit across from him and repeat my earlier question. "Why are you here?" I want him to think I am annoyed. I want him to feel unwelcome.

In a guarded manner he pulls the package up from the floor and slides it across the island. "I want you to have this."

Great. A gift. His idea of an apology? I open it and am surprised to find that it a photo of us from the shoot. The photo is beautiful. You can see my face. It's the perfect shot. This should have been the album cover. This must be some sort of peace offering. Maybe Ken called and told them all off.

"Victoria, I wanted to explain about the photo that was chosen for the album cover." He offers, almost apologetically.

Standing my ground and keeping my "I don't give a shit" attitude, "I get it. I understand. It is your album and cover. You did not have to come here and explain anything to me. Thanks for the photo." I discard the framed photo to the side as if it means nothing to me.

"But I did have to come here. I needed to tell you in person that you were the right choice for the cover. I need to make this right between us. I know you are pissed at me. When we sat down to pick the cover photo I wasn't prepared for what I saw in the photos. Some of the photos were so revealing and I am not talking about our bodies. I am talking about the raw illicit emotions that came through in them. Sitting with my marketing team and my wife I felt like I needed to protect you. I chose the photo. I picked the one that shows no connection between us." He voice is filled with regret.

Continuing my flippant performance, I stop him before he can say another word. "Protect me? I don't need your protection. You owe me no explanation and I really don't want to hear any more." I wanted to tell him how much this hurt me and how I felt used. I wanted to tell him I felt I was not going to get the recognition I deserved from doing the shoot. Instead I keep this all to myself. What's the point? Telling him all of this will just reveal to him that I am weak and that he meant something to me. I don't want him to know any of this. I want him to leave. I want this part of my life over. I want him to be a memory. A bad memory.

He stops and just stares at me from the other end of the island. His eyes connect with mine and I cannot break the hold he has on me. Again those eyes. They're so seducing. I am overcome with contrasting emotions. I'm confused, turned on, and pissed off, all at the same time. I can feel the salty sting of tears starting to well in my eyes.

I will not cry in front of this man. Before those eyes accomplish what they set out to do to me, I push my stool away from the island. "Sonny, I appreciate the gesture, but this whole thing has left a really bad taste in my mouth."

"I have something else I would like to say." He announces. Instead, he drops his gaze and stares down at the counter, saying nothing. Hmm. It appears the Latin

Superstar may not be quite as smooth as he thinks.

Really? What else does he want to use me for? Another video? More photos? Maybe give me another lecture about how I should learn to speak and understand

Spanish. No, I am done with the you, Sonny de la Cruz. If only I had the guts to say these things out loud.

The silence between us is becoming unbearable. I think I'm going to ask him to leave. Just as I am about to open my mouth, his eyes find mine. When will I learn? His eyes are my weakness. I am taken in and seduced. His eyes, my kryptonite.

Drawing in a breath so long and deep it's audible, he begins. "Victoria, I am a believer of living my life to the fullest. I regret nothing. If something is on his mind, I say it. I don't walk away from any emotions that I am feeling. I don't back off from anything."

What the hell does any of this have to do with me? Is he that egotistical? Why is he sharing this with me?

I think he can sense my annoyance. He draws in another deep breath and begins, "My wife has been the only woman in my life. The only woman I have ever loved. She is the reason I am who I am in the Latin music world. Without her I would be nothing. But like I said I don't turn my back on anything including my feelings and that is why I am here. I am tired of struggling and ignoring what I am feeling. I can't turn my back on it any longer."

What the fuck? He just had to drag her into this! I get it, he loves his fucking wife. I am going to put a stop to this, now. He needs to leave. But the look in his eyes changes just as I am about to speak. My heart is pounding. How can one man's eyes have such an effect on a person? I grab my wine glass and drain it. I am not prepared for what he says next.

"I cannot walk away from what I have been feeling these last few months. I constantly think about you. My mind is always occupied with thoughts of you, Victoria. Thoughts of you follow me to my dreams. The memory of the first time I saw you dance will not leave me. The passion with which you dance is the same passion I feel when I am writing or singing. I felt the connection the instant our eyes met on the dance floor. Thoughts of your naked body haunt me. The feel of your skin touching mine during the photo shoot ignited something I haven't felt in a very long time. There was a spark between us. I tried ignoring it, but I can't turn my back on what I feel. And this, Victoria, I feel is real. Right or wrong. I want you."

Oh. My. God! My biggest want and my biggest fear has just materialized. He has been feeling the same things I have these past few months. So it *wasn't* just something I had created in my head! The feelings were mutual and very real. Fuck! I should have sent him away and refused to see him. Now what? I just sit here frozen. My heart is pounding out of my chest. I am gulping for air. Oh God, he is waiting for me to say something? My mind is reeling. I can't think. Again, silence and staring into each others eyes. I am afraid to respond because I know where this will lead, and I am not prepared. He is married. I keep telling myself over and over in my mind. If I remain silent, maybe he will leave.

The silence drags on for what feels like several minutes. He starts to become and look very uncomfortable. He finally drops his eyes away from mine. "I am sorry. I should never have said anything. Forget everything." His mood shifts, and he seems almost agitated. I think he may even be embarrassed.

He continues with a melancholic tone. "I truly believed there was a connection between us. I see now that I read you all wrong." He gets up from his stool and turns to leave.

Still frozen in my seat and afraid to speak, I make no attempt to say or do a thing. But my mind is in overdrive, trying to process everything. If I let him leave, it will be the end. But if I speak up, it will open a door to something I am not sure either of us is ready for. I know in my heart where it will lead. I know where I will always stand in his life. But if I don't speak, he will never know how I feel. My mind rewinds back to the time I first fell in love with Blake. As much as I try to fight what I am feeling for Sonny I remind myself I wouldn't have missed a minute of what I shared with my husband. I don't want to miss this chance no matter what the consequences. I realize I can't let this man walk away without telling him how I feel. Even if it is wrong. I want to become his muse.

Pouring myself another glass of wine I take a long drink hoping it will give me the nerve to speak. Just as he reaches the door I yell out, "Sonny!"

He stops with the door handle in his hand, but keeps his back to me.

"You are not alone in your feelings. I felt something between us the first time you put your hand around the small of my back to learn the dance. That was the moment everything changed for me." I blurt out, forgetting to breathe as the words fly from my lips.

I stand up and take another gulp of liquid courage and prepare to bare my soul to this man.

My voice is shaking as I force the words out. "I have been feeling the same way for the past few months and you haunt me in my dreams. I have danced with several men over the years, but never have I felt or danced the way I did with you. It was hard to try to mask those feelings in front of everyone, especially your wife. But when I was in your arms, I was able to put all that out of my mind and just enjoy the moment."

Sonny turns around to face me. His dark seducing eyes find mine and I open up to him about what I have been feeling. "I tried convincing myself what I was feeling was nothing more than simple flirting between us. But I knew it was more than that. No matter how many times I reminded myself that you were married I couldn't stop what I was feeling. Sonny I am not proud of myself but I don't know what to do." It was like the floodgates were opened, and I couldn't stop. "When you took me into your arms the first time we danced it was one of the most intense feelings I have ever experienced. It felt so amazing to be that close to you in the photo shoot and smell and feel your body touching mine. I didn't care that the photographer and his assistant were there. I felt the passion between us then. No matter what I told myself, I could not stop myself. But it's been such a long time since I have felt that way. I wasn't sure if it was real. I have spent the last few months consumed with doubt.

I glance down at the beautifully framed photo and I see our bond. This photo clearly reveals the connection between the two of us. I can't take my eyes off of it. I don't even notice that Sonny has made his way across the room and is standing behind me. Before I know it, he has his strong hands around my waist. He spins me around to face him and without any warning or chance to stop it, it happens. Sonny de la Cruz kisses me. Hard.

It is amazing and surprisingly not awkward in any way. His lips are just as I imagined them. Full and soft. He has me leaned up against the kitchen island, because without the support I would probably sink to the floor. He has one hand resting on my hip and the other has made it's way up the back of neck to cradle my head pulling me even closer to him to control the depth and angle of his kiss. When he does I can't stop the moan that escapes my mouth. He responds with a growl deep in his throat. We continue kissing and I am not cognizant of anything. My breath hitches reminding me to breath. His delicious lips and tongue continue exploring every inch of my mouth. With each stroke of his tongue on mine, my mind goes twirling like my best pirouette. He's commanding my each and every move, my loss of breath, my outpour of emotion. It's our first encounter, yet it's as if this man's kiss is all I've ever known. He is a maestro; he knows exactly what he is doing and he does it well. This seems so insane and at the same time it feels so right. I feel safe in his arms. I want more, but he seems to be in no hurry. He is pushing up against me and I feel the hardness through his jeans. Ken may be right. It feels *huge*. My breathing is heavy and my heart is pounding. What the hell am I doing? What am I getting myself into?

I want to drown in this man's kiss. I don't care that he's married. I don't care what anyone thinks or if anyone wants to judge me. The only thing I care about is how I feel right now. I know I'll regret letting this moment slip away if I don't give into what I am feeling. It's the first time I've felt this alive since Blake's death. I want this. I want to feel alive again. Nothing matters to me right now except this man's kiss. It's as though time is standing still. I will never forget this kiss.

He pulls away and slows his breathing and says, "Relax, Victoria. It's just us. No one is watching and we don't have to hide the passion. Just let it go."

Thank God he did not say this in Spanish. He returns to my lips and it is different this time because I do just as he requests - I relax and let go. Every thought about holding back or stopping this leaves my mind. The kissing is so intense. You can feel sparks igniting between us. He starts moving his hands and unzips my sweat shirt to pull it off. The first thought that pops in my head is...thank goodness I have on my dance heels. I am kissing the man I have been obsessing over for months now and all I can think of are dance shoes. Oh, Victoria you are in big trouble. The heel is the perfect height and I don't have to stretch to put my arms around his neck. He then starts to run his hands along the sides of my breasts. Just skimming the sides of each one with his finger tips. I think I am going to melt and slide down this granite island. The feeling is amazing and my nipples react. I think I may just die right here. I'm fucked!

He stops and backs up for a moment, and our eyes are locked. He slowly slips my camisole straps off my shoulders and glides it off in one smooth sweep. I notice his grin when he recognizes the La Perla bra I am wearing. He remembers it. He returns to my lips. More tongue dancing. This man is patient and loves kissing. I feel his hands around the waist band of my capris. No zippers! He rolls them down and while doing so he drops to a kneeling position and helps me step out of them. On his way back up, he pauses and runs his hands over my hips and as he pulls himself up and drags his hard cock along the front of my body. If he is not too careful I may just explode right here. I am standing in just my La Perla lingerie and dance heels. The only thought that registers in my head is I am so glad I took that shower earlier.

OK, it's been a while but that doesn't mean I don't remember what to do. Not only am I a great dancer but I have also been told I am great in bed. Reminding myself of this, I figure it's my turn. I think I remember how to undress a man. I pull his T-shirt up out of his pants and over his head. Not as graceful and sexy as he was with me, but I got it off. I can't control myself as I run my hands all over his arms and down the front of his chest. This makes him smile and makes me blush. Good, he liked it. I can do this. I want this. This time I take control of the kiss. His lips feel so amazing I can't help myself and I bite his lower lip and draw him closer into me. He pulls away and moves his lips to my neck. My neck and ears are one of my weaknesses. A moan escapes my mouth. This urges him on and his lips trail down my neck to my breasts. He stops and kisses the top of each of them before he pulls my bra straps off my shoulders and with one snap it falls to the floor. I know he has seen everything before but it feels different this time. He takes my breast in his hands and pinches my nipples between his fingers. In comparison to my neck and ears, my nipples would be my sexual drug of choice. It's the thing that will send me over the edge. I not only like it, I need it. I crave it. He finds this out quickly when he takes one nipple in his mouth and gently sucks and bites it. I arch my back and let out another uncontrollable moan. He notices and take the other nipple in his mouth and repeats the same thing. He stops only to whisper, "I see I have discovered something you like." The whispering is such a turn on. I have no idea if I should say anything back. So I decide to just enjoy this moment. My hips thrust out and he pushes me back hard against the kitchen island and whispers, "Not so fast, Victoria."

My turn. I run my tongue up the line of his neck before I capture his lips. My tongue slips in-between. I grab his belt buckle and undo it. I unzip his pants and hope he is going commando. Yes! I discover quickly he is. His pants drop around his ankles. Even though I cannot see it with my eyes, I can feel that he is huge. He is pressing up against my stomach. I push back. I want to feel this man and I want him inside of me now! He whispers, "Slow down and breathe, Victoria. I am going to fuck you and trust me we will get to that, but I also want to enjoy this first time with you." I cannot believe he just said he is going to fuck me. More kissing, more nipple biting. He has me standing here soaking wet, and just about to lose control.

He steps back and puts his hands on my waist. He pulls my panties down and I hold on to his shoulders to support myself as I step out of them. Halfway back up, he stops and kisses me on my *other* lips. Thank God I have kept up with my Brazilian since the photo shoot.

"Victoria, you're already so wet for me. You smell amazing."

Oh God. Is it that obvious? It must be. Again I thank myself for taking that shower.

Sonny steps back, looks my body up and down, and says, "Do you have any idea how hard it was for me to control myself when I first saw how beautiful you are? Then to have to hold you so close in those dance positions, so close that it took everything I had in me to control and fight what I was feeling? I don't want to control myself any longer. I want you and I want to touch every inch of your body."

Not sure if I am just caught up in the moment or it's the wine talking but I can't help myself. "Sonny, I want you. Inside me. Now!"

He puts both of his hands around my waist and pulls me close and whispers

"Victoria" as he returns to kissing me. His one hand leaves my waist and before I know it I am letting out a loud moan. He has slid his fingers into my lips and is stroking my clit. He stops kissing me and whispers again, "Victoria you really need to relax and breathe. I am going to make you come. I want you to enjoy it."

Really? Relax? Are you kidding me? Come? I think I have come a million times since he started kissing me. His tongue is amazing. Concentrating on how good it feels as he kisses me, I finally relax as he manipulates my clit with masterful fingers. I am sure he can tell by my breathing I am enjoying it. He is good. Oh God, I just said good. What the fuck, Victoria. Good? Try, fucking incredible. I have stood for hours at a time in these dance heels, but this is the first time I'm aware that I'm having trouble balancing. My legs are noticeably shaking. He has to know the effect he is having on me. Driving me to the point of insanity. He stops just before I am about to come and repeats this several times. He knows exactly what he is doing. The kissing stops and he concentrates on my nipples. The combination of him biting my nipples and stroking my clit with his fingers has me reeling. When he feels he has pushed me to my limits he pulls away and whispers again, "Victoria you need to look at me. I want to watch you come." Before I can say anything or look at his eyes the stroking of my clit continues but this time he doesn't stop. He takes me all the way. My heads drops back and I am sighing and pushing hard against his fingers until I come, and I come hard. It seems to last forever and I let out a long moan. It's been a while since I have felt a release like this and I hope I don't sound too desperate. His touch is better than anything I could have imagined.

When I return to my senses, he is staring at me. Once again his lips capture mine and the kissing intensifies. This time I feel it is my turn to return the favor. I take his huge and I mean huge dick in my hands. I am happy to hear him moan into my mouth. I pull away from his lips and begin kissing his chest and working my way down his stomach. Before I can reach my destination, he stops me and grabs both of my wrist and pulls me up. Pushing hard against me he whispers, "No, not this time." He then asks me, "Does this beautiful apartment have a bedroom or am I going to have to fuck you on this kitchen island?"

"Yes, I have bedroom," I laugh. He pulls his pants back up as I grab his hand and I take him down the hallway toward my bedroom. It's a long hallway. Half way down he stops and grabs me and pushes me against the wall, but I am not facing him. He has me pinned with my cheek flush with the wall.

I can't help if I seem anxious. It's been a long time since I have felt this way about a man. I've never shared anything like this with another man. Not even with

Blake. I know it's wrong but its like I'm on a carnival ride and there is no getting off until the ride is over. I tell myself to relax and calm down. I take in a long, deep breath.

He spreads my hands out so I can support myself and then he spreads my legs wide apart. I am standing here completely naked in my dance shoes spread eagle with this hot Latin man standing behind me. I am a little unsure of what he is about to do, but I am so caught up in the moment that I really don't care. He starts kissing my back and reaches around to pinch my erect nipples between his fingers. With his other hand he reaches between my thighs and inserts first one, then two, then finally three fingers inside of me and begins feverishly thrusting them in and out, while he drags his thumb in circles around my swollen clit. Just as I am about to come again he stops and turns me to face him. I want to fucking kill him this time! Damn this man. His lips and tongue continue their assault on mine. He continues to push himself up against me. This man is slowly driving me insane. I can feel his hardness and I'm eagerly grinding my hips against him. I want this man inside of me. This pushing and kissing goes on for several minutes and he *knows* I am about to come again and pulls away from me. He takes my hand and leads me down the rest of the hallway into my bedroom.

It's hard for him not to comment on my bedroom. The bedroom is the best part of the apartment. One wall is filled with floor to ceiling windows and the other wall is covered in mirrors. The floors in my apartment are all stained concrete except for my bedroom. They are done in refurbished hardwood flooring. My bed is huge and covered in white linens, the kind you would expect in five-star hotels. Other than the two night stands and a bench at the foot of the bed, there is no other furniture. So the bedroom is massive. He guides me over to my bed and sits me down. He stands in front of me and slowly removes his boots and then his pants. Then he walks over to where I am sitting on the bed and squats down between my legs and removes my dance shoes. Sonny looks up at me through wantonness eyes and asks, "Victoria do I need to use a condom or are you on birth control?"

Oh shit! Wait, I got this covered. Think Victoria. I am happy to tell him he will not need to use a condom since I am on birth control. Not that I am sexually active. The pill helps regulate and lighten my period. I'd like to say that this was an awkward question but I understand and I certainly do not want any accidents.

My Latin Superstar spreads my legs open and slides his fingers into me. I prop myself up on my elbows and lock eyes with him as he brings me to the brink of another orgasm. My head is swimming and watching him work his magic has me entranced, but just as I think I'm about to come -- he stops, again. Fuck! What is he trying to do to me? He pushes me all the way back on my bed and entrails kisses from my ankles all the way up to my mouth. His breathing is heavy in my ear and with his strong hands he pushes my legs open and guides his huge, hard dick inside of me and I immediately go slick around him. In an eager and shaky voice, he whispers in my ear, "Oh God, Victoria, I have been dreaming about how you would feel." And before I can moan, he does. I lose all inhibition and let myself go, matching him stroke for stroke. No fantasy of mine could possibly compare to how good it feels to have him inside of me. The kissing intensifies and the only time he stops is to take my nipple in his mouth. He pulls away and breathlessly whispers, "I want to come with you at the same time. Tell me when, Victoria..."

No more kissing, he is looking straight into my eyes. Straight through me. With each thrust he pushes hard as I grind my clit into him. Our eyes lock. I am raising my hips off the bed to meet his strokes. I am almost there and I am about to get lost in the moment when I dig my nails into his back and sigh, "Come with me, Sonny." He pushes in deeper and presses hard and slow against me. With just two strokes I feel everything tense up and I shake as I begin to climax. I feel myself tighten around his dick as I feel the warmth of him pulsating inside of me. He collapses on my chest and buries his head in my neck, whispering in my ear, "Eres tan hermosa cuando vienes. Puedo mirar a los ojos para siempre y se pierden."

What the fuck did he just say? Damn, I am going to have to learn Spanish.

We lay for several minutes while he is still inside me. He pulls out and grabs my waist to lay behind me. Neither of us are sure what to say. He is the first to break the silence.

"When are you leaving for competition, Victoria?" I am surprised to hear he knows I am leaving. Seems like he has been doing some internet research of his own. Interesting.

"I leave in 4 weeks." I reply. I'm uncomfortable with the suddenly casual feel of this conversation. One minute this man is making me come, and the next minute he's practically asking if I've read any good books lately.

"I want to see you before you leave. I will be returning to NYC in three weeks. I will call you and let you know what day I can see you."

I don't need to answer him because he knows I want to see him again. We don't need to talk about it. We both know what has started here.

"I am sorry, Victoria, but I need to get dressed. I can't stay."

"I understand." I am not sure what I should say. I knew the minute we started kissing what I was getting myself into. It's too late now. I am in this deep and I don't want it to end.

I lay in bed and watch him as he dresses, admiring the view. I can tell he is enjoying this and takes his time getting dressed. He then takes my hand and leads me to the front door.

"I will see you in three weeks. Tonight was amazing Victoria." He says to me.

"It *was* amazing. I want you to know I have no regrets, Sonny." He gives me a reassuring look. I think he feels the same way. I am not sure why I chose those words. Now everything feels awkward between us.

Then he pulls me to him and whispers, "Ahora tengo el recuerdo de esta noche para llenar mis sueños y atormentar mi corazón aún más."

I return the whisper and say, "Why do you continue to torment me with the Spanish? I want to know what you are saying to me."

"Then I suggest you learn to speak Spanish, Victoria." He smiles.

"Maybe I *will* learn. Then I will know all your secrets." I say taunting him.

Pulling me to him for one final kiss, he whispers, "Maybe that's not such a good idea."

After I lock the door I slide down the wall and just sit there for what seems like forever.

When I awake I have to remind myself that what took place last night was real and not a dream. I know it was real. My lips are swollen from all the kissing. I can still smell him. His scent is all over my body and my bed. It was amazing. For a minute I ask myself, what the hell have we started here? Then I remember last night and all I can think about is that I get to see him in three weeks. I need to shower and get back to reality. In the shower, I discover my nipples are swollen and there are red marks all over them. For some reason this makes me smile as the memories of last night replay in my head.

Staying busy over the next three weeks is helping to take the edge off of waiting to hear from Sonny. If it weren't for me being occupied preparing for competition season, I'm not sure how I would get through these days. I haven't talked to him since our evening together. I don't know what to expect. Hell, we hardly talked that night. What do I really know about him? I never dreamed I would be in this position. Having an affair with a married man is nothing I would ever had imagined myself doing. To me, it isn't just some affair. But yet it is just that, an affair. I have become the other woman. Though I can't control the way I feel about this man. It's wrong on so many levels. I simply cannot walk away. Okay, so I wasn't expecting a dozen long-stemmed roses the next day, but I had hoped for at least a phone call. Nothing. I have no idea how I feel about that.

My days are filled with practice. It keeps my mind and body busy, but in the evenings when my Bose headphones are filled with the music from my Latin Superstar, my mind drifts to that night. I keep telling myself not to put too much thought into it. It is what it is. But exactly what is it, anyway? Is it just sex or is there something more? What have I gotten myself into?

Ashley seems to sense something but knows better than to ask. The day after his visit she was far too inquisitive. That morning she questioned why I was so happy. At one point she even told me I *looked* different. Oh, if she only knew. She would kill me. The one thing about Ashley, when I shut her down she knows not to cross the line with me. The only thing I shared with her about that evening was that he had come to apologize about the album cover and he brought me a beautiful framed photo from the shoot. I told her I was ok with it and did not want to discuss it any further. For now I will keep my Latin Superstar to myself.

It was incredibly difficult containing my euphoric mood the day after Sonny's visit. I constantly had to check myself and make sure I wasn't smiling too much. But damn, I was floating on cloud nine! Throughout that next day I replayed every moment over and over in my head. I am sure there were times I was blushing from the images. Making love with him--or to put in Sonny's terms, *fucking*--was far superior to any fantasy I could have conjured up on my own. The only disappointing part of the entire night is his use of that word. Maybe I need to check more than the smile on my face and realize that may be all I truly was to him. Just a fuck. Nothing more than a fuck.

Even Mateo comments on my mood while we are practicing. "You seem very happy this morning Baby Girl. Something you want to tell me about?"

I ignore his question but he pushes me and catches me off guard. "Ashely told me Sonny de la Cruz was here last night at the studio."

I shut him down quickly. "Ashley talks too much. She needs to learn to keep her mouth shut about things that don't concern her."

"Relax Baby Girl. It's me, sweetheart. Mateo. You know I would never judge you."

"I know that, but there is nothing for you to judge. Let's get to work."

I need to lighten the mood and get his mind off Sonny's visit to the studio so I pull him into a dance position, spin myself around, fall into his arms, and say, "I am just happy to be back in your arms again, Mateo." Then I plant a huge wet kiss on his lips.

Mateo is laughing so hard he has trouble getting the words out. "Victoria, you really need to find a man. Clearly I cannot meet your needs."

I guess it must be obvious. I *am* happy. I know it's wrong and I should never have started any kind of a relationship with Sonny. The whole thing is just too surreal. When I'm with him, it's as though I have known him for years. But right now, I feel like I don't know him at all.

A few evenings later, Ashley and I are having Chinese take-out in my kitchen and she notices the framed photo still sitting on my island. As she shoves chopsticks filled with Shrimp Lo Mein into her mouth and shaking her head, she fires off some questions, "Is that the photo he gave you? Did he think that would satisfy you? He really has no idea who you are, does he?"

As I open a container filled with Kung Pao Chicken I answer her. "Yes it was a gift from him and yeah I think it was his way of saying he was sorry. I'm not sure there is a man out there that will ever really know me. My Blake knew who I was. He knew everything about me. And I'm not sure I want to ever share that part of me with anyone again. I have no time for a man. I really don't like talking about this Ashley."

"I'm sorry I brought it up. I understand how painful it was losing Blake but at some point you are going to have to let your guard down and let a man into your life. You need to open your heart to *someone*. Just not a married man, please. I don't think I could handle the drama."

"This from a woman who has no man in her life either. We are a sad team girlfriend."

I can't get that evening out of my mind. As we sit here having dinner I can't help but think this is where it all started that night. Right here at this very island in my kitchen. Which is now filled with at least 8 containers of Chinese take-out food. Thinking about it elicits the beginnings of a small smile on my lips. I shake my head. I need to stop daydreaming before Ashley wonders what I'm thinking about. I'm dying to share the story with her. But I can't. Not yet. I know she is my closest and most trusted friend. But I also know she will protest. She is fiercely protective of me. My story would not meet with one ounce of her approval.

Mateo and I have been working hard on our new routine and it seems to be shaping up to be one of our best. But no matter how much I throw myself into our practice sessions I can't stop from feeling anxious about Sonny's return visit. Well, I *hope* it's a return visit. I haven't heard from him and he is coming tomorrow. Maybe he lied and I will never see him again. Maybe he did just want to fuck me. Those *were* his words. Why do I have such a hard time with that word? Why can't I just accept what this is. An affair! I crossed a line that I thought I would never cross.

The day Sonny is supposed to arrive, I awake feeling like I never slept. It was one of the most restless nights I have had in a long time. Uncertainty and anticipation hang in the air like a thick fog. As I head down to the studio, my cell phone rings. It's a number I don't recognize, but the area code is from LA. It's got to be him. Right? I answer, and when I hear his velvety smooth voice it immediately sends chills through my body. Wait! How did he get my cell phone number?

"Buenos días, Victoria. I am headed into a meeting and then this evening I have a dinner to attend. I would like to see you later please."

Wow. I don't even have a chance to wrap my head around the idea that it's him. But he is here, just as he promised. "Good Morning. Yes, I'm free this evening. I'd love to see you as well." Oh God! Could this be anymore awkward?

"I'm sorry. I didn't mean to assume you were available tonight. It's just that I am always surrounded by people and it's hard to talk sometimes. Victoria, I've missed you." His deep husky voice is low and full of promise.

"No worries. I understand. It's just early and I was surprised to hear from you. I've missed you and I want to see you, too." There I said it. I do miss him and I want him to know.

"Victoria, I've not only missed you but I need you. I'll see you sometime after nine."

Before I can respond back he ends the call. I am still in shock over the fact that he called me, but I am also excited. It's hard to keeping myself from smiling. I can't help but feel like a teenager who has just been asked out by the hottest guy in school! I want to jump up like a lovesick girl! I throw a fist in the air like a Jersey Shore Guido. Thinking over and over - He called me! He called me! I am so excited he called me! Now I really sound like a teenager in love. Love? Probably not a good choice for words. Lust, maybe? I don't know what to call it. But he *did* say he missed me. He even said he needed me. What does that mean?

 Now I just have to get through this day.

When I walk into the office I tell Ashely I need to be finished by 6pm. She picks up on my mood immediately and wants to know why I am so happy again. I reveal nothing to her and just smile and run the day through my head. It will be a full day of practice with Mateo, a costume fitting, then a meeting with Ken and Ashley to complete the competition itinerary. I will need time to shower and get dressed in something more attractive than my dance clothing. This time I know what he is coming for, and I do not plan to disappoint.

Practice with Mateo keeps my mind busy and our routine is looking incredible. We work on polishing it to perfection. I really concentrate and work hard on this rehearsal hoping Mateo will not notice a mood change in me and start asking questions like Ashley.

The costume designer is on time and I keep counting down the hours until 9 o'clock in my head. This is the last fitting for my finals costume. The costumes from the previous years championship competitions will get used during the 12 weeks of preliminary competing. But what I wear for the finals is always new and show-stoppingly fabulous. Mateo and I always wear black for the finals. I worked closely with the designer and we came up with a halter style body suit. It is completely covered in black Swarovski crystals and then trimmed out in silver crystals. The feather detail in the skirt I designed is the WOW! factor for this costume. The feathers skim my waist to create the look of a skirt and the plume effect in the back of this design makes my ass look amazing. Mateo of course will be wearing traditional black pants but his shirt always reflects the look of my costume. So they have added black crystals to his shirt and trimming it out in the silver crystals. Our designer is beyond amazing. We are always the envy of every couple on the circuit. You'll never see my photo on People's Worst Dressed List, or dissed by E!'s Fashion Police. This year is no exception -- my costume is breathtaking.

I keep ticking today's itinerary off in my head. Somehow wishing it will make the day go by faster. Next up my meeting with Ken and Ashley. Throughout our meeting, I can't keep myself focused on anything but what tonight will bring. Ken is the first to speak up. "Victoria are you feeling all right? You seem preoccupied about something."

"Tell me about it! But it's no use asking. I've already tried," Ashley chimes in.

Do I really look that different? Is it that obvious?

"You guys, I am fine." I say, exasperated with all the speculation. "I just have a lot on my plate today, that's all. Chill."

Up next, a coaching session with an up-and-coming Bachata couple. I can't recall a thing about their routine, nor what music they danced to at practice. I just go through the motions. Tell them they look great, and I'll see them in Miami next week for our first competition. Normally, I more than earn my high coaching fees. But today, I feel like I robbed these two blind. My heart and mind are on other things.

Just a few more annoying tasks to blaze through before I get the day over with and the night started. I quickly finish up my paperwork, return some calls, and respond to my e-mails. I am practically pushing Ashley out the door before 5 o'clock even rolls around.

"Why are you rushing me?" Ashley protests. "Do you have a hot date tonight or something?"

"No, Ashley. Not a hot date." I laugh. "My friends Scott and Stevie are in town and they want to take me to an early dinner." I know this is a lie, but I have to tell her something so she won't be curious and start asking for details.

"Ugh. Not *those* guys." Ashley rolls her eyes. "The last time they were in town I thought I was going to have to bail you all out of jail."

"Don't worry, *Mother*. We'll keep it PG-13 tonight," I smirk.

Well, she is right about Scott and Stevie. They have been my two best friends since high school. They *are* a bad influence. We've been known to cause a ruckus every now and then. We have been good friends for years and they have gotten me out of a few tough jams while traveling for competitions. My first year with Mateo I lost my passport and I would have missed the finals that year if it weren't for my boys stepping in and handling everything. Then the incident in Caracas when my luggage got switched with some drug smuggling guy from Cali. What a nightmare that was. Once again my boys took care of everything. Let's just say they both hold some very high ranking government credentials. Since Blake's death I have never worried about anything knowing those two were always there for me. I wonder what those boys are up to these days. I don't think they'll mind me using them as an alibi for what I'm really up to tonight. They owe me. I've covered for them many, many times over the years.

On her way out, Ashley warns, "Don't call me tonight from some jail. Behave yourself, and tell the guys I said hello."

"Will do. I have you on speed dial just in case I need you! Have a great evening."

Now that I'm alone and I don't have to hide my excitement. I run up to my loft taking two and sometime three steps at a time. My mind starts to overload with thoughts about tonight. Time to shower, grab something light to eat and prepare for tonight. Heading to the kitchen I plug in my phone and put some music on, Sonny's music. Then I stop by the kitchen to see what's available in the fridge. I find a fruit and cheese platter I picked up at the local gourmet grocery store. Perfect. I can nibble on this while I get dressed.

On his last visit I didn't get to doll myself up the way I'd have liked. This time I want to look smokin' hot. I want him to see what he's been missing. I know I spent 20 minutes showering with my favorite soap from Shiseido. It's called a honey cake. It's the best soap to travel with. You can use it on your face, body and hair.

Mateo is always pulling me in close to sniff me. He says I smell like the first day of Spring. Now I'm wondering since we live in NYC, how would Mateo know what the first day of Spring smells like?

I need to stop overthinking everything, I need to chill and unwind. Time for some wine. I open a bottle of Moscato d'Asti and pour myself a glass. This should help me relax. I'm going to wear my black cotton maxi dress by Vince Camuto. The dress accents all my curves and shows off my cleavage without looking like I'm trying too hard. It's very casual so no heels this time. I think I'll go barefoot and show off my new manicured toes done in my favorite burgundy OPI polish. I go soft on the makeup. No jewelry, except some silver hoop earrings. I had a spray tan done yesterday which is a little darker since I am getting ready for competition. I may being going for a casual look, but I did make a special trip to Neiman's for something new from La Perla. Since he clearly has an eye for expensive lingerie, I might as well give him something he can appreciate. Besides, it's fun. I haven't put so much thought into what I am wearing under my clothes in years. I have chosen a beautiful black mesh bra and panty set. The panties are a cheeky boy-short style and the bra is an underwire Demi cup, so my breasts spill over the top just a little. The fabric is stretchy and has silver metallic thread running through it. Nothing fancy with my hair. I blow it out, flat iron it and let it hang perfectly straight. Why I am so worried about what I am wearing? He is coming here to fuck me, not my dress, not my La Perla lingerie or my fucking hair. Just me.

It's a few minutes before 9 and I'm completely ready. Now the waiting and wondering begins... Could time tick by any slower! It's 10 pm and there's no sign of my Latin Superstar. At 10:15, I begin to feel stupid. Did I really think he would come? At 10:20, I realize I drank the entire bottle of moscato. I know I didn't imagine his feelings for me that night. No one could make that up; no one could do what we did without real feelings. Could they? I am so unaccustomed to being unsure of everything like this! In the middle of running all of this through my mind, the intercom buzzes alerting me that someone is requesting access to my private elevator. I had the elevator installed when I gutted and remodeled the apartment. I spared no expense when it came to safety and convenience. The elevator cannot be accessed without punching a code into the monitoring system - except with a key. Besides myself, Ashley is the only person with a key. The elevator opens directly outside my four inch steel, reinforced front door. You should never put a price tag on your safety. Thanks to my state-of-the-art system, I can see on the monitor that it's Sonny! It's him! Oh my God, it's really him!

I open the door and I almost forget to breathe when I see him. Damn, he looks hot.

In a soft, seductive yet apologetic tone he speaks his first words to me. "Victoria, I'm sorry I am late. The dinner meeting ran much longer than I expected."

"Don't apologize. It's fine. It gave me time to drink an entire bottle of wine." I say, smiling, feeling warm and just a little bit tipsy.

"So, you are drunk?" He says, playfully rubbing his palms together as he enters the loft. "If so, can I take advantage of you?" His voice is sexy even when he is teasing me.

"You think I need to be drunk for you?" I tease back. I wonder what he has in store for me tonight. It doesn't really matter. I'm starving for whatever this man is serving.

He looks amazing. He is dressed in business attire rather than his usual rugged look. From his wool dress pants to his shirt and blazer, he is a vision in all black. I love his signature leather boots. Even the uncharacteristic Burberry scarf draped stylishly around his neck. Burberry? He's usually so casual. I am taken aback when I see him showing a little fashion sense. But then my mind rewinds to the photos Ashley found of him wearing exquisite designer suits. Add that to his appreciation for my La Perla lingerie, I guess it's safe to say my rugged Latin Superstar has a taste for luxury, too. Another side of him I appreciate. I want to reach out and touch him. I want him to kiss me. It may not be our first time, but I'd never initiate the first move. It's been so long I really don't remember how. Even after drinking an entire bottle of moscato, I don't have that kind of confidence. We start walking into my loft when he grabs my hand and pulls me toward him.

"Not so fast, Victoria. I've missed you." He nuzzles his face against my neck, runs his hands down my back and over my ass and whispers, "This *body*." He breathes into my ear as he pulls me in with such force that I fall against him. His eyes are smoldering. I love his cologne, and have been trying to determine the brand ever since our first meeting. I've stalked several department store fragrance counters, spraying and sniffing until I gave myself wicked headaches in search of his scent. All I know is it has to have notes of patchouli, mandarin orange, maybe even cedar? One of these days I will find out. Wait a minute. Did he just say he missed me?

He pulls me closer, his lips are on mine and this time he doesn't have to tell me not to hold back my passion. Kissing is what we seem to do best. His lips and tongue continue their pleasurable assault on me. The only sound echoing in my loft is sound of our labored breathing. I could kiss this man for hours, but I want more. I am immediately turned on and want to rip his clothes off. Because of my moscato buzz I have a little trouble controlling myself. I'm eagerly grinding against him. I want him naked and deep inside of me. Now!

Abruptly, he pulls away to draw in air. "Why are you always in such a hurry?" He whispers. "You need to slow down and learn to enjoy this, Victoria." Damn it. I must look desperate. I need to relax. The whispering is my favorite part. I hope he doesn't whisper to me in Spanish. Even though I find it very sexy, I want to *know* what he is saying. Every single word. His lips don't leave my ear. He starts kissing me there and trails down the side of my neck, and back up, breathing heavily, gently nibbling at my lobe. I smile to myself. I love that he remembers how hot I get when he kisses my ears and neck. Let's hope he remembers my other weakness.

The wine is freeing me up from my earlier shyness. Making me feel very sexy and flirty. I decide I will be bold tonight. I want him to know I can take charge. Before giving him the opportunity to assume control, I grab his belt buckle, release it, and unzip his pants. I reach in, run my hand down the length of his shaft. I find he is already rocked up for me, standing strong. Okay. I want him so bad, but I have hatched a new plan for what will go down next. *Me*.

I release my hold on him, pull off his blazer and begin unbuttoning his shirt. Dragging my lips up and down his neck peppering him with kisses while I completely undress him. His eyes darken and become even more seducing as he stares into mine. His stare is so intense I have trouble concentrating. I need to focus. I have some skills of my own to show him. It's been a while, but I know what I'm doing. I take hold of his beautiful, hard cock and begin to stroke him while I continue kissing his neck and chest. He starts breathing heavily and leans his head back against the wall. I drop to my knees and just as I am ready to make this man very happy, he grabs my arms, pulls me back up and says, "No."

Did he really just say no? What man turns down a blow job? I am good at this Damn it! Maybe he doesn't like it. That can't be true. Maybe Latin men don't like blow job. I will have to ask Mateo. I'm confused. He then whispers in my ear, "Not like that. Victoria I need you. I've missed you. I want to be inside of you." He still has my arms and spins me around until I am the one pinned against the wall. His eager lips find mine as he pulls my dress up and over my head. Sending it flying down the entryway.

Sonny notices my lingerie immediately. He spends what seems like an eternity staring at my body, admiring my new La Perla bra and panties. A grin forms across that beautiful mouth. A sexy grin. Then he surprises me with his question. "Victoria, how do you know about my obsession for beautiful lingerie? It's La Perla again, is it not?"

Thanks to the wine I have found my confident side. I am not afraid at all to tell him the truth. "There is all kinds of information on the Internet. Even about you, Sonny de la Cruz. Yes it is La Perla."

He laughs, cups my chin in his hands, and kisses me sweetly. He then rolls my panties down and helps me wiggle my way out of them. When he is done he stays down there and spreads my legs apart and squeezes my ass. His eyes once again connect with mine and I get lost in them, "Victoria, you really do have a great ass." The wine has given me the edge to reply. "Glad you like it. I work very hard to keep it that way." Damn, did that sound as stupid as I think it did? It must because he laughs and says, "Yes, I know. It must be all those eight hour practice sessions you are so great at." I knew it. It was stupid. He is teasing me. I need to work on my sexy side.

He grabs my full attention when he spreads my lips apart and strokes my clit with his tongue. A moan escapes from my mouth. There is no point in trying to control what I'm feeling. My breathing increases with the intensity of each one of his strokes. I feel like I am already about to explode. I can't help myself, I am on the verge of coming. I remove my hands from the wall, grab hold of his hair and grind my hips hard against his tongue, pushing his face in deeper. His tongue is working magic on my clit, and he knows it. How could he not? Moaning uncontrollably, I must have said his name a thousand times while I came harder than I've come in a long, long time. Thank God I am leaning against the wall because I am having trouble holding myself up. He grabs my waist and spins me around until I'm facing the wall. He unhooks my bra and reaches under to pinch my nipples with his fingers. Oh God, my nipples. Yes! He leans in and his mouth is directly on my ear, "Bedroom. Now. I want my cock inside of you. You need fucking," he says, through clenched teeth. Fucking. I know this word is a problem for me. But damn. This is so hot! I don't care how many times he says he wants to fuck me.

When we reach the bed, he grabs me, pulls me to him, and kisses me deeply. His kisses are aggressive, and I like it. A lot. He holds nothing back as he assaults my lips. Our tongues dancing to a tune all their own. I try to pull him onto the bed, but he stops me and pulls me back by my neck. I'm a little nervous, but the forcefulness really turns me on. He is behind me now and trailing eager kisses up the back of my neck. Breathing heavily into my ear. He pushes me toward the bed and orders me on it. As I start to climb onto the bed, he says, "Stop. I want you at the edge of the bed, on your hands and knees. I want to fuck you from behind." I do what he wants and he positions himself right behind me. Oh God, what does he mean "fuck me from behind?" Figuratively or literally? Shit! He reaches under and rolls my nipples between his fingers. Surprisingly, he *gently* slides his rock hard cock inside me. Fuck! I felt every inch of him slide into me. It felt better than anything I have ever experienced before. OK, he just meant he wanted to stand behind me and fuck me. I breathe a little sigh of relief, which I'm sure he takes as just another moan. Damn, this way feels amazing. He is balls deep inside me, gripping my hips and digging his nails into my skin with every thrust. He may have slid into me gently at first, but that is where the gentleness ended. Sonny is now plunging that thick cock deep. I welcome the pain and meet every stroke throwing myself right back at him, faster, harder, moaning his name. At this pace and intensity, I'm sure he is about to come. I know I am.

Just when I feel myself begin to tighten around him, he stops and withdraws. Oh, fuck. My legs are shaking and if I move right now the orgasm that was building might just happen. How does he have such control? He stretches himself out across the bed. I don't have time to think about what he has in mind, because he motions to me and says, "Come here, I want you on top of me." No problem, I think to myself. I love to ride. I like being in control.

Then he says to me, "Victoria, I want you to fuck me. I want you to make me come the same time you do." There's that word. I am not sure I like him saying it -- it really isn't a turn on for me. I do as he says and straddle him. Since I am still reeling from what he just put me through, I let out a long, soft moan as I slide his thick shaft into me and start to ride him. At first, I slowly raise my hips up so that I slide all the way up to the tip of his cock, then quickly drop down until he's deep inside of me. It's hard to keep anything close to a steady rhythm because it hurts. It hurts so bad, but in such a good way. I know in the morning I am going to pay for this. It feels so good, and I'm trying to hold off as long as I can and enjoy this. I stop kissing him so I can concentrate and not come. But after a few minutes, I can't hold off any longer. I *need* to come. Thanks to the wine I'm not afraid to tell him.

"Sonny, I can't hold on any longer. I am about to come," I whimper breathlessly.

"You don't have to wait, Victoria. You are the one that is in control."

I start fucking him harder and faster, grinding my clit against him, watching him gaze at my efforts with hooded eyes licking his lips meeting each stroke. I get lost in the moment and begin to come. "Come now, Sonny. Come with me. I'm ready" knowing I can bring this man to orgasm with me. "Yes, oh yes, Sonny, come with me, " I'mmoaning louder, and shaking as I climax. With every stroke I tighten around him and I can feel his warmth pulsating inside of me. Finally, I collapse on his chest. He wraps my sweat-soaked hair around his hands and pulls my face to his, kissing me sweetly. "You are fucking incredible, Victoria." We both lay there, exhausted. I slide off and lay beside him, still breathless. He gets out of bed and says he needs some water. I think I just might have worn this man out. As he leaves the bedroom, I can't help but smile and say, "That was good."

Laughing, as he walks out, he turns to look at me and replies, "No, Victoria, that was great."

A few minutes later, he returns with a glass of water and sets it on my nightstand. He is standing there, still naked, looking around my bedroom. He seems intrigued by something. I am not sure what it is because I can't seem to take my eyes off the defined lines of his torso. He definitely has the v lines. God he is gorgeous. The last time we were together I didn't take the time to appreciate just how well built this man is.

"Tell me about these mirrors, Victoria. Are you obsessed with looking at yourself or do you like to watch in the mirrors when I fuck you?"

OK, there is that word again. I can play this game as well.

"The mirrors have nothing to do with *fucking*, Sonny. I had them installed along with the hardwood floors so I could dance in here. Some nights when I can't sleep I work on some new steps, I dance in my bedroom. When I can't sleep, dancing is the perfect way to relax." I put a lot of emphasis in my tone on the "nothing to do with fucking" part, and I think that has caught his attention.

Remaining cool, he tries to ignore it and asks, "Do you only do Latin dances, or all types of dance?" But I know by his reaction I have gotten his attention. Maybe now he will stop referring to it as fucking.

"When I dance to relax or work out, I usually just freestyle. I do know all the Latin dances. But I only compete in the traditional ones."

"Is this room wired for music?"

"The entire loft is wired for music. I had speakers installed in every room when I remodeled. There is a system here in the bedroom and in the living room where I can use my iPod to play music"

What he says next surprises me. "I want you to put on some music and teach me that dance the couple was doing the other night in the studio."

"Do you mean Kizomba?"

"That's it. You said you had to have a lover to dance Kizomba. So now you have a lover. Teach me how to do this dance for lovers."

"So you are my lover, are you? Well, I don't dance with anyone naked. Put your pants on and I will teach you."

He ignores my question. Maybe I should have said, "So, I am the woman you fuck?"

He must want to learn this dance because he quickly finds his pants and is standing there waiting. I step into the bathroom clean up a bit before putting on some capris and a camisole, and, of course, my dance shoes.

I go over the basics and show him the general steps. I tell him he must lead because my head will be on his chest the entire dance, and I cannot see the floor or know what my partner will do next. I tell him I will push up against him and he will need to push back against me and lead. He will also need to count the beats of the music with his wrist that is positioned right above my ass and I will move my hips and ass to his beats of the music. This part he likes.

He is a great dancer and picks up moves very quickly. After about 30 minutes he announces, "Ok, we are ready for music."

"You think so? One lesson and your ready for music. Remember you have to lead. Let's just see how good you are." The good comment has us both laughing.

I have chosen my favorite Kizomba song "P'ra Ti" by To' Semedo. It is a slow and very sensual song. I cue the music and he leads me across the floor as I push against him with my hips.

He whispers in my ear, "You should see how hot your ass looks in these mirrors when you dance."

"Behave, Sonny." I scold him like a teacher. "You are supposed to be leading not looking at my ass."

"Tell that to your ass, Victoria," he laughs. "But don't worry I can lead and take in the view at the same time. When I am alone with you, there is no reason to behave."

I can't believe how quickly he has picked up this dance. He is really doing a great job. You can tell he has had formal dance training. He even counts the beats of the music with his wrists like I showed him. I can't help but take a peak in the mirrors of us dancing. We look hot dancing together. This is a very sensual and sexy moment. Dancing can be very intimate and this certainly is one of those moments. Toward the end of the song he pushes me back toward the bed. He strips out of his pants and takes my clothes and shoes off. He pulls me to him and we fall back on to the covers.

"I know why that dance is for lovers. It makes you want to fuck."

I just laugh and shake my head. Taking control I lay him on his back and climb on top of him, kissing him. I feel him beneath me and he is hard again. I decide now is the time. He had no problem going down on me, and I am eager to return the favor. I kiss my way down his neck, chest, and stomach. He seems to let go and relax, and I think he is giving in to me. I am almost there and he pulls me back up and says, "You're sure you want to do this?"

Mocking his words I say, "You need to learn to relax and just enjoy this."

He releases my arms, lays his head back and gives me a soft, sexy laugh. The music continues to play in the background. My lips graze his ear and I whisper, "Relax. I've got this under control." He surrenders himself and laughs again. I can feel it's vibrations on my finger tips as I make my way down his gorgeous naked body. I reach my destination, and this time he is not attempting to stop me. I stroke his hard cock a few times, my hand looks so small around it. He is huge. I raise it up so that I can glide my tongue along the bulging vein that runs underneath it, pushing down as I lick my way slowly from the base to the very tip. I stop there and encircle the head with long, soft strokes. I gently kiss the crown of my Latin King, and then devour every inch of him. As his cock disappears into my warm, enthusiastic mouth, my always controlled Sonny begins to squirm and moan. This gets me hot, and I'm sucking and stroking him, fast and hard.   Between the music and him responding to me, I am completely turned on. I know he is about to come. He is now thrusting his hips up while I am working his gorgeous cock. I take him even deeper in my mouth and this sends him over the edge. He leans forward and grabs my head and pushes me further down on him. "Yeah, oh yeah, just like that...don't stop." His breathing is uneven. I know he is almost there. "Ay dios mio," he begins to say, over and over again, and then it happens. He explodes in my mouth. I continue to stroke and swallow every drop. When he is finished, his breathing begins to slow down. I am thankful for the glass of water he brought back with him from the kitchen. I drink the entire glass as I sit on the side of the bed. He puts his arms around my waist and pulls me to him.

He whispers in my ear while kissing my neck. "Usted está haciendo muy difícil salir esta noche . Eso fue increíble."

That's it! I am learning Spanish.

Then I hear him say the words I dread. "Victoria, I need to go. I wish I could stay, but I can't. People will wonder where I am and start asking questions." I say nothing.

We both remain silent while he dresses. When he is finished, he asks me for my cell phone. When I get out of bed and try to put clothes on, he grabs my pants from my hand and throws them, shakes his head no, and says to me. "Don't get dressed. Let me enjoy looking at you. It's going to be a while before I get to admire that amazing body of yours."

Of course I do as he says. He has this weird power over me. Without even thinking of why he wants it, I retrieve my phone from my handbag and hand it to him.I see him punching numbers in it. I figure he needs to make a call. Maybe for a ride back to his hotel.

He hands it back to me and says, "I have entered my cell number in your contacts under the name 'Lover'. If you ever have an emergency, you can reach me."

"I would never do that, Sonny. 'Lover'? Really?"

"If you ever have an emergency, you are to call me."

"I won't do that. I know and understand what our relationship is about. I would never do anything to jeopardize your marriage."

We stand in silence, staring at each other. It's the first time either of us has spoken about his wife. I can tell by the look in his eyes he believes me and understands.

"Victoria, I don't know how else to say this. We need to set some rules."

"Of course. I understand. Rules." The reality of the rules start to set in and so does the guilt. I guess it's expected with what we are doing.

"We can't have any contact with each other through email or texting. No one is to know about us. You can't tell anyone."

I am not sure what to say so I nod my head in agreement.

"But if you ever have an emergency I want you to call me. You have to promise me you will call if you need me."

I have no idea what type of emergency I would ever have that I needed to contact him about. But I nod in agreement with his request.

Just when I think the rules are set, Sonny grabs me by the waist and pulls me to him. He looks me directly in the eyes.

"Victoria, you must promise me you will not sit around and wait for me. You must continue with your life. Don't close yourself off from finding someone. I want you as my lover, but you are not to give up on finding love. I want you to be happy."

"Sonny, I have no time for a relationship right now, but I promise." I am left wondering what does he mean by being my lover and not to give up on finding love. Is there a difference? Does this mean this is only sex and he could never love me? Damn, I am so confused. I keep my thoughts to myself.

He questions me about my plans. He wants to know how long I will be traveling and competing. I tell him he can follow my travel plans on the International Latin Dance website. It will show him where I will be competing for the next 3 months. We make no promises to each other. He says with the new album out there is talk of doing some concerts. He is not sure of anything yet and mentions that touring may start soon.

"Promise me one more thing, Victoria. Learn to speak Spanish please."

This breaks the intense feeling that is going on between us and makes us both laugh.

"I'll try. Now is not a good time. I am going to be very busy for the next 12 weeks trying to defend my title."

I walk him to the door and we have one last kiss. Circling my waist with one hand he pulls me into his body. He then brings his other hand up to fist my hair and pull my chin so that he can work his magic along the line of my jaw and across the curve of my neck before he assaults my lips. He has to pull himself away because the kissing once again becomes very intense. Before he releases me, he whispers one final time, "Me estás volviendo loco. Me as robado el corazón, y la idea de verte que con otro hombre me mata. Pero, no perteneces a mí - y no te pertenezco a tí."

Before he can pull completely away from me I whisper to him, "Sonny, that's not fair. I don't understand what you are saying. I want to know what you are feeling."

"Remember what you said to me. Maybe there is some truth in that."

My mind is racing. What the hell did I say? Is he referring to my comment I made to him after the photo shoot? The thing about hiding his feelings by saying it in Spanish. I did understand two of the words he just whispered to me. Loco and corazón. One means crazy and one means heart. I have to learn Spanish, this is driving me insane.

When the door closes, I know it will be a while before I see my Latin Superstar again. I am at peace with that. If I never see him again, I almost believe I will be satisfied with the two nights we shared. They were beyond amazing. Who the fuck do I think I am fooling? I will *never* be satisfied with just two nights of being with this man. I want more of Sonny de la Cruz.

Chapter 12

Of course the morning is when the reality of everything always hits me. Ever since Blake's death the mornings are the hardest. I can't help it. I always wake up early and lay here and think about everything going on in my life. It's just my way of remembering that morning. Sometimes I think I'm afraid, if I get out of bed bad news is sure to follow. I know it's silly but that morning still haunts me. But this morning my thoughts are different. What is running through my mind is what took place in this bedroom last night. I can feel the heat rise in my cheeks as I remember our evening together. I can't believe Sonny wanted to dance with me. Oh and the blow job!

I am up and in the office before 9. I have so many things to do in this last week before we leave to start the competition tour. Ashley is very inquisitive about my evening. I ignore her because I have too much to do. Besides, I feel great about last night. It was amazing. I don't want her questions to get me second-guessing things. Trust me I have enough guilt going on in my head. After I dodge a few comments, she soon forgets everything and is back to business. She tells me Ken is on the line and needs to speak to me.

"Good morning, Ken." I say with a little too much enthusiasm in my voice for even my taste. I can't help it. I am still on a high from my rendezvous with my Latin Superstar. Rendezvous? Now there's a word I never thought I'd be using. Still, I can't stop thinking about our time together last night. Oh, and the blow job.

"And a good morning to you, Victoria. My, don't we sound cheerful? Really out of character for you so early in the morning. Glad I caught you in a good mood. I want to see if I would be interested in a judging gig right after the competition tour ends."

"Judging what, and where?" I quiz Ken with reservation in my voice.

"It's the Junior World Latin Dance Championships. Your competition tour ends in Venezuela and the job is in Cali, Columbia. You would fly directly there before heading home. It is really good money with amazing accommodations. You would have three days to rest and relax before the two day judging event. Everything would be paid for including your flight home. It could also lead to more judging work. I know how much you love to support these young dancers."

I really want to say no. After competition season ends we are exhausted and just want to return home. We are gone for twelve weeks and living in a hotel room for that amount of time gets really old. Besides, what if Sonny wants to come and visit me. I did promise him I wouldn't sit around waiting. It does sound like a great opportunity and I need to start thinking about what I am going to do after I stop competing. Ken did say great accommodations and pay. In addition, they will pick up my tab for the flight home. The pay is not an incentive for me. I may have money but I also save whenever I can.

With some hesitation, I agree to do it. "OK, set everything up and make sure

Ashley gets all the information for me. Thank you Ken for always looking out for me. What about Mateo, is he coming to judge as well?"

No. He turned down the job. You were my second choice."

"Oh really, Ken. I see where I rank with you."

"Remember Victoria, I have known Mateo a lot longer than you. Besides, didn't I save the job that required you to strip nude with a hot Latin singer just for you?"

"Gee, Ken I really appreciate that. But let's be real, you just wanted to know how big his dick was," I say, my voice laced with sarcasm.

"Whatever," Ken snaps."I will send all the information to Ashley."

Ashley doesn't travel with me during competition season. She stays in NYC and continues to run the studio. I have a team of dancers that teach classes year-round. She makes sure everything I need is downloaded on my iPad, and sends me updates daily. All I need to do is show up at the airport, board the plane, land and dance.

Repeatedly, for the next 12 weeks. We will be traveling to 12 different cities internationally for competition. I will travel in the US and Canada, then on to Puerto Rico, the Dominican Republic and South America.

The finals are held in Caracas, Venezuela. You must be in the top 6 to make it to the finals. Each competition in which you place earns you points to make it to the finals. Then it's a clean slate and you compete in the finals to be #1. I guess the trip to Cali will be just what I need at the end of the season. I am also going to use the next three months to learn Spanish. I bought that expensive Rosetta Stone program. Mateo promises to help me. If I am ever going to understand what Sonny is whispering in my ear it's time I learned some Spanish. I want to know what this man has been saying to me.

We are off to Miami for our first competition. Mateo and I travel together so there is no chance of one of us missing a flight. Since we are defending champions, we will be very busy, even outside of competing. There is a great deal of PR work to be done including several interviews, appearances and dinners. While I don't mind the PR schedule, unlike many dancers, fame is not my motivation. It's the competing that has my heart. Competing is my favorite part of dancing. Mateo is just like me, and hates to lose, too.

We arrive in Miami early Thursday morning. January is the best time to hit South Florida. The weather is warm, yet comfortable, and hurricane season is months away. We have two days to settle in and rehearse before the first round is under way. After a quick check in at the Hilton Bentley, we head over to the convention center. Individual rehearsal rooms are available for everyone. We are also assigned a time slot to practice on the main floor, where the competition will take place. You have to be on time for these pre-booked sessions or you will lose your slot. We are a tough group of dancers. Very competitive and with many cliques. We are here to dance and win, nothing else. Russian couples are commonplace in the Ballroom dance world, but they are also starting to take over in this genre of dance competition.

It's late in the evening when we return to the hotel and all I can think about is a hot shower, room service and some sleep. I tell Mateo I will see him in the morning. I am exhausted from our early morning flight and practice. Mateo tells me he is going to hit some of the gay bars but promises he will not be out late. I spend a few hours listening and practicing to my Rosetta Stone CD's. When I finally fall asleep, my dreams are filled with memories of my Latin Superstar.

Mateo is waiting for me in the lobby and seems very happy this morning. I am assuming by the grin on his face he had a great evening. "Good Morning, Victoria. We are going to start every morning with a new Spanish word. You will learn to say it and understand the meaning. Then you will use it in a sentence."

"By the enthusiasm in your voice I gather you had a great time last night. What is our new word for the day?"

"Oh yes, I did have a great evening! I got laid. So, today's word is sexo caliente!"

"Mateo, that is two words, not one. It means hot sex."

"¡Muy bien! Very impressive! All right, here it is in a sentence, smarty-pants: Yo tenido sexo caliente anoche!"

"Funny, Mateo! I get it, you had hot sex last night."

"Muy bien hecho, Victoria. Maybe someday you'll actually be able to use that phrase yourself."

Smart ass. If he only knew.

We practice for three hours in the morning and then have some lunch. The World Latin Dance Organization takes great care of us at these events. Lunches as well as snacks and drinks are available for us during practice sessions. The food is always healthy and really delicious. Today they served us caesar salad with roasted chicken. My favorite thing was the chocolate chip cookies. I made sure I snagged an extra one for later. After lunch we have the floor from 1-2 for practice. As we approach the floor, I recognize the couple that is finishing up. They're from Miami. José and Angela

Rodriquez. Married, which is not unusual. Mateo has reminded me time and again that being married doesn't mean a thing. He thinks every man in the dance world is gay. They are young and inexperienced, but in a few years they could become the couple to beat. But not until I retire. Nobody is knocking this title out of my hands.

We exchange greetings and a little small talk before our time slot. "I was surprised Victoria to see you dancing in a music video," José comments, condescendingly.

"Well, José, it was obviously a good career move since I have gotten a ton of recognition. It seems I got your attention as well!" Mateo chuckles out loud. He knows no one is a match for me. Even so, Mateo is very protective and watchful. He knows I don't speak nor understand Spanish, so he let's me know what people are saying about me. But I am working on rectifying that. Neither of us understand Russian, yet we know they talk about us all the time.

Chapter 13

This evening we have a formal reception and dinner to attend at a private home of a very wealthy businessman. Fred Horne who is well known in the Latin dance community. He owns a chain of dance studios all over the world. Mateo is waiting for me in the lobby when I step out of the elevator. He seems to approve of what I am wearing tonight because his eyes light up and a huge smile comes over his face. I have chosen the dress from the video shoot. It's too beautiful to waste, and it was a gift from Sonny. I am wearing my hair pulled up and a very dramatic look with my eye makeup. I have added a lot of bling tonight. Unfortunately, it's all fake. I really am quite frugal. I would love the real thing, but cannot fathom spending that kind of money on myself. Rhinestone bangle bracelets with large rhinestone hoop earrings. I am wearing my Christian Louboutin high heeled sandals in metallic silver. I know I said I was frugal, but designer shoes are my weakness. I can't help it. It's an obsession of mine and always has been. So, designer shoes is where I have no problem dropping the bucks. I own more than I am willing to admit. Let's just leave it at that. Mateo looks very handsome in black tuxedo pants, a crisp white dress shirt, and an ivory dinner jacket. My favorite touch is the bow-tie. Mateo is truly precious.

"Wow, Victoria you look amazing. Is that the dress from the music video?"

I can't believe he recognized my dress. "Why thank you, Mateo. You look muy caliente yourself." He grins. He's so proud of his little gringa learning Spanish. "Yes, this is it. It's such a beautiful dress, I can't just let it hang in the closet forever."

The house where tonight's party is being held is stunning. It's out on what they call Star Island. The night sky is clear and star-filled, and it's living up to its name. Many local celebrities and some industry people from the Latin music world are here. I think several are singers, but I am not familiar with them. Other than my Latin Superstar, I really don't know much about Latin music. I wonder if anyone will recognize me from the video. They certainly won't know it's me on the album cover.

Our host Fred and his wife Audrey greet us graciously, and she asks if they could possibly get us to perform later when they open the patio for music and dancing. I tell her I am not prepared with the proper dance shoes, but I will do my best. She is delighted. Cocktail hour is in the huge foyer. According to Mateo, the foyer is the size of his entire apartment. Our hosts announce dinner is going to be served in the main dining room and there is assigned seating.

Main dining room? There's more than one? Wow. I am so out of my element. I could afford two, hell, three dining rooms...but why?

The "main" dining room is massive. I didn't take a head count, but there are easily seventy-five of us in here. There are several wait staff available to help us find our seats. Mateo is sitting on my left and I notice a place card for the person sitting to my right. It says Alejandro Perez. The seat is empty, so maybe he is not coming. That would be great. Then I can quiz Mateo about the Latin music people here tonight without having to worry about who's listening. I notice Mateo looks up and seems to be excited when he sees a gentleman being guided toward us. Whoever it is, he must be hot. I've seen that look before on Mateo's face. I whisper sarcastically, "Great, looks like Alejandro Perez is showing up after all."

Mateo whispers back excitedly, "Did you say *Alejandro Perez*?"

Before I can answer, they are seating this tall and extremely handsome man next to me. I mean *extremely handsome*. He looks like a concoction of Antonio Banderas and William Levy, with a little splash of Enrique Iglesias for added flavor. This man is breathtaking. Holy shit! I don't remember the last time I saw a man this handsome. Tall, broad shoulders and extremely well built. Even his skin is perfection. Now I totally get the look on Mateo's face. I'd say he is at least five years older then me. He is showing the first signs of greying in his thick, jet black beautiful hair. He is dressed in a custom-made tuxedo. Probably Armani or Gucci or some designer I've never even heard of but definitely custom-made.

Before I can say anything, or at least introduce myself, he speaks.

"How am I so fortunate to be seated next to the most beautiful woman in the room?" He asks me as he is staring directly at me. His eyes are scanning me up and down, but somehow this does not seem offensive. This man exudes class and style.

OK, I admit I'm blushing. Not only is he gorgeous, but he's so smooth and confident. He's just intriguing. The way he spoke sent chills up my back. I don't know many Latin men but this guy got the best of everything in the looks department. His features are striking. This man is movie star beautiful. What strikes me the most other than his gorgeous good looks are the color of his eyes. Turquoise! I never thought I would ever see another man with the same breathtaking eyes as my Blake. There is no mistaking it even in this lighting. Damn! It's hard for me to not stare directly into them as I respond to his comment.

"Thank you, but the room is filled with many beautiful woman. I am Victoria Moore and this is my dance partner Mateo Chavez." By the smile on Mateo's face I can see he is thrilled that I have introduced him.

"Good evening, Victoria and Mr. Chavez. My name is Alejandro Perez. You are right Victoria, the room is filled with many beautiful women, but what I said was the most *beautiful* woman in the room" Mr. Perez points out. I can feel the heat rising in my cheeks. This gorgeous man said I was beautiful? Wait, he said I was the most beautiful woman in the room! And it didn't sound like some pick up line. Hmm...who is this Alejandro Perez and why does he have me blushing?

There seems to be a lot of interest in this man, and several people are staring in our direction. He is very handsome, but the looks are as though people here know who he is. I have no idea but I can tell by the way Mateo is acting, he must.

"What do you mean by dance partner, Victoria?" Mr. Perez quizzes me.

Mateo leans in and explains to Mr. Perez that we are competitive Latin dancers and are in Miami for the first round to defend our title as World Latin Dance Champions. Mateo also tells Mr. Perez that he is sitting next to the reigning Queen of Latin Dance. Really Mateo. I am sure this gorgeous, obviously very successful man is not going to be interested in hearing about my dancing. I'm very proud of my dance career. But I don't like Mateo drawing all this attention to me. My already flushed cheeks feel even more flushed. I just hope it's not obvious to Alejandro Perez. Why is Mateo embarrassing me like this?

"I had no idea the beautiful woman in Sonny de la Cruz's new music video was such an accomplished dancer." Mr. Perez says with surprise in his voice.

I find it odd that this incredibly handsome, well-spoken man knows I am the dancer in a video and he knows who Sonny de la Cruz is. I just hope Mr. Perez doesn't recognize that the dress I am wearing tonight is the same one from the music video.

"Mr. Perez, are you from Miami? What do you do?" I ask in an attempt to deflect some of the attention from me.

"Victoria, please call me Alejandro." My name rolls off his lips as he stares straight into my eyes.

Holy shit! How can a man so gorgeous also have a voice that makes everything he says sound so damn sexy. This mans voice drips of sexiness. Mr. Perez goes on to tell me he owns a record company. He grew up in Miami, but also has a home in LA and an apartment in NYC.Mateo fleshes out Alejandro's resumé by informing me that his record company has all the top Latin music stars signed to his label. It's the largest Latin recording company in the world. Well, now I know why Mateo is so excited for this man to be seated with us and now I know why he is getting so much attention.

"Mr. Chavez, I have an incredible staff of people and that is why my company has so much great talent. We work very hard to go after the best talent out there," Mr. Perez adds modestly.

Well, not the best talent. After all, Sonny de la Cruz is not signed to your record label, I think to myself.

"Please call me Mateo. You do have some of the best in the Latin music world. I really like a few of the new reggaeton artists that have signed with your label recently." Wow, Mateo knows a lot more about Latin music. What the hell is reggaeton?

"Thank you, Mateo. Reggaeton has become such an important part of the Latin music scene recently. The company has grown so much these past few years as the result of Latin music becoming so popular. Subsequently, we are expanding and will soon be opening a new state of the art recording studio in South America. There is a lot of great talent coming out of there."

He is very humble and not at all arrogant. I find this extremely attractive. We spend the rest of dinner talking and getting to know each other. It was refreshing to have someone ask me about my career. He seemed very fascinated by my story. I have to keep reminding myself about these feelings that keep surfacing while I am talking to Mr. Perez. Maybe 'remind myself' is not a good choice of words. More like I have to fight off these feelings that keep surfacing.

After dinner everyone is asked to gather on the patio for drinks, music and dancing. As we all begin to exit the house, Mr. Perez asks if he may join us for the rest of the evening. Of course I can't say no, as that would seem rude. Besides, I really enjoy his company, even if he does have me keeping myself in check. The man is gorgeous, but his personality and demeanor are what really intrigue me. Just when I decide that it would be harmless, Mateo leans in and whispers to me, "Alejandro Perez has the hots for you." I give his arm a pinch and shoot him a look that shuts him up.

It turns out that this is not your average backyard patio. It is an amazing space that has been transformed into an outdoor night club. Complete with a huge dance floor, lights, and cozy spaces for socializing. A well-known reality TV star turned DJ is spinning records. Mr. Perez asks if he could get me a drink. I tell him I will have whatever he is having. When he returns with the drinks, I notice he has chosen Crown and ginger ale. I am intrigued by his choice but I am not going to comment because Mateo will point out that Mr. Perez and I have some things in common. He's such a little instigator. We continue talking and enjoying the music. After about half an hour, our host takes over the microphone to thank everyone for attending. Then hands the microphone to his wife Audrey. She explains that she is very excited to have two special guests, and she has asked them to honor everyone with a special dance performance.

"Everyone please give a round of applause to the reigning World Latin Dance Champions: Victoria Moore and Mateo Chavez. They are in Miami this weekend competing to defend their title in the first round of the competition." The guest break out in applause.

Mateo and I have a unique routine that we use just for these type of special occasions. It is a blend of salsa, meringue and samba. We perform it to a Pitbull song called "Bon Bon".Mr. Perez offers to hold my drink. As we approach the dance floor, I remind Mateo that I am wearing four inch Louboutins and he needs to take it easy on me. In his best RuPaul impersonation, he quips, "Like that ever stopped you before. You better *work it*, girlfriend!" That's Mateo. I'm surprised he didn't follow that with a diva triple-snap. But he is right. I can out-dance anyone in heels.

When the music starts, the guests go crazy and we begin to dance. Mateo loves moments like this; he is such a show-off. Playing to the crowd is a very important part of competing but he is really playing it up tonight. I know Mateo so well that I know someone in the crowd has caught his attention. He is really grandstanding this performance. He is absolutely in his element, and we finish to a standing ovation.

Apparently our performance has inspired our host. As Mateo and I rejoin Mr. Perez, he asks the couples to please join he and his wife on the dance floor for a tango. Mr. Perez extends his right hand and asks, "Miss Victoria, may I have this dance?" I am surprised by his request, but before I can answer, Mateo blurts out,

"Victoria adores the tango and would love to join you for a dance."

Damn you, Mateo!He knows I hate being paired with someone when I know nothing about their dance capabilities. But how can I refuse? Mr. Perez is standing with his hand extended for me to join him. I hope this man can dance the tango and doesn't step on my foot and break a toe. I reach out to accept his invitation.

Once on the dance floor, we take our place and wait for the music to begin. Mr. Perez takes my hand and puts the other around my waist. And there it is...an immediate spark. No way! No fucking way can this be happening. Not twice. Who is this guy? He probably can't even dance? Then the music begins and the magic happens. Not only can the man dance but he is an expert in this dance. How is that possible? He is very well versed in the Argentine Tango, and makes an excellent partner. Argentine Tango is improvised. Every step being a spontaneous, and with the partners focused on each other and on the music. I can tango, but it is not my area of expertise. The man is so good that I am beginning to believe he could compete. We immediately draw the attention of the other guests, as they crowd around us and we take over the dance floor.

Dance comes very natural to me, as effortless as breathing. But I am forced to concentrate to keep up. I am certainly at a disadvantage in these heels. In tango there is a 'leader' and 'follower'. Through the embrace, the leader offers invitations to the follower for where and how to step. Tango is sharing a moment of intimacy and understanding with another person. I am starting to feel that connection and intimacy dancing with him. Then it happens. Without warning, the dance takes over. As he leads I fall under his spell and that of the dance as we become one. Dancing

157

this close, I can feel every hard muscle in his body. I can feel his warm breath on my neck and he smells amazing.

It's truly magic, how two people can really move as one. So connected with each other and the music. I feel his breathing and he feels mine. He leads without direction, and it just happens without effort or prodding. There is a feeling of "One body, four legs." It's intoxicating. The way he looks at me with those turquoise eyes he sets me into a trance, it's blissful and it's magical. To deny the connection would be to go against everything I believe about dance. I let go and surrender completely to him. He owns this dance and me.

I forget where I am and who is watching and just let go and enjoy. I don't even notice that we have completely cleared the floor. When the music ends, the applause and whistles from the quests brings me back to reality and I begin to blush. It takes me a few moments to return from the subspace I entered.

"Thank you for honoring me with a dance that apparently made me look better than I am," Alejandro smiles as he scans and gestures his hand toward the crowd that surrounds us.

"*I* am the one who is honored, Mr. Perez. It is *you* that made *me* look good."

We rejoin Mateo, and he says, "I see why they call this beautiful woman the Queen of Latin Dance." I feel the heat rising in my cheeks. I really hope it isn't obvious.

We spend the rest of the evening chatting on a beautiful oversized sofa. The outdoor area has several intimate seating areas, which gives everyone privacy. We are seated farther away from the music than everyone else, so we can easily talk. After a few moments, Mateo abandons me to go mingle and dance. Whoever caught his attention earlier is where I am sure Mateo is headed. Some friend. Not that I don't enjoy Mr. Perez's company, but I'm simply not comfortable with how this man makes me feel. Our conversation is varied and effortless, so my worries are baseless. Our only interruption is by the wait staff, who kept the drinks flowing throughout the entire evening.

There is one point during our conversation that I completely blank out because I can't stop staring at Alejandro's eyes. When he turns his head a certain way the outdoor lighting highlights their gorgeous turquoise color. I am mesmerized by the similarity in his eye color to that of Blake's.

"Victoria? Victoria, are you all right?" Alejandro raises his voice to pull me from my trance.

Embarrassed by this and before I am fully aware of what he is asking me I say, "Your eyes are the most unusual shade. They're quite beautiful."

Chuckling he says, "They're turquoise. When I am enjoying the company of such a gorgeous and interesting woman the color becomes more intense. You say my eyes are beautiful, it's only because I am looking at you."

To break the intimate connection I laugh saying, "Mr. Perez, if I didn't know better I would think you were flirting with me. I wonder how many times you have used that line on other beautiful women?"

Immediately the color of his eyes change and they darken to an even deeper shade and his voice becomes serious. He makes sure his eyes connect with mine while he replies to my comment, "Let me assure you Victoria, I don't use lines on other women. There are no other women in my life. Do not be mistaken, I am flirting with you."

After a few minutes of complete silence between us and nothing but our eyes speaking for us, something changes. I become hypnotized and transfixed by this man's stare. I know this man is being completely honest with me. There are no other women in his life and he finds me beautiful. Shaking my head I pull myself from the trance and return to my senses and our conversation.

As we notice people begin leaving, I sneak a glance at Alejandro's elegant wristwatch and am surprised by the time. Three hours have passed and yet it felt like 20 minutes. We talked about everything. From where I was born to where I am today. I told him that I was a widow. Even after five years it's hard for me to use that term. He shared that he was married but has been divorced for several years. We didn't get into the intimate details about our past marriages. But it was as though we were both putting it out there that we were single. He told me he grew up dirt poor in Miami and what it took for him to build his empire. Even though we come from different cultures, our lives are similar in many ways. We both were blessed with supportive and loving parents who have had a profound impact on our lives.

Mateo returns, and we all agree it's time to call it a night. Is it just me, or was Alejandro somewhat reluctant to end our evening? Still, the party is winding down, and we don't want to be the last to leave. Tomorrow is competition day and we have to get some rest. When I thank Mr. Perez for the dance and tell him I enjoyed meeting him, he insists that I call him Alejandro. "Very well. Good night, Alejandro," I say, turning to leave.

Before I can step away, he takes my hand, pulls me to him and gives me a kiss on both cheeks and whispers in my ear, "Thank you for a truly mesmerizing evening. Good night, and good luck this weekend, Victoria." Wow! I was not expecting that. And I certainly wasn't expecting how it has left me feeling.

My stomach is tying itself into tiny little knots. I want to forget this feeling, but there's really no ignoring it. It's there. His good looks are one thing, but the hours and ease of talking with him is what I can't shake. There was something very intimate about our evening together. I feel more exposed emotionally than I have felt in long time. I have never opened up to anyone so quickly. What is it about him?

On the drive back, I am hoping Mateo doesn't bring up Alejandro Perez. We are almost back at the hotel when Mateo mentions how taken Alejandro Perez was with me.

"Mateo, shut up. You are wrong. Mr. Perez was just being polite."

"That was not just being polite. You both cleared the dance floor. It was amazing. Teasing me he adds, "Girl, something is going on between the two of you."

"It was just a dance." I snap back at him.

"That Baby Girl, was not just a dance."

I jokingly punch Mateo and tell him to shut up.

In my room I am alone with nothing but my thoughts. I am missing my Latin Superstar; yet my mind keeps drifting off to Alejandro. I kept telling myself Mateo is wrong and it was just a dance. Nothing more. If it was just a dance, then why can't I get to sleep?

The first day of competition is a long one. I bring my headphones along so I can spend the downtime working on my Spanish. We slide effortlessly through the preliminary rounds as expected. After a quick dinner in the hotel restaurant, I am thankful to be back in my room, standing under a hot shower. My mind begins to wander. I keep thinking about Sonny and our two nights together. I recall the way he kisses me and how he knows exactly how and where to touch my body. My breathing begins to intensify just thinking about this man. Damn it, Victoria. This is going o be a long three months.

It's day two. We are set to go on at 7:30 in the evening. It's vital that we win the first round in this 12 week competition. It's our way of declaring that we ARE the ones to beat. We take the dance floor promptly at 7:30 and execute a flawless routine. The audience goes wild, cheering and applauding. We are honored with a standing ovation and take first place. Mateo and I celebrate at the hotel bar with some of the other dancers.

We have one day off to enjoy the Miami sun before we continue our travels. I am to meet Mateo in the lobby for a day at the beach. Just as I am ready to head down to the lobby, there is a knock at my hotel room door. It is a member of the hotel staff carrying a stunning bouquet of the most beautiful long-stemmed red roses I think I have ever seen. There must be 50 of them in a beautiful crystal vase! I know who they are from before I even open the card. It has to be Sonny. I told him he could follow my itinerary online and he probably saw Mateo's blog post about our win last night. I open the card, "Congratulations on your first victory of many. Thank you for your lovely company and the beautiful tango the other night. Alejandro." The card falls from my hand, "Damn you, Mateo." You started this! "Oh, Victoria just adores the tango and would love to dance with you," I recall him saying. He warned me Alejandro was attracted to me, but I didn't believe him. I decide not to tell Mateo about the flowers. I hate it when he's right, and I don't want to be subjected to one of Mateo's "I told you so" conversations.

I leave Miami without contacting Alejandro Perez to thank him for the flowers, although it truly was a thoughtful gesture. For the thousandth time, I tell myself it was just a dance and it meant nothing. It doesn't matter how many times I say it, though. It's a lie.

Once we start the circuit of competing, all the cities and rounds start blending into each other. There are days I have to remind myself which city we are in. Mateo says my Spanish is getting better every day. We practice all the time. When he laughs, I know I have fucked it up. This is just what we needed on this tour. It takes our minds off the competition and has brought us even closer. We are so in tune with each other. We are fearless and flawless on the dance floor. In our down time we have been spending time exploring the different cities and doing a lot of retail therapy. Hell if I can't have Sonny at least I can buy shoes!

I can't believe we are nine weeks into the season. I guess it's true what they say...the older you get the faster time seems to pass. The weeks are passing quickly but the traveling is really getting to me. I am missing Sonny. My body is craving him. He has awaken something in me that I didn't think I would ever feel again. A need. A need for him. At night my thoughts drift to those two nights we spent together. I wonder if he does the same?

All the shoe shopping in the world can't keep my mind from the memories of him. I miss him. I miss his touch. Hmmm…never thought I would say that about another man. I follow any information I can get on him. But all I find are updates on his album. The critics say it will definitely be a Latin Billboard contender for Album of the Year. I had no idea they had Latin Billboard Awards. The music video should also get several nominations. But nothing has been mentioned about a tour.

It's the final night of regular competition and we are in San Juan, Puerto Rico. We don't even need to perform tonight to qualify to make it to the finals. There is no couple even close to the points we have accumulated. When I asked Mateo if he would like to sit this one out, he looked at me like I was crazy. Mateo never passes up an opportunity to show off. Besides some of Mateo's relatives live here in San Juan and they will be attending tonight's performance. I know he enjoyed our time here. There was no shopping for us. Instead we spent time with Mateo's family. My favorite evening was having dinner at his Aunt Rita's house with all the relatives. It was a great opportunity to practice my Spanish. I loved seeing him surrounded by his family. They are all so proud of him and you could just feel the love between them. I would say I was a little bit envious, but everyone made me feel so welcomed. They treated me as familia.

I was happy to hear Mateo did not want to skip this last performance. We want to sweep the entire tour. After tonight we have a little break-six days off until the finals in Caracas, Venezuela. We have a delicious dinner at the hotel restaurant before changing into our costumes. Neither of us could decide on what we were hungry for so we ordered a variety of dishes from the menu. Mateo insisted since it was his last day in Puerto Rico he wanted some local favorites. We had monfongos with garlic sauce, chillo entero, bacalaitos and carrucho. My favorite was the bacalaitos. They are cod fritters that came with this amazing dipping sauce. We are slated to go last around 10:30 p.m. But first we have to dance the preliminary dances. Then we wait for our turn to dance the final round.

I use the down time to check my e-mail for my daily updates from Ashley. She let's me know how things are going back at the studio. She also keeps me current on all the information and travel plans for my judging gig in Cali, Columbia. The end of the email is what catches my attention. She says that an envelope arrived from the Latin Superstar's management team. I immediately click on reply and send her a message telling her to open the package. Within seconds of sending it I get a reply.

Hello Victoria,

Really? You even had to ask? I've already opened it. It's a CD of the photos from the shoot. They are amazing! Really sexy! I already scanned them to another e-mail so you can see them. Look for the subject 'photos'. Miss you!

Ashley

Shaking my head not in disbelief but in what I call true Ashely form. I quickly close out her email and scan the rest for the one marked 'photos'. Of course she opened it. Duh, it's Ashley.

Miss Nosey herself! Let's see…Neiman's Lingerie Sale. Several from Ken. Facebook updates. Twitter. Blah, blah, blah…I found it! Ashley left one word out. The subject was' Sexxxy Photos.' Typical Ashley. I click it open and wait for the photos to appear. Wow, she's right. They really are sexy. Some of them are not exactly hiding my private areas very well. I can't stop staring at Sonny. Those dark seducing eyes. I miss him even more now. I wonder if he sent the CD or if it was someone from his management team. Probably his management team. But I prefer to think he had something to do with it. He wanted me to see these photos. He wanted me to remember our nights together. Oh boy, my imagination is taking off again.

I close out the photos and check the rest of my emails. I don't even open the ones from Ken. He is wordy, and I don't have that kind of time. I assume he had words with Sonny's management after the album cover came out. Ken doesn't let things like that go unnoticed. He makes sure he looks out for his client's best interest. There is another one from Ashley and the subject is Miami. I click on it and the email reads:

Victoria,

I found this photo of you on line. It appeared in Ocean Drive magazine. Looks like someone had a great time in Miami.

So…who is this gorgeous Alejandro Perez you are dancing with?

Ashley

I click to open the photo and it's of me and Alejandro dancing the tango. It is a great photo. It totally captures the moment.We look like a couple. Oh God! I wonder if anyone else has seen this? Of course they have seen it. If it's in Ocean Drive then I can bet it's in other magazines. Shit!

I still have time for a Spanish lesson and I make Mateo practice with me. It's 9 p.m. and we begin to stretch and warm up. We run through the routine one last time in the practice area. As I gather my things and get ready to head up to the main floor, I notice Mateo is bending and stretching his right foot, grimacing.

"Mateo is everything OK? We can sit this one out if your foot is bothering you."

"Estoy bien. Vamos a mostrarles que es número uno."

Laughing I answer him. "Bien, entonces vamos a patear algunos culos."

We step onto the floor promptly at ten. I try not worry about Mateo's foot, but it is on my mind as we dance. I keep an eye on him to make sure he is showing no signs of a problem. When he pulls me to him in a turn, he whispers, "I am fine, stop worrying." I try to put my mind somewhere else and just enjoy the dance. If we can get through this routine, he will have six days to rest his foot before we compete in the finals. We finish and it is a flawless routine. The audience is brought to their feet applauding for us. I grab Mateo and throw my arms around him and whisper to him, "Are you OK?"

"I am fine, Baby Girl. Stop mothering me." He may be saying that but I can see the pain in his eyes. He is just putting on a brave face for me and the crowd.

We take first again at the awards ceremony, and have swept the entire tour.

"Mateo, there will be no celebrating tonight. It's back to the hotel for you. You need to rest your foot." I announce as we are packing our stuff to leave.

"Victoria, I think it will need more than some rest. It's not good," He admits finally.

The ride back to the hotel is in complete silence. I am afraid to even ask him how bad it really is. When we arrive Mateo screams in pain as we step out of the car. I run to the other side and find him on the ground. Through clenched teeth, he looks up at me and orders, "Hurry and get me in the hotel so no one sees me."

The hotel sends someone out to help me get Mateo to his room. He cannot put any weight on his foot. I ask the hotel concierge to call for a doctor. We don't have to wait long. The doctor examines Mateo's foot, and explains that without an X-ray he can't be certain whether it is broken, fractured, or sprained. Mateo refuses to get an X-ray. The doctor leaves him with some pain medication and tells him to ice it down and stay off of it for as long as possible.

"I'm fine, Baby Girl. Please stop looking at me like that." Mateo tries to reassure me. But I can hear the agony in his voice.

"Mateo, you and I both know without an X-ray we don't really know if your foot is fine."

"I do not want to discuss anything further about my foot. This is not going to change our travel plans and we will be dancing in the finals." By the tone in Mateo's voice I know not to challenge him any longer on this. I know by his determination, we will dance in the finals.

I got very little sleep worrying over Mateo. In the morning I call Ken and tell him what's going on. He suggests we continue on as planned, and see how things are in six days. So it's off to Caracas, Venezuela.

The pain medication made traveling for Mateo easier. The airline was gracious enough to move us to first class. Before leaving for Caracas I cancelled our original hotel reservation and booked us in a hotel that is nowhere near the convention center. We are staying at the Cayena. It's in the most exclusive part of Caracas. A true 5 star luxury hotel. I don't want anyone from the dance circuit to know about Mateo. There will be no practice for us and Mateo is not to be on his foot for the next four days. He assures me we will dance in the finals and implores me stop worrying. We are both fatigued from traveling and turn in early. Although I am exhausted, I can't sleep. I spend another restless night worrying about Mateo.

The next day I retrieve the package Ashley has sent me from the hotel concierge. Mateo is resting in his room. The hotel we are staying in is really beautiful. It's much more expensive than what Ashley usually books but I wanted Mateo to be comfortable. There is no point staying in my room. I might as well enjoy this gorgeous hotel. I can still keep a low profile and enjoy myself at the same time. The hotel is far enough away so I don't worry about running into any other couples. Besides they would never pay a night for what this place is costing me. I decide to stop in the hotel restaurant to sit and look over the information about Cali while I drink a glass of wine. When I order, I try my Spanish out on the waiter.

"Buenos tarde. Puedo por favor tener un vaso de vino blanco y un poco de fruta."

He brings what I asked for, so I know I got it right. I'm amazed that I am able to understand most of what he saying. He also speaks English, and I explain to him I am learning Spanish. As I return to the stack of information Ashley has sent, I notice a table of men dressed in business attire. They appear to be having a meeting. They are speaking both Spanish and English. I try to follow their conversation. From what I can gather, they are discussing something about building permits and contracts. There is one voice that sounds familiar to me. His back is to me and I can't see his face.

Perhaps he is someone from the dance committee and that is why I recognize the voice. The men seem to be finishing up their meeting as they stand and shake hands. Now that they are standing, I notice they are all are all dressed in expensive designer business suits. The one with his back to me turns to reveal his face. Now I see why I recognized the voice. It is Alejandro Perez.

I'd forgotten how handsome he is. Seriously, this man is ridiculously gorgeous. I feel myself blush as he spots me, catching me staring directly at him. I can tell he

instantly recognizes me by the huge grin that begins to spread across his face. He excuses himself from the rest of the men, and makes a beeline straight to my table. I feel my pulse quicken and my heart begin to race. This time I can't ignore it. The minute he spotted me and those turquoise eyes zoned in on me I felt the physical change in my body. Honestly I don't want to ignore what I am feeling. As I stand to greet him, he gives me a warm hug and a peck on each cheek, as though we are old friends. Alejandro looks unmistakably gorgeous in his navy pinstriped suit. It looks like an Armani. I may be thrifty, but I'm secretly a closet fashionista and know the major designers.

"Buenos tardes, Victoria. Is that all I had to do? Travel 1,300 miles to get the pleasure of seeing you again?" He says in a very soft voice, with just a hint of flirtation.

Yep, there it is again. But this time it's not just my pulse and heart. This man has just made me blush and I can feel my entire body tighten and tingle. Just the sound of his sexy ass voice has me feeling like a wanton woman.

"Buenos tardes, Alejandro," I say, showing off my Spanish. "This is such a surprise. I can't believe I'm running into you here in Caracas." I'm trying to ignore how handsome he is, which proves impossible as he stands there, staring at me. I'm relieved that I did my hair and makeup this morning and that I'm wearing something other than my usual dance wear. I am wearing a white cotton sweater and a pair of dark indigo skinny jeans that fit me like a glove, and my black Havaianas.

Casual, but cute.

"It's fate, Victoria. Fate is what brings most people together in life."

"I don't know about fate. The reality is I am here to compete in the World Latin Dance finals this weekend."

"Victoria, don't ever fight fate. My reality is I've come to Caracas for a meeting to discuss the building of a new recording studio. We are expanding our search for artists in South America and want to provide a studio where they can record. I am staying at this hotel during my visit. It seems now I am also here so I could have the pleasure of seeing you again. Which is so much more interesting to me than the meeting I just attended."

"Then I won't fight fate. I want to thank you for the beautiful flowers you sent me in Miami. I apologize for not calling and thanking you, but I didn't have your number."

"You did not need to thank me. They were my way of thanking you for a lovely evening of conversation, dance and the company of the most beautiful woman in the room."

"Would you like to join me for a glass of wine?" Did I just invite this man for a drink? I am not sure where that came from but I am drawn to this man.

"I would love to. If you would please excuse me for a minute while I tell my business associates goodbye."

Watching him walk away I realize how comfortable I am around him. I only had one encounter with this man at a dinner party and yet something about it has me wanting to learn everything about him.

When he rejoins me he asks, "Victoria, have you eaten lunch?"

"No, actually, I just sat down."

"My meetings are finished for the day. Would you have lunch with me?"

"Well since Mateo has hurt his foot and is holed up in his hotel room I am free for the next three days, so yes, I'd love to have lunch with you."

Alejandro tells the waiter we would like to order lunch, but he requests a more private table in the outdoor patio area. I gather my papers and put them in my tote as we move outside to a beautiful private cabana on the patio. Wow! The outdoor area of this hotel is breathtaking. The patio is filled with oversized pots overflowing with the most fragrant and colorful flowers. The cabana is like having our very own outdoor dining area. It seems very intimate. I can tell by the way the staff is catering to Alejandro's request he must be a VIP guest at the hotel.

"Victoria, would it be all right with you if I order our lunch? I promise you will like it." I agree, Alejandro and the waiter speak solely in Spanish while I try to follow. The waiter turns to me and asks in Spanish if there is anything else I would like to add.

"Sí, por favor. ¿Podría traerme un vaso de agua con limón. Gracias." I reply with great pride in my voice.

"I see since we last met you have mastered the Spanish language. Very impressive." Alejandro comments and with a big grin on his face as he winks at me.

I can't believe he remembers me telling him that I did not speak Spanish and wanted to learn. This is new territory for me.

"Please tell me more about Mateo's foot. Has he seen a doctor since you arrived in Caracas?" Alejandro seems genuinely concerned.

"No, not since we arrived yesterday. Before we left Puerto Rico, a doctor from the hotel examined his foot and prescribed some pain medication. He is resting his foot for the next few days. I just hope he will be able to dance on Friday."

"I might be of some help with Mateo's foot. I know some doctors here in Caracas. If you wish I will place some calls and see what I can do."

"Thank you Alejandro." I am very surprised by his generosity and kindness. Since I know no one in Caracas I am happy to accept help from Alejandro. I want to dance in the finals, but I don't want take the chance of hurting Mateo's foot any further if there is damage already.

This eases my mind. I give in, relax and spend some time having a delicious lunch. I am not sure of some of things I'm eating, but it's all really good. The wine and conversation is also wonderful. I check my watch and can't believe two hours have passed. It seems like only fifteen minutes.

"What are your plans for the next few days since Mateo is out of commission for a while with his foot?" Alejandro ask.

"I am trying to keep a low profile. We don't want the other dancers to know we are here and question why we have not been to the practice center. Before we arrived in Caracas I changed hotels. There don't seem to be any dancers staying at this hotel."

"See, it is fate. Changing your reservations led us to meet again. I would love to show you Venezuela and some of my favorite places. It has been months since I have had some time for myself, and this would be a perfect time to do that with you. I don't have to be back in Miami until Thursday."

"I would really enjoy that, but I don't want to take you away from your business."

"What I came to do in Caracas is done and you would not be taking me away from anything. You would be doing me a favor. I could use a few days of relaxation."

"I have to admit I was wondering what I was going to do for the next few days. I would love to see Caracas with you as my guide."

It's all settled. I'll be whisked around Venezuela for a few days by this wonderful man. A man that is starting to enter my head with thoughts and feelings I didn't think I wanted. He invites me to dinner, which I gladly accept and we make plans to meet in the lobby around eight. Before I return to my room, I stop in the hotel boutique and buy a beautiful dress to wear tonight. The only dress I brought with me on this tour is the dress I wore to the dinner party in Miami. I don't want to show up tonight wearing a dress Alejandro has already seen. Since this is an upscale hotel they have a cute boutique shop that seems to carry a little bit of everything including a nice selection of ladies dresses. I was lucky and found the perfect dress for tonights dinner. It's just a simple white fitted sheath dress. It's made out of a gorgeous knit fabric that's completely lined. Sleeveless and with a deep v-neck that shows off not only my tan but my great cleavage. It's simple but perfect for the weather here in Caracas.

I am back in my room getting ready when the phone rings. It's Mateo. He said he was shocked to receive a phone call from Alejandro. He explained to him that he ran into me in the hotel restaurant and I told him about his foot. He has arranged for a doctor who specializes in sports medicine to examine Mateo's foot and see what can be done. He can't believe we ran into each other and that he has offered to help him. I tell him I am going to meet Alejandro for dinner later and that we're going to spend the next few days touring the city. Of course Mateo can't help himself as he drops the old "I told you so" on me! He then tells me the doctor is at the door, so he has to go. "I hope he's cute!" he adds just before hanging up. Typical Mateo.

When I get to the lobby, Alejandro is waiting. Gone is the suit and tie. He is dressed in taupe linen pants and white linen shirt. He looks much younger in casual clothing. I can fight it all I want, but I find this man incredibly attractive. When he sees me again that grin appears on his face. He greets me with a hug and a kiss on each cheek. I am liking the way his hands and lips feel on my skin. His touch reminds me of something I am missing. Something even Sonny doesn't give me.

Alejandro pulls me to him and he whispers in my ear, "Victoria, you look lovely. The dress is beautiful, but it's your shoes that caught my eye." Once again I can feel my body react and I welcome his touch, his warm breath and heat of his body. The length of the dress is almost to my ankles so I wore my nude gladiator Gucci heels. Clearly Alejandro has great taste in shoes. A man after my own heart.

"Thank you. I'm impressed you noticed my shoes. When I was getting dressed Mateo called me and told me what you did for him. I can't thank you enough."

"I noticed more than your shoes, Victoria. The doctor's visit was for you as well. If we are going to spend a few days together, I want you to be able to relax. He is in good hands."

Wow! Now he has me blushing. He noticed more than my shoes. Duh, of course he did. I really need to stop ignoring what is happening here. This isn't just him being nice. I don't want to lead him on but I don't want it stop either. Again he reminds me of things I have been missing. The company of a man. A man that takes notice of me.

We go to a local restaurant that is a favorite of his. I think to myself, what must his life must be like? I mean, how many people do you know that can say they have a favorite restaurant in Caracas, Venezuela? When we step outside there is a chauffeured car waiting. I have become accustomed to nice things in life, but nothing to this degree. Still, I am not one to be impressed with wealth. I have money. It makes life easier, but it doesn't make it perfect. I would trade everything, and I do mean *everything*, to have my husband and our simple little life in Florida back.

The restaurant is not far. We are greeted at the door and it is apparent that they know Alejandro very well. He introduces me to the owner, Luis, and we are given a table in a private area away from everyone. This restaurant is known for it's steak and that's what we have. It's by far the best steak I have ever eaten. We also dine on baked and fried yucca, delicious tamales which are wrapped in maize husks, fried maize cakes and a variety of cheeses. The food, wine and conversation is amazing. We continue to chat, learning a lot about each other. We say goodbye to the owner and the car is waiting for us outside. When we arrive back at the hotel Alejandro tells me he has a day of sightseeing planned for us tomorrow. We agree to meet in the lobby at 10 a.m. He asks me to dress casually.

"Thank you for such a lovely evening, Victoria. I've been so busy with the company that I haven't taken much time to simply relax and enjoy myself as I did this evening. I haven't shared an evening like this in such a long time. I forgot how nice it was. The food and wine were wonderful but having the company of a beautiful woman that has captivated me from the first night I met her made the evening perfect." Taking my hands in his he pulls me in for a kiss on each cheek as he says goodnight.

Chapter 16

Back in my room I have trouble getting Alejandro out of my mind. I keep thinking about what he said and it has me wondering. He said it's been a while since he enjoyed himself. I'm sure he dates. The man is gorgeous. I bet the women in Miami are throwing themselves at him. I hate to admit it, but tonight was the first time I was able to relax and be myself with a man in a long time. Even with Sonny, I was always keyed up and our time together was filled with intensity with definite limits and boundaries. Tonight, however, was just easy. I'm so glad Alejandro feels the same way.

This morning, I surprise myself when my first thoughts are not of my Latin Superstar. Instead, I'm excited about spending the day with Alejandro, and wondering what sights he plans to show me. I know this isn't really a date, but it kind of feels like one, at least to me. Before I head down to meet him, I place a call to

Mateo's room to see how he's doing. He tells me the doctor must be at the top in his field because he knew exactly what to do to ensure that he will be able to dance in the finals. He also told him he has set him up with a doctor in NYC for treatment when he returns from competition. He has to stay off his foot until we go in Friday for practice. Before I hang up I ask him if the doctor was hot. "Really, Victoria!" he laughs, playfully adding "is that all you think about?", He inquires about my dinner with Alejandro and I tell him it was lovely. He laughs and says, "You just refuse to admit this guy has a thing for you, don't you?"

"There is nothing to admit," I say, exasperated with his prying. Yet I can't help but wonder if I'm only fooling myself. I also place a call to Ken and he is happy to hear Mateo is on the mend. I tell him nothing about Alejandro. I know better.

Alejandro is waiting for me in the lobby and is dressed in khaki cargo shorts, a turquoise T-shirt and deck shoes. I swear his t-shirt has made his eye color more intense and harder to resist. Dressed like this he looks even younger than he did last night. I have chosen black knit capris, black camisole and my black Havaianas. I also brought a blouse to pull over my camisole if it gets chilly. He tells me we are going to see Caracas by the best way possible.

Before we go I take his hands in mine and look directly into his gorgeous turquoise eyes, "I want to thank you again for what you did for Mateo. I was really concerned. I was ready to tell him we were going home because I didn't want him to further his injury. Mateo is so stubborn. I know he would have danced no matter what the consequences. The doctor has assured Mateo if he follows his orders he will be able to dance by Friday."

"Your welcome. So today you belong to me. I don't want that beautiful head of yours thinking or worrying about anything."

A car is waiting for us and after a short drive we pull into what appears to be a small airport. To my surprise we will be seeing Venezuela by helicopter. Alejandro is right, this is the best way to see the city. From above, the view is breathtaking. Among many sights, we flew over the Avila National Park alongside the mesmerizing turquoise Carribbean Sea, the Miraflores Palace, and the Pico Naiguata. If we'd have visited these places on foot, I don't think I'd have come close to recognizing how beautiful they really are.

Over the headset, Alejandro informs me we are going to land for lunch before heading back to the airport. Where could we possible be landing for lunch? We land on the roof of a skyscraper in the business district of Caracas. He helps me out of the helicopter and right there on the roof awaits a tent with a table for two. The tent is beautiful and filled with plants and beautiful flowers. Inside is a team to tend to our every need. There is a chef and his assistants to prepare our meal. A head waiter to tell us what the chef has prepared for us. Then there is yet another waiter that serves our food. I keep telling myself something my Mom taught me years ago: When you experience new things and they are things that are beautiful and extravagant, act as though you have already experienced it before. OK, well this is really to hard to do. First, a helicopter ride over Caracas, and then lunch on the rooftop of a high rise. The best part about all of this is that

Alejandro is in no way trying to impress me. It just seems to be a natural way of life for him. He is not an arrogant man; in fact, he's quite humble about his wealth.

Lunch is beyond delicious and quite the new experience. Instead of sitting directly across from me Alejandro sits next to me and the chairs are turned so we are facing each other. Once the food is served Alejandro moves forward on his chair so he is even closer. His knees are actually touching mine. Alejandro describes the different dishes then offers me a bite of each from his fork. Just his voice alone describing the food and how delicately he places the fork in my mouth is something I have never experienced before. It's very decadent. It's such an intimate gesture and incredibly sexy. I can't help but notice how his eyes never leave mine. I think he is enjoying this as much as I am. The connection between us just adds to the intimacy. Who knew eating lunch could be so sexy?

We had something called Cachapa which is similar to a traditional pancake but it's folded over and filled with some sort of soft white cheese. These just melted in my mouth. We did have one of my favorites and the only dish I recognized, caprese salad. My favorite was the Pasticho, the Venezuelan version of lasagna. Dessert was something called Bien Me Sabe. It's a sponge cake bathed in liquor and layered with coconut cream filling and topped with meringue. Alejandro called it 'a little slice of heaven'. I laugh and say I would call it 'better than sex' cake. This has Alejandro raising his brow and winking at me as he slides the fork into my mouth.

I lose track of time. It is effortless to be with him. Before I know it lunch is over and it's time to go.

As he is strapping me in the seat of the helicopter a look of disappointment comes across his face. His eyes meet mine and for the first time I feel and see the emotion in them. "I am sorry I will not be able to see you this evening. It's hard to step away completely from work. I have a business dinner to attend tonight with a new artist that I am interested in signing."

Completely taken back by this feeling and the realization of it, I am only able to mutter, "No problem. I completely understand." I am relieved when he finishes strapping me in and the connection breaks between us. I need to watch myself with him. I am starting to feel this is more than just a little innocent flirting going on between us. My body is certainly telling me it's more.

When we return to the hotel he says, "I have tomorrow's plans all set. Is 11 a.m. good for you?"

"It's perfect."

"Do you have a bathing suit?" he asks. I nod yes, and he tells me, "Good you'll need it. I'll take care of everything else."

Once again we part ways with a friendly hug and a peck on each cheek. Before he releases me he whispers, "Thank you for another lovely day. I hate that it has to end early. Get some rest beautiful."

Truthfully, I am thankful to have the evening free because I am exhausted. I think I will finally be able to sleep knowing Mateo's foot is healing and we will be able to compete Saturday. I take a long, hot shower and my mind drifts to my day with Alejandro. But as always thoughts of Sonny make their way into my head. My body is craving his tonight. I need to see him. I let the water from the shower wash over and warm my skin. Running my hands over my body I am reminded how much I miss Sonny's touch. I also find my mind drifting and becoming filled with thoughts of what Alejandro's hands would feel like. How different would his touch be? Would his touch have the same affect on me? Could I give myself over to him? Damn it! What am I doing? What am I getting myself into? Too many questions. I need to shut everything out of my head tonight and just sleep.

I awaken excited to find what Alejandro has planned for us today. Before I leave my room I call and check on Mateo. He tells me his foot is feeling great but will continue to follow the doctor's orders and stay off of it. He says he has been sunbathing nude on the balcony. This does not surprise me.

When I get down to the lobby Alejandro is waiting for me and I can tell by his surfer style shorts there will be water involved in today's adventure. I am wearing a matching Trina Turk black paisley printed bathing suit, lounge pants, and cover up. Again he greets me with a hug but instead of a kiss on each cheek he leans in and just gently brushes his lips over mine. He then pulls me to him so I am resting my hands on his firm, hard chest and he whispers in my ear, "I see you slept well. You look gorgeous this morning." Chills run up my body as I feel his warm breath against my skin. Before he pulls away he places his full, soft lips against my neck stealing a kiss.

As usual, a car is waiting and we take a short drive to a marina. As I scan the bay, I have a strong feeling that the biggest boat is the one we are going out on. My assumption is verified as

Alejandro leads me directly to it. The 'boat' as Alejandro calls it, is magnificent. It is staffed with a full crew. There is lunch and champagne awaiting us on the top deck. With the breeze blowing off the water and the sun shining down it's a perfect day. The water is the most magnificent shade of blue. This 'boat' is so big I don't even hear the engines or notice we are pulling away from the marina.

I didn't think anything could top the lunch we had on the roof top or the dinner at Alejandro's favorite restaurant but I may be wrong. The spread they have laid out for us is stunning. It's like food porn. Fresh fruit of all types cut into intricate shapes displayed like works of art. Shrimp cocktail the size of my hand and a tray of spectacular looking sushi. All different types to pick from. Everything is so fresh and delicious. After lunch we go up on the sun deck where there is more champagne. On the deck is a beautiful enormous lounger, large enough for several people. There is a basket filled with sun products and towels. Alejandro tells me if I'm going to remove my cover-up I should put on some sunscreen. Thank God I am comfortable with my body since the only bathing suit I brought on the road was this skimpy bikini. I can feel Alejandro's eyes checking me out even through his sunglasses. He is right; I will need some sunscreen. My so-called "tan" is spray-on, and I cannot afford to burn, or have tan lines at the finals. I'm not comfortable enough to go topless in front of Alejandro, so sunscreen it is. Alejandro seems very comfortable as he strips out of his shorts and revealing a black Speedo-style bikini. Typically, seeing a man in a Speedo would make me gag, but this bathing suit fits Alejandro's style and personality perfectly. Besides, his body is amazing and I am thankful I am wearing sunglasses so he can't catch me checking him out.

I choose a spray on sunscreen and after applying it to everything within reach, I ask him if he minds applying some on my back. I lay stomach side down on the lounger and Alejandro sits down next to me on the edge to put sunscreen on me. Before applying it Alejandro asks, "May I untie your top so I can apply the spray evenly over your back?"

Giggling I respond, "Of course you can. I really can't have any bathing suit marks on my tan before the finals. But my bottoms stay exactly where they are. You got it?"

Pulling the two strings on my top and pushing them to the sides Alejandro laughingly remarks, "I got it! Can I at least enjoy the view? Why are you worried about bathing suit marks? Your tan is so even."

"Yes you can enjoy the view! The reason my tan is so even is because it's not real. Hate to tell you this but it's fake. For competition season I get spray tanned.

Welcome to my world."

"Well the tan might be fake but your skin beautiful. This spray doesn't seem to be going on evenly. May I use my hands to blend it in?"

"Really Alejandro? Just admit your dying to touch me."

"Can you blame a guy for trying? No, really it needs blended in. I am afraid the spray is missing places on your skin."

"Then by all means blend away. I don't want to burn." The minute Alejandro's hands touch my skin I tense. I didn't meant to it just happened.

"Relax, Victoria. I'm just blending in the sunscreen." Oh shit he noticed. Taking a deep breath I force myself to relax and just enjoy the moment. Like he said he is just blending in the sunscreen. Regardless, I can't stop the way his hands gliding across my skin has me feeling. My core tightens as his hands glide down my legs blending the product in. His hands feel so good sliding up and down and across my skin. Unexpectedly a small moan escapes my lips. I finally let go, relax, and enjoy this man's touch.

We enjoy the rest of the afternoon on the deck drinking champagne. I guess it was all the champagne and the warmth of the sun that made me fall asleep. When I wake, Alejandro is laying next to me, watching.

"I am sorry for falling asleep. I think it was a combination of good sun and even better champagne." I say apologetically, feeling embarrassed that this man has watched me sleeping. I hope I didn't snore.

"Victoria, you don't have to apologize. I am happy that you are relaxing." He reaches over and touches his hand to my cheek. "You are even more beautiful when you sleep."

We are laying very close to each other and I can feel some sexual tension beginning to develop. Since we have been spending the last few days together getting to know one another, we have become very comfortable. I know what is beginning and I just can't allow it. I get up before it can happen. I just can't let this man into my life. Not now. I am so confused. I am standing, looking out over the ocean when Alejandro comes up behind me.

Alejandro leans into my body wrapping his arms around and whispers. "Are you all right, Victoria?"

Thank God I have on really dark, huge sun glasses because I can feel tears forming in my eyes. Lying I answer him, "Yes, I am fine." I think about what Sonny said to me about not giving up my life just to be his lover. In conversations Alejandro and I have shared over the last few days, we have learned so much about each other and it has been made clear we are both single. I would never tell him about Sonny. I know it is only natural for him to want to take this relationship we seem to be building to the next level. But I am so confused. I don't know what to do or what I want. Alejandro catches me off guard, turns me around to face him. He then pulls me to him and wraps his arms around my waist.

"I will wait until you are ready." He doesn't have to explain. I understand exactly what he means.

"Alejandro, I'm not sure if I'll ever be ready." I let the words fall from my lips, in almost a whisper.

He pulls me to his chest and whispers, "Then I will just have to wait until whatever is stopping you is gone."

What is it with these Latin men whispering in my ear? Damn, they know my weak spot.

"I hope you are man with a lot of time on your hands." This make Alejandro laugh out loud, which also makes me laugh.

"I am a very patient man and I know you will be worth the wait."

After returning to the marina we head back to the hotel. We decide to meet in the restaurant for a late dinner. Dinner is different this time. I am more relaxed and so is he. We both are casually dressed; Alejandro is wearing jeans and a Polo shirt, and I am wearing my black knit Vince Camuto dress. As I was dressing in my room, I realized I haven't worn this dress since my last evening with Sonny. I hate that I am constantly reminded of things about Sonny but he is a man that is impossible to forget. No matter what I am feeling for Alejandro, Sonny always finds a way into my mind and my heart.

Alejandro is waiting for me in the lobby with a single rose. As he hands it to me he leans in and brushes his lips softly over mine. Wow! I wasn't expecting that.

We dined on a light dinner of Caesar salad and roasted chicken paired with the most delicious white wine I have ever tasted. After dinner, Alejandro tells me they have set up an area on the patio for us to have drinks. It is beautiful and obvious Alejandro arranged all of this. Inside the cabana are two oversized chairs. The cabana is filled with candlelight and flowers and a bar set up with two champagne filled buckets and a variety of desserts including my favorite chocolate covered strawberries. It's really romantic and for the first time I feel this more than just a casual evening Alejandro has planned.

"Mr. Perez, are you trying seduce me?" For once I think I made him blush.

"Is it working, Victoria?"

"Let's just say it's tempting." We spend the next four hours talking. Talking about everything. In between talking I indulge

Alejandro once again to let him feed me dessert. He really seems to enjoy this. The chocolate covered strawberries were so good I could have eaten the entire tray. I am surprised coming from two different cultures how much we actually have in common. During those four hours Alejandro remains a complete gentlemen. He has managed to take my mind completely off of everything going on in my life. It was one of the most enjoyable evenings that I have ever spent with anyone. But in my mind I know that Sonny de la Cruz is not just anyone.

Alejandro walks me to the elevator to say goodnight. "I'll be leaving in the morning around ten for Miami."

"Thank you so much, Alejandro, for the past few days. I had a wonderful time. Thank you for showing me the beauty of Caracas. I enjoyed our talks and getting to know you. But most of all thank you for what you did for Mateo."

He places his business card in my hand and says, "Promise me you will call when you return from your trip to Cali. What I did for Mateo was nothing. Good luck this weekend and safe travels to Colombia." He then pulls me close, puts his arms around me and runs his lips up the side of my neck with soft kisses before he whispers in my ear, "I meant what I said, when whatever is stopping you is gone, I will be waiting for you." He looks in to my eyes then gently kisses my forehead right before he releases me.

It's really late when I return to my room but I can't seem to relax enough to get to sleep. After such a beautiful evening with Alejandro I am beginning to question a lot of things. Why does Alejandro make me feel this way? At the same time how can Sonny make me feel a way that I can't stop craving? How and why has fate sent these two men into my life? Yeah, I am a huge believer in fate. I didn't want to admit that to Alejandro the other day in the restaurant. But I knew he was right. Fate brings people together for a reason. Now I just have to figure out the reason.

I awake in the morning and panic when I check the clock. It is 9:45. I can't believe I have slept this late. I quickly pull my hair back in a knot, throw on sweat pants and a

T-shirt and brush my teeth. I call down to the desk and ask if Mr. Perez has checked out. They tell me he is checking out now and I tell them not to let him leave, that I am on my way down. On the elevator ride down, I'm still not sure what the hell I am going to do. When I reach the front desk he is waiting.

"What is wrong, Victoria? Is everything OK? Is it Mateo's foot?" Alejandro asks with concern in his voice. I pull him aside so we are alone.

"Mateo's foot is fine. I am fine. I just want to give you something before you leave. Something to remember me by." I can't believe I am standing here in the lobby of this hotel, about to do this. This time I am letting go. I decide to let my heart speak for me.

"Victoria, what is it?" he asks, an expression of confusion on his face. Because I am barefoot, I have to stand on my tiptoes and stretch to put my arms around his neck. No turning back now. I give him a kiss. A deep, passionate kiss. Even though I have caught him completely off guard, he responds immediately. With his hands on my hips he pulls me close, leans down, accepts, and returns it. My heart is beating so fast and my stomach is doing flip flops. This kiss feels amazing. When I try to pull away, he pulls me in even closer this time and says, "Now let me give you something to remember *me* by." He kisses me long and hard. I allow him to take over the control this time. His tongue slips past my lips and dances with mine. His kiss is slow and deliberate. Filled with desire, it seems to last forever, and I savor every second of it. When we finally part, he holds me sweetly, and whispers, "Remember, Victoria, I am waiting for you."

On the elevator ride up I am unable to stop smiling, feeling lightheaded and giddy from his kiss. There is this feeling in the pit of my stomach. A good feeling. Different. Alejandro is right, after all. Maybe, just maybe, this is fate.

I spend the last day of rest with Mateo. We worked on my Spanish. He is impressed, and says the time I spent with Alejandro has clearly helped. "You are rolling your r's better," he tells me. Of course he is relentless with the questions about Alejandro. He wants to know what we did and where we went. I tell him half-truths, and keep the best parts to myself. Mateo and I sunbathe on the private balcony. He suns completely nude, but I prefer to go topless, just to ensure no tan lines when I perform in my dance costume. After a while we head inside to shower and relax. We order room service and watch movies in our fluffy white oversized hotel robes until we are both tired and ready for sleep.

It's Friday, practice day, and Mateo is on his feet for the first time in four days. I am sure people have been wondering where we've been. We have the floor for an hour at 1pm to run through our dance. When we arrive at the convention center, we are both sun-kissed and look rested. We hear a few whispering that they thought we weren't going to show up. One couple had the audacity to ask if we thought we were too good to practice. Of course Mateo and I ignore all of this. We go to our assigned practice room, stretch, and warm up before we dance. I ask Mateo if he is ready. "Of course, Victoria," he assures me, and then Mateo dances as if he had never been injured. After lunch we make our way to the floor for our 1 p.m. practice session. We notice we are not alone. Clearly everyone has been wondering about us and speculating where we have been. Nearly all competing couples have shown up to watch us rehearse. Mateo shoots me a smug grin, and whispers, "Looks like they all want a show, so let's give them one." Then that is just what we do. We dance like it's the final round and not merely a rehearsal, making it quite plain that we have come here to win and that we will be leaving with our title as champions.

When we return to the hotel, Mateo tells me that the doctor is coming by to check on him and give him a shot, if needed. We are both exhausted, but very happy with how things went in practice. We make plans to meet at 10 a.m. in the hotel restaurant for breakfast before heading to the convention center for the preliminary rounds. It will be a long day, so I will not have a chance to work on my Spanish and catch up on emails as usual. I open the door to my room and am surprised to find it is filled with flowers. Arrangement after arrangement, no two alike. There must be 15 vases filled with the most beautiful flowers I have ever seen. In the largest vase are red roses, with a card attached. I don't even need to open it to know who has sent me all of these flowers. I open it anyway; curious to read what is written. It reads:

Victoria,

I will be waiting!

~ Alejandro

I feel myself smile. So this is what it feels like to have a man want me completely. Not just when he can sneak away to be with me. There will never be flowers from Sonny or dinners or anything. It's an affair and nothing more. If it's so clear and defined and simple to put into perspective why can't I convince myself to walk away from him? What is this hold he has on me? What is the connection I feel for him? How did I allow him to crawl into my head and my heart and take up residency where I had allowed no one to enter since Blake's death. I'm stupid for even dwelling on these things. I should be enjoying and appreciating the flowers from the man that wants me in his life. Shaking my head I crawl into bed. The scent of flowers fills my room and my senses. Tonight I will not think about what the future holds for me only about what my heart is feeling. I pray for sleep so I don't torment myself.

We take advantage of the breakfast buffet the hotel offers before we start the long day of preliminary competition. We'll needs the calories to get through today's dancing. The convention center is having trouble with its Internet connection. Looks like I will spend the down time working on my Spanish. I tell myself I will have plenty of time when I arrive in Cali. Then I can catch up on email and see if my Latin Superstar is up to anything.

We fly through the preliminaries and head back to the hotel. We are meeting Rafael and Lily for dinner in the hotel restaurant, La Sibilla. They serve a menu of delicious authentic Italian cuisine. We dined on insalata caprese, an Antipasti platter, grilled vegetable salad and rolled beef carpaccio. The food lived up to it's 5 star rating. Mateo and I mention nothing about his foot.

After dinner we all say our good nights and Mateo whispers to me, "I am having another treatment from the doctor on my foot." He knows the look I give him.

"Foot treatment? Really, Mateo."

"You need to stop giving me that look or I will be moving to Caracas permanently." Mateo snaps back at me.

We don't have to be at the convention center until 7:00 pm so I spend most of the day by the pool relaxing. Mateo finally shows up at noon and I tell him, "No nude sunbathing here." Bending down giving my cheek a kiss he laughs, "Happy Birthday baby girl. Looks like a perfect day to celebrate it and defend our title."

Smiling it dawns on me. It's my birthday! I can't believe I forgot. After Blake's death I dreaded my birthday. But since meeting Ashley and Mateo I have learned to enjoy it and celebrate it again. I am thankful Mateo is in a chatty mood and keeps my mind occupied with stories about his new doctor friend. After a day of sun and laughing with Mateo I am in need of a shower. We agree to meet in the lobby for a light early dinner at 5 then head to the convention center.

We are set to dance last since we have the highest score going into tonight's competition. We will be wearing the new costumes that we had designed just for tonight. We are also changing our music for tonight. It's time to shake things up a bit. I work on my Spanish to pass the time. Then we are called to the floor. We are announced as the reigning 2015 Latin Dance Champions Victoria Moore and Mateo Chavez. The audience loves us here. When they cue the music the audience reacts to it right away. It is a remix of Pitbull's "Don't Stop the Party." We bring the audience to its feet. Mateo is really laying it on thick. We both enjoy the moment and dance a flawless routine. We know before the song is over we have this. As the song ends, we collapse in each other's arms, and Mateo whispers in my ear, "If they only knew!"

We spend the evening celebrating our win and my birthday with all the other couples. Rafael and Lily also won in the Kizomba division. It's a great close to an incredibly long 12 weeks. We are all sad to see it end, but happy it is over. Between the traveling, dancing, interviews and guest appearances, we are exhausted. We say our goodbyes. Some of the couples we will not see again until next year. Mateo and I head back to the hotel.

Mateo and I both have early flights. He will fly to Miami and then home to NYC. I am off to Cali, Columbia. What was I thinking, agreeing to be a guest judge right after competing for twelve weeks? I want to go home. I miss Ken and Ashley. I miss my Latin Superstar. I miss my time with Alejandro. Now I am *really* confused. A year ago I had nobody in my life, and now I have not one but TWO men. Two Latin men, at that!

Chapter 17

Mateo and I say our goodbyes at the airport. Our flights are only 20 minutes apart. When I get back from this judging gig we plan to have a celebration dinner. I remind him to follow up with the doctor in New York. "I wonder if this one is hot," he says with a smile.

I arrive in Cali, Columbia and the hotel has sent a car. We pull up to a beautiful grand hotel that is buzzing with people. I notice so many young dancers staying here for the competition that will take place this weekend. Ken told me that the accommodations alone would be worth it, and I can see that he was right. I am escorted to my room. I guess room would be an understatement. It's a penthouse suite on the top floor, bigger than my loft in New York. It is amazing. Maybe this is exactly what I needed. A little time to clear my head before returning home. On the table in the living room there is a gorgeous bouquet of roses in an exquisite crystal vase. There must be 200 hundred roses, in a variety of colors. There is a card, but I already know who sent them. I open it anyway, and it simply says: Congratulations, Alejandro. This man has a way sneaking himself into my thoughts and stealing away moments of my day. Now not only do I have memories of Sonny filling my head. But after that kiss I am fighting to keep him out as well and if I am being totally honest with myself my heart.

There is a knock at the door. The hotel concierge has come to introduce himself and ask if there is anything I need. His name is Javier Rodriguez. He presents himself in a very professional manner and seems to take his job very serious, yet I can sense a playful side to him. He is also quite handsome. I'd say he is in his early 30's and basically he's tall, dark and handsome. But I don't think he would have any interest in me, maybe Mateo, but not me. Javier is warm and friendly, and we have an instant connection.

"After you have freshened up, a spa day has been arranged for you." He goes over what appears to be an itinerary. He is very dramatic about what awaits for me this afternoon, as though he is selling me a car or a million-dollar estate. I love his personality.

"I can't believe they treat their judges to a spa day. That's a first."

"Oh, but they don't, Ms. Moore," Javier quickly points out. "It is a gift from a Mr. Alejandro Perez. If there is nothing else you need at the moment, I will leave you to settle in. Please do not hesitate to call me for anything," he adds.

"Thank you. I can't think of anything." I mumble, gazing at the roses. I am taken aback by such a lovely gesture from Mr.

Perez. I feel like a princess. "Did you speak with him by phone?" I ask.

"If you are referring to Mr. Perez, yes I did speak with him. I helped him arrange everything for you this week. He is a very generous man." Javier answers. "Wish I had one like him," he adds with a wink.

"Oh, Mr. Perez is just a friend. A good friend," I say, trying to convince Javier I am not some kind of kept woman. What must he think of me?

After twelve long weeks of touring and dancing, a spa day was just the ticket. Mr. Perez went all out for me; I received the royal treatment from head to toe. I began with a cedar enzyme bath and salt scrub, a full body four-hand massage, a luxurious facial, some very much needed waxing, ending with a mani-pedi. I enjoy a little time alone. Time to think. So much has happened in these last few months. I went from being utterly single, to having two men occupying different spaces in my heart. I have a man who wants me that I am not ready for, and a man I cannot stop thinking of who belongs to someone else – a man I can never have. They truly are polar opposites. One is dark and seductive, offering me mystery, intensity and passion. The other is handsome, has killer turquoise eyes and that sexy as hell voice. Not to mention successful, and generous, offering me a sense of safety and security. My head swirls at the thought of my two Latin men.

After my day at the spa, I am physically relaxed, but mentally exhausted. I check in with Ashley and Ken before going to bed. I tell Ken about my incredible penthouse suite.

Ken is surprised. "How did you manage an upgrade like that Victoria? I know you were to have an executive suite, but not the penthouse."

He has caught me off guard, but I recover quickly. "Oh, well the hotel had an overbooking situation. I guess I lucked out." I realize now where the upgrade came from. Another generous arrangement from Alejandro Perez.

The next morning I am awakened by the phone. It is Javier. "Good Morning, Miss Victoria. I hope you slept well. What time would you like your breakfast?" he cheerfully inquires.

"Good Morning, Javier. Yes, I slept very well. What time is it?"

He tells me it is 10, and I can't believe I slept that long but I feel rested and refreshed. I tell Javier I'd like some fresh fruit and a diet Sprite, and ask him if there is a pool at the hotel. He laughs and says, "You have your own pool. If you open the doors to the balcony you will see it." I hop out of my king-sized bed, draw the curtains and am surprised to find a beautiful infinity pool, complete with a built-in Jacuzzi and waterfall. "Perfect," I say, not so much to Javier as to myself. It is completely private, so I can sunbathe nude.

Within minutes Javier is at the door with a beautiful spread of fresh melons and berries, with my soda. He apologizes that I was unaware my suite had its own pool.

"Is Mr. Perez responsible for the upgrade in accommodations?"

"I am not at liberty to say, but if you put two and two together, I think you will come up with the answer," he tells me with a grin. His attempt to use an American cliché is precious.

"Two and two equals four, Javier," I laugh, which makes him blush. Javier resonates a great warmth. I'm not big on reading people's auras, but I can feel his positive energy and it is contagious.

"What do you have planned for today?"

"The weather is gorgeous," I say, watching the sun shimmer across the blue water of my private pool. "I think I'll just relax in the sun." Then I add, "I want to go shopping tomorrow, and I'd like you to take me. Can you get away for the day?"

Enthusiastically, Javier tells me he can. Remembering that I don't have a car, I ask if he can arrange one for us.

"Mr. Perez has arranged a chauffeured car for you for your entire stay here in Cali," he informs me.

Pleasantly surprised, I ask Javier if there is anything *else* Mr. Perez has arranged for me.

"You'll see," he smiles, revealing very little. "I don't know who this Mr. Perez is, but I would love one for myself," he adds. I bet he would.

I spend the rest of the morning and early afternoon by the pool, sunbathing and relaxing. Javier brings me a Greek salad for lunch, before I even had to ask. It's just what I wanted, something light. He anticipates my needs and is right on the money, every time. I want to steal him away from Cali, and take him back to New York with me. Wouldn't Ashley just love that!

Just as I decide I've had enough sun for the day, the phone rings and it's Javier. "It is time for another one of Mr. Perez's surprises. Go ahead and shower, get comfortable. You are in for a real treat."

After I've bathed and put on a pair of pajama pants and camisole, there is a knock at my door. When I open it, I am greeted by a sturdy woman in a navy button-front dress and white apron, standing in front of a large covered cart. At first I think she is from housekeeping, but she introduces herself as Paola, and tells me she will be cooking authentic Columbian cuisine for me this evening. Alejandro Perez has sent a personal chef to cook for me! This really is a treat, something I would never do for myself.

Paola isn't really a talker, but her demeanor is sweet and friendly. She wheels her cart into the kitchen and gets to work. As she prepares the food, she hums. It is obvious that she loves what she is doing.

"I present you this night with Bandeja Paisa, a most popular dish in Colombia," Paola says, her thick accent quite endearing. Now I know why she doesn't say very much. Her English is a bit broken, but I am no stranger to Latin accents, and find her easy to understand. "I hope the lady is hungry," she laughs.

When my meal is served, I realize the meaning behind her last comment. Bandeja Paisa is no joke! It is a hearty meal served on a platter, consisting of grilled steak, fried pork rinds, chorizo sausages, all on a bed of red beans and rice, topped with a fried egg. As if a side dish is even needed, there are sliced avocados and sweet banana chips. I am grateful that I ate light today, because this is a lot of food! But it is rich in flavor and absolutely delicious, and I eat until I am stuffed. Paola cleans the kitchen and wishes me a pleasant evening as she leaves.

Completely relaxed, full and content I brush my teeth and head straight to bed. I can't remember the last time I crawled in bed to just relax and unwind. I even picked out a cheesy dance movie to watch. Just as I settle in and get my pillows exactly how I like them someone knocks on my suite door.

Ugh! Really? Now what? As I pull myself out of the comfy cocoon and look through the peep hole to see it's Javier and he has a huge grin on his face as I open the door.

"Buenas noches, Victoria. I hope you enjoyed your dinner this evening."

"Bueno noches, Javier. Yes I did. It was delicious. It reminded me of something we call comfort food."

"Ahh...yes I have heard of this saying. I am so happy you enjoyed another one of Mr. Perez's surprises."

"Indeed I did. By the look on your face and the box in your hand I am betting you are here for another one of Mr. Perez's surprises."

"Yes I am. Mr. Perez gave me very specific instructions. I was to hand deliver this package the minute it arrived. I am sorry. I should have asked if I was disturbing you."

"No, Javier you are not disturbing me. Please come in."

Javier and I sit down on one of the two mink colored upholstered sofas in the living room area. This penthouse really is spectacular. The color palette is done in grey, whites and minks. All the decor is contemporary and very luxurious. There is a living room space, a dining room with a table to seat at least eight. A private state of the art kitchen and the large outdoor terrace with the infinity pool is truly breathtaking. At the end of a very long corridor is the master bedroom which features one of the most opulent dressing room and en suites I have ever seen.

"Miss Victoria, this is for you" Javier says as he places a beautifully wrapped package in my hands. I already know by the size of the box it's got to be jewelry. Hey, we women know these things.

After Javier places the box in my hands I sit there just staring at it. I'm not sure I am ready for jewelry from this man. After a few uncomfortable awkward seconds Javier rises from the sofa.

Clearing his throat Javier breaks the silence. "I will let you have some privacy to open your package. Before I leave is there anything else I can do for you this evening?"

Shaking my head no I say, "Oh hell no! You are not going anywhere until I open this box. I know you are dying of curiosity to know what's in it. So sit that ass of yours back down."

Flopping back down on the sofa Javier lets out an audible sigh of relief. "Well thank God you asked me to stay. You're right, I am dying to know what's in the box. I was just trying to be discreet."

"I appreciate that Javier."

I begin to untie the white organza ribbon from the box and then tear into the silver embossed foil gift wrap. Inside I find a black velvet box with a small gift card attached to it. Taking in a deep breath I open the envelope. I swear by the way Javier is squirming around on the sofa he is more excited than me. The simple white card has Alejandro's monogram on the front in silver raised lettering. I open it to find a hand written message from him.

Victoria,

Every Queen should have a crown! I hope the color of the stones reminds you of something. Remember, I am waiting for you.

~Alejandro

I smile as I slide the note back into the envelope. I pause for just a moment to prepare myself for what's in the box. Javier has now moved to the edge of the sofa as I pull open the box.

His eyes grow big and a gasp escapes his mouth before blurting out, "Mierda. Eso es jodidamente hermosa. Usted es na mujer muy afortunada."

"You do know I understood every word you just said?" I can't help but laugh. So much for Javier being discreet!

"Please forgive me, Victoria. It's just that it's so beautiful. I couldn't help myself."

He is right. It is fucking beautiful. I can't believe what I am looking at. Its' a crown pendant covered in different shades of turquoise gem stones. The crown is attached to a elegant, fine intricate chain. I am sure by the quality of the piece, it's platinum. It's gorgeous.

"Mr. Perez is not only generous but he has exquisite taste." Javier says.

He certainly does. After tasting his kiss in Caracas I realize right then and there Alejandro is *exquisite*. I can't think of a better way to describe him. I can only imagine what his exquisite hands would feel like on my body. Oh Victoria Moore you are in such big trouble for thinking these thoughts.

Pulling me back to the moment Javier asks, "Would you like to try it on? I can help you with that before I go."

"Oh yes of course. Thank you."

Javier stands to assist me. Carefully I take the necklace from the box and hand it to him. After he figures out the clasp he reaches around my neck and fastens it. The crown falls right below the base of my neck. Javier directs me to the huge mirror in the foyer.

I don't know how he did it or where he found it but it's perfect. It's just the right size. The gem stones sparkle brilliantly when the lights reflect off them. We both stand in silence just admiring the way it looks.

"Well Miss Victoria if there is nothing else, I'll leave you to enjoy the rest of your evening and your gift from Mr. Perez."

"Of course. No there is nothing else. Thank you."

"My pleasure. Call me in the morning when you are ready for your breakfast and our day of shopping."

After Javier leaves I continue to stand in front of the mirror admiring the necklace. Alejandro Perez is certainly making sure I don't forget him. It's a little extreme on his part but I find it very sweet. Now I just have to figure out if I should call and thank him for his gift. Not calling would be rude. I bet it is part of his plan. He knows I won't let the gesture go without a proper thank you. So his plan is working.

I find where I left my handbag and dig into my wallet to find his business card. Since Cali is an hour behind Miami it's not too late to call him. Switching on my phone I think about what I am going to say as it powers up. Without another thought I dial his number. As it begins to ring I feel my pulse quicken and my heart pound against my chest. It rings three times and now I am thinking this was a bad idea. Maybe I should hang up. What if he is busy? Oh shit, what if he is with a woman? Just as I am ready to hang up he answers.

"Hello."

"Alejandro?"

"Yes this is Alejandro Perez."

"Hello. It's Victoria."

"Oh, Victoria! What a wonderful surprise. How are you? Is everything okay? Are you all right?" I could melt just hearing him say my name. His voice has my body awakening and feeling things I have tried to ignore. You can hear both the excitement and the concern in his voice.

"Everything is fine. I'm fine. I was just calling to thank you for my wonderful surprise!"

"It was delivered? Do you like?"

"Yes, Javier just left. No, I don't like it," I pause before I finish. "I love it. It's perfect. I just don't how you did it."

Laughing Alejandro says, "I have my ways, Victoria." He continues in that sexy tone I am growing to love. "Did the color remind you of anything?"

"Yes. It reminded me of those insanely beautiful turquoise eyes of yours. How can I ever thank you for such a beautiful gift?" My pulse and my heart begin to race thinking about how he just made me feel.

"You just did by saying that you loved it and it's perfect. But you could let me into your life. I want to know more about the beautiful woman that captured my attention the first time I laid eyes on her."

"I can't promise you that. But I can see you are not going to give up trying."

"No, I won't give up until you let me in. When I see something I want I go after it."

"I'm sorry I can't give you what you want right now. I need time."

"I'll wait. I am willing to be patient for something I want and I want you, Victoria."

There is an awkward moment of silence between us. Wow! He wants me. I don't know what else to say so I decide to end the call. "Thank you, Alejandro. Thank you for everything. I am so touched by all the wonderful things you have done for me."

"Your welcome. Just don't forget I am waiting for you."

"I don't think it would be possible to forget and I don't think you'll allow me to. Good night Alejandro."

"Good night, Victoria and sleep well."

As I crawl back into bed I don't even realize I am rubbing the crown pendant between my fingers feeling the detailed cuts in the stones. So much for my evening of relaxing and unwinding. I try every trick in the book to block what is filling my mind. There really in no sense in trying. Alejandro has worked his way into my head and now I have to figure out if I should let him into my heart. Is there room for him with thoughts of Sonny always filling my head? Have I let Sonny capture my heart and that is why I can't open it Alejandro?   As I lay here trying desperately to escape these thoughts I can't help the feeling that comes over me. It's eerie, a feeling that sends noticeable goosebumps up my arms.

I awake at 9 am, I am eager to go shopping. I have been holed up in this luxury penthouse for far too long, and although it is beautiful, I am ready to venture out into the city. I need to clear my mind of both Sonny de la Cruz and Alejandro Perez. Well for at least one day. There is no better way to do that then with some retail therapy. I call the concierge desk and Javier answers.

"Buenos dias, Javier.   What time can we leave to go shopping?" I ask.

"Ah, we are up early this time! We can leave whenever you like, Miss Victoria. The driver is here and waiting. I will order a light breakfast of fresh fruit and yogurt for you to enjoy while you are dressing." I am thankful Alejandro has arranged for a car for me. It is my first time to Cali and I do not like traveling alone in unfamiliar cities.

I meet Javier in the lobby. As we walk to the car, I tell him it's been a while since I've been shopping and I need some new clothes. I show him a list of things I'm looking for. I am famous for my lists, and often I drive Ashley and Ken crazy with them.

"There is a great shopping district. It is filled with boutiques and restaurants so we can also have lunch." Javier enthusiastically explains to me. I think he is more excited about the shopping.

First order of business is to find a new pair of jeans. I end up finding three great fitting pairs that I can't decide among, so I buy them all. There are designers here that I have never seen nor heard of, not even in NYC. I tell Javier I want some great leather boots; one pair to wear with jeans, and a black pair that extend over the knee. He tells me there is a local Zapatero, Mr. Jiminez, whose custom shoes are beautifully handmade. Since Zapatero sounds a lot like zapato, the Spanish word for shoes, I quickly recognize it means shoemaker, and smile, proud of how far my Spanish has come.

Javier knows what he's doing when it comes to shopping. The shoes in Mr. Jiminez's shop are gorgeous. Made of the softest, most luxurious leather I have ever seen. I choose a pair of brown distressed leather western style boots with a very pointy toe and a high heel. The other is pair of black leather thigh-high boots. They have a flat heel, but are very sexy. Behind the knee area is an elegant leather lace-up detail. Javier says they will look hot with leggings or with jeans tucked in.

After we leave Mr. Jiminez's shop, I announce that it's time for lunch and some champagne, my treat. Javier selects a trendy, upscale café in Palmetto Plaza that is abuzz with beautiful young people. Javier makes me feel comfortable enough to practice my Spanish with him during lunch. He tells me about his family and growing up in Cali, and I am excited to find that I understand every word he says. Just as it was with Alejandro, I discover that although we come from different worlds, there are also many similarities between us. This is one thing that I have learned from many years of traveling – no matter where you go, if you pay attention, you will find that people are not all that different. We all have our struggles, but we make it through with families and/or extended families who give us love and support. Sometimes, it's just the scenery that is different.

After lunch, I tell Javier I want to look for a few new blouses to go with my jeans. He insists that I get some black leggings to wear with the black thigh-high boots and maybe a black blazer. As we exit the café, he tells me he feels like we are in a scene from the popular film from the early 90's, *Pretty Woman*. This makes me laugh. "Too funny, only I am not a prostitute!" He blushes and says, "I only meant the shopping part." I have to admit, all these surprises Mr. Perez has lavished upon me do make me feel like I'm in a movie. I just don't want it to be *that* one.

Javier takes me to a trendy designer boutique and I find everything I want and then some. He picks out a fabulous pair of black leggings that, according to him, make my ass look amazing. There is even the perfect black blazer, a Carolina Herrera cotton and silk faille that is, dare I say it? To *die* for! After we are rung up, I tell Javier we are done because I am officially broke. Of course that is not true. I have simply reached my personal limit for the day. "Perhaps I should have suggested that Mr. Perez throw in a shopping spree," he jokes. I remind Javier I am not a kept woman. "Me either," he laughs. "But a girl can dream!"

On our way back to the car I see a massive three-story music store with giant posters on the windows. As we get closer, I notice the entire store front is plastered with posters of Sonny's album cover. I stop dead in my tracks. Confused, Javier asks if I'm okay. I ignore him, standing next to a poster advertising a concert here in Cali. If my Spanish is correct, the concert is tomorrow evening at the convention center. Just to be sure, I ask Javier to read what it says, and find that I am right. Tomorrow night. Sonny de la Cruz in concert. Special engagement. One night only. I feel lightheaded. Javier, more interested in the posters themselves, looks closely at one of them, then turns to look at me. "Is that YOU, Miss Victoria?" he asks. Ignoring his question, I ask him if he knows of Sonny de la Cruz. "Oh yes, of course, he has a huge fan base here in Colombia. He's doing one show here, then two more in Puerto Rico, and…" Javier stops and looks at me again. "Would you like to go to the concert?" he asks. I tell him yes, and that I need a ticket for the front row, center. "Of course," he replies. I love that he does not ask questions, even though I am clearly behaving suspiciously. Still awestruck, staring at a poster, I ask, "Javier, is Sonny de la Cruz booked to stay at my hotel?" Javier explains he knows for a fact that he is not. He would have had special instructions given in advance for such an esteemed guest. "I am good friends with the concierges in all the upscale hotels in Cali. If Mr. Cruz is staying here, someone will know."

I press him about the ticket, "So you will be able to get me a seat in the center of the front row? It has to be as close to center stage as possible. I will pay whatever it costs."

Javier puts on his best American Diva accent, saying, "Calm down, girlfriend! Javier can do *anything*." This breaks my trance momentarily. I tell him we have to get back to the hotel. There is much to do before tomorrow night.

"I don't know what you're cooking up, sister, but I am in! Let's get moving," he says, practically pushing me into the car. Then with with great drama in his voice, "Javier needs to work his magic."

When we arrive back to the hotel, Javier joins me in my suite and gets busy contacting his connections for concert tickets and sleuthing around to find out where Sonny is staying. There is a knock at the door. A bellman is standing there with another huge vase full of flowers. This time, they are lilacs. My favorite. I know who they are from. It was one of the memories I shared with Alejandro about my hometown. How I loved the fragrant lilacs that bloomed early each Spring. The arrangement is gorgeous and the scent brings back that time. I open the card and it reads, "I would love to become one of your favorite memories. Alejandro.

Damn, Alejandro. Not now! I must have said it out loud, though, because Javier asks if the flowers are another surprise from Mr. Perez. I nod yes, thinking about Alejandro's timing. Javier must sense my uneasiness about the delivery and he immediately removes the flowers from where we are sitting in the living room area. He carries them to the bedroom out of my line of vision and my thoughts. He can move them all he wants. The fragrant lilacs leave behind their intoxicating scent. Once again Alejandro is trying to slip into my space, my head and my heart.

I'm trying to wrap my mind around the fact that Sonny is going to be right here in Cali. Alejandro steals a moment to remind me that I have something secure and real waiting for me. My head is spinning. If Javier is able to get me the seat I've requested, what is my next move going to be? I can't just show up at his concert in the front row if his wife is there.

"I am waiting to hear from my connection on the ticket. I know Sonny de la Cruz will be staying in the hotel directly across the street. He arrives in the morning and is only booked for the night." Javier says with pride in his voice. Wow! He really does know how to work some magic.

I don't ask Javier if he knows if Sonny's wife is traveling with him. That would be far too obvious. The phone rings and Javier answers it, suddenly he is speaking lightning-fast in Spanish. So fast that I can't understand what he's saying. He hangs up and dials an extension within the hotel. He tells the person on the other line to send a messenger to pick up a package in his name and gives the address. He tells them when the messenger returns to have someone bring the package up to my suite. When he hangs up, he has a wide grin on his face. "I got it!" he exclaims, proudly.

A rush of excitement mixed with trepidation washes over me. "How much is it?" I ask, reaching into my handbag for my wallet.

Javier waves his hands in the air and tells me now to worry. "A friend owed me a big favor," he says. I tell myself to make sure I take very good care of Javier before I return home. I do need to find out if Sonny's wife is traveling with him. But that will have to wait until morning when he checks in to his hotel.

"Will you help me put something together to wear to the concert?"

"Girl, put on some music and let's have a fashion show!" Javier replies, rubbing his palms together like a mad scientist. This is clearly right up his alley. "So what look are we going for? Sexy siren showing lots of skin, with big hair and dramatic makeup? Or the hot rocker chick with a sultry edge?"

"Let's go with the rocker chick. I like sultry," I decide, and we get down to work.

"Let's start with the black leggings and thigh-high boots," Javier says. I don't hesitate and strip down in front of him. "Damn, girl! You have a rockin' body. You need to show it off." He says no to the boots and leggings, and orders me into the deconstructed denim skinny jeans and the distressed high heeled boots with a point. It's fun to watch Javier as his mind goes into action. He is totally into this, and I love it. I feel like a living Barbie doll. "Try the indigo blue blouse you bought today." I was hoping he'd say that. This shirt is very sexy. It has a plunging neckline with beautiful beaded work. The sleeves are three quarter length with cutouts that fully expose my shoulders. It is form-fitting and shows just enough cleavage. I ask him, "Is too much? Does it look like I'm trying too hard?" I have gotten to the point where I know I can say anything and Javier won't ask questions.

"Sister, if you want him to notice you, this is IT." Javier tells me, looking me up and down. I have to agree. The outfit is perfect. For makeup, Javier suggests some dark smoky eyes in either wine tones or deep browns. I tell him he should become a stylist. "One day," he sighs.

It's late and I order room service. During dinner I inquire as to why he hasn't asked me anything about Mr. Perez or why I need information on Sonny de la Cruz and a concert ticket. "Discretion is what makes me one of the top hotel concierges in the area. My business is to meet your every need and to make you comfortable, not to ask questions and pry." I thank him for being so personable yet professional. What an asset he would be to me in New York. Before leaving, Javier tells me that he will call me in the morning when he gets more info from the hotel on Sonny's check-in time. Just then there's a knock and the ticket is delivered. Javier checks to make sure it is front row center. It is. He then leaves me to get some rest. Ha! Rest? My mind is racing and I can't keep up. I decide to take a late-night swim to clear my head, but all I can think about is seeing my Latin Superstar. It has been so very long. I need to see him, to be with him. Can I really pull this off? What will he do when he sees me in the middle of his performance? I drift to sleep, letting the lingering questions swirl above me.

The next morning I am anxious and not doing a good job of waiting for Javier to call. I'm dying to know what he is able to find out. I order some breakfast to be sent up, and then I open the drapes and the French doors to my balcony. Another beautiful sunny day in Cali. A day that could turn out any number of ways. The phone rings, jarring me out of my little daydream. I nearly fall rushing over to answer it. It is not Javier on the other end, but I do recognize the voice. It is Alejandro. Damn. I hope he doesn't pick up on the eagerness in my voice when I answered.

"Good morning, Alejandro. I just got up, but it's great to hear your voice." Why did I say that? I am not thinking!

Before he can reply, I begin to thank him for everything he has surprised me with this week. I tell him it was not only thoughtful but exactly what I needed before I return to business as usual in New York. "As much as I love the necklace, the lilacs were my favorite. The scent brought back so many memories. I can't believe you remembered about my love for them!" I said, gratefully.

"I am delighted to hear you are enjoying yourself. Of course I remembered the lilacs, Victoria. I loved talking with you and hearing about your past. I hope I managed to steal a few moments this week to bring a smile to your face. I want you to be thinking about me."

"Yes, Alejandro, you have stolen more than just a few moments from me this week. I have been thinking about you."

He doesn't push for any information or ask if I plan on calling him when I return home. He never asks me for anything and he never makes me feel obligated. He simply does what he does to get my attention, and he has succeeded. Unfortunately – and unbeknownst to him – someone else has my attention too. I am so torn and perplexed by this whole thing. I cannot lead this man on, and yet I'm not ready to let him go, either. I simply don't know what I want. I wish I could put him in a little box and save him for later. Which makes me feel like a horrible woman.

"I hate to cut you off but I have a boardroom full of people waiting for me to begin a meeting," he says, hurriedly. Then he pauses and as though he has just read my mind, he says, "Victoria, I am not going anywhere. I will be here waiting for you when you are ready. Take as much time as you feel you need. I will remind you from time-to-time that I am waiting. Please don't make me wait too long." He hangs up without saying another word.

"Damn, damn, damn" I say out loud. He is really tugging at my heart. Why now? Why did he have to call and tell me all of this?

The morning is almost gone before I finally hear from Javier. Instead of calling, he comes to my suite. When he said he can work magic, he wasn't kidding! He tells me the hotel concierge from across the street will notify him the minute they check in. He has also arranged a hair and makeup artist to come this afternoon. I feel like Cinderella, and Javier is my Fairy Godmother. I just hope it doesn't end up with a pumpkin and missing a shoe at midnight.

Javier surveys the outfit we have put together for tonight and asks if I'm carrying a handbag. I didn't even think about that. I may love my shoes, but when it comes to handbags, I only have a select few, and when I travel, I only carry my classic monogram canvas bag by Louis Vuitton. Javier tells me it will not do for tonight, and that he will take care of finding me the perfect bag.

"You need a tiny cross-body bag to wear. Just big enough for your ID, room key, and lipgloss. The hotel boutique will have exactly what we're looking for. I'll have them send up a few pairs of earrings and some bangles to choose from, too." With that, Javier makes a few calls and tells me those items are on the way up.

"I need to ask you for something. This one is not easy but I have to ask." I really hate bringing this up to him, but I have no choice.

"Victoria, whatever it is, just ask. I think it is a little late to start being shy."

"I need an extra room key."

He then pulls a small envelope out of his jacket pocket. The hotel name and room number are on the outside and the key is inside. When he hands me the envelope he says, "I will also ring your room tonight when the key holder arrives at the hotel."

I am stunned, but before I can say anything, the phone rings. Javier speaks in Spanish, and I can understand everything he's saying. Sonny has arrived. I hear him ask if Mr. de la Cruz is in his room. He says thank you and if they ever need anything don't hesitate to call.

When he hangs up he says, "Sonny de la Cruz and his entourage have checked in. So now what is our next move?"

"I need to find out who he is traveling with." I know I can tell Javier anything, but I just don't know how to come right out and ask if his wife is there. I have not even come to terms with it myself. Sonny de la Cruz is a married man. It hurts my heart to even think it to myself. What kind of woman have I become?

Javier interrupts my thoughts before I talk myself right out of this. "I tried to get that information for you, but it was such a large group that they were not sure. They did say there were mostly men in the group, but whether any women were there is not clear."

"I have his cell number, but I am only to use it for emergencies." For a moment, his eyes grow wide, but only for a moment. Nothing truly shocks Javier. He has probably seen it all.

"This is definitely an emergency, Victoria," he says, plainly. "You cannot show up at the concert if his wife is there."

Wow. I guess he *does* know what's going on here. I get my cell phone from my handbag and scroll through my contacts to find his number. I had forgotten it was listed under "Lover." I write his number down on a piece of paper and put my phone away. Javier shakes his head at me in disbelief and says, "Victoria, really? This is exactly why I am here." Now I look confused. "Sweetheart, you cannot call from this hotel. He will know you are somewhere in South America by the caller ID. It most likely will say Cali, Columbia. Do you have international phone access on your cell phone?"

"Yes, Javier. That I do know. I am sorry. I am just not thinking clearly. I am nervous as hell about making this call. Thank God you are here."

"Let me see your phone, Victoria. It's an iPhone so we need to go into settings to make sure your location app is turned off." He hands it back to me and says, "I'll give you some privacy while you make the call. I need to check on a few things downstairs, anyway."

After he leaves, I take a deep breath, pull up his number, and hit call. It takes several seconds before it begins ringing. It rings once, twice, three times and just as I'm certain it is going to go to voicemail, I hear his voice say, "Hello."

I feel like I am going to either pass out or explode. I struggle to form the words, but finally am able to manage a hello.

"Victoria, are you okay? Is something wrong?" He asks with urgency in his voice. Oh, that voice. That seductive voice. I have missed it.

I make sure my tone gives emphasis to what I say next. "If you are not alone and can't talk just hang up."

"It's OK, Victoria," he says with concern. "Talk to me. Is something wrong?"

Again I stress to him. "I'm serious. If you can't talk just say so or hang up."

"Victoria, I said it's fine. Please tell me now, what is wrong?"

"There is nothing wrong and I am fine. I know I should not have called. It's not what we agreed on."

"Victoria, relax I am alone. Where are you? The connection is very clear."

"I am in New York City at my apartment. I am sorry for calling. I should not have taken the chance."

"Would you please just relax? I told you I am alone."

"You sound very clear as well. Where are you?" I thought saying this would make sure he was not thinking I was close to where he was.

"I am in Cali, Columbia. We are doing three shows to try out some of the new songs before we officially kick off our tour in the US."

"You are probably busy then. I should let you go."

"Victoria, please. I am alone on this trip with the band. Maria is in Puerto Rico, I won't see her until tomorrow. Now let's get back to why you are calling me."

"I'm sorry. I shouldn't have called you. It's not an emergency."

"If it's not an emergency then what is it? Tell me, Victoria!"

"I miss you." There I said it. I can't believe I had the nerve to say that to him. I had to tell him something. I don't want him to catch on.

He laughs and asks me, "What is it you miss, Victoria? Tell me what you miss."

"You. Everything. I miss everything." Now I feel stupid and embarrassed.

He pushes me. "Really? Everything? I think since you have taken this chance to call me there must be something you specifically miss. Tell me what it is." Now he is playing with me. He knows exactly what buttons to push with me. He knows he's turning me on. So I am going to go along with him and tell him what he wants to hear.

"I miss your lips on mine. I want you."

He laughs a very sexy laugh, "Victoria, just my lips? I have missed more than that. I've missed you. It's been too long. I will be in NYC in about three weeks."

"I will be here. Competition season is over and things are back to normal for me at the studio. I hope the concert goes well for you tonight and I am sorry for calling."

"You don't need to apologize. It was a welcome surprise hearing your voice on the phone. It's been a while since I performed live but I am looking forward to it. I am a little nervous about trying out the new songs." I can tell someone has come into the room because I can hear them telling him they need to leave for a sound check. Before he hangs up he says, "I got to go. Congrats on your win. See you in three weeks. I promise."

After I hang up I jump up and down like some crazy teenaged girl. I call down to Javier and he asks if everything is still a go for tonight. I tell him yes and he says he'll be right up. He brings jewelry and the perfect little cross-body bag that looks more like a piece of jewelry than a handbag. Javier wasted no time getting what I needed for tonight. Everything is perfect! He tells me to relax and that he has ordered me some food and to make sure I eat something because it will be a long night for me. He says hair and makeup will be here around 5 pm and the car will take me at 7:30 pm to the venue. It is a short ride and the show is to start at 8 pm He tells me my suite will be sparkling clean and ready when I return tonight. This guy doesn't miss a beat.

I try really hard to rest before it's time to start dressing but I just can't. I still can't believe I am going to see him in a few hours. Oh, no! I realize I'd forgotten about picking up some new lingerie for tonight. Then a smile forms across my lips. Why give him something he expects, like a new set of La Perla lingerie? No, Mr.

de la Cruz. Victoria Moore is not the predictable woman you think she is. I laugh to myself, how bold I am when no one is around!

Hair, make-up and Javier arrive all at the same time. Javier has champagne delivered to help me relax. Champagne is nice, but damn what I wouldn't give for some Crown and ginger ale! There is some debate on how I should wear my hair. We all finally agree on wearing it down, kind of messy and carefree. That is the last decision I am in on. Javier has taken complete control at this point, putting me and my look at his mercy. My makeup is soft, my lips glossed in neutral, but my green eyes are dark and smoky in deep shades of wine. Everything fits into my tiny bag. My ID, ticket, hotel key, lip gloss and cell phone. Javier instructs me to put the other key in the pocket of my jeans for easy access. I have no idea how I am going to pass this little envelope to him, but no time to worry about that now.   Hair and makeup are finished, it's time to get dressed "The outfit is *perfect*, Victoria! You look amazing!" Javier declares. "You are going to have a hard time not getting noticed. The good thing is the look is so different from the album cover, posters, and the video. You look younger and hotter, as if that were even possible!"   I am just hoping no one makes the connection. If someone asks me, I'll just look at them as though they were crazy.

It's time to go and Javier tells me my car is waiting. The concierge from Sonny's hotel called earlier to say they'd all left already a few hours ago. Javier says, "Victoria, take a deep breath and have fun. Enjoy the concert. I will call you later if your guest arrives."

I thank him for everything. I am so excited and nervous because I have no idea how this is going to go over with my Latin Superstar.

The driver drops me off and tells me he will be waiting in the same location when the show is over. I am overwhelmed and embarrassed by the men staring at me as I make my way into the concert venue. I can even hear some of their comments. I understand every word. I am trying in vain to blend in with a crowd that is 99.9% Latin. At least so far no one has recognized me from the video. I'm sure I must be beaming from ear to ear, but I can't control how exciting all of this is for me. I am going to see my Latin Superstar, Sonny de la Cruz, and he has no idea I'm here! My stomach reminds me just how nervous I am, but my heart tells me to forget everything else going on and just enjoy this chance to see Sonny perform live. I am just hoping all this effort will be worth it. What if he doesn't notice me?

The venue is sold out and I have no idea how Javier got this ticket. I owe him big time. My seat is front row, center, exactly what I asked for. It does feel a little strange being here alone, but I am so excited and busy looking around that I really don't care. I can see the roadies and stagehands running around, making sure everything is set up and ready. It's 8:15. *Please start this concert*, I think to myself. A moment later, the lights go out, and everyone jumps to their feet, applauding and cheering. The curtain is raised and the band begins to play. I recognize it within only a few chords. I cannot believe they are opening with the song we danced to in his video. Sonny walks out on the stage and the fans are going crazy. He is gorgeous. In worn jeans, boots, and a white V-neck T-shirt, my rugged Latin Superstar sounds even better live than I imagined. I almost forget I am standing right in front of him. I wonder how long it will take him to notice me.

Halfway through the song, it happens. I can see in his eyes something has caught his attention. The soft flutter in my chest confirms it. Slowly, the sides of his mouth curl up to form a broad smile, and I know he has spotted me. As his eyes shift in my direction, his grin widens. Even Sonny de la Cruz cannot mask his emotions. He moves to the edge of the stage and smiles down at me, shaking his head in disbelief. When he finishes the song he speaks to the audience in Spanish. "Thank you all for coming. I hope you enjoy my new songs. Cali is a magical place, and you never know what might happen here," he says with a wink in my direction. Little does he know I understood every word he just said.

The crowd goes wild. I had no idea the effect this man has on his fans. Javier is right, they really do adore him. The concert is, as Sonny put it, magical. He performs some new songs and some old ones. Even though I am sitting right here in front of him, he is not completely distracted. He is a true artist and gives these people a great show.

Then while he's singing his last song, he comes to the edge of the stage and leans down to greet his fans in the front row. Some of the people shake his hand and the women all want to hug him. I have been so lost in enjoying the music and the excitement, I almost forget about the envelope with the key. I retrieve it from my pocket just in time. As he leans down before me, I extend my hand and slide the little envelope into his. Seamlessly, he slides it right into the pocket of his jeans. Mission accomplished!

Of course these fans will not let him go without an encore. After only a few moments of thundering applause, Sonny returns to the stage and sings his final song. In between verses he thanks us all for joining him tonight, and tells them Cali was the perfect place to begin his tour. Then he walks to the edge of the stage, and standing right before me, tells the audience, "I told you Cali is magical. Amazing things happen here." I hate to see the concert end, but I'm eager to get back to my hotel and see what the rest of this night brings!

The driver is waiting for me precisely where he dropped me off. Thank God, because the traffic is ridiculous with everyone leaving the venue. I arrive back at the hotel and stop by the concierge desk to speak to Javier. He is working late just for me.

Javier is ecstatic to see me. "Victoria! How did it go? Was your seat perfect? Did he spot you? Were you able to pass your room key to him?" Javier barrages me with questions, Ken-and-Ashley style.

I hate to be rude, but I'm kind of in a rush. "Everything was perfect, Javier. Yes, I was able to pass him my room key. I need to get up to my room in case he tries to call me."

"Princess, your suite is ready. Get up there!" Javier understood my rush, without my even saying a word. That's what makes him so good at what he does. I thank him for everything. As I turn to leave, he calls after me, "Girl, I bet you were the hottest thing there!" I giggle as I head toward the elevator. My Latin Superstar has such an effect on me. To see him perform live took this to another level. The way he connects to such a large group of people is amazing. It's such a turn on. I can only imagine how it makes him feel.

When I walk into my suite the smell of jasmine fills my senses. My suite has been completely transformed. It's so beautiful and romantic. Javier has filled it with scented votive candles. There are so many that I'm almost afraid it will appear that I'm trying too hard. I decide I don't care, because the ambiance of the room reflects exactly my mood. I intend to seduce my Latin Superstar. My balcony doors leading outside are open and there are several large candlelit lanterns surrounding the pool area. On the coffee table in the living room, there are a couple of bottles of champagne chilling and a platter of fresh fruit and assorted cheeses. Javier has thought of everything. I open the champagne, hoping it will calm me down. I hope I don't have long to wait.

The concert finished around 10:30 and I was back at the hotel by 10:45. So now it's a waiting game and again I am not even sure if he will show up. At 11 the phone rings, startling me. I jump up to answer it, and it is Javier. He has called to tell me that the other hotel informed him that Sonny has arrived back at his hotel and went directly to his room. I have more waiting ahead of me. I will not call him. If he wants to see me, he will make it happen. I make a trip to the bathroom and brush my teeth, freshen up and make sure my hair and makeup still looks good. About 15 minutes later my cell phone rings. I scramble to find it and realize it is still in the little bag I carried to the concert. The caller ID says 'Lover', and it takes a moment for my mind to register that it is him. I am not accustomed to him calling me. When I answer, he wastes no time getting straight to the point. "I am on my way over to your hotel and I want you naked when I arrive." Then the line goes dead.

Those feelings return to my stomach. I am both nervous and excited. I stand there frozen for a moment, and then realize what he has said. I start stripping my clothes off. I can't decide if I should be waiting for him at the door, on the sofa, by the pool…where? I look around the suite and see my huge king-sized bed with its fresh linens and decide that it's perfect. Javier has thought of everything. Including removing the vase filled with lilacs. The bedroom is dimly lit with only a few candles. Lying here exposed like this, both my head and my stomach have me questioning myself. What the fuck am I doing? I must look ridiculous. But he said he wanted me naked, so naked is what he's getting.

The phone on my nightstand rings and it is Javier. He tells me Sonny has just arrived at the hotel and is on his way up. "Don't do anything I wouldn't do, and girl, just between you and me I have done it all. Enjoy!" he giggles, just before hanging up.

Minutes later the door to my suite opens, and I can hear Sonny walking around. I can't tell if he's looking for me, or just checking everything out. He even goes out to see the pool area. The anticipation builds up inside; it feels like it's taking him forever to get to me.

Finally, he makes his way into the bedroom, carrying a glass of champagne in one hand and the bottle in the other. This is the first time I have ever seen him drink. I can tell he has showered and changed his clothes, because his hair is slightly damp and he smells of soap and cologne. That cologne! I still haven't figured out what he wears! He has on his signature attire: jeans, a T-shirt, and of course, those boots. He looks amazing, and I want this man, now! I am tired of waiting. I go to pull myself to the edge of the bed, but he stops me, and firmly tells me to lay back. "We're going to do this my way tonight," he says. Usually, I'm not the submissive type, but something about Sonny de la Cruz makes me do as I'm told. He throws back the entire glass of champagne, pours another, and sets the bottle on the nightstand.

"I hope you enjoyed the concert tonight. It certainly was a surprise when I saw you in the front row. Lucky for me no one else recognized you. That might have been a little hard to explain." I try to speak but he shushes me before I can get the first word out. "This is different for me, Victoria. Usually after a concert, I go out with the band. Performing live in front of such a large audience is very stimulating. I am wired after doing a show, so you are going to have to help me with that. Let me warn you now, I am not going to go easy on you."

I understand what he means by this. After a competition performance in front of thousands of people Mateo and I are wired. Exhausted but wired. Sometimes it would take me several hours to unwind. I am definitely up for this challenge and will be happy to help him with this.

He tosses back another full glass of champagne. Then he pours another one, but this time he hands it to me. "Drink this. All of it," he orders. I oblige, figuring I am probably going to need a little cushion to my already present buzz. Worried that Sonny thinks I'm following him around the country I try to explain to him how I ended up here in Cali. "Sonny, I really want you to know that I had no idea you were coming to Cali," I say between gulps of champagne.

"Oh, I am wondering about that, and how you have this amazing penthouse suite. But before you explain anything, I need to fuck you." There's that word again. But at this point I am so turned on I don't even care.

He is standing about three feet away from this huge bed. I have the perfect view of him. He starts to take off his clothes. First, he kicks off his boots. Then, he slowly pulls his T-shirt up over his head, and lets it drop to the floor. His smooth, chiseled chest and tattooed biceps are such a welcome sight. Next he unbuckles his belt and slowly pulls it out of his belt loops. One loop at a time. Slow like honey. He's killing me and he knows it. He unbuttons and unzips his jeans and lets them hang off his hips while he pours himself yet another glass of champagne. He has to be feeling this by now. He stands and stares at me while he drinks it. The look in his eyes is one I've never seen before. Is he trying to tell me something? As he slowly begins to pull his jeans down off his hips, he exposes his huge dick. He is rock hard and ready. *Damn, he is good*, I think to myself. It's been weeks since I have been with him. His cock is a beautiful welcome site to my eyes. I am dying. I want to reach over and touch him so bad. But I sit patiently, propped up on my elbows, enjoying the show even more than tonight's concert.

He lets his pants drop to the ground and steps out of them. I think he is going to walk over to the bed now, but he doesn't. Instead, he stands in front of me, staring. He takes his thick, hard cock in his right hand and begins to stroke it. I think I'm going to die. I can't take any more of this. I try again to pull myself to the edge of the bed, but just as I reach him, he steps back, holds up his left hand, smiles, and says, "just watch, baby." I can't take my eyes off of him as continues to stroke himself. Then, I figure two can play this game. I run my hands over the curves of my soft breasts and roll my very erect nipples between my fingers. It feels so fucking good. I let out a soft little moan, and slide one hand down, part my wet lips and begin to stroke my clit in swirls with two fingers. While he strokes his cock, his eyes never leave mine. "That's my girl," he says. I can tell he loves to watch me get off just as much as I love watching him. I'm getting close, so close I feel like I'm about to explode, and I think it's pretty clear by the look on my face and the sounds I'm making. He steps toward me, takes my arms and pulls me up to him. He is standing at the edge of the bed and I am on my knees in front of him. Abruptly, he pulls me even closer to him and that's all I am conscious of: our breathing and his hands on me. My hard nipples brush across his chest. I lose control as I eagerly run my hands over his beautiful, muscular tattooed arms and then wrap my arms around his neck. He cups his strong hands around the sides of my breasts, pushes them close together, and slides his tongue in between them, sending shivers all down my naked body. It's hard to explain this moment. We are just staring into each other's eyes and feeling the electricity crackling between us. At this very moment I don't care about anything else except being right here in his arms. In one swift movement, his lips are on mine, and he takes over my mouth. Oh, those lips and that tongue! I know how much he likes kissing, and we kiss for what seems like an eternity. Is it possible to experience ecstasy without even coming? If so, then that is what this feels like. I even have to remind myself to breathe.

I get my first seductive whisper of the night, but it's not in Spanish. "I've missed this amazing body of yours, and you...Victoria, I've missed you. Do you have any idea how badly I want to throw you down on this bed and fuck you right now?" I shake my head yes because I can't get words to form. Even if I could speak, I wouldn't have the chance because he is kissing me again, kissing me hard and deep. He leaves my lips only to take my nipple in his mouth as he teases it with his teeth. He knows what this does to me. Why he is making me wait? No. I can't wait any longer. Kissing him, I pull him down to the bed with me, take one of his hands off my waist and guide it down between my legs. He stops so I can see his smile. "So wet...I see you have missed me, too. I love that you aren't afraid to show me what you want," he says with a grin as he slides one finger deep inside me and my breath catches. As he drags that finger in and out of me, he asks me, "Is this all you want? Do you want more?" I can't get a word out but I shake my head yes as I bite his lower lip and grind against his hand. Two fingers find their way inside me, filling me with pleasure, and he teases me again with rhetorical questions. "Is that enough? Tell me if you want more." But I don't have to tell him a thing, because I am straddling him now, riding his fingers while he slides another one in. My clit is grinding hard against his hand now, and I'm pushing myself down on him faster, harder, so close to coming.

But of course he won't let me come. Not yet. He lifts me up off of him and stands back in front of me again. "Please don't stop," I beg. "I want more. I want you to make me come. Please Sonny, I have missed your touch." He smiles and continues to kiss me while he returns his fingers between my legs and begins to rub my clit. It feels so good that I concentrate on the kissing to hold off. I do this over and over, taking in deep breaths to control my orgasm. He knows what I'm up to and it turns him on even more. I can feel his hard dick touching the top of my thighs. Then I let it happen. He brings me to a climax and it is beyond amazing and seems to last forever. I am literally trembling in his arms.

I am still mid-orgasm as he pushes me back and drags his rock-hard cock up the length of my body. Without warning, he slams his cock deep inside me, and I let out a loud moan as my lingering orgasm continues. I have never experienced anything like this before. He whispers in my ear, "This is turning out to be a great way to unwind. I know I just made you come, again. Now it's my turn." He is pounding into me with long, hard strokes, then abruptly pulls out of me and flips me over. He roughly grabs me at the ankles and spreads my legs wide apart, stretching my dancer's body to new limits. He then slides himself into me from behind. My clit brushes against the bed linens and with every stroke I feel even more aroused. I come close to coming again, but he stops and pulls out. I think this is his way of making it last. His way of controlling himself. This time, he stands on the side of bed and pulls me in front of him and makes me kneel with my back to him. He is at the perfect height because I can feel his hard dick against me. He reaches under and pinches my nipples while kissing my back. He slides several fingers in and out of me. He then bends down and uses his tongue on me. He is kissing everything and even moves to run his tongue in an area I was not expecting. I don't have time to decide if I even like that or not, because now he has positioned himself behind me. My mind is reeling and I don't know what to expect, but then I am relieved as he slides his cock deep inside me and pounds hard with each stroke.

This man definitely meant what he said. He is not taking it easy on me at all. He roughly flips me over to face him again, and as he begins fucking me, he says, "I want you to come again for me when I come. Come on baby, give me one more." His words send me over the edge and I don't hold back and it isn't long before I'm breathlessly moaning, and he is right there with me. Right on time. I don't have to say a word. He knows when to let go. Our bodies are in perfect synch with each other.

Then it happens. He whispers in my ear again but this time it is in Spanish.

No es de sorprender por qué yo no puedo sacarte de mi mente y pensamientos. Usted es embriagador y no puedo conseguir bastante de ustedes. No consigo ningún alivio incluso cuando duermo porque persiguen mis sueños.

This time I know what he says so I translate it in my head. *It is no surprise why I cannot get you out of my mind and thoughts.*

You are intoxicating and I can't get enough of you. I get no relief even when I sleep because you haunt my dreams.

Now it's my turn to surprise him with my Spanish.

¿No entiendes por ahora que tiene el mismo efecto sobre mí. Eres como una droga que no puedo conseguir suficiente. Mis noches no son perseguidos por usted, pero mis sueños están llenos de usted.

Do you not understand by now that you have the same effect on me. You are like a drug that I can't get enough of. My nights are not only haunted by you but my dreams are filled with you.

I have caught him completely off guard. He is silent. Finally, a smile breaks across his face and he says, "I see you have learned to speak my language. I will have to keep my thoughts to myself." I think he is bothered that I know his true feelings. Not sure he likes me reading his inner thoughts. I think he feels he has revealed too much.

We lie there and he begins to quiz me on how and why I am in Cali, Columbia. I tell him everything except the part about Alejandro and our time in Caracas. I am totally unprepared for his next comment.

"I didn't know that you were friends with Alejandro Perez." I can feel the heat rise in my cheeks, and I hope he doesn't notice. "What are you talking about?" I ask. He tells me that several Latin entertainment web sites featured a photo of me and Alejandro dancing at a party in Miami. I know exactly what he's referring to, and tell him that we were only seated next to one another at a dinner party and nothing more. He goes on to inform me that Alejandro Perez is a well respected and powerful man in the Latin music business, but I act as though I am not interested. Really? Did he have to bring up Alejandro Perez's name while he is bed with me?

I kiss the subject away, hoping for more sex and less talk. I glance over his shoulder at the clock and can't believe it's already after one in the morning. I'm not sure how long he's going to stay. Then, he stops kissing me and says, "Let's go try that pool out." He jumps up and pulls me from the bed.

The outdoor pool area is truly romantic. The huge candlelit lanterns are perfect. Just enough light. The pool light illuminates the beautiful turquoise water. We are close to the pools edge when suddenly he grabs me, holds me tight, and jumps into the pool. It is a shock to my body, but the water feels incredible. I splash him for throwing me in, I swim to the side of the pool to catch my breath. He swims up behind me and pulls himself close, turns me around and wraps my legs around his waist. I can't wait to try him out in this new change of scenery, but apparently he has other things in mind. He cups his hands underneath my bare ass, lifts me up, and tosses me right over his head, sending me screaming into the deep end! When I come up for air, he is laughing, a sound I am not used to from him. I like it. Sonny de la Cruz has a playful, boyish side! Giggling, I swim over to him, slither my way up against his body, and begin to kiss him. But just when he kisses me back, I reach my hand up over his head and push him down into the water as I swim away, laughing. He swims over to me, and wraps his arms around me in a strong embrace. For a few sweet moments, we are silent, just standing in the shallow water, holding one another. When he pulls away, that boyish playful side is gone. "I'm afraid it's time for me to go, Victoria," he says. "Much as I don't want to, it's getting late, and people will begin to wonder where I've been." I nod my head to show I understand. We step out of the pool and wrap ourselves in towels to dry off.

We go back into the suite because he needs to get dressed. "I will be in NYC in three weeks. I will call and let you know when I can see you." We discuss nothing else. We don't need to. We know it is what it is. We both also know it can be nothing more. He knows I do not expect it to be.

Although he gets dressed, I remain naked. I remember the last time we were together, I tried to get dressed but he wouldn't have it. At the door he turns to kiss me and his lips and tongue take over every inch of my mouth. I wish he didn't have to go. I'm pushing up against him and can feel him get hard. I want him again and he knows it. This time I don't wait for him. I undo his belt and pants and pull them down, drop to my knees to take him in my mouth. He falls back against the door and moans out loud.

He lets me have my way for a while but then he pulls me away and says, "No, I need to fuck you." He pulls me up by my arms, spins me around, and pushes me up against the wall. Hard. He spreads my arms so I can support myself and then he tells me to spread my legs. I do, but he says wider. He then grabs my waist and pulls my hips to meet his. He is behind me, hard and ready. He teases me and rubs his cock against my ass. I am not sure what is going to happen. We are both breathing heavy. He leans in and slides his dick in me and starts to pump in and out. I am dripping wet at this point. Freeing one hand from my waist he reaches around and stroke my clit. He then whispers, "One time I am going to fuck that sweet, little ass of yours." I surprised both of us when when I whisper back to him, "What are you waiting for?" He stops immediately. I can tell I've shocked him because his touch has changed. He is not sure what to do. He slides out of me and rubs his dick against my ass. I don't know if I am ready for this but I am so turned on that I don't care what he does. Next, he slides two of his fingers into my mouth. "Suck." He orders. "I need these wet." I suck his fingers and after a few seconds he pulls them out of my mouth, and slides one slowly into my ass. Then, he adds another, stretching them apart to loosen me up a bit. His breathing is rough and labored, as though his animalistic side has taken over. He pulls his fingers out, and then he slides his cock slowly inside my ass. "Oh fuck, you feel so fucking good…" he says this over and over. I feel like I am being torn as he begins to pump in and out. It feels good but it hurts all at the same time. With each stroke, I relax a little more. I can tell by his breathing he is holding himself back. But I am letting myself go, as I start to move with every stroke. This catches his attention and he increases the intensity. It's the most intimate moment the two of us have shared. It's raw and uncensored. I am unaware of the moaning that is escaping my mouth. It's as though are bodies have molded into one form. Wrapping one hand around my waist he uses the other hand to reach around my neck pulling me back to him as he begins to run soft sensuous kisses up and down my neck. And we both get lost in this moment. There is no reason to prolong it – he is ready to come as he fucks me even faster. Then it happens. It is the strangest feeling when he comes inside of me. He moans louder than I've ever heard him moan before. Just the thought of how good this feels to him turns me on.

When he is done he pulls out, turns me around to face him and draws me close as he whispers, "Victoria are you all right? Did I hurt you?"

Clutching my hand around his neck and trying to slow my breathing I whisper back, "I am fine. You didn't hurt me."

I have mixed emotions that I don't want him to see right now. He must sense that I am feeling this way. He releases his hold on me and steps back into my suite. When he returns just a few moments later he is carrying a wash cloth and towel. Gently he begins to wipe and clean me and while doing so he assures me that it was amazing, something he had never done before. "Victoria I am not saying that to make you feel bad. I just want you to know when we are together things get very heated. We enjoy each other and we should not feel guilty for doing so." This makes me feel a little better, but it also makes me wonder. What have we crossed over to? Tonight was so different from our other times together. The need to be as intimate with each other as possible took over both of us. I don't have to question this and doubt if he felt the same way. That feeling was there and there is no denying it or mistaking it for something else. We have become so comfortable with each other's bodies that we lose ourselves completely.

"Victoria, I am sorry, but I really need to get back to the hotel. I'll see you in three weeks," he promises. After planting one last kiss on my lips, he rushes out the door, shouting "sweet dreams," behind him.

As I close and lock the door, I turn around and lean against it with a sigh. So much swimming in my head, I can't contain it. I head down the hall into my bathroom, drag myself under the shower, and as the water pours, so do the tears.

Waking I am not sure last night was a dream or if it all really happened. But when I go to move, my body reminds me that it was quite real. Let's just say I am more than just a little sore after last night's escapade with my Sonny. Just the thought of all that we did makes my cheeks burn. I feel I have nothing to regret. The time I get to spend with him means something to me. Sure, we had some hot moments. Some very hot ones. The evening was ours and despite our situation, what we share together is special. But what about the tears last night? I can't hide what I am beginning to feel for Sonny. I just need to keep those feelings in check or else I am really going to get hurt when all this is over. Over. I let that word linger for a moment in my mind. It is going to be over one day. I can't believe I have accepted that.

Luckily, I am rescued from these thoughts as the phone in my suite rings. It's Javier, calling to see if I'm awake. I ask him what time it is, and when he says it's almost 11, I am stunned. I can't believe I slept this late! I feel as though I have been up all night. Javier senses the panic in my voice and tells me he'll bring up some breakfast while I shower and get ready. I have to be in the hotel ballroom at noon for preliminary judging. I'm grateful that the competition is right here in the my hotel, so I have plenty of time. Javier arrives with a huge breakfast - exactly what I need. I can't even remember when I last ate. There were hotcakes, sausage links, bacon, fried plantains, and my favorite: fresh fruit. While I shovel the food into my mouth, Javier poses a few basic questions about my night. I can tell that what he really wants are all the dirty details, but he is very careful not to pry. It's his job to be discreet about things like this.

Cautiously, he begins his questions. "Was the evening all that you had imagined it to be?"

"It was and more." I reply between bites, the memories of last night flashing through my mind. The heat rises in my cheeks, and I'm sure he's noticed.

"Oh my, Victoria. That good?" I think Javier is even blushing himself when he reads the look on my face. It's hard to hide how I feel this morning. I am still floating on cloud nine. What a night! It still feels a bit surreal, although my aching body won't let me forget how very real the whole evening was.

"Victoria, are you all right?" Javier asks, puzzled.

"Better than all right. I'm great." I say with the biggest grin on my face, reminiscing. But there's no time for this right now. I have to get myself downstairs and checked in to the judge's panel. This is going to be such a long, long day. Although my heart is elsewhere, I am thankful to have this distraction.

After day one of judging is over I look forward to going to bed. I am beyond exhausted; and drained. I did not get much sleep after Sonny left last night. After I showered and got in my bed I just couldn't unwind. I wanted to be in bed with his arms wrapped around me. Instead, he was across the street in a hotel room. I will never know what it is to go to bed and wake up with this man on a regular basis. What I wouldn't give to know that feeling again. When I return to my suite, I find that Javier has left the local Cali newspaper on my bed. He has a paged turned down and marked with a yellow post-it note which reads, "thought you'd enjoy this." It is a review about Sonny's concert last night. The critics loved him. They said Sonny remained true to his roots with his new music. There is an envelope with something in it. The outside reads, "This was found by the cleaning crew this morning in the hallway by the door." I open it to find a leather bracelet with three small carved beads on it. I recognize it right away and know it belongs to Sonny. I remember seeing it on his wrist the first time I met him. Every time I've seen him since, he has had it on. It must have fallen off when things got crazy. I put it on my wrist, thinking I'll give it back to him when I see him in three weeks. It feels kind of nice to have something that belongs to him right now. It's like I have a piece of him with me.

The next two days are busy and filled with long hours of judging. I will be so happy when this week is over and I can get back home. I miss my life in New York. I have been away too long. I am thankful there have been no more surprises from Alejandro Perez. I don't think I can handle anymore from him without feeling guilty. I know he doesn't expect anything in return, but I need room to breathe.

There is a ton of young talent coming up in the Latin dance world. It seems that the popularity of dance competition TV shows have piqued people's interest in the sport. I love to meet young dancers who tell me how dance has changed their lives. I lived it and I know what they mean. People love to hear my story. I think it gives them hope that they can change their lives at any age.

It is my last night in Cali so I take Javier out for a late dinner after judging the finals. He takes me to his local favorite spot. I can tell already that after dinner there will be dancing, because I see a DJ setting up on the lower level dance floor.

I tell him that I will forever be indebted to him for everything he's done to make this week one I will always remember. When I tell him that I've already agreed to judge here next year, a smile crosses his face. I invite him to come stay with me sometime in New York so I can return the favor and show him a great time. I hand him an envelope with a cashiers check for $5,000.00. Ken will of course be very unhappy when he discovers my extravagant token of appreciation. I have just given Javier my entire judging fee. I can tell by his reaction that he is stunned.

"Victoria," he stammers. "y-you must have made a mistake and put too many zeros, right? This can't be! It's too much!"

"It's no mistake, Javier; you are worth that and then some. I could never leave Cali knowing that I did not take care of you properly. You went above and beyond the call of duty with all that you did for me this week. I know Mr. Perez was responsible for the extras at the hotel. But you were the one that made it possible for me to have one of the most magical evenings I have ever had in my entire life."

"Victoria, it was my pleasure. It was one of the best weeks I have ever had. I don't know Mr. Perez, but I think you should keep the door open to that relationship. You need to be very careful with Sonny de la Cruz. Latin men may wander but they will never leave their true love. I don't want to see you get hurt."

He isn't saying a thing I haven't said to myself time and again. Still, those words sting a little, and I try to conceal it. "Thank you, Javier. I will keep that in mind. If you don't mind, I may call you from time to time for relationship advice ok?"

"Call me anytime, Victoria," he says. I can tell he is being genuine. I can also tell he does not like to get too sentimental. "Now before I start blubbering, we need to head downstairs for some dancing. I want to see if you really can move like a champion."

They are beginning to clear the tables and transform the restaurant into a night club. We head to the lower level where I meet several of Javier's friends. They are all as colorful and interesting. The music gets started and Javier can't wait to hit the dance floor with me so he can make everyone in the place envious. When people get together after a long work week, they want to forget their worries and just dance...that is when you get to see *real* dancing. No one is judging for correct footing or proper technique. They are free to be themselves and let loose. I am inspired by everything that is going on here tonight. It's not just about the dance; it's about the music, the style, the fashion, and most important, the passion. It's such a great way to conclude my stay here.

It was after 4 in the morning when I finally got back to my suite. Javier arranged to have hotel staff pack my bags for me. He told me there will be a car waiting to take me to the airport in the morning. I'm saddened that I won't get to see Javier. But we said our goodbyes before I left Sabor Express, a Colombian version of Denny's. We had such a fun last night together, and I can't wait to return the favor when Javier comes to see me.

It's early but I am looking forward to returning to the states. I'm taking the red-eye to Miami and then it's home to NYC. Because my layover in Miami is two hours, I toy with the idea of calling Alejandro to see if he'd like to meet for lunch. My flight has wi-fi so I began checking some of the Latin entertainment sites for new stories about Sonny. I find far more than just one new article-- there are several, and photos, too! Most of the photos are from the concerts in Puerto Rico. There are some of him on stage, with fans, a few celebrities. The usual stuff. There is also a photo of him and his wife Maria. It's hard for me to look at the two of them smiling together, looking so happy. The night before this photo was taken, he was in bed with me. Although I've accepted what we are and what we'll never be, I don't believe I'll ever get used to seeing him with her. But it goes with the territory of this kind of relationship. Relationship? Is this really a relationship? I need to call it what it is. An affair.

Something in the photo catches my eye. I look at it closer and notice something on Maria's wrist. My hand automatically goes to the bracelet I'm wearing. It's the same bracelet. She is wearing the exact bracelet. Oh, God. My stomach turns. I feel as though I am going to throw up. I signal for a flight attendant and ask him to bring some water. Then I pull off the bracelet and shove it into my handbag. They must have bought them together. Maybe she gave it to him for a gift. Who the hell knows? It just makes everything real. Too real and too hard. And so hard to accept. In one article, they ask him what it was like performing his new songs in Cali for the first time. His answer gives my stomach a moment of relief. "The trip to Cali was one of the most magical times he had ever experienced." But before a smile could break, I open a link to another article in which he speaks of his wife as his muse. "It is my wife who inspires me to write and continue to sing. Without her love and support, I would be nothing." So, I think to myself, Sonny de la Cruz has everything he wants, doesn't he? A magical time in Cali and a loving and supportive wife waiting for him in Puerto Rico. I close my iPad. I can't take another second of this. Javier may be right. Am I closing myself off from something real and honest with Alejandro, in exchange for something temporary and apparently quite meaningless with Sonny?

My hand makes its way up to my neck to touch the crown necklace from Alejandro. Rubbing my fingers over the cuts in the gemstones I am starting to understand my place with the two men that have entered my life. I'm the mistress to one. Nothing more. To the other I am everything. If I can't walk away from Sonny there will be no chance of a relationship with Alejandro.

When the plane lands in Miami I decide to call Alejandro's office and see if he would like to meet me for lunch during my two hour layover. His assistant tells me he's in LA for business. She does ask if I would like to leave a message, and I do. When I tell her who is calling her whole demeanor changes and I have caught her attention. "Oh, Miss Moore, Mr. Perez said if you called he wanted me to be sure to tell you he was sorry he was not here in Miami. He had to make an unexpected trip to LA. He left his cell number for you if you would like to have it. I jot it down and consider trying his cell but decide against it. Instead I use the next two hours thinking about the differences between Alejandro and Sonny. Comparing them. I can't call Sonny just to say hi and on the other hand Alejandro not only wants to talk to me but he has his staff on alert if I call. My relationship with Sonny will always have to be hidden while Alejandro was more than happy to show me around Caracas. What I have with Sonny, will it be enough for me? I know Alejandro can give me so much more. Not only love but a real out in the open relationship. Not an affair I have to hide and keep to myself. Wow, give me two hours alone and I can pick apart anything. I still have no answers for what I need to do, but I was touched by Alejandro's message for me. He stole another moment of my day. I'm more confused than ever. They are calling my flight and right now I just need to get home and back into my familiar routine. I need to surround myself with the people and things that I *can* be sure of and depend on.

It's after six when I get back in the city. I go straight to the studio to find Ashley is still working. There is also a class in session. All the familiar sounds of music and dancing bring me great comfort. There is a banner in the studio from the dance instructors and students. It reads, "Congratulations Miss Victoria Queen of Latin Dance."

Ashley jumps up from her desk and greets me with a great big, uncharacteristic hug. "It's great to have you home. You have been gone too long."

"I missed you, too. It feels good to be back. But right now all I want is a hot shower and my bed. I'll see you tomorrow, okay?"

"Oh no you don't. You're not going any where until to tell me where this came from." Ashley picks the crown up off my neck and examines it and waits for me to answer.

"What does it look like? It's a necklace. Just a gift."

Dropping the crown from her hold she looks me directly in the eye as if she is searching for something. "Ok then. You're tired. I understand. Get some rest. Tomorrow we will talk about the necklace. You can't come home from weeks of being away wearing a gorgeous, obviously expensive piece of jewelry and think we aren't going to notice it."

"We aren't going to talk about it. Not now and not tomorrow."

Ashley looks a bit deflated, but she knows when to back off. Before I leave the office she tells me that Alejandro Perez called only a few moments before I walked in, and that he was sorry he missed my call.

"Damn," I say to no one in particular, and keep walking.

I feel one hundred percent better after sleeping in my own bed. I'm looking forward to getting back to teaching and my routine. I know in three weeks Sonny is coming. I also know that I need to keep this relationship in check and not forget that "it is what it is" and will never be anything more. I also need to figure out if that is enough for me. For now, I know it is, but I'm not sure how much longer I can keep going like this. My need for him grows more each time we are together. I head downstairs to the office to find Ashley. She is waiting for me and has a stack of mail to go through.

Halfway through the mail she ask, "Victoria are you sure everything is all right? You don't seem to be yourself."

"I'm fine," I lie. I think I just have a little jet lag. Give me a few days and I'll be back to normal."

"Sorry, but you know me. Now, I just have to ask. Who the hell is Alejandro Perez? Does he have anything to do with the necklace?"

"The necklace is none of your business. He's just someone Mateo and I met at a dinner party in Miami. He owns a Latin music recording company. Why do you ask?"

"It's the guy you were dancing with in that photo from Ocean Drive magazine, isn't it?" Ashley is beaming. She's such a romantic.

"Yes, it's him. We danced the tango together at the host's request."

She wants more information about him but I quickly shut her down. We finish going through all my mail. I ask her to call Mateo to set up a dinner for us one night this week. I let her know I'll give Ken a call later and see what's new. As I get up to walk out, she stops me and asks where I'm going.

"To do something I have missed. To dance." I open the door to the studio and plug my iPod into the sound system. The music comes on it's one of my favorites by Annie Lennox: "*Precious*." I freestyle barefoot across the hardwood floors of my studio. This one of my favorite ways to unwind and shut the world out. But the lyrics to this song are really getting to me, I was lost until you came. Oh Annie, you are so right.

I push myself into it more to get lost to escape. This is the one place I can be completely honest with myself and put all my emotions into the dance. Then it happens, the dance takes over. It is so freeing and healing. It's just what I needed, I needed to dance. My drug. My escape from reality.

Back in my office, I ring Ken to catch up on things.

"Hello stranger," he says as he answers the phone.

"Funny, Ken. I *have* been a little busy. You know, defending my title and all."

"Yes, you have and you have been getting a ton of recognition and calls for work. We should meet soon so I can run some of these offers past you and see what interests you."

I tell him I'm free tomorrow and we agree to meet for lunch.

"Your treat since you seem to be in a spending mood," Ken says. "I want to hear what happened in Cali and why you spent five thousand dollars."

I'll have to limit what I reveal to Ken. Nobody can know about Sonny. My business. My secret. My magical night.

Ken and I meet at Bouley's in Tribeca. His choice of restaurants puzzles me. Not that I can't afford it, but Ken knows better. Usually we run out to Sal & Carmine's on Broadway for a slice of pizza when we do lunch. As soon as I sit down, I start in on him. "Bouley's, Ken? Really? What's up with this place?"

"Well, I figured since you can afford throwing around money in Cali, five thousand here, five thousand there, your ass has gotten a little too precious for Sal & Carmine's. Now, are you going to tell me what that check was about, or not?" He asks.

"Or not." I smile sweetly as I refuse to answer his question. Ken cannot stand secrets, which makes this even more fun. We order lunch and get down to business. He has several job opportunities. Some we pass on. Lots of judging opportunities. There is even a request to be a guest judge on a television dance show.

Before we part ways Ken pushes one more time for information about the five thousand dollars. "You really aren't going to tell me about the money are you?"

"Nope!" I say holding my ground.

"Look I know you don't confide in me about your personal life but I want you to know I am here if you need to talk. Don't shut yourself off from all of us. If you are going through something, we can help you. I know I'm your manager, but I also like to think I'm your friend."

"Well I see you have been chatting with Mateo and Ashley. I know you are more than just my manager. I consider you a friend as well. There is really nothing to share. It's just not the right time."

"When you feel it is the right time I'm available. Try not to forget we are all here for you. By the way, nice piece of jewelry. Don't think I didn't notice it. Oh, and thanks for lunch. I like spending your money."

"Thanks, Ken. I really appreciate that. Don't get used to it. Next time it's back to Sal & Carmine's." I ignore his comment about the necklace. It's none of his business.

Later that evening over a light dinner with Mateo I fill him in on the judging gig in Cali. How impressed I am with up and coming talent in the junior division. We both agree the interest in ballroom dancing has increased due to all the dance shows on television. It's also brought us both increased business at our dance studios. I am happy to hear his foot is completely healed. His doctor gave him the go ahead to dance again. His tone then grows concerned and asks me if everything is all right. He has always been able to sense when I'm troubled. I try to shut him down like I did when Ashley asked, but he just doesn't buy it. Mateo knows me too well, even better than Ashley or Ken.

"You've been thinking about Alejandro Perez, haven't you?" Something went on between the two of you and you are trying to fight it. You can't lie to me, Baby Girl! There is something different about you. For starters where did that gorgeous piece of jewelry come from? So starting talking."

My hand flies up to touch the crown necklace. Shit. "There is nothing different about me, Mateo. Ok, yes, I have been thinking about Alejandro, but it's just not that simple. The necklace is just a gift."

"That necklace is not just a gift and I can bet I know who gave it to you. I know you better than anyone. Why does everything have to be simple with you? Love is never simple. Don't be afraid to take a chance with him. You know you can tell me anything, and you always have. Don't start holding back on me now. I got your back, always! Now get out there and start dating at least. I love you Victoria, I want to see you happy."

"I love you too Mateo," I assure him, "and I'll be honest. I think you're right. I do need to start dating. Maybe I will. If anything develops, I won't hold it back from you." I also ignore his comment about the jewelry.

Mateo and I enjoy the rest of dinner and walk around the city, laughing and just having fun together. For the first time since I've returned, I feel light and carefree.

It's great to be back and back to my life. I throw myself into work and even take over teaching some classes I had passed on to other dance instructors. I need to keep busy. Ashley buzzes the phone in the studio and says, "Alejandro Perez is on line two. You know the guy who gave you the gorgeous necklace you don't want to talk about. That Alejandro Perez."

"Not funny Ashley." I take a deep breath and I am not sure if I should answer. I tell myself to pick it up. I need to either explore a relationship with him or end it now. Taking in another deep breath, I click on line two with no idea what direction I will go. Maybe I will leave it up to fate.

"Hello, Alejandro."

"Victoria, hello. I am truly sorry I missed your call." The sound of his voice immediately makes me happy that I chose to take his call. The familiar sound and sexiness of it sparks something in me.

"Me too. I had a short layover in Miami and I thought we could have met for lunch. Maybe next time?"

"Definitely next time. Yes, unfortunately I was in LA when you called. After Caracas, I was looking forward to seeing you again."

"I wanted to thank you again for all you did for me in Cali. The flowers, the necklace and everything else was just so thoughtful. I really appreciate it, Alejandro." I am careful not to mention the upgrade on the penthouse because Javier said it was a secret.

"I was calling to see if you would like to have dinner Friday or Saturday evening. I am going to be in the city for business. I have a meeting Friday and I don't have to be back in Miami until Sunday."

"I am free *both* nights, Alejandro." The words are out of my mouth before I can stop them. Why did I say both nights? Face it Victoria, this man intrigues you.

"Then let's have dinner both nights," you can hear his smile in his voice. "I'll call you Friday."

"That sounds great. I will talk to you on Friday." I hang up and start to think, what am I getting myself into? It's time to follow my heart but I am not sure where my heart will lead me.

It's Friday, Alejandro called early to say Good Morning. He is going to pick me up at 8 for dinner. It felt good to hear that sexy voice. I suggested we have drinks at my loft. I am wearing a simple but sexy black leather dress from Gucci. It's a few years old, but one of my favorites. Since Alejandro is tall, much taller than Sonny, I am wearing a 5 inch pair of black leather Louboutin classic stiletto pumps. The look is very sexy, so I guess I'm putting myself out there tonight. I am really anxious and excited to see him.

As always, Alejandro arrives on time and looks every bit as handsome as I remember. He greets me with a quick hug and just one kiss. A kiss on the lips and then he comments on my look and tells me I'm beautiful. He's wearing a dark navy pinstripe suit, crisp white dress shirt and navy and turquoise striped tie. He is one those men that can make a suit look casual. The suit look has always been a turn on for me. My mind flashes to the magazine article that I first saw of Sonny. The photo spread where he is wearing all the designer suits. I shake the image out of my mind. I owe Alejandro all my attention tonight.

There is a few moments of awkward silence, as though neither of us are not quite sure what to do next. But his gorgeous turquoise eyes find mine and I notice the warmth in them and I am calm. Alejandro is the first to speak.

"My meeting ran late and I was not able to change before dinner." Alejandro apologizes. I see no need for an apology. I could stare at him dressed like this for hours.

"You look amazing to me. If you would be more comfortable, go ahead and take your tie and jacket off." This seems to put him at ease and he removes both. After giving him a brief tour of my loft we end up in the kitchen area and we take a seat at the granite island.

My mind flashes back to the first night Sonny came to my apartment. We also sat here that evening. Tonight I will sit next to Alejandro. There is no need to have distance between us like that night with Sonny.

"Would you like a drink?"

"Do you have any Crown Royal?"

"I most certainly do, since it's my favorite." I laugh. "How would like your Crown?"

"Ginger ale?"

Then I remember the first drink in Miami when we first met and it was Crown and ginger ale. I laugh out loud. "What do you find so amusing Victoria? Share with me."

"It's just that my drink is crown with ginger ale."

"I told you it was fate." We both laugh. One drink turns into two, then three, then four and we forget to go to dinner. Thank God I had laid out some fruit and cheese to have with our drinks or I would be feeling these even more than I already do. Just like our time in Miami and Caracas it just passes without us even noticing. We never seem to run out of things to talk about. Something Sonny and I have never done. Talked. It's getting late and I can't believe three hours have passed.

Alejandro glances at the beautiful watch he is wearing. "Oh Wow! Victoria I am so sorry. I forgot about the dinner reservations I made. I can't believe it's after eleven already. It's too late to find a decent restaurant serving dinner, even in this city. I feel awful. You must be starving. I promise I will make it up to you tomorrow evening."

"There is nothing to make up for. This evening was wonderful. I'm fine. Really. I loved catching up with you on what's been going in our lives since we were together in Caracas."

Smiling, he says, "I've missed you.I was hoping you were feeling the same." The awkward silence from earlier returns. He then extends his hand out to me as though he is asking permission. I don't hesitate and let him take my hands. He pulls me off the barstool and over to where he is seated. I am standing directly in front of him. I know what is coming and I am so confused and don't know what to do. He leans in and gently brushes his lips over mine in a sweet and gentle kiss. It's nice. It's very nice.

"Would it be all right with you if I kiss you again?"

"Alejandro, you don't have to ask me that."

"What I meant to say was, are you ready for me to kiss you again? I was wanting to know if whatever was stopping you before, is still there?"

I shake my head no as he slides his arms around my waist and draws me closer. I slide off my heels and wrap my arms around his neck. I am the perfect height standing in front of him. Then he kisses me sliding his tongue in to take a taste. Taking in a deep breath I give in to his touch.

It's not easy to just let go. The kissing is slow, gentle and controlled. Alejandro moves one hand from my waist and gently grips the back of my neck pulling me closer to him. A low moan like growl rises in his throat as he continues to kiss me pulling me even closer. We are both aware of what this could easily lead to, but with my guard up and him being the gentlemen he is, that is not going to happen. He pulls back, stops and releases his hold. He takes my hands in his and stares deep into my eyes.

"It's late and we both know we've had too much to drink. I will pick you up tomorrow at seven for dinner." He places a sweet kiss on my forehead as he releases his hold on me. Before he leaves he says, "Victoria you are very hard to resist. I just want this to be what you want. You need to tell me when you are ready." He knows nothing about Sonny but he knows something is holding me back. He is very intuitive and doesn't pressure me.

Alejandro is behind me as I walk him to the door. When I open it for him, he does something unexpected. He reaches over my shoulders and pushes the door closed. He grabs my shoulders and spins me around to face him. I am pushed hard against the door and kissed with a fire I'd not experienced from him before. I'm sure it's the alcohol that has my head spinning. But damn, with the same quickness he overtakes me, he also releases me. I am standing before him, dumbstruck.

"When I walk out this door," he begins, his voice serious and even, "I want you to think about how that kiss has you feeling at this precise moment. I want to be the last thing on your mind and on your lips as you lie in bed thinking about tonight. Sleep well, Victoria." And then, with nothing more but a simple smile, he walks out, closing the door behind him.

Damn. Damn. Damn! I am so fucking confused and have no one to talk to about this. Wait, yes I do. Retrieving my handbag from the foyer table I dig until I find the business card from Javier. I dial the hotel in Cali and ask for the concierge desk. The phone rings and I hear that familiar voice. "Hello, this Javier, how may I assist you?"

"Hello Javier. It's Victoria. Is it a bad time to talk? Are you busy?"

"I'd like to say I am thrilled to hear from you, which I am, but the sound of your voice has me worried. What's going on Victoria? I know you didn't just call to hear my handsome voice."

"Your right I didn't just call to hear your handsome and might I add sexy voice. I need some advice. You are the only person that knows everything."

After telling him what is going on he lays into me. "You need to stop comparing the two. Stop comparing two men who couldn't be less similar. I know that's what you are doing. You need to stop it right now. Victoria, how can you not see what is right in front of you? If you don't give Alejandro a chance you'll never know what it could be." He goes on to say, "There all types of lovers in this world. Each will bring something different to your life. Forbidden love is always hot. It never gets old because it never has to deal with reality. Real love, you will carry with you, forever. You have experienced it once and lost it. You are afraid to give in for fear you will lose it again. With the forbidden love you never really have it or own it so you can't lose what you don't have.

Victoria, don't turn your back on real love."

"Javier, when did you get so smart? I miss you so much. I knew you would open my eyes."

He laughs, "When it comes to Latin men I know what I am talking about. You know you can call me anytime you need me."

That night in bed I think about what Javier said. I know he is right. But if he felt the raw passion that I felt with Sonny he might just change his mind. I know it's hard to understand but if you ever get the chance to feel that way with someone, do it. But be careful, because it is a feeling that you may never get over. Everyone should experience the honesty of raw passion at least once in their lifetime.

As excited as I am for tonight's date with Alejandro that's not what got my ass out of bed before 7 am on Saturday. I am about to drag Ashley kicking and screaming from her apartment to a different type of dance studio. Today we start our pole dancing lessons. A six week crash course in the art of stripper pole dancing. Mateo offered to go with me. But I really don't want him to show me up in class. Remember it's Mateo I am talking about and he can be such a diva.

Since I returned from competition season I have decided to cross another thing off my, for lack of a better term, bucket list. Actually it was an assignment that Dr. R. had me do in Cartagena as part of my therapy. Not only is it a list of things I want to do in my lifetime. It's also a list of things my husband wanted to do but we ran out of time. Last year I crossed off a Nascar racing experience. The year before that I bungie jumped off the bridge at the New River Gorge in West Virginia.

When we arrive for class I am pleasantly surprised to find Mateo waiting outside. He is grinning from ear to ear. Shouting he says, "Did you really think I would let you two have all the fun ? I hope you both brought your best stripper heels. Cause your going to need them. I am about to show you bitches how to work a pole."

Rolling her eyes Ashley starts begging me, "Please don't make me do this. Let me leave before that bitch shows the two of us up."

Putting my arm around her and holding her tight so she can't get away, I'm laughing as I say, "Oh hell no. You are not getting out of this. If he is going to make me look bad you are going to be right there with me sharing in the shame. I need you for support."

Of course Mateo was the center of attention in class. But it was Ashley that really surprised me with her pole moves. Maybe there is more to Ashley then she lets us see. It's going to be an interesting six weeks with these two. OK, I have to admit it. I am good at this. The instructor even asked if I had worked at club before. We all got a good laugh from that.

This was just what I needed to take my mind off of everything. After class we headed to our favorite breakfast diner, Tom's, to chow down on all the bad stuff we shouldn't be eating. But I'm sure we burned a ton calories in class. Our table looks like a buffet of breakfast food. There is everything from a fully loaded omelette, hash browns, strawberry and blueberry pancakes and Mateo's favorite, corn beef hash.

Just as we are digging into the food and my mind is completely free of all thoughts except for this spread of food in front of me, Mateo ruins the moment. "So you have avoided the elephant in the room long enough, Baby Girl. I want the 411 on that fabulous crown you are wearing around your neck. And don't you dare say it's nothing."

We all stop eating and both Ashley and Mateo are staring at me. Before I have the chance to defend myself Ashley pipes in, "Mateo trust me I have tried to get that information from her. She has shut me down twice. My hunch is it's from Alejandro Perez."

"Ashely you're probably correct. If you would have seen the way he looked at her during the dinner party we attended, your hunch would be right. But I think she is hiding something or someone else from us." Mateo's tone of voice is one that expresses his concern and curiosity.

Ashley is intrigued. She raises her brow and opens her mouth to say something but I cut her off before she can articulate a single word, "Ok, both of you stop it right now. Yes it was a gift from Alejandro Perez. Yes I had drinks with him last night and I am having dinner with him tonight. But it's just dinner. We are just friends and the necklace was nothing more than a trifle gift. Nothing else is going on with something or someone. Nothing." I put emphasis on my last two sentences.

"So you finally admit you like Alejandro Perez. I knew it! And that necklace is not just a trifle gift. Really Victoria, trifle? Who uses that word? I bet the necklace is a thank you for some really great sex you had with him." Mateo says as Ashley looks on shocked by Mateo's comments.

"Fuck you Mateo! I'll use whatever words I want. I have not had sex with

Alejandro Perez. He did not give me a necklace as a thank you for sex. Really Mateo? How rude! Alejandro is not that kind of man."

"No sex? What the hell are you waiting for girl? Fuck the man and then give us all the details. As uptight as you are about answering a few questions from your very concerned, wonderful and amazing friends I think you could use some sex." Mateo has now managed to leave Ashley speechless as she continues to stare in disbelief as to what he has said to me.

"It's none of your business if I plan to fuck Alejandro Perez or not. And if I do I will not be sharing the details with the two of you. This conversation is over. Now can I please get back to stuffing my face? After all I may need the calories for energy tonight when I may possibly fuck Alejandro Perez."

"OMG! This conversation between the two of you is better than any episode of my favorite Real Housewives show." Ashley says with a little more enthusiasm than needed. She is relishing the exchange between me and Mateo.

I give them a look that they both know very well. It's a look that tells them this conversation is over and don't even attempt to cross me on it. After a few awkward minutes Ashley breaks the silence with some mindless chatter about the time she ran into some of the women from the Real Housewives of New York at a restaurant in Soho. Like I said she is like a sister to me and knows when I have had enough. Mateo continues his stare as if he is trying to read my mind and figure out what I'm thinking. He knows me and he knows when I am hiding something.

I would love to able to share what is going on in my life with my two best friends, but I'm just not ready yet. Also I promised Sonny we would tell no one. Maybe after I see how tonight goes with Alejandro I will share some details with them. I know they would love him. Mateo already thinks he's the perfect man for me. I don't need any outside influence to cloud my judgement. Who knows what will happen. I'm not even sure what I want. But I don't get away without Mateo noticing I am lost in my thoughts. After breakfast we all go our separate ways for the day. I've made an appointment at the spa for a little pampering before tonight's date.

Chapter 23

We are having a casual dinner tonight so I decide to wear the black leggings I got in Cali. I tuck them into my 5 inch, platform, black suede knee high boots. Alejandro seems to like high heels. I choose a black knit camisole and wear my new black blazer also from my shopping trip and I accessorize with some silver jewelry. No La Perla lingerie tonight. Nothing underneath. Thinking about being naked makes me feel sexy. I like the all black look. I think Alejandro will like it as well.

Alejandro arrives promptly at 7 and when I open the door he gives me a look that I have never seen from him. If I had to describe it I would say he was undressing me with his eyes. A look that has left me blushing and tingling in areas and that is going to have me regretting my decision to not wear panties. He is wearing jeans and a white collared shirt, black Gucci loafers with a black leather jacket. No matter what this man wears he looks handsome. Alejandro is always very sophisticated looking and seems very unaware exactly how good looking he is. Wrapping his arms around my waist he greets me with a kiss, pulls me to him and says, "Victoria, you look gorgeous. I think you are purposely trying to drive me crazy." Before he releases me he removes his hand from around my waist and moves toward my neck capturing the crown pendant between his fingers. Fingering the cut edges of the stones he says, "I like this. I noticed you were wearing it last night as well. I love seeing you in something that I picked out for you."

"Good evening, Alejandro. Nice to see my plan is working. Yes I love it as well. I haven't taken it off since the night you had it delivered to me." I reply smiling but also knowing I just lied to him. I took the necklace off the night of the concert in Cali. I didn't want Sonny asking me about it. It felt wrong to wear it.

As I gather my handbag and we make our way down the steps of my loft, the sexual energy builds. There is no denying it or hiding it. It's there. When we exit my building there is a driver and a car waiting for us.

We have a great dinner at Pulse in Rockefeller Center. I have the lobster risotto and Alejandro has the sliced hanger steak. After dinner we have a few more drinks and more conversation. It seems he is purposely taking his time and stalling leaving the restaurant. I ask him, "Alejandro, are you trying to avoid taking me back to my apartment?"

"With what you are wearing and the effect that has on me I think it is safer if we stay here. You very hard to resist. I am not sure I can control what I am feeling much longer." I want him to know he doesn't have to control himself with me and decide to take this as my cue. I slide my hand up his leg and before I reach my destination he grabs my hand, and kisses it. He then calls the waiter over for the check.

On the ride back to my apartment we are both very quiet. I know I should wait for him to make a move but I'm tired of waiting. I take my hand and attempt to run it up the front of his thigh but before I can reach my destination he stops me again. This time he pulls me in closer to him wrapping his arm around me and kisses my cheek. You can feel the sexual tension building. It's hard to ignore. Sensing my frustration he leans in and whispers to me, "You are making this very hard on me. When we get to your apartment. I have no plans to resist you. Victoria, I am not into putting a show on for the driver. Please be patient until we get to your place" Wow! I felt like I just got scolded. Hard on him? I have yet to discover if he is hard! I guess Alejandro is very reserved and measured about public displays of affection.

When we arrive back at my place Alejandro has a conversation with the driver, but I am not sure what is said. Instead of going to the kitchen I take him in to sit in my huge living room area. I ask him if he would like a drink. He says he is fine and takes off his jacket. I put an R&B mix on my sound system. I know it's not Latin music, but the only Latin music I have is Sonny's. This man owns the largest Latin recording company in the world and I am playing R&B music for him. I hope the music doesn't seem cheesy or look like I am trying too hard. I just want him to relax a little. Why am I so nervous all of a sudden? Why does all of this seem so awkward for me? He sits down first in the corner section of the huge modern sectional sofa. When I go to sit down beside him he takes my hand and pulls me down to him so I am facing him. Before I have a chance to say anything he leans in places one hand around the back of my neck and draws me to him and brushes his lips softly against mine. Snaking his other hand around my waist he pulls me even closer and kisses me again. When he kisses me the third time it changes and he seems to relax a bit and deepens the kiss. His tongue slides past my lips joining mine as our tongues begin a slow circling dance.

Abruptly he releases my mouth and pulls me away from him, "Victoria, I really want you. Are you sure about this?"

What the fuck? If I didn't want this I wouldn't be sitting here with him. I thought I had made myself clear in the restaurant and in the car. I guess it's time for me to show him that I do. I get up and take off my jacket and my boots. I then literally straddle him on the sofa and kiss him and not just any kiss. I take control of the kissing. If he can't tell by this kiss I don't know how else to tell him. It's my tongue that slides past his lips and explores every inch of his mouth. When I go to pull away he pulls me back and kisses me hard taking back the control. The kissing gets heated and we are both wanting more. He reaches up and pulls the straps down on my camisole and kisses my shoulders. We start to lose ourselves in the passion of the moment. He runs soft kisses up the side of my neck. Making his way down to my shoulders and then the front of my neck. Since I am sitting on his lap I feel him getting hard under me. My heart starts racing and I can hear my own breathing. I can't believe the effect this man is having on me. Everything in my body is awakening to what his kisses are doing to me. I take in a deep breath to gain control.

He reaches up and pulls my camisole over my head. I am not wearing a bra and he runs his hands along the side of my breast allowing his fingers to graze the side of them. "Victoria, you are so beautiful." This makes me tense up and pull away and I know why. It's the same way Sonny touched me. It makes me question if this is what I want. Can I really do this? Why now of all times do I have to think and be reminded of Sonny's touch?

Sensing my sudden change in behavior Alejandro positions me so he is looking directly into my eyes, "Victoria I want you, but if you can't give yourself to me completely nothing will happen here. I can feel your body tense up and pull away from me." If he only new how hard I was trying here. Desperate for him to know that I want him, I get up and strip off my leggings.

Standing here naked I tell him, "Alejandro, I want you. What more do you want me to say?"

"Victoria, you are going to have to tell me what you want. I am here waiting for you to tell me what to do. I need to know you want this as much as I do."

"Alejandro, I want you." Then out of no where and and beyond my control I begin to cry. I feel completely broken down and confused. Where did all this come from? I feel stupid. My heart is filled with confusion. I am torn over what to say and what to do. I know what my heart is saying, but I just can't give this man my heart. If I can't give it to him who am I waiting for?

He jolts me back to reality and says in a very harsh tone, "I am going to ask you one more time. Tell me what you want from me. If you can't tell me then there is no point in going any further in this relationship. I want more than just to be able to kiss you."

In a very angry tone, between sobs I announce to him. "I want you to fuck me, Alejandro. Is that what you wanted from me?"

He pulls me down to him, wraps his arms around me and stares me directly in the eye and says, "No that is not what I want. Victoria that's the problem, I don't want to fuck you. I want to make love to you." I pull away from him and stand back up. Wow, I was not prepared for that! This man wants to make love to me.

"Victoria I am here. I want you, but you need to decide if this is what you want. If it is I am here."

I stand silently and close my eyes and remember again what Javier told me. I take a deep breath and open my eyes. Then I take his hands and pull him off the sofa and lead him to my bedroom. When we get in the bedroom I pull him on to my bed and with tears rolling down my cheeks I tell him. "Alejandro, you need to understand it's been a long time since I have given my heart to anyone. I am trying here. I do want you. Please, make love to me."

Wiping the tears from my cheeks he kisses me and this time it's like the kiss in Cali. It is long and passionate.Our lips collide, his tongue slides in and connects with mine. Not breaking our connection I help him unbutton his shirt and take it off.

Releasing my mouth he stands up and I can see and remember how amazing his body is. He unbuttons his jeans and unzips them and slides them off. He has on black knit tight boxer shorts. He takes his boxers off and I can finally see the size of him. Wow! He is definitely hard and ready. I think he is enjoying this. The sight of his naked body makes me forget everything else. I hear him laugh softly as he caught me staring and it's not his face I am checking out. He walks over to the bed and pulls me up to him. His lips come crashing down on mine. This time it is even more intense than the last kiss. He then whispers to me, "Victoria I am going to make love to you. I want that more than anything. I know you said you wanted me to make love to you, but you need to open up your heart and let me. I want the part of you that you refuse to give. I want all of you. Stop shutting me out and ignoring your feelings."

I want him to know this is what I want so I look him in his eyes and tell him in his native language, "Alejandro, por favor hacer me encanta. Necesito sentirte dentro de mí.

With a smile and a sexy laugh he replies, "Oh mi dulce y bella Victoria quiero dentro de ti también. Quiero ser enterrado tan profundo dentro de ti."

The passion and the intense need for each other takes over. I can't help myself and I reach out and grab his very hard cock and stroke it. He lets me have my way with him for several seconds before he gently pushes me back down on the bed and then climbs up the length of me while spreading my legs. He is very attentive. Making sure he takes his time as he runs kisses up the length of my neck before capturing my lips in a kiss so intense he steals the breath from me. Breaking the kiss he moves to my breast taking one of my nipples in his mouth. He bites gently on it and I moan out loud, surprising even myself with my response. He picks up on my desire for this and repeats the same on my other nipple. I am totally lost in his assault when I feel his cock push against me and slowly make his way in. He is sweet and gentle and gives me time to adjust and accept his size. My body relaxes completely as he slides his full length into me and begins to thrust slow and deep. I began to match his strokes and raise my hips up to meet him trying desperately to rub my clit against him. He is so attentive to my needs he picks up on this and he whispers in my ear, "Victoria, what do you need from me. I want you satisfied. I want you to come."

"It's fine. Please don't stop." I beg him.

"I don't want to stop, but I am not a selfish lover. You have needs. I want you to come. Please tell me what I can do for you."

DAMN! He wants me to tell him? OK. Taking in a deep breath I whisper to him, "I need you to touch me."

He slows his pace and pulls out of me dragging his body from mine and settles himself kneeling between my legs. I miss the feeling of him inside of me. Just as I am about to protest the absence my eyes fly open in surprise to the intense feeling as his fingers begin to stroke my clit. Moaning I lay my head back down and close my eyes and let myself enjoy his touch. It's mind blowing to say the least. He knows what he is doing. He is good at this. Really good! I attempt to hold off from coming too quickly but my body is not going to cooperate with me. Within seconds I feel the orgasm build in me and I can't stop it. My back arches off the bed as my whole body quivers and the orgasm leaves me grasping for breath and crying out his name. Before I have the chance to fully enjoy the moment Alejandro slowly drives his cock back in to me. This only intensifies what I am experiencing. My entire body reacts to the feeling and sends chills up the length of me as a moan escapes my lips. Alejandro joins me and moans in pure satisfaction. I can't form the words to thank him for how incredible that was. As he begins to thrust hard and deep into me he whispers, "You are even more beautiful when you come. I want you to touch yourself while I make love to you."

Shocked and unable to stop the words I blurt out, "What?'

"I want you with me when I come. Touch yourself."

I hesitate for just a few seconds then I slide my hand down between my legs and before I start stroking my clit I let my fingers run up and down the length of his cock as he slides in and out of me.

Moaning he whispers again to me, "Come with me. How much time do you need?"

Caught up in the moment and feeling the second orgasm already building I tell him, "I'm ready, Alejandro. Now. I don't need anymore time. Please."

His strokes quicken and I feel his body tense as he starts to come. His entire body is reacting to his release. I increase the stoking of my clit and let go. My pussy tightens around his cock and he whispers unconsciously, "Buena mujer señor. Su coño es magia." I can barely translate in my head what he whispered because this second orgasm is more intense than the first. I am not aware of the moaning and his name escaping from my lips. Alejandro brings my orgasm down by slowing his thrust and whispering, "Victoria, let the magic happen. Let go of your heart to me." He buries his face in my neck and sighs. We lay together for few minutes as we both try to slow our breathing. He then pulls out of me and lays beside me.

Sonny flashes immediately in my mind. I try to shake the image but I can't. I want to get up from this bed and go some where and cry. I feel like I have just betrayed Sonny. What is wrong with me? I tell myself to stop it. Instead I stay and let him put his arms around me and hold me. I feel safe. The love making was beautiful, but it was also safe. Is it passion I have with the Latin Superstar or is it pure lust? He has never said the words make love to me. I am sure he makes love to his wife, but he just fucks me. Is there a difference? I fall a sleep with this in my mind wrapped in Alejandro's arms.

When I wake in the morning he is still holding me. I can't believe how well I slept. After we made love I fell into one of the deepest sleeps I've had in a long time. It's early and he is awake. He pulls me to him and kisses me and says, "Buenos días. You are so beautiful when you sleep." He smells really good and his hair is damp. He must have helped himself to my shower.

I pull away from him and tell him, "I need to use the bathroom. I will be right back." I know it was rude but I need my space and time to think. I am at a disadvantage here. He has showered and looks great. I step away from the bed I notice the time. It's only 7:30. Once in the bathroom I splash my face with some water, brush my teeth and check my appearance in the mirror. Not bad, actually. Standing there staring at myself in the mirror I realize I am just fooling myself about everything. This wonderful, gorgeous man has spent the entire night just holding me. He did not have to leave in the middle of night so no one would notice. I need to let this man into my heart. I grab my robe off the back of the door and pull it on as I exit the bathroom.

When I walk back into the bedroom Alejandro is out of bed and getting dressed. Surprised and puzzled I ask him, "Where are you going?"

"My plane is scheduled to take off in a few hours and I need to get back to my apartment before heading to the airport. Victoria. Last night was amazing. I am sorry I have to leave. I will call you when I land in Miami."

Feeling weird and desperate to make this right I blurt out, "I enjoyed last night and thought it was amazing as well." Omg!! How stupid must that have sounded. OK, I need to fix this. Now. I reach up and give him a very passionate and intense kiss. He returns the kiss, with one hand around my waist supporting me the other slides up the back of my neck. Using his hands he pulls me into his body encompassing me completely with this kiss. He takes control of the moment and I release my body to him. I can feel his arousal thumping lightly against my thigh. I shift slightly so my robe falls open so he understands my intentions. Instead he unexpectedly pulls away from me leaving me just standing there exposed to him.

"Victoria, I really have to go. The flight cannot be changed." Confused and not willing to let this end this way I use my hands to pull his face down to mine devouring his lips. I claw my fingers into his shoulders so he understands my intentions. I am trying to tell him something with this kiss. Again he pulls away from me.

"You are really making this difficult for me to leave. I can't stay. I really have to go."

"You can go Alejandro, but the next time I will not take no for an answer." I smile releasing him. Before he walks out the door I get nothing more than a kiss on the forehead.

After he leaves I am left wondering did he really have to go? Surely a man with his power could have changed his flight time and stayed. I wonder if I have ruined what could have been. Maybe last night is not what he thought it would be. Maybe he was just being polite. My stomach is turning sick and I feel like I could pass out. What the hell is wrong with me? I was supposed to listen to my heart. I am pulled back to reality when there is a knock at my door. Retying my robe around my waist I go to it.

When I open the door I am shocked to find Alejandro standing there. Without hesitation he grabs my hand and pulls me down the hallway back towards the bedroom. He stops in the middle of the hallway turns me to face him setting his hands on my shoulders and looking straight into my eye he says, "Victoria, I am not used to living my life where I just change things at the drop of the hat. My life is very scheduled.

Appointments and itineraries are set in place to keep."

I stop him before he can say anything else. Allowing my robe to fall open I put my hands on my hips and ask, "Alejandro, did you come back just to explain your busy life to me or was there something else you wanted?"

Alejandro gives me a puzzled look and then a smile. We both stare at each other and start laughing. He then says, "Victoria, I have 15 minutes before I need to leave. Do you want to stand in the hallway here or can I take you to your bedroom and make love to you before I have to leave?"

I stand there putting my finger to my lip acting like I need to think about it for a minute. He grabs me and throws me over his shoulder and carries me to the bedroom and tosses me on the bed.

A giggle escapes my mouth. He removes his clothes quickly. It's as though he can't get undressed fast enough. He crawls on my bed and pulls both of my ankles towards him while spreading my legs open. I slide quickly across the soft satiny sheets earning him more giggles. My robe slides completely off in the process. This time is different. There is no sweet and gentle. We both know we want each other and are holding nothing back. Without warning he thrusts his hard cock into me. Before he begins his relentless assault on me he gives me a few seconds to adjust.

"Victoria, you are so beautiful." He is deep inside of me as he begins stroking in and out and it feels amazing. This time he is not as gentle with me or my nipples. My breathing becomes heavy and so does his. I don't wait for him to tell me to touch myself. He did say we only have 15 minutes. This time he doesn't have to ask me if I am ready, the look in my eyes says it all.

When he is getting redressed he looks at me and says, "You need to know that was not my style. Just know the next time we are together we will not be in any hurry. We are going to spend some time getting to know each other."

I smile and say, "Well, Mr. Perez maybe I need to teach you how to be more spontaneous."

He replies with a huge grin on his face, "Maybe I need to teach you how to trust me with your heart!" Before he leaves he tells me he will call when he lands in Miami.

I spend the rest of the day trying to figure out what the hell I have gotten myself into. As I go through my Sunday rituals of laundry and cleaning I can't stop thinking about everything. Am I really going to open my heart to this man? Can I let go of Sonny to be with him? At some point I will have to make that decision. Not yet. I am not ready to give up one for other.

Just like he promised Alejandro calls when he lands in Miami. It has been so long since I have felt so appreciated and desired. He tells me, "I would love for you to come to Miami and spend some time with me at my home."

I don't hesitate even a second before I answer him, "I would love to."

"Could you fly down Saturday?"

This week is when Sonny is going to be in town but he said he would be here Wednesday.Without another thought I tell him, "Saturday will be perfect."

"Can you fly down and stay at least a week? I will show you Miami. It will give us a chance to get to know each other better. I will cook for us and we can just hang out at the house."

"Yes. A week sounds great! I will call later this week with my flight time. Alejandro, I want you to know I really enjoyed last night and this morning!"

"I did as well. Thank you for allowing me into your life. Now I just have to get you to open your heart for me. I promise you more wonderful evenings like last night. Sleep well my beautiful, Victoria. I will see you soon."

After I hang up I decide to take a long bath. Just as I am undressing my phone rings again. I answer it thinking it is Alejandro and giggling say, "I know you miss me but Saturday will be here soon." The familiar voice on the other end says,"Who is missing you and where are you going Saturday?" It's not Alejandro. It's Sonny. I freeze because I am caught off guard. His voice immediately sends shivers down me. I quickly recover, "I thought you were my dance partner Mateo calling me back. I am going to have dinner with him on Saturday." I lie.

"Just make sure you are home this Wednesday. I will be there around 9."

When I don't respond right away he ask, "Victoria, are you OK? Are you still there?"

"I'm sorry. I'm just tired."

"Get some rest because you will need it. I've missed you. Sweet dreams, Victoria." Before I get the chance to respond he hangs up. Really, he misses me? He just had to add that. My head is spinning. I need to get off this emotional roller coaster soon. Not quite yet. I cannot give him up just yet. That feeling returns to my stomach. I want this man, but what is it I really see in him? I am not sure if I will be ever ready to walk away from him and I am not sure how long Alejandro will wait for me.

It's Monday morning and Ashley is already in full work mode when I come down. I am so thankful that she handles things so well and is fiercely loyal. She points at a huge vase filled with the most beautiful shade of purple lilacs and says, "Those were just delivered. There is a card there with your name on it. I guess your dinner Saturday night went well with Mr. Perez." I don't need to open the card to find out who they are from, but I do. The card reads, "I told you we could create some beautiful memories together. Alejandro."

"Ashley I need you to book a flight for this Saturday to Miami. Also I need you to clear my schedule for next week." Picking up the vase off I head to my office before she has a chance to start drilling me with questions.

"Oh no you don't. Hold up there chica. You don't drop that in my lap this morning without some kind of explanation. What is going on in Miami?"

I confidently announce to her, "I am going to see Alejandro Perez."

"What do you mean you are going to see Alejandro Perez?"

"Maybe now would be a good time to tell you about everything."

"Yeah I think it would be. It's not like you to hide things from me. I feel like I have been left in the dark. I don't want to pry for information. I want to be here for you if need to talk about anything. I've missed our chats. I noticed you have been very quiet the last few months. Ever since your trip to LA for that music video thing."

Wow! I had no idea I was acting any different. I didn't realize it was noticeable to others. I need to take care of this. We do need to talk about some things. I tell her to get herself a cup of coffee and join me in my office. Over several cups of coffee I tell her everything. About Miami, our time in Caracas, what he did for me in Cali. I tell her how he helped Mateo with his foot. I tell her about this weekend. She can know about

Alejandro. But she can never know about Sonny. She is shocked but happy to hear about this and to see me smile. But I am not prepared for her first question.

"Are you in love with him?"

"Don't be ridiculous. It's too soon for that."

"What do you know about this Alejandro Perez?"

"I know what is important. He's good man. I know he would do anything for me."

"Just to be on the safe side I will see what I can find about him. How is this good looking, very successful man still single?"

I laugh and say, "Sometimes Ashley you are just too efficient."

"It's better to be safe than sorry. I don't want to see you get hurt. What time would you like your flight to be on Saturday?"

"Early in the morning." Alejandro is not one that will hurt me. Oh, if Ashley knew about Sonny de la Cruz she would kill me.

The next few days have dragged as I anticipate Sonny's visit. I did make a trip to Neiman's for some new La Perla. My heart is torn over seeing him tonight. After this weekend with Alejandro I am even more confused. I don't really have an issue about seeing two men at the same time. I'm an adult and know what I am doing. What I don't know is if I can handle it. The issues are much deeper and more confusing than ever. But I can't give up my Latin Superstar yet. The desire and craving for him is too strong. After all no one knows about us and it will always be this and never anything more. All this thinking is giving me a headache.

It is hard for me to concentrate on work today. Something feels wrong. I think I am just feeling anxious for his visit. I already know it will be amazing. I won't have to hide my desire and needs from him. It seems to be the one thing that binds us together. It may not be much, but it is strong and very powerful.

My last class is at 5 and Ashley says she needs to leave early because she has plans for tonight. I am thankful I don't have to run her off tonight and have her asking questions. After class I lock down the studio and it's time to shower and get dressed. I decide to wear my favorite designer deconstructed jeans and a simple white T-shirt. Underneath will be my new champagne colored La Perla. It is beautiful. It is flesh colored so it looks like I am wearing nothing. Up close the lace details are gorgeous. Hair natural and soft makeup. It's still only 8:30 so I open a bottle of wine and try to relax. At nine the nerves and the excitement of knowing he will be there soon has me on edge and excited. 9:15 and I am still waiting. I check my cell phone. No missed calls. I tell myself he is probably just running late or it could be traffic. 9:30 and nothing. 10:00 and still nothing. I realize there is no way I can call him because I don't know who he is with. There is nothing I can do but wait. I finish the bottle of wine. By 11:00 I am starting to feel disappointed and hurt. The fact that I drank an entire bottle of wine doesn't help. I fall asleep on the couch hoping I will hear a knock at the door.

I wake up on the couch still in my clothes. My head is pounding. I can't believe I was stood up. Yep, stood up by Sonny de la Cruz, a man I have no way of contacting. A man that I really know nothing about except what he likes in the bedroom. What was I thinking? Involve yourself with someone who doesn't belong to you and what do you expect? I have to stop this madness. My heart is aching. I need to get changed and get busy working and stop wasting my time with someone that was never mine. As I step out of my clothes the tears begin to fall. They continue as I step into the shower, where I began to sob controllably.

When I arrive in the office Ashley starts in on me as soon as she sees what I look like. "You look awful. What happened to you? Did Scott and Stevie come back into town?"

"No. I've just had too much drink. I drank a whole bottle of wine and passed out on the couch. I feel like shit."

"You tied one on by yourself last night? Why? What's going on Victoria? There is something you are not telling me. I can feel it."

"Yes I tied one on by myself. I just had a rough night. Leave it alone and stop putting your nose in where it doesn't belong. Just shut the fuck up for now. My head is killing me."

"Well I can take a hint. You don't have to be rude. I have your flight itinerary and some background information on Alejandro Perez. When you feel like being nice again maybe I'll share it with you."

"Ashley I'm sorry. I didn't mean to be rude. It was just a bad night and there is really nothing to discuss. Can't girl have a bad day once in a while?" Now I feel like shit. Why did I jump on her ass. She had nothing to do with Sonny not showing up.

"Of course you can have a bad day. But I'm here if you need me. Since you apologized here is the info I got on Alejandro. There really is nothing bad to report on Alejandro Perez. He was married once for about five years. Divorced and no children. Worked hard to be where he is today. Very well respected in the Latin music business. You have my approval on this guy. Oh and your flight leaves from LaGuardia at 7am Saturday."

When I give her a dirty look about the time. She snaps at me with,"You said early Saturday. Next time be more specific."

"And just where did you get your information on Alejandro?"

"Scott and Stevie are my friends as well. I just made a few phone calls. They were more than happy to help me and very surprised to hear you are dating someone."

"I appreciate your approval but I told you he was great guy. I'll see you tomorrow. I am going back to bed."

"I hope you are not getting sick," are her final words as I drag myself back up to my loft.

As I crawl into my bed the tears begin to fall again. Why does this hurt so bad? I still haven't heard anything from Sonny.

Feeling a little better today I begin packing for my trip to Miami. My phone rings and I scrabble to answer it praying it's Sonny. When I answer I realize it's not. It's Alejandro. He ask if I am ready for a week of being pampered in Miami. I tell I am ready for a week of just being with him, I tell him I don't need to pampered. I just need to be with him. He ask if everything is OK. I tell him, "It will be when I am back in your arms."

There it is. That sexy laugh of his. "Victoria, I am looking forward to having you back in my arms as well. I am also looking forward to having you in my bed. But remember there will be no quickies. I want to spend a lot time making slow beautiful love to you."

"We will see about that, Mr. Perez. Being spontaneous has it's benefits as well." He says he will be waiting at the airport.

I finish things up Friday in the office and tell Ashley if she needs anything to call me. "Victoria, please go to Miami and relax and enjoy this time. I promise everything is in good hands."

I go to bed early because of the ridiculously early morning flight. When I get in bed there are no tears tonight. I am thankful for this trip to Miami. I need to get away and clear my mind. I need to be with someone that can spend more than a few hours with me, not only when it is convenient. Who I am fooling? I knew what it was going to be like going into this relationship with Sonny de la Cruz. If he called tomorrow I would jump at the chance to see him. To be with him. To kiss the man that I can't get out of my head.

I awoke feeling content about going and leaving everything behind me -- including my relationship with Sonny. If I'm being brutally honest with myself, the word relationship does not even apply. He was never *mine*.

Although I jumped on Ashley's case about scheduling such an early flight, I am now happy she did it. I had accumulated so many frequent flyer miles she upgraded me to first class. Since I am going to Florida for a vacation, I dressed accordingly with bright red skinny jeans, black form-fitting off the shoulder top and my black Michael Kors platform sandals. I slept through the almost three-hour flight, feeling relieved to leave all the drama and melancholy behind me. I am going to Miami with a clear head and an open heart. I am excited to see Alejandro. I won't allow any thoughts of Sonny de la Cruz to muddle up my mind.

As I exit the plane, I almost immediately spot Alejandro at the gate. Every time I see him, I feel a school-girl rush. He is so handsome and refined. Dressed down in jeans and a T-shirt, I am surprised at how much younger he looks. His gorgeous turquoise eyes are hidden by a pair of classic Ray Ban aviators. When he spots me, I see a huge grin form on his face. I smile right back. I decide I owe this wonderful man a proper greeting. To *feel* how much I missed him and how happy I am to see him. As soon as I approach him he opens his mouth to say something, but I throw my arms around his neck and pull him in for a long and passionate kiss. Even though I can sense his surprise, and he quite happily accepts and returns it. Somehow I need to learn how to reel myself in with this man; to wait and let him take control. I am sure he would have greeted me with a kiss, but I didn't give him the chance.

"Welcome to Miami, Victoria," he says pulling away. Taking his aviators off and hooking them in his T-shirt I get my first glimpse of those sexy as hell eyes.

We walk to the baggage claim engaging in some small talk about the flight, and since he knew my flight was such an early one, he asks if I'm tired.

"The flight was great – I slept right through it!" I tell him. "I'm not tired at all, but I am starving!" I tell him with a smile.

"Ah, well I know the perfect place for breakfast," he announces, as we stand arm-in-arm at the baggage claim. Then he adds, "I am really happy you are here. I have missed you."

He loads my luggage in his Land Rover. Before I get in on the passenger's side, I pull him to me for another kiss. Then I whisper in his ear, "I think breakfast can wait, Alejandro. I need you to take me to your home."

Alejandro pulls me closer to him and whispers back, "Victoria, we have all week together. There is no need to rush. We're going to get to know each other and I am going to share my beloved Miami with you. Slow down love, and enjoy."

Damn him and his slowing down! I have missed him and I want to *be* with him. I would have thought he would feel the same way. Sometimes I wonder if I think more like a man than a woman when it comes to sex. Oh well, I sigh to myself. I *am* starving, so I guess I'll feed my belly first. But after we eat, he had better plan on taking me directly to his house so I can feed my other needs.

Alejandro takes me to the Front Porch Cafe on Ocean Drive and the setting is perfect. Miami is beautiful. The people here are beautiful. It's almost too much. Miami is so different from the Central Florida area I lived in with Blake. Sure the warm, sunny weather is basically the same but the people, the energy and the vibes of Miami are nothing like the slow paced area we had lived. I have always said coming to Miami is like leaving the U.S. and traveling to a foreign country filled with exotic, eccentric people. The smells, the buzz and the atmosphere here is mesmerizing to me.

We are seated on the patio of the restaurant, which is already buzzing with locals and vacationers. He orders a little bit of everything for us: poached eggs, thick-sliced hickory smoked bacon, sage sausage, fresh fruit, fried plantains and even blueberry-smothered pancakes. I eat voraciously; I guess I was hungrier than I thought. I think Alejandro is surprised by my appetite, which had left me since the night the Latin Superstar failed to appear. I can't remember the last time I ate a proper meal. We top off breakfast with a few rounds of mimosas -- an ideal way to wrap up the morning. The mimosa takes the edge off, and I settle in to a far more relaxed frame of mind. I am trying very hard to let Alejandro have control here, but I am having trouble keeping my hands to myself.

When we arrive at his home in the Venetian Islands, I am dazzled. It is so utterly breathtaking; I can hardly believe it to be real. Perched so that it appears to be overlooking Biscayne Bay. His house is a vision of architectural refinement. Completely encased in floor-to-ceiling glass windows, it sparkles in the Miami sun. Inside is equally as stunning. The estate appears to be a combination between minimalism and coastal chic. The palette is starkly white with clean lines throughout, peppered with sumptuous shades of turquoise, emerald, coral, and fuchsia in its artwork, furnishings, and accents. Surely this is the type of home you would find featured in Coastal Living or Architectural Digest magazine. In fact, I'm willing to bet it has been.

"I am going to put your bags in my suite. Please go ahead and look around. Make yourself at home," he says with a wink as he disappears up the glass staircase.

While he does, I just stand there slowly turning taking everything in. Although clean and crisp in its design, this home is incredibly welcoming. You don't get that feeling that you can't touch anything. It has warmth. It feels like a home not just a house.

"Since it's the weekend and we have the house all to ourselves," I hear him say before he reappears from upstairs. I am at first a bit confused, and then realize he must be referring to some type of staff that works for him in the house -- maybe a chef and a housekeeper. We exit out onto the beautiful lanai.

I am surprised to find there is no pool, "I'm shocked. No pool. A Florida home without a pool huh?"

"It had an infinity pool when I bought it," he explains, "but I had it filled in to extend my lanai out to the bay. Who needs one with a waterfront view such as this?", he declares with a smile. I kind of get his point. The lanai features an al fresco bar and grill and is generously furnished with luscious, oversized outdoor furniture. There are several different sizes and types of containers filled with plants and flowers.

We spend most of the afternoon on the lanai just talking. I love our talks but I am starting to get restless and I may have to jump him at this point. I have missed him and I am running out of patience waiting to have him. Maybe that's his plan to make me wait until I lose control.

"Victoria, why don't you take a shower and lay down for a while? I am going to start preparing dinner for us."

A shower and a nap? Really? No, I don't want a shower and nap. I want him! This is ridiculous, but I've got to control myself. Maybe a shower would be a good idea. Not so sure about the nap.

"Alejandro, that would be great," I lie. "I think the early morning flight is starting to catch up with me." He takes me to his bedroom which is *beyond* luxurious. There are floor to ceiling windows with a gorgeous view of the water. The décor is very modern and chic. The California king-sized bed features a sculptured teak headboard that reminds me of a piece of coral. The linens are a crisp white, and the rich turquoise coverlet that I recognize instantly -- it is by one of my favorite designers, Trina Turk. I had just been admiring it in New York a few weeks ago.

The bathroom is equally impressive and Alejandro shows me where everything is placed. There is a steam shower that features a glass wall and a large wide bench. The shower is enclosed in rugged, tumbled soapstone, with a trio of brushed chrome shower-heads that would make you feel as though you are showering under a waterfall. For a moment, my mind wanders off as I imagine the fun we could have in that shower later. But my fantasy is interrupted the minute I catch a glimpse of the gigantic bathtub that is perched upon a platform in the center of the room. It's like it is on it's own miniature stage, very unusual.

After surveying the space and seeing the huge tub I ask him, "Would you mind if I take a bath instead?"

"You don't even have to ask. Mi casa es su casa." He replies taking me into his arms and placing a soft kiss on my cheek. Releasing me I feel a sense of warmth and welcome from him.

"Muchas gracias, Alejandro," I say with a smile, impressed with my Spanish. "Me siento muy cómodo aquí. Gracias por invitarme."

It takes forever to fill the tub, but is well worth the wait. The moment I step into the warm water, lightly fragranced with vanilla and lavender bath oils, I am whisked away to a state of total relaxation and serenity. After some time I catch myself nodding off and decide it's time to get out. I step out towel off and wrap myself in a soft bath sheet. Stepping into the bedroom, I notice that Alejandro has turned down the bed for me. Although originally didn't feel I needed a nap, I change my mind and yield to his suggestion. Maybe I should just surrender completely this week, and let myself be pampered. Although I wish he would join me, I slip off my towel, slide into bed, and fall asleep admiring the dazzling view.

I am awakened by a bad dream--something about the Latin Superstar. I can't recall exactly what happened; only that it has left me with an eerie feeling. It takes a few moments to remember where I am. I wonder how long I have been sleeping. Outside, the sun has begun its descent, disappearing into the horizon. I feel like I've been a terrible guest, sleeping the majority of the day away. Hastily, I throw on my favorite torn, faded jeans and a white cotton v-neck sweater. I may be awfully casual on the outside, but underneath I am wearing beautiful lingerie. I make sure of that. I'm well aware that Alejandro has an affinity for high heels, but tonight I go barefoot. After all, I am on vacation, right? I haphazardly throw my hair up in a clip, spritz on a little Coco Mademoiselle, and head back to the main part of the house.

This place is so big that I practically have to follow my nose to locate him in the kitchen. Whatever he's cooking smells fantastic. I'm a little embarrassed when I walk in – I'd been asleep for hours! He is standing over a stove, stirring something, still wearing jeans and a T-shirt, and he, too, is barefoot! "Well, hello my sleepy girl," he says with a smile. "I checked on you earlier, but you looked so content, I did not want to wake you."

"I can't believe I slept all day," I say, apologetically. "I honestly didn't think I was that tired. I think it was the bath that did it."

"Victoria, stop." he interrupts. "There is no need to apologize. It makes me feel good that you were able to relax enough in my home to sleep." And then he adds, flirtatiously, "Besides, it's good you got your rest. You will need it later."

This makes my cheeks warm, and I almost say something provocative back, or even approach him with a kiss, but then I remember that Alejandro is different. I wouldn't call it old-fashioned, but he does prefer to be in control. I can allow that; it just takes a little restraint on my part. Since Blake's death, I have had absolute control over my life and everything in it. Just then, something dawns on me. For the first time since I met them, I see something that Sonny and Alejandro share. They both enjoy and assume control. Sonny, especially...clear down to the precise moment I'm going to orgasm. Perhaps that is why I am so drawn to them both. I shake my head to stop myself from thinking further. I need to erase Sonny de la Cruz from my mind.

Especially now. Maybe a drink or two would help.

"We are going to have dinner on the lanai," he announces, sending my thoughts even further away. "How about a glass of wine?"

"That is exactly what I need," I tell him, not surprised that he has apparently read my mind. I offer to help, but he sends me and my glass of wine out to the lanai to take in the sunset while he finishes up in the kitchen. He insists on doing everything himself, which I admire. This man has more money than anyone I personally know. He probably has a full staff of help who could have taken care of all of this – but no, he does it all on his own. I find this trait incredibly appealing.

There is a breathtakingly romantic table awaiting us on the lanai. A rustic driftwood table for two is set beautifully, with an arrangement of fresh dahlias in red, purple, and white in the center. The space is flanked by oversized white candlelit lanterns. There must be ten of them. They remind me of the lanterns around the pool at my suite in Cali. "Stop it, Victoria," I whisper to myself. No more thoughts of Cali. No more thoughts of *him*.

Everything is perfect, right down to the weather. I am beginning to wonder if there is anything this man can't do. Dinner was delicious. He tells me his grandmother and mother loved to cook and they each taught him a great deal. We have fire-roasted vegetables, broiled swordfish, and seasoned rice that is like nothing I've ever tasted, his grandmother's special recipe. He delights in watching me devour everything on my plate, and is clearly quite proud of himself.

"I hope you have left enough room for dessert. I made you my favorite. Flan."

I almost tell him I thought *I* would be dessert, but I reflect on what I realized about him earlier, and stop myself. "Flan? I am sorry what is flan?"

"If you have never had flan then you are in for a delicious experience. I make a killer flan. Another one of my grandmothers recipes."

I discover flan is a strange but delicious version of a custard like spongey substance. We are having vanilla flavored that is covered in carmel sauce. Scooping up the last bit of flan from my plate scrapping it clean I remind myself to ask Mateo why he has never introduced me to this delicious, little slice of heaven. If I didn't think I would embarrass myself I would pick up the plate and lick it clean. It was that good.

After dinner I am hoping things will soon progress to the bedroom. Instead, he goes back inside and, after a few moments, music is playing. He returns with a bottle of wine and two glasses. Other than the two kisses I got at the airport and the peck on the cheek in his bathroom, there has been no physical contact between us. What the hell is going on here? Again, I have to remind myself to slow down and just enjoy everything as it comes. The man singing has a rich, velvety voice that I love.

"This music playing is beautiful. The singer has an amazing voice. Is he signed with your label?" If I am going to date a man in the Latin music business I think need to figure out who some of these artist are. And what type of Latin music I like. I wonder if I would like that reggaeton that Mateo talked about?"

"He is a new artist that we have recently signed," he replies, a hint of pride in his voice. "This is the final cut of his debut album, which is slated to drop in a couple of weeks. He is young and very talented. I'm glad you agree."

We sit and chat a while, enjoying the music and wine. I wanted this man *before* I started drinking, and after several glasses, that feeling has multiplied. We're making small talk, and all I'm thinking about is getting him in bed. I don't know how long I can keep this up. Maybe I will yawn and he will get the idea. Before I have to take such drastic measures, he says, "It's getting chilly out here. I think we should go inside." I am relieved and jump up from the table a little too quickly, which makes my head spin a tad before I regain my composure and walk inside. He doesn't seem to notice, and I'm relieved.

Once inside, Alejandro stops in the living room and motions for me to go ahead on to the bedroom, "Go on up and get comfortable and I will join you in a few minutes. I need to make a few calls first. I'll be up soon."

Oh, how romantic, I think to myself. Go ahead without me? What does he expect me to do? Get undressed and sit on the bed in my beautiful lingerie, and just wait for him? He does not know who he is dealing with. I don't wait for anyone. Well, not anymore. This is killing the mood, as I plop myself down on the bed, fully clothed and a little exasperated.

Fifteen long minutes later, Alejandro reappears. "Did you need anything Victoria?" Ha! I think to myself, yeah, I need to you to come here and fuck me hard. But God forbid I say anything like *that* to this man. He wants me to be ladylike? I can do that.

"No, I'm fine. I don't need anything," I say, in what I thought was a pleasant tone of voice, but the moment the words leave my mouth, I can practically taste the sarcasm.

"Victoria, is there something wrong?" Alejandro asks in a just as concerned-yet-sarcastic voice.

"Like I said, I'm fine. Just laying here waiting for you." I don't attempt to hide my frustration at this point.

"OK," he says, a little too matter-of-factly for my taste. "I am going to take a quick shower. I will only be a few minutes." And with that, he disappears into the en-suite.

Unbelievable! I say nothing. When I hear the water running in the shower, all I want to do is march right in, and join him. Maybe I will just sneak in there and stare at him while he is showering. I giggle to myself at such a thought, and just stay put. Several minutes later, I hear the water turn off. He enters the bedroom with nothing but a towel wrapped around his waist. He stops at the foot of the bed and begins to dry off his gorgeous chiseled, naked body, right in front of me, like it's nothing. Really? It takes every ounce of self-restraint I have within me not to pounce on this man and devour him! I admire his beautiful golden-brown physique, shimmering with droplets of water that disappear with every stroke of the towel. He is clearly taking his time; it almost seems as though he's putting on a show for me, teasingly testing my dwindling patience.

Just then, he confirms my suspicion. "Victoria, has this been hard for you today?" I pretend to have no idea what he's talking about. "I don't understand what you mean, Alejandro," I say. There is nothing hard in this room, including him.

"Victoria, really," he chides, as though I were a little girl who'd just got caught in a lie. "Do you mean to tell me this was not frustrating for you?"

All right, Alejandro Perez, I think to myself. Two can play this little game.

"Nope I am not frustrated at all," I respond, as nonchalantly as I possibly can. "I honestly have no idea what you're talking about." I slide off the bed and begin to peel off my own clothes, proving I am better at this game than he is. He is the one with the dick that will soon be rock hard, and there's not a thing he can do about it! I begin by slowly pulling my sweater over my head and letting it drop to the floor. Then I unzip my jeans and wriggle them down, stepping out of them once they fall around my feet. Within moments, I am down to my irresistibly beautiful LaPerla lingerie. My lavender laced demi bra is so skimpy that I'm spilling out over the top of it, and from the way he is admiring me, it is quite clear he loves what he sees.

"I think I'll go wash my face and brush my teeth," I say, making sure I brush past him as close as possible without touching him. As I turn, I notice I have definitely had an effect on him. He can pretend that he's patient all he wants, but his dick tells another story. In the bathroom, I busy myself with brushing my teeth and washing my face. I don't see him when I first enter the bedroom, but as I turn to get in bed he grabs my arm and pulls me to him. He is naked and more than just a little excited. "So Victoria," he asks. "Was relaxing and enjoying the day without rushing so difficult?"

I look up at him and see fire in his eyes. "Alejandro, I really don't know what you are talking about," I say, trying very hard to appear indifferent.

My attempt at being flippant is clearly in vain. "Victoria," he chuckles. "I told you long ago, I don't hurry at anything and I certainly don't hurry my love making. I want to get to know you. Sex is a very important part of a relationship, but so is the intimacy of just spending time together. Simply talking and laughing with you brings me great pleasure. I didn't invite you here just to bed you all week long. I want to build a relationship with you. But make no mistake, it is not easy for me to keep my hands off of you. I want you as much as you want me."

I stand there for a minute and then let out an exaggerated yawn. "Alejandro, I am really tired. Can we talk about this tomorrow?" I pull away from him and walk to the edge of the bed, trying my hardest not to giggle. Slowly, I remove my bra and wiggle out of my panties, making sure I take my time, giving him a show before I slide into bed. I can feel his eyes on me the whole time, but I don't dare make eye contact. I think he is well aware that his charade has backfired. But when he walks over to get in on his side of the bed, I can tell he is no longer excited. *Shit*, I think to myself. *Maybe it's my charade that has backfired*.

"Thank you for a beautiful day and a delicious dinner," I say, clearly defeated. "Good night, Alejandro."

He rolls over and grabs me around the waist and pulls me towards him and I start laughing. He then says, "Not so fast, Victoria," he commands. "I think we have gotten to know each other enough for one day."

I turn over and whisper in his ear, "Just so you know, there is a lot we can learn about each other in bed as well." This makes him laugh, and he whispers back, "Well then, let's see what we can find out about each other tonight. My way."

Alejandro wastes no time pulling me in close and kissing me deeply and passionately. In fact, several moments go by where all we do is kiss, and it becomes so intense that I begin to feel as though this is all I need from this man. *Relax*, I tell myself. *Let him be in control*. The way he is kissing me is all too consuming to take in. His lips feel like velvet as they assault mine. I can't seem to get enough of him and wrap my hands around his neck drawing him in closer.

He rolls me onto my back so that he's on top. I can feel he is rock hard again. I think he's going to enter me, but the kissing continues. No grinding, no rushing, just long, slow, amazingly passionate kissing. I don't think I've ever enjoyed kissing as much. This must be what I miss out on when I rush things. Slowly, he uses his knee to spread my legs open. I am so into the kissing I don't even notice. Then I feel his hand slide down guiding his cock as he pushes into me. I stop kissing only because I have to catch my breath – that's how intense it feels. As cliché as it may sound, it's as though our bodies were designed for one another. It feels *that* good. "I do hope this was worth all the waiting I put you through today," he murmurs. Even though I am lost in the thrill of this moment, I have to respond. "Oh, yes, Alejandro," I sigh. "This was definitely worth the wait."

This is nothing like the first time. Not that the first time wasn't great, but now we are relaxed and so much more at ease with each other. This is beautiful and – dare I say it? -- Romantic. He never stops kissing me as he slides all the way in and all the way out at his own, slow rhythm, which only multiplies the intensity. The feeling is amazing. I feel like I'm having orgasms in tiny, pulsating ripples each time he pushes into me. The wait was beyond worth it, I tell myself. I don't want it to end, but I can't help but wonder how he can keep going for so long! I am enjoying this so much I can't think of anything else. I am lost and have no idea how much time has passed. Just when I think this couldn't be any better, he pushes deeper and with a force so great I begin to quiver as I come one final time as he climaxes inside of me. The feeling cannot be put into words. I never knew it could be like this. When he finally stops, I am completely drained. "Alejandro, promise it will be like that every time we make love," I sigh. "I promise it will," he whispers back. "I also promise it will get even better if you just open your heart to me."

I fall asleep easily after making love with Alejandro, exhausted and very content, wrapped in his arms.

I wake very early the next morning to find Alejandro is still sleeping. I tiptoe to the bathroom to pee, brush my teeth, and wash my face, returning quietly so that I don't disturb him. It's still dark outside. I can't help but lay there and stare at his sleeping gorgeous face. Something has profoundly changed between us. What we shared last night was the real thing. Our lovemaking was so intense, like nothing I have had with any other man. Including my late husband and the Latin Superstar. It's a bit frightening, to be truthful. When you have experienced this kind of intimacy, you never want to lose it. I'm afraid there's no turning back now.

After Alejandro wakes up, we have a quick breakfast and get dressed. We spend the majority of this gorgeous day driving around Miami in his Porsche. We stop for tacos at a downtown street vendor, and walk around the city hand in hand, window-shopping. It's a carefree kind of day filled with laughter and light conversation.

When we arrive back at his house Alejandro says, "Let me draw a bath for you while I take care of some work in my office."

"Mmm, I would *love* that. That bathtub of yours is amazing." I say, smiling.

Alejandro prepares my bath before retreating to his office, filling the bathroom with the most exquisite scent. It's very soothing to my senses. He's even lit a few votive candles and dimmed the beautiful Murano blown glass chandelier. As I undress, I hear music. Only then does it dawn on me that I have not seen one television in his entire house. Stepping into the perfect temperature of steamy hot water my body immediately relaxes. Laying back and resting my head against the padded headrest my mind and thoughts slowly drift.

I was soaking forever – my fingertips look like prunes! When I finally get out, I decide to lie down while I wait for Alejandro to finish working. Again, I have fallen asleep. When I wake I know it is late because Alejandro is in bed next to me, asleep. I scoot my body closer to him. He is naked and I want to feel his body against mine. I want him next to me when I sleep. I am so very drawn to him. When I move closer, I accidentally wake him. "Is something wrong, Victoria?" he asks in a sweet, sleepy voice.

"No, Alejandro, everything's fine." I tell him. "I'm sorry I woke you."

"No, don't apologize for waking me. If you need something please don't be afraid to ask. I am here for you. Just let me know what you need."

Oh! Wow! He wants to know what I need. Come on Victoria tell the man what you want. Just tell him you want his cock inside of you. Stop holding back. Open yourself up to him. Tell him your needs and desire. Okay, I'm doing this. It's now or never.

"I need...I need you to make love to me," I say, shyly stuttering. "I need to feel you inside of me. Please make love to me."

He doesn't answer me. Instead he lifts his arm and pulls me in close. Wrapping his tan, strong arms around me. I feel safe, warm and wanted. His lips are on mine before I have a chance to break the silence between us. His tongue slips past my lips and begins a slow delicious dance. I love the way this man kisses me, devouring my entire mouth. Drawing the breath from me I am left with a need to draw him in closer. I get lost in his kisses. Just as I feel myself floating away he whispers, "I don't want you touching yourself."

What the fuck? Confused I say, "I don't understand."

"I will make you come. I need you to relax and let me give you your orgasm."

"Oh. Okay." I respond. Not really sure what else to say.

Alejandro turns with me in his arms and lays me on my back. His strong, lean body is draped over mine pinning me to the mattress. As he kisses his way up my neck and to my ear he whispers again, "Spread your lips open for me." I don't hesitate for even a second before sliding my hand down between us. Just as I use my fingers to spread my sodden folds open for him he slides his cock into me. Pulling my hand from between our bodies Alejandro takes them and stretches them above my head securing them. As I take in a deep breath he begins to move. Slow and steady never separating his body from mine. Fuck! This feels amazing. My lips are wrapped around his cock. With every stroke I feel the connection between us. When he slides and grinds into me he is simultaneously stroking and stimulating my clit. My breathing increases and so do his strokes. I feel him harden and the head of his cock swell. He is close. Sensing I need something to take me over the edge he dips his head down taking my right nipple in his mouth. My body arches as he bites and sucks. Everything all at once becomes blissfully hazy around me as my orgasm rips through me. Releasing my nipple Alejandro cries out my name as his own orgasm releases. Several minutes pass as we lay there waiting for our breathing to slow. Alejandro pulls himself up from my body. It's only then that I realize the entire weight of his body was pressing down on me. I wince as he pulls out and I feel the wetness of our releases between my legs. Alejandro tells me to lie still as he heads towards the bathroom. Returning a few minutes later he spreads my legs wiping me clean with a warm wash cloth.

As he climbs back in bed he wraps his arms around my waist pulling me into his body with my back to his chest. Just as I feel myself drifting off I get one more whisper from him, "Better? Now go to sleep my love." I lay there for a few minutes, trying to memorize the feeling. Nothing has ever felt so right.

The next few days slip by, filled with shopping, wonderful dinners, and a trip to a luxurious spa at the Mandarin Oriental

Hotel. Alejandro booked us a couple's suite for six hours. This by far was one of the nicest and most romantic things anyone has ever done for me. Oh, and sexy as hell. We did this couples mud treatment. The spa personnel explained everything before leaving us alone to indulge ourselves. First there was a mud bath, where we got to apply a mud mixture of volcanic ash, hot spring water, natural minerals, with peat moss to each others body. It was very erotic and playful. Then we showered to rinse off followed by a soak in a bubbling mineral bath. Finally some quiet time in the steam room. We were then escorted to one of their blanket wrap rooms. Here we relaxed to some soothing aromatherapy. We cooled down, with the scent of lemongrass and eucalyptus essential oils. I think we both drifted off to sleep.

We had several more treatments, but my favorite of all was the Oriental Harmony

Signature Four-Hand Massage. Four hands work in perfect unison in a remarkable experience. Two therapists work together in time and movement, first providing a warm scrub that smooths and replenishes the skin and then a massage that balances the body. The treatment left my body energized and my skin exotically fragrant.

Talk about ecstasy. Wow. I think I could really get used to this pampering thing.

Dinner one night was held at the home of one of Alejandro's friends. Everyone was very welcoming. They also seemed surprised that Alejandro had a date, which was surprising to me. I guess it's true – before me, he had been keeping to himself. They were all interested in my dance career. Some recognized me as the dancer in Sonny's video and asked many questions. The evening ended with some impromptu dancing on the patio. Everyone wanted me to give them lessons!   It was fun to experience Alejandro interacting with his friends. I've never felt more at ease.

We spent another day shopping at Bal Harbor, where several people knew him by name. I used to think shopping with men was a bore; well, straight men, that is.   But shopping with Alejandro was actually quite fun. He has great taste in clothing and he let me pick some things out for him.   To return the favor, I indulged him and allowed him to treat me to a sexy pair of red patent leather Mary Jane's at Gucci. High heels *are* his weakness.

The entire week has been simply magical. Some nights are filled with intense and beautiful lovemaking, while others were spent with us cuddling in bed. It was a perfect blend of passion and intimacy. No matter what we do, evenings always end perfectly with me wrapped in Alejandro's arms. My only complaint is that it is going by much too fast.

When we wake on Friday Alejandro says he needs to go by his office to sign some papers, and would love for me to accompany him. I decide wear a simple floral print wrap dress from Diane von Furstenberg and my new red patent Gucci shoes. It must be business casual Friday at the office because he is wearing a pair of pinstriped flat front trousers and a white button down dress shirt with no tie. During our week together I have discovered Alejandro is a bit of a clothes horse. His style and taste are amazing.

On the ride he mentions his plans for this evening. "Victoria I have somewhere special I'd like to take you. Something I think you are going to like."

"Do you think you could be a little more specific. I need to know what to wear."

"You will need shoes and clothing that you can dance in, but casual."

"What do you mean by dancing shoes?" I quiz him.

"Victoria, relax," he laughs. "I remember your heels from the dinner party. Those will not be good for tonight. You are going to need some real dancing shoes tonight."

"Well, Alejandro, you are lucky. I always travel with a pair of dance shoes in my suitcase. But allow me to remind you, I *was* able to keep up with you that evening in *those* shoes."

"No, Victoria, you are the lucky one because you are going to need your dancing shoes tonight. You may have kept up with me that night, but let's see how you can handle what I have in store for us this evening."

Now he really has my interest piqued. I know he dances the tango but can Alejandro really dance?

His offices in Miami are beautiful and filled with beautiful people. Everyone was friendly and polite, and seemed pleasantly shocked to see Alejandro showing a woman around. We head down a very long hallway to his office. The hallway is lined with photographs framed in brushed chrome. I ask who all the people are in the photos and as we walk he points out each artist and tells me about them. They are all signed by his record company. Some of names I recognize, but most I don't.

Then he points out one photo and says, "All but this one. I do not represent him any longer." I look closely at the photo and its Sonny de la Cruz! Before I can stop the words from coming out of my mouth I ask, "What happened?"

"My divorce happened."

I'm confused. "What did your divorce have to do with Sonny de la Cruz?" The words pop out my mouth before I stop and think about what I am asking.

What he says next shocks me and makes me feel sick. "I was married to his wife Maria's sister, Adrianna. After we divorced, it was not pretty. Maria insisted Sonny get out of his contract with my label. It's been several years now, but my relationship with Sonny has never been the same."

As we walk into his massive office I want to know more, but I am still in shock about who his ex-wife is so I don't ask anything else. I do ask him what happened to his marriage. We have talked about so much this past week I feel comfortable asking. He also knows my very painful story about Blake. I didn't think it could be any more tragic and sad. He tells me she desperately wanted children, but they found out they were unable to conceive. He told her they could adopt or use a surrogate, but she would not hear of it. She wanted her *own* children. Once it was determined that it was because of him she wanted out of the marriage.

"Where is she now?" I ask.

He laughs and says, "She is married to a wealthy investment banker she met in Spain. They have three children."

Then he turns to face me, and with a sad tone to his voice, "I guess this is the time I should tell you, if you want children, Victoria, I am not the man for you."

He searches my eyes, as I step closer and take his hands in mine. "You are the perfect man for me. I don't want children. I am sure that would have been a possibility years ago, but when my husband died I shut my heart off from any man. As time passed my life went in a completely different direction and becoming a mother was something I never thought about. Life takes us on different paths and some things like children are part of some people's lives. But for others, they are not. It doesn't mean our lives are less fulfilled. I love my life and my career and I have never felt like I missed out on anything." Then I smile, and tell him, "You should feel the same."

As he thanks me, I can tell he is relieved that we had this talk. But more importantly it was something he needed to share.

I can't seem to wrap my mind around the fact that his ex-wife was Sonny's sister-in-law. No matter where you go in life, things like this make you realize how small the world really is.

When we get back to the house Alejandro tells me we will have dinner around eight and then will need to get dressed. He says I should really consider taking a nap before dinner because I will need my energy.

As I walk away, I tell him, "You should rest as well, because you are the one who will need the energy when we get back tonight."

Laughing, Alejandro says, "We will see how much energy you have left after the evening I have planned for you."

Just as I suspected, he does have a chef. Dinner was prepared for us and served outside on the lanai. This is a lifestyle I could become accustomed to. I am going to miss all of this when I go back to New York. After dinner I tell him I am going to get dressed but I need to know what I should wear. He says to put on something casual that I can easily dance in. I roll my eyes. "That doesn't help much, Alejandro."

Since I don't even know what type of dancing we are going to do, I decide to wear a pair of black form-fitting capris and a black fitted camisole. Over that I slip on a sheer white blouse that can be removed if needed. I add a silver low slung belt and put on several silver bangle bracelets, just to dress it up a bit. I figure the less jewelry, the better. I wear my hair down and punch up the drama on my makeup. Then I get my dance shoes out. I have brought my classic black ones with the highest heel I can dance in. This particular pair can be worn anywhere, not only for competition. I travel with this pair every where I go. Even though I dance for a living I still like to go out and dance for fun. All of my other shoes are custom made for competition and I would never wear them on any other surface then a dance floor.

Alejandro is in the living room waiting for me. He is wearing jeans, a black V-neck T-shirt and black boots. This man looks so sexy whether he's dressed up or dressed down. "Come closer and let me see you," he says, motioning me over with his hand. He looks me up and down as if he's inspecting my outfit and asks, "Will you be comfortable taking the blouse off if needed?"

I laugh because that's precisely why I wore it. He drops his gaze to my shoes. "Hmm," he says. "Do you think you can dance in those heels all night?"

"Do I need to remind you what I do for a living?" I quip with some attitude.

"No," he laughs. "You don't need to remind me. I just want you to be comfortable and enjoy yourself tonight." What happens next catches me off guard. He smacks my butt and says, "By the way your ass looks amazing in those pants."

It's about ten o'clock and I'm not sure where we are heading. We seem to be going to an older part of Miami. Gone are the big homes and the high-rise buildings. We pull in to a parking lot where we are greeted by two young men who know Alejandro by name. They tell him not to worry they will take good care of his car. I see him slip them some cash. One of the young men opens my door. As he helps me out I can feel his eyes running up and down my body. I am sure I heard him make some suggestive comment under his breath in Spanish, but I couldn't quite make it out. The other guy also looks me up and down. Alejandro notices and smiles. Apparently he finds this amusing.

They ask him in Spanish, "Mr. Perez, are you taking this beautiful women dancing this evening?"

"Yes, I certainly am." He replies proudly.

The one that helped me out of the car asks Alejandro in Spanish if he thinks I can handle their style of dancing in these shoes.

What is the deal with these shoes?

Alejandro can tell from my expression that I understood exactly what they said, but before I can answer them back, he says with a twinkle in his eyes, "Gentleman, you have no idea who this beautiful woman is. She may just put everyone to shame tonight." Both men look at each other and then look at me and smile.

We walk about a half block. As we approached a large single story brick building I started to hear music. It's Latin music, definitely Latin dance music! I may just be a *gringa*, but my entire soul responds to Latin music. There are people standing outside smoking and hanging out. When we approach, I can tell they know Alejandro. Some greet him with, "Good evening, Mr. Perez." They all seem surprised to see him with someone, just like the people at his office and at the dinner party the other night. They all have their eyes focused on me. When we enter the club, I am once again taken back to Cali. It reminds me of the club Javier and I went to that evening. The music is loud. The place is packed and the dance floor is elbow room only with people dancing. Alejandro is watching closely for my reaction.

I turn to him and with a huge grin on my face and excitedly say, "Mr. Perez, I certainly hope you know how to dance because I don't plan to sit here all night waiting for them to play a tango."

He laughs, "There won't be any tangos played here tonight, mi amor."

We make our way through the club and there is a remix of Gloria Estefan & The Miami Sound Machine's Conga playing and the place is jumping. The vibe of this club is intoxicating. I am completely mesmerized by this place. It is amazing. As we are walking to find a table, I can still feel people's eyes on us. First I thought it was because of Alejandro, but then I realize they are staring at me. I don't necessarily fit in here, and they don't seem to have any idea who I am. Alejandro is clearly enjoying all of this. We find a table and Alejandro excuses himself to get us some drinks. He must have judged by my reaction that I'm not too sure about him leaving me.

He pulls me to him and whispers in my ear so I can hear him over the music, "You will be fine, Victoria. I will be right back."

There is so much to see. The people, the clothing and the dancing – everything is just so colorful! There are couples of all ages here. So many different styles of Latin dance. I try to appear casual, but people are staring and some even pointing at me. Although I pretend not to notice, I do overhear someone comment that I look like the girl from the new Sonny de la Cruz video. They are playing old school Latin music as well as all the new Latin artists. It is all dance music and remixes. The energy in here is reminiscent of what I saw in Cali. The dancing is unstructured and raw. No one is judging them on proper stance or footing or hand placement. Nobody cares if their toes are pointed or flexed. There are no score-keepers or judges here. Just a pure, organic love of dance.The talent here is spectacular. When Alejandro returns with our drinks, he can quickly tell that I am loving this place.

This time I pull him to me and whisper, "You could have prepared me for this."

He whispers back, "I wanted you to be surprised."

"I am." I reply, a huge beaming smile breaking across my face.

He lets me watch and soak everything in for a few songs. I am having trouble sitting still. It's been a week since I danced and I can't contain myself! At the same time, I feel anxious about it. This isn't competition dancing. Will I stand out on the dance floor, too?

Then Alejandro leans in and asks if I'd like to dance.

He can tell I am a little hesitant. "Relax, you know how to dance," he assures me. "But, if you are wondering whether I can dance, let me assure you Victoria, I can."

I have never been so nervous or intimidated about stepping onto a dance floor. I have competed and performed in front of thousands of people the world over, but never in a settling like this. Cali was different. Javier and his friends were so warm and welcoming. I feel like an outsider here. I try to tell myself this no different from Mateo and I goofing off dancing together in the studio.

Alejandro yells over the music so I can hear him, "Victoria are you going to sit there all night or are we going to dance?" He is standing in front of me with his hand extended and I stand to take it.

There is no warm up or practicing here. Everyone will judge me as soon as I step out onto the floor. *Alejandro better know how to dance or I will kill him.* As we approach the dance floor the DJ is starting to blend the next song in and it's Ricky Martin's "La Bomba". I swear everyone in the club is staring. Alejandro does not seem the least bit concerned and seems very confident. Now if I don't fall in these heels it will be a miracle. Damn, now I know why he asked me about the shoes. I see some women pointing and staring at my shoes and I know what they are thinking. Does she really think she can dance in them? I am counting on Alejandro to lead and he better be good. I remember the first time I competed, if it wasn't for my dance partner leading me those first steps, I probably would still be standing there. Frozen.

The minute we step onto the dance floor, Alejandro slides his hand around my waist and takes my other hand, leaving me no room to change my mind. We are off and traveling this dance floor. Alejandro has completely shocked me. He *can* dance and is actually quite good. It feels natural to him. The heels are not a problem. Trust me, there are some things I do best and dancing in heels is one of them. I am known for wearing dangerously high heels in the dance circuit. I quickly learn I do not have to be worried about technique at all - I just need to feel the music and move naturally.

I have no problem keeping in time with him. When I say we are traveling the dance floor, I mean it. There's no specific pre-conceived pattern here – you just sweep in and out of people's way. Alejandro is whisking me effortlessly across the floor. I can tell everyone is watching, even the couples dancing among us. Within seconds I begin to relax, stop doubting myself, and turn it up a notch. It's what I do. There isn't a dancer here that could clear the floor and out dance me. Alejandro immediately senses how relaxed I become and steps it up himself. Of course he knows it isn't a challenge for me. Not only can I keep up – I can match him, move for move! My dancing progresses and builds with the music, and I am now in complete control. The people are no longer staring to see if I'm going to fall flat on face. They are staring at me, the dancer. I am in my element, and I love it.

When the songs ends, Alejandro pulls me in close and whispers, "I love how happy you are when you dance."

I whisper back, "Are there other talents you are hiding from me?" He laughs, pulls me closer and kisses me passionately. His kiss leave me feeling like a teenager on the first date. I can't stop the giggles. The stares from people watching Alejandro openly show me affection have me feeling like the sexiest woman in the building.

When we leave the dance floor, it is clear that I'm no longer an outsider. Now they are trying to figure out who this woman is coming into their club and taking over the floor. Back at our table, I take off the white blouse off. Alejandro laughs, smiling with approval. He can tell by my expression that I have no plans to sit still tonight.

Before we can return to the dance floor, a guy who appears to be in his early 20's approaches Alejandro and leans in to say something. I can't make out what he says. Then I hear Alejandro ask him, "Can you handle dancing with her?" This makes me laugh.

The guy tells Alejandro he promises to try his best.

"Victoria would you like to dance with this young man?" Alejandro inquires.

I love the confidence Alejandro has to allow me to dance with someone else. Without thinking or knowing anything about this young man, I agree. I have no idea what to expect. I did not notice him earlier, but then again, I was in my own world and Alejandro was along for the ride. I'm pretty sure he has no formal training. His dance style is what he has probably learned from dancing in clubs like this and from his parents.

As the DJ is blending the next song in, I stand with my hand extended, and he leads me to the dance floor. Daddy Yankee's hit "Limbo" is playing; a song I'm grateful to have danced to with Mateo during rehearsals. This song is much faster-paced song than the one I just danced to with Alejandro. I'm impressed to see the young dancer bob his head to the music counting the beats as we stand on the edge of the dance floor. He takes control on the first step. He is an aggressive dancer and not afraid to push me. But I have a few things I can teach him. I don't usually lead into moves but I want to see what this kid is capable of. Giving me back just enough control of the dance I decide to teach him a few things. Let's see if he can take direction.

Within moments, it is apparent to me that he is eager to learn and follow my lead. This young man is just what competitive Latin dancing needs. I decide to take him through what we call reverse samba rolls to see if he can follow me. He struggles through the first one but by the third one he has got it. Normally this move would take months -- even years for some dancers to learn, but he has the rare ability to feel his way through. A smile forms across his face, as he settles into the flow.

When the song ends he bows down to me over and over and pulls me to him to whisper in my ear, "Wow! You are amazing! Seriously, Miss. It was an honor to dance with you." Then I notice that everyone is on their feet, applauding us.

The rest of the evening is just as wonderful. Alejandro and I dance together several times. A handful of men ask if they can dance with me, as well. Happily, I oblige. Alejandro, I think, is very proud to be with me. Later in the evening, just when I think I may have a bit of a break, a man much older than the young men dancing in this club approaches our table. He smiles at me, and then turns to Alejandro. "May I have the pleasure of dancing with the reigning Queen of Latin dance?" *Ah*, I think to myself. *This one knows who I am.*

As we approach the dance floor he says, "It is such an honor to dance with someone from my world." The DJ plays an old school song: *Magalenha*, one of my favorites. His style of dance is more refined and measured, very much the style of dance that I am accustomed. He handles himself very well, even through the faster tempos of the song. He also takes a very firm lead. I am under his full control in this dance. By the end of the song, there is no one left on the dance floor. The entire club has stopped to watch us. It was one of the highlights of the night for me, and I think for him as well. It quickly spreads throughout the club exactly who I am. We dance very late into the night. It is one of the best nights of my life.

Before we leave, I ask the young man that first asked me to dance for his number. He seems confused but doesn't hesitate to give me his cell number. I tell him I would love to talk to him about dance. He says he is looking forward to hearing from me and would love to talk about more than just dancing with me.

On the drive home I cannot stop talking and thanking Alejandro for the wonderful evening. "It is the most fun I have had in years. You are seriously making me dread going back to New York!"

He raises an eyebrow and smiles. "I see my plan is working."

Back at the house I am so wired from dancing. I should be exhausted but it always has had the opposite effect on me. My body is in full adrenaline mode. I hope Alejandro is feeling the same way. I'm not ready for this evening to end.

"I don't know about you Victoria but I could use a shower. Would you like to join me?"

"Sounds great!" I reply.

Really Victoria? That's the best you could come up with? Why don't you tell this man the truth. More like, Oh fuck yes I want to shower with you! Hopefully the seductive grin on my face reveals what I'm really thinking. Honestly, I was tempted to suggest that we shower together. But I'm working on relinquishing control to Alejandro. Maybe he does have a dominant side! Hmm...this could turn out to be an interesting way to end the evening.

We make our way to his massive, amazing en suite and strip out of our clothes. I am granted several playful and sensuous kisses along the way. My mind is buzzing and my body is so hypersensitive. With every kiss and touch of his hands on my skin he takes me closer to where I want to be. It's time to let go and just let this man have his way with me.

Just when I feel myself let go and relinquish that control my delicious thoughts and desires are just that. Thoughts. Nothing more. I guess when he asked me to join him in the shower he meant just that. To shower. He is at one end and I am at the other end showering. This is not what I had in mind at all. The only contact between us has been him passing the shampoo and conditioner to me. I am not giving up on my fantasy. Time for a little show.

As we are rinsing the last of the shampoo and conditioner out of our hair I ask Alejandro to hand me the great smelling soap he uses. After he passes the bar to me I begin to lather my body. Sliding my hands over my skin I reach my breast and brush my fingers over the tips of my erect nipples. I begin to squeeze and pinch them. Rolling and pulling them. I purposely let out an audible seductive moan that rattles deep in my throat. Bending to run my hands over the length of my legs I turn my back to him. Taunting him with a great view of my ass.

It's his turn to moan and it's long and sexy as hell. An almost purring noise comes from deep within him. Before I have a chance to finish my little show he reaches out for me. Grabbing me by my elbows Alejandro swings me around and drags me towards him. He places me on the long bench. Before I know what is happening he has me positioned so my ass is on the edge of the bench and my legs are swung up over his shoulders. He doesn't ask for my permission as he leans in separating my folds with his long slender, elegant fingers. He then swipes his thick long tongue over my exposed clit.

"Este enthrone hermoso coño mío," as he continues to lick and suck.

Closing my eyes I smile to myself as I translate his words. I lean back against the tumbled stone of the shower submitting to him completely. I enjoy the cool feel of the stone against my skin. Reaching out I thread my fingers through Alejandro's wet hair attempting to draw him closer to me. I am desperate for release as I grind my sex against his delicious mouth. My body is covered in chill bumps from the divine feeling of his tongue assaulting my clit. Sensing that I am on the verge of coming, Alejandro takes two fingers and slides them deep turning and hooking them to find my g spot. My moans turn to whimpers. I am so close but can't seem to find my release. Alejandro leans back and demands of me, "Come for me Victoria. Come now mi bella reina preciosa."

Just like that, on command, I explode. I lose complete control of my body and senses. One of the most amazing and intense orgasms. I feel myself slipping into a blissful state. Fuck! What the hell just happened?

He lifts me up in his arms and rinses me off again. We step out and he grabs a big warm fluffy towel from the heated towel bar. Another thing I love in this bathroom. He even helped me blow dry my hair. It's certainly not something I am use to but I think I could get there if I would just open my heart to him. Before Alejandro dries himself off, he walks me into the bedroom, turns down the bed and motions me to get in. While standing at the foot of the bed drying off with a towel, Alejandro makes it apparent that sleep isn't on his agenda. "We are not going to get much sleep tonight, are we, Victoria?"

Propped up on one elbow, I jokingly give him the once-over like the valets at the club. "Well, you are the one that said you don't hurry your lovemaking," I tease back.

He laughs as he pulls back the sheets to get in bed. I owe him one for such a fabulous night. Oh and I owe him one for that mind blowing orgasm he just gave me. Before he can even approach me, I decide to make the first move. He is lying on his back, naked and clearly vulnerable to what I want to do next. Taking him by surprise, I straddle him. Immediately, he pulls me down to kiss me, but I place both hands on his firm chest, push him back and hold him down. I am surprised at how quickly he surrenders. I begin to kiss his neck. Then I kiss my way to his ears and whisper, "So, Mr. Perez, do you think you can let me drive just this once? Can you let me have control tonight? Hmmm?" I purr, kissing my way back down his neck.

"That depends on what you have in mind," Alejandro says with a nervous laugh.

"I'd like to return the pleasure you just gave me." The look on his face is confusing. "I will enjoy the process of giving you that pleasure." I answer, as I continue to torment and tease him with kisses up and down his neck and shoulders.

"You should know by now that I cannot resist you, Victoria." Alejandro replies in a low, soft, sexy voice.

"I assure you I will be completely satisfied by doing this for you and I do not want to be interrupted," I say, with a little authority in my voice. "Do you understand?"

I stop my kisses for a second, looking directly in his eyes. This makes him smile. "I completely understand," he tells me.

"Good," I say. "Now, I need *you* to lay back and just relax." I kiss his lips and let him explore my mouth with his tongue before I pull away and start kissing his neck again. It is no mystery that he is incredibly turned on already. I feel him get hard beneath me. My kisses travel the length of his neck, his chest, his abdomen. When I reach my destination, his cock is hard and ready. After some teasing and stroking I take him deep inside my mouth. He lets out a moan, jerks forward and grabs my shoulders.

I shake his hands from my shoulders and push him back down while I make my way back up his naked body. I whisper in his ear, "Please relax and let me do this for you." I see pleasure form in his eyes this time. He still does not look comfortable letting me have my way with him. I am beginning to think it's been a while since he has experienced this.

I start my way down again, kissing and licking his muscular stomach until I reach his cock. I take it in my hand and stroke the length of it as I kiss the head softly. When I take him in my mouth he moans and starts to pull back up, but this time he stops himself and lies back down. As I stroke and suck him gently, I can feel him relax as his breathing grows heavier and more labored. I begin to go faster, take him deeper and more aggressively. I can tell he is working to retain control, but I can hear the pleasure escape from his mouth as he begins to grind his hips upward. I know he is very close as he gently places his hands on my shoulders. As he comes, I take him as deep as I can into my mouth, forcing him to give up the fight to control his pleasure. Moaning, he grabs two fistfuls of my hair and pushes me to take him deeper still. I feel his entire body tense up until he finally lets go with a strong shudder. I take it all until he is finished. Then he releases my hair, pulls me up to his chest and holds me. Breathlessly, he whispers in my ear, "I have never experienced that kind of pleasure before, Victoria. That was amazing. You have no idea what you are doing to me." I can't help but smile into his chest. This man has the money and the power to buy whatever he wishes, yet he tells me I have just given him something he has never experienced.

I excuse myself to the bathroom to get some water. When I return, he wraps his arms around my waist and pulls me to him. There is no more talking. There is nothing more that needs to be said. Alejandro falls quickly to sleep with me wrapped lovingly in his strong arms.

Chapter 28

The next morning, I awake to an empty bed and the aroma of breakfast cooking. I'm not sure what's on the menu, but I definitely smell bacon. I'm famished, so I grab one of his T-shirts and pad all the way to the kitchen to find him standing in front of the cooktop, turning strips of bacon. On the buffet is a stack of blueberry pancakes, already buttered, and a bowl of the fluffiest scrambled eggs. Dressed in nothing more than black sweat pants he looks as delicious as the food he has laid out or us. His pants are slung low on his hips exposing the v's on his lean muscular body.

"How are you feeling this morning?" Alejandro asks, embracing me as he plants a sweet kiss on my lips.

"I have been dancing for years, but never have my feet hurt like this! Maybe I should have heeded your warning about my shoes," I joke. "Thank you again for the most fun I've had in such a long, long time"

"You are welcome, but I think I am the one that needs to thank you for a memorable evening. I apologize for falling asleep," Alejandro replies.

This makes me blush. "There is no need to apologize," I tell him with a smile. "Didn't I say I would get just as much pleasure as you?" His turn to blush.

Alejandro quickly recovers and changes the subject. "It's going to rain all day and I thought we would stay in and watch movies."

"I was beginning to wonder if this house even had any TV's." I say, grabbing a piece of bacon and nibbling on it.

"There are several," he laughs. "You just can't see them. One is behind the mirror in the bathroom and there's one that comes up from the foot of my bed. I also have a media room," he says. "But anyway, I thought we would also spend the day getting to know each other a little more intimately...like last night."

Maybe I am wrong! He *isn't* changing the subject, after all. "Would you like a repeat performance of last night?" I challenge, coyly.

Shaking his head, he says, "You are making it so very hard for me to let you go back to New York."

"Mr. Perez, did I just see you blush?" I tease.

While he finishes preparing breakfast I tell him I need to call the dancer from last night. I want to make him my protégé. Maybe groom him to be the next Latin Dance Champion.

"What about your partner Mateo?" he asks.

"The guy from last night is years away," I explain. "He has a raw talent, though. I'd love to see where I could take him, if he's interested."

I dial the number and it rings several times. Finally, he answers, quite rudely. "Who's this?" he says. I tell him my name is Victoria Moore, the woman he danced with last night.

"I danced with many women last night," he says flatly.

"Really?" I say. "As I recall, there was only one woman that kept up with you and taught you a few things herself."

The light bulb apparently switches on. "Ohhhh, yeah!" he exclaims. "The beautiful one they call the Queen? Hey! Sorry for being rude before. My name is Robbie Santos, by the way. Listen, how did a gringa from up north learn to dance like that, anyway?" he asks. I tell him one day I will share my story, and ask him if he is interested in learning competition style Latin dance. "Like that ballroom dancing shit?" he replies, abruptly, which makes me laugh. This boy is definitely rough around the edges. I explain to him the difference, but he doesn't seem to be very interested. He claims he doesn't have time. When I ask what it is that takes up all of his time, he tells me he works for a luxury car detail shop in the city. "What if I told you that you could make real money dancing and travel to places you only dreamed of – and some you've never even heard of?" I ask. "Well if that's true, yeah, I might be interested," he tells me, but when I mention working out a plan to get him some training, he cuts me off. "No disrespect, Miss, but I already know how to dance." I don't let the arrogance deter me. I know it comes from immaturity and lack of experience.

"There is a difference between dancing at the club and competing," I explain. "It will take discipline, but if you commit, I can make a champion out of you. I'm sure of it."

"Why me?" he asks. "There were a lot of good dancers out there last night. What's so special about me?"

His resistance is exhausting. Is he fishing for compliments? I don't enjoy games. I decided to say one more thing, and then leave the ball in his court. "Not one person in that entire club came close to the raw talent you possess. Don't question my instinct. But if you doubt that I'm capable of getting you there, do me a favor and pull me up on YouTube. Victoria Moore. Google it." I give him my phone number, and make him repeat it to me to be sure he's written it down. "So, when you call me next week – and I know that you will – we will see if I am the real deal. Until then, Robbie Santos," I say, then hang up the phone before he can utter a word.

After breakfast, I help Alejandro in the kitchen, washing dishes and tidying up. He tells me how much he loves to cook for me. "It's hard to find a woman who truly loves eating the way you do," he says. I guess most women are more conscious of what they eat, but I don't have that problem. One of the perks of being a dancer.

Even though it rains the entire time, my last day in Miami with Alejandro is perfect. As promised, we spend most of the day in his media room watching movies, telling each other stories and laughing. It is the most comfortable I have ever been and it seems he is equally at ease.

After we shower and get in bed, Alejandro seems a little pre-occupied. I ask him if there's something up, and he tells me in a very measured, serious voice that he does want to talk with me about something important. I swallow hard. I have no idea what this could be about. He clears his throat and begins by telling me how much this week has meant to him. "For the first time in years, I have enjoyed myself. I typically get so wrapped up in my work that I forget how to relax and have fun. But with you, it's just so simple." I open my mouth to say something but he puts his hand up and stops me. "Victoria, I don't want you to go back to New York," he says. "Ever."

I am stunned. "Alejandro, slow down."

And then, the man who always tells *me* to slow down can't seem to do it himself. "Victoria, I want you to move to Miami. You can live here with me. I don't want to be without you, not even for a day."

I can't believe what I am hearing. "Alejandro my life is in New York City. My time with you this past week has been amazing. This is all new to me, too. I have not been in a relationship for years. And dancing! Dance is my life! I have a studio to run and a title to defend."

"You can do all of that here!" he tells me. "I'm not asking you to change your path or who you are. Only your address."

"I don't want to rush things. I want us both to be sure. I know that long distance relationships can be challenging, but at this moment, that is all I can offer. But there is only one man who could ever make me want to leave New York – and that man is you, Alejandro. I just need time," I say, hoping my voice gives him the reassurance he needs.

His voice becomes even more serious and this time filled with doubt as he asks, "Is something there still stopping you. Or should I say someone?"

Oh shit! What the fuck do I say to that. I need to be honest with him and in reality, myself. How can I even think there this something or someone? There isn't.

There's certainly not *someone* that belongs to me. *That* someone belongs to another woman. *That* someone stood me up. That someone doesn't even think enough of me to call and tell me he's not coming. I need to move on. I need to stop fighting with all these emotions and open my heart to a man that is here and wanting me now.

"No, Alejandro. There is nothing stopping me. I just need some time to think things through. Please give me the space I need to make that decision." I say in a sincere, pleading voice.

Reaching across the bed Alejandro pulls me into his arms and his lips descend onto mine. His kiss is warm and comforting. But that's not what I want. Wrapping my hands around his neck I pull him closer. I deepen the kiss. It's my tongue that takes over control. He softly sighs and relinquishes control. I want him to feel the need and desire I have for him.

I pull my body from his warm, tight embrace. Placing my hands on his upper arms I push him down into the mattress. Then straddling him I take complete control. I position my hands against his chest for support. I lean in and whisper in his ear, "My love, have no doubt that I want you. Let me show you how much this week has meant to me. Lay back, relax, and just enjoy the ride."

I remove one of my hands from his chest and wrap it around his very hard, erect cock stroking it a few times. He relaxes and closes his eyes. A deep erotic sounding moan escapes his lips. I raise my body up just enough so I can position the swollen head of his cock at my entrance. Slowly and seductively I slide onto him. I don't stop or hesitate until I am completely filled. I give us both a few seconds to enjoy how damn good this feels before I start to move. Raising my body I slide his dick in and out of my greedy pussy. Sitting back just a bit, I settle into a sultry, slinky paced rhythm. In this position I am able to use my hands to caress and squeeze my breast. A soft purring moan is all I can verbalize as I pinch and pull my nipples. My purring moans turn into whimpering sounds. Alejandro continues to relax allowing me complete control as I ride him. Throwing my head back, I close my eyes and get lost in this feeling.

Pulling me from my hypnotic trance Alejandro says in a begging tone, "Victoria, I'm close. Come with me. I need you with me."

I feel his cock swell inside me. Fuck! I know his release is close. Sliding one hand down I begin to massage my swollen clit with my finger tips. Within seconds I feel my orgasm starting to build. I increase the rhythm. Riding him harder. Intent on bringing us both to fruition. My heavy breathing fills the room as the first wave of my impending orgasm tears through me. Alejandro jerks up to an almost sitting position as he yells out my name over and over again clinging to me as he empties his hot seed into me. Pulling Alejandro closer, I ride out the rest of my orgasm.

Several minutes pass. Still wrapped in each other's arms Alejandro says, "I meant what I said. I need you with me. Here in my Miami. In my bed. Every night. Please, Victoria."

I remain silent enjoying the moment. Pondering what to say to ease his need for me. My mind drifts. Even after this intense, beautiful moment between us thoughts of Sonny invade my head. Why now?

Pulling me from my thoughts Alejandro reminds me, "Just like I told you in Caracas, in the interim, I'll be doing everything I possibly can to ensure that you decide to move to Miami to live with me." I have seen the persuasive side of Alejandro Perez. I am quite sure he is not joking at all.

Time to lighten up the mood. "Now that the serious talk is out of the way, can we have some fun?" I ask, peppering his neck with kisses.

I think he's relieved as he smiles and asks, "Victoria, what do you have in mind?"

"I would love some ice cream!" I tell him.

"Ice cream, huh?" he teases back.

"Yes, ice cream! Does that fancy refrigerator have any ice cream in it?" My turn to tease him.

"As a matter of fact it does. And I can do better than just plain old ice cream. I'll make you an ice cream sundae."

"Oh Mr. Perez! Ice cream sundae's! Would there be some hot fudge to go with that?" I squeal out in delight.

"It wouldn't be an ice cream sundae without the hot fudge." Lifting me off him he pulls us both from the bed. "Let's get you cleaned up. Then ice cream sundae's."

After a hot fudge sundae, with bananas and a cherry on top it's time for bed. Wrapped up in his arms, just before falling asleep, Alejandro whispers to me. "This is where you belong every night, Victoria. Good night, my love."

The next morning I am jolted awake by another dream about Sonny. In a panic I am having trouble catching my breath. Once my body catches up with my mind I realize Alejandro is not in bed. I hear him in the bathroom. Thankful I don't have to explain what has shaken me so. I try to recollect exactly what the dream was about, but I can't remember. Only that it has left me with another inexplicably eerie feeling.

As soon as Alejandro steps out of the bathroom, he notices the look on my face and rushes over. "Victoria, what's wrong? What happened? Are you all right?" I guess there was no hiding how this dream has upset me.

"I am fine. Nothing happened. It's silly really." I say trying to assure him. "I was just scared when you were not next to me when I awoke." I lie to him.

He pulls me into his arms and just holds me. As my breathing begins to return to normal and my body relaxes into his he whispers, "It's not silly to me. Please consider moving to Miami. I don't want you to ever wake up without me. Right here is where you belong."

"Slow down, Alejandro." I need to think of something quick. After the dream I just had I can't be talking about uprooting my life and moving to Miami. It's all just too much, too fast. Desperately trying to change the subject I use the one thing I know will change the mood. Sex!

"Well lover boy! Since it's my last few hours in Miami maybe you should be thinking of something that will change my mind." I say in a seductive voice.

Still with his arms around me holding me close he throws back his head and laughs, "Lover boy? Really?" Pausing, his tone changes and his voice comes out dripping of sexiness. "What did you have in mind, Victoria?"

Giggling I try, without success, to squirm my way out of his arms. "Oh no! I'm not giving you any ideas. You want me in Miami? Then convince me to stay."

"Convince you? No. Let me show you." Pulling me close so he can pepper sweet, soft kisses up my neck, he stops when he reaches my ear and nips at my earlobe. This man is quickly learning my weaknesses and turn ons.

Setting his eyes on me he whispers, "I'm going to show you to the point you will be begging to never leave my bed." The look in his eyes was so intense. I swear I stopped breathing for a few seconds. I could feel my pussy tingle. I knew I was wet. I turn my head to break the stare between us but Alejandro grabs my chin pulling me back to his lust filled eyes.

"No. Eyes on me. When I am done showing you I want to see the satisfied look in those eyes. I want to burn that look to my memory so I never forget this moment." He says in an almost purring tone to his voice.

Oh fuck! I am so screwed. Those fucking turquoise eyes. I swear they turn the deepest, most gorgeous shade when he is aroused. Staring into them I get lost, give in and submit to his demand.

"Good girl. I want you to lie back and relax. But don't take your eyes off mine. Do you understand Victoria?"

Fuck! I can't think straight let alone answer him so I just nod my head in agreement, never taking my eyes away. Laying me back Alejandro adjusts the pillows behind me so I am almost sitting up. After he is satisfied with the position he settles himself between my legs spreading them open. He waste no time showing me how much he wants me to stay. Spreading my lips open with those long slender fingers he leans in swiping his tongue across my swollen clit. His eyes never leave mine. He works his magic by flattening his tongue as he glides it across my clit applying just the right amount of pressure. He is relentless and I feel the orgasm already building inside of me. Just as I throw my head back and shut my eyes lost in complete ecstasy he stops. Fuck! My eyes fly open pulling me away from my bliss. I return my focus to his eyes. "Good girl. Don't do that again. Eyes on me." He demands in a low sexy as sin voice.

This time he uses his delicious full lips on my clit. Sucking on it and nipping it with his teeth. I can't hold back any longer as the most amazing, satisfying orgasm rips through my entire body. My breathing is out of control. I hadn't even noticed my fingers twisting and pulling my nipples. I was so focused on his eyes, I forgot where I was.

Before my body can recover from the breathtaking orgasm he brings himself up over me sliding his cock easily into my hot, wet pussy. The feeling is exquisite. Still his eyes never leave mine. He begins a slow, steady grinding of his hips as he slides his cock in and out. His stare is intense and filled with passion and lust. It's so damn sexy. I fall deeper under his spell. His movements are flawless and riveting. The moment is so fervent I feel the tears sting my eyes. It's almost too overwhelming and I feel the need to look away and break the connection.

"No, Victoria. Don't you dare. Eyes on me." Alejandro says through gritted teeth.

How the hell did he know what I was thinking? It's as though he was inside my head and had my heart in his hand. Blinking away the tears I return his gaze. He increases his strokes and I feel another orgasm building. Using my hands I pull his hips to mine as he grinds against my sex. I wrap my legs around him pulling him closer. Grinding my clit against him with each stroke. Arching my back off the pillows I pull

Alejandro to me and our foreheads are now touching. Our stare never breaking. My orgasm is the first to detonate. Then his erupts chasing right after mine with each grinding stroke. The sound of our heavy breathing and the scent of pure lust fills the room as we both begin to descend from our shared bliss. Tears are sliding down my cheeks. There are no words needed. Alejandro is right. This moment will be burned into my memory as well.

Breaking the intense bond Alejandro captures my lips and slides his tongue in. Lavishing me with several passionate, all too consuming, kisses before pulling out. The silence between us is getting uncomfortable. At least for me. I am at a loss for words. As if it could feel the awkwardness, my stomach rumbles. We both start laughing. The laughing becomes uncontrollable as Alejandro pulls me out of bed hauling me over his shoulder.

"You would think after all the treats you had last night and then again this morning you would be satisfied. But it's seems my girl is hungry. Let me make you breakfast." He says roaring with laughter as he carries me into the shower.

The mood has definitely shifted, but the need for Alejandro to prove he wants me here in Miami hasn't. We both know what just happened was a game changer. During our shower he washes every inch of my body. The oversized shower is filled with his essence. It's a delicious modern blend of citrus, floral and sensual musk. He continues to caress my body. Just his touch is becoming my new kryptonite. He has also burned into his memory what turns me on and he is definitely using it to his advantage. Swaying me with his loving touch he fondles my breast, pinching and pulling at my sensitive nipples. All the while lavishing me with the most luscious kisses up and down my neck.

"I can't let you go. I won't let you go. I want to start everyday like this. With you my arms. Let me show you how good it can be." He says in a sexy voice. Moaning against his neck I give in and my need to feel him inside me has me behaving like a wanton, desperate woman. Grinding my body against his semi hard cock. I want him to know how badly I want him. I'm rewarded with a satisfied moan.

His next move totally catches me off guard, "I want you on your knees. I want those gorgeous, sexy lips wrapped around my cock." Pushing ever so gently on my shoulders. I drop to my knees. Taking his cock in my hand I stroke him until he is rock hard. I am eager and ravenous as I take his shaft in my mouth. First teasing him by circling my tongue over the slit before taking him deep. Alejandro begins to thrust forward with his hips as I allow him to fuck my mouth. The moment of absolute intimacy has me forgetting I have a flight back to NYC. The way he is pumping deep into my throat has me forgetting everything and anything that would stop me from returning to Miami. I need him. I crave the control he is casting over my body.

Precipitously he pulls his cock from my throat. Grasping my shoulders he hauls me up into his arms. His voice is deep, controlled and filled with dominance as he whispers what he wants, "Turn around and go to the bench. I want you on your hands and knees with your ass in the air for me." It takes me a few seconds to register what he wants. Sensing my confusion he guides me to the bench and helps me into position. Completely lost and caught up in the moment a whimpering cry escapes as Alejandro slams his cock into me. He takes one of his arms circling it around my waist pulling my body up to meet his. Then taking his other arm he wraps it around my shoulders and buries his face into my neck whispering, "You have ruined me. You have danced your way into my life and into my heart. You have awakened something in me. Something I haven't felt for a long time. I need you Victoria." Moving his hand that's was wrapped around my waist he slowly glides his fingers across my very sensitive sex. A needful moan escapes my lips and I cry out, "Make me come, Alejandro. Please." Jutting my hips out I silently beg him to stoke my clit. Sliding his fingers in between the folds, he begins a slow, seductive assault on my clit. Whispering over and over again, "Mi reina let me show you how good I can make it ."

After a few minutes, I am lost to another place. I lose track of everything as

Alejandro pounds his hard cock into me. It feels so damn good. Eager for my release I throw my hips back to meet his strokes. Both of our bodies tightened as we soar towards our impending orgasms. His cock swelled and my pussy clenched milking him for everything. The hair on the back of my neck stood up and my entire body shivered as my orgasm rocked through me. Alejandro collapsed on top of me wrapping both of his arms around me. He then turned and sat down on the bench placing me on his lap and cuddling me close.

"You really are trying to convince me to stay aren't you Mr. Perez." I say trying to catch my breath.

"How am I doing?" He asked, while trying to bring his own breathing under control.

"Great. Really great."

"Good. Now let's get is out of this shower before we both shrivel up like a couple of prunes."

Leaving me wrapped in a towel he pads off to his closet to pull on a T-shirt and jeans. He comes back to ask me what I would like for breakfast and all I can concentrate on are his bare feet. I never noticed until now how sexy they are. Before leaving me he tells me we will have breakfast out on the lanai. While I am getting dressed he goes down to cook. When I join him the rain is long gone and has left us with a beautiful blue sky. Another thing I miss about Florida living. It can be pouring down one minute and then a minute later the sun will be shining so brightly you forget it ever rained. I forgot how much I enjoyed the feel of the Florida sun against my skin. He has made me fresh squeezed orange juice all week -- I could really get used to this. It's the first time in years that I have even considered returning to Florida. I guess I have busied myself so much with dance and competing that I never really took the time to even think about all the things I have been missing.

Then it happens. Alejandro is reading the entertainment section of the newspaper. Just as I take a bite of cantaloupe, he mumbles to himself, but out loud, "Oh no. I can't believe this." As if I am not even here, he continues to read and mumble. "This does not sound good, not at all," he says. I ask him what it is he's reading, then he reads the headline to the story out loud.

"Latin Singer Collapses at Home in Los Angles." He pauses for a second, and continues. "Latin music artist Sonny de la Cruz collapsed at his home in Los Angeles last week. He was preparing to leave for a business trip to New York City last Tuesday when he became ill and had to be rushed to the hospital. Preliminary tests indicate kidney failure. Doctors have only revealed that de la Cruz has contracted a rare virus that has attacked his kidneys and other parts of the singer's body. A kidney transplant is imminent. If his condition does not improve, doctors say he may not even benefit from the operation. They have placed him on an emergency transplant list. Before the transplant can take place they have to rid his body of the virus before it does further damage. His PR manager, Armando Diaz, kept this information from the press until they were sure what Sonny was facing. Diaz is asking everyone for their prayers at this time for the Latin singer. He is hopeful and optimistic that de la Cruz will make a complete recovery."

Thank God Alejandro had the newspaper in front of him. I remain quiet, but my face is telling another story. I can feel panic building inside me. My forehead beads up with sweat, and my hands are trembling. I feel as though I may have an anxiety attack. I try to calm myself down and recover as much as I can before he notices. I can't get any words to come out of my mouth because it has gone completely dry. My stomach is churning and I'm afraid I may vomit.

Alejandro continues to read the newspaper and make comments. "I feel bad about this. I know we have had our differences since my divorce but I have always liked Sonny. He is a good man and an amazing artist. I almost feel sorry for even Maria having to go through this."

Somehow I finally get words to form. "I'll be right back. I need some water." When I get to the kitchen, I am close to hyperventilation and fighting back the tears.

Sonny did not stand me up, after all! He has been sick – deathly ill – all this time! There was no way for him to call and let me know what happened to him. Fuck! I knew something was wrong. I could feel it. My whole body is trembling and I can feel the tears welling up in my eyes. I have to get a hold of myself before Alejandro notices. I go to the bathroom and splash water on my face. Then I grab my sunglasses to cover my eyes before I head back out to the lanai.

When I return Alejandro asks me, "Where is your water?"

"Oh, that," I say, nervously. "I just needed a drink of water and I wanted to get my sunglasses." Thank God my flight is in a few hours. I don't know how long I can keep up this charade. What I really want to do is get online and see if I can find out more about Sonny's condition. I can't concentrate on anything. I am trying hard to appear as though nothing is wrong, but inside, my whole heart is breaking. I could win an Academy Award for my performance. My mind is racing as I try to remember verbatim what Alejandro read to me.

"I hate to even mention this since my trip to Miami has been so amazing.I need to pack and get ready for my flight. Thank you for another delicious breakfast." I say rising from my chair while grabbing my plate to help clear the table. I am relieved when we get back inside the house and he tells me he has some work to do while I pack.

Perfect, I can be alone. When I get to the bathroom, I notice Alejandro has put on some music. As soon as I shut the door, I feel myself getting sick. I kneel before the toilet just in time. When I can't throw anything else up, I sink to the floor and begin to sob. The crying becomes uncontrollable. I am hoping the music is drowning it all out. *I have to get a grip here.* All this time, I simply thought he didn't care. But all the while he was lying in a hospital, fighting for his life. After several minutes, I find the strength to pull myself together, wash my face, brush my teeth, and finish packing.

After a short while, Alejandro comes in to tell me it's time to leave for the airport. He has his driver take us. I try to keep my focus on Alejandro on the way to the airport, in spite of all the emotions and concern I am feeling for Sonny. I do want Alejandro to know how much I enjoyed myself and how wonderful it was spending time together. I can't help but wonder how all this could potentially change my feelings about Alejandro. Until this morning, *he* was the center of my world and Sonny De la Cruz, a distant memory.

Alejandro uses the drive to the airport to tell me he will be working hard to make sure I return to Miami very soon, and permanently. At the airport things become uncomfortable for me. I'm not sure what to say. My head is spinning and I feel like I am going to have another anxiety attack. Taking a deep breath, I try to calm myself. Alejandro notices my uneasiness and gathers me in his arms. He buries his face in my neck and whispers in my ear, "Stop overthinking everything. Open your heart to me. Come back to me." Tears threaten to spill down my cheeks. His words aren't soothing like I had hoped. More confusion fills my already overfilled mind. I welcome the airline personnel's interruption informing us the lines are long at the security check-in area and I really need to head there. They will be calling my flight soon for boarding.

We say our final goodbye at the security check with a long passionate kiss. Just like the one I gave him when I arrived. I struggle as I etch in my memory the feeling of his lips and how they feel against mine. I don't want to forget how safe I feel being held in his arms. I want to remember his smell and those amazing turquoise eyes. I'll need these memories as I sort out what the future holds. Before releasing me he whispers one final time, "I hate letting you go back to New York. I want you here with me in Miami. I hope you will miss my arms around you tonight and realize that *this* is where you belong. Call me when you land. I need to know you are home safe."

"Yes I'll call. I promise." The tears return and I'm thankful to be wearing sunglasses. I wonder if I will ever return to Miami.

While I am waiting to board, I notice there is a Latin news station on the television. A news report comes on about Sonny de la Cruz. It's the same information that Alejandro read to me from the newspaper. I need *more* information. Thank God they are calling for us to board.

When the pilot gives the all clear for us to use our electronic devices, I begin to scour the web. I do find one Latin entertainment website that has an updated statement from his management team. They say that Sonny is resting comfortably with his wife at his side. They ask that everyone please join them in prayer for a complete recovery. I find myself praying silently.

On the taxi drive drive back to my loft, I battle whether or not I should call Alejandro and let him know that I have arrived safely. I promised him I would. Sonny is weighing heavy on my mind and I am not sure if I want to talk to anyone right now. But my heart wins. As I pull my cell phone out to make the call, it rings. I immediately recognize the number. It's Alejandro. As I answer, I take a deep breath and try to sound calm and happy to hear from him.

"I hope you are missing me as much as I am missing you." Alejandro says before I can even say hello.

"It's only been a few hours since I left, but I have to admit I am dreading being alone tonight. I am going to miss your arms wrapped around me," I reply.

"It makes me very happy to hear that mi bella reina preciosa. Maybe after a few nights alone you will realize where you need to be and what you are missing."

I can't help but giggle and blush when I mentally translate in my head his comment referring to me as his beautiful, lovely queen. "Oh, I know what I will be missing. I just need some time to be sure it is what I want," I tell him.

"What are you saying? You are not sure you want me?" He sounds concerned.

"No, Alejandro, that's not what I meant. I just need to make sure Miami is where I want to live. I already know that I want you. Please give me the time I need to make the right decision for me." I say, trying to soothe his concerns and buy myself some time.

"I will give you the time. But let me remind you I have an apartment and offices in New York as well. Just like your time in Cali, I will be reminding you from time to time what is waiting for you mi bella reina preciosa."

"Thank you. I promise I will not make you wait very long. I just need to work out a few things. Right now I need to get unpacked and settled back in again. I'll talk to you later, okay?"

"Of course, Victoria," he says. "I will be thinking about you tonight while I am alone in that big bed. Goodbye, mi amor."

I'm so thankful to be back at my apartment. I am missing Alejandro, but my mind is on Sonny. It's not good for me to be alone tonight. I have no one to talk to about this and I really need it. I could use some advice or even a distraction. As I climb into bed, my cell rings and my heart begins to race. When I answer, the tears begin to fall. It's Javier. He knows about Sonny and me.

"Oh my God, Victoria. It's all over the news media here in Cali." You can hear the true concern in his voice. I know the concern is for me.

"Javier, are they broadcasting anything different in the Cali news media than what is being reported here?" I ask but he has nothing more than what I already know.

"There are fans being interviewed saying they would give him a kidney if they were a match." He adds trying to make me feel better.

Javier and I talk for over two hours. I tell him about my relationship with Alejandro and about the week I'd just spent with him in Miami. He urges me to focus on that relationship.

"I warned you once about Latin men. You need to forget about Sonny. He belongs to another woman. He will never leave her. You should be chasing something that has a future. Not stolen moments." His voice is filled with concern.

"Don't you think I get that? I just wish I could get my heart to understand it. Thank you, Javier. Your call came at a time when I really needed to talk to someone. I have no one else I can talk to about this."

"I will pray for Sonny. If you need to talk please don't hesitate to call me." Before hanging up I make him promise to call if he hears anything reported there. No matter what time of day it is. We hang up and again I am alone.

The tears and emptiness return.

When I arrive in the office the next morning, Ashley is ecstatic to see me. But her face falls as she picks up on my mood.

"Victoria, I thought when I saw you this morning you would be glowing with happiness, but you look so sad. What's going on? " she asks.

I give her the safe story – tell her I'm missing Alejandro and I had such a great time that I really didn't want to leave. *If she only knew the truth*, I think to myself. She tells me she wants all the details over lunch. She is going to order something because we have a lot of business to catch up on. It's good to be back and busy because it helps keep my mind occupied, and free from worrying about Sonny. I can't help thinking that if something happens to him I will never get the chance to say goodbye. My mind occasionally drifts and I wonder if he thought about me sitting here that night waiting for him or what I'm thinking now that the news has broken about his illness. I don't know if he is even well enough to be aware of anything. Is he trying to figure out a way to call me and reach out to me? Does he even care? I only know what we have shared. Maybe I am nothing more to him than a woman he fucks. Then I think back when he came to see me the first time. How he told me I even haunt his dreams. I try to assure myself that *he* came to *me* first and told me how he was feeling. That he doesn't turn his back on his feelings. Look at me, trying to convince myself that any of this matters.

I shake my thoughts and get back to work. "Ashley, I need you to get Mateo on the phone."

She let's me know when Mateo is on line two. Before I can even get a word out he says, "I was going to call you today Baby Girl." In a reserved, concerned tone, he continues "I'm not going to be able to do the workshop circuit with you as we'd planned this season. My foot has been giving me problems again. The doctor has told me if I want to compete this year I have to stay off of it. If I don't do as the doctor says I will need surgery and could be out a full year."

"I understand. You need to do everything the doctor says."

"How was your trip to Miami?" He seems eager to change the subject.

"I see Ashely has been running her mouth again!" I reply, with sarcasm thick in my voice, "Miami was amazing. I had a wonderful time. We went to this club to dance and I met this young dancer named Robbie Santos. Just a kid from Miami. But the talent he has is off the charts. I think with proper training he could really be a threat to the professional Latin dance world in a few years."

"Baby Girl you are crazy to even think you can take a kid with no formal dance training and make him into a dancer for one, and for two that he could compete at our level. Especially a street kid with attitude."

"You haven't seen him dance, Mateo. I have. Do I need to remind you how I became a dancer? I'm happy I didn't meet you years ago when I first wanted to train." My tone of voice lets him know it's futile to argue with me when I set my mind on a project.

"Are you going to bring this street dancer to New York to train?"

"I'm not sure what the plan is just yet. I am still working out the details." We go back and forth on Robbie for a few moments, and in the end, Mateo relents as usual. He tells me to let him know once I've figured things out.

Next, I have Ashley get Ken on the phone. "Where the hell have you been?" are the first words out of his mouth.

"It's only been a week, Ken! Calm your ass down. " I say in a teasing tone.

"Did you hear about Sonny de la Cruz?" He blurts out with great concern in his voice.

"Of course I have. It's been ll over the entertainment news shows as well as every social media site. Do you know anymore than what they are all reporting?" I ask cautiously trying not to sound overly worried.

"No. But I thought about calling Sonny's management offices, but after the ass chewing I gave them regarding the album cover, I doubt they'd return my call, much less tell me anything."

To change the subject, I bring up the young dancer. Ken also has doubts about me having much success with this kid. I do my best to sell Ken on my idea that he could become a real contender in the Latin dance world.

Before he responds, I tell him, "His aggressive style of dance has something new and refreshing to offer. He has a personality that truly sets him apart. He is just what the professional Latin dance world needs. A true breath of fresh air."

Ken pauses, and after a deep breath, he says, "I will see what I can do on my end to get this kid into some formal training classes in Miami. I have some connections there. I think it's best not to bring him here, at least not now." I give him Robbie's name, number and age. Ken says he sounds like a real piece of work but will do what he can.

"I just hope your intuition is on the mark with this one." He says with doubt in his voice. Before we hang up, he promises to call me in a few days with some plans for my new protégé.

A few hours later Ashley buzzes me to tell me our lunch has arrived. I realize I haven't eaten anything since breakfast yesterday before I left Miami. My appetite disappeared when I heard about Sonny. Ashley is excited to have some quality time with me and wants to hear everything about my trip and Alejandro.

"Tell me everything, Victoria. Don't leave any details out about your trip to Miami. Okay, wait, you can spare me the sex stories. But I'm sure Mateo would love to hear them." Ashley is perched on the edge of her chair just waiting for me to spill my guts.

In between scarfing down the delicious chicken caesar salad I divulge most of the details. I tell her it was amazing, trying to make sure I share all the wonderful things we did while sparing her the sex stories. She loved hearing about the spa day we shared at the Mandarin Oriental Hotel. I wait till the end of sharing to leave the best detail for last.

"Alejandro wants me to come live with him in Miami!" I blurt out. My voice is filled with excitement and apprehension. I can't believe I just shared that with her.

In an instant she gushes, "I am so ready for sunshine! Wearing flip-flops to work every day sounds very appealing."

Before I can say anything, she looks at me very seriously and says, "If you think for one minute I am going to stay here, you are crazy." She talks about how easily I can open a studio in Miami just like I did in here in New York. For the first time since the subject was ever brought up, I start to agree. All that raw talent I saw at the clubdancing that night! I could really do something big there.

Ashley's next question comes right out of left field. "Victoria, be honest with me.Are you in love with Mr. Perez?" Nervously, I laugh, and tell her it's just a little too early to be using the L word. "But," I add, "he is someone I think I really could fall in love with." That statement just dangles in the air a moment, as Ashley scrambles to change the subject once again.

She brings up the news about Sonny de la Cruz, asking if I'd heard about his illness. I tell her I'd just learned of it yesterday, and then I tell her who Alejandro's ex wife is. She finds this every bit as shocking as I did when I first learned of it. "It really is a small world, huh Victoria?" she says. "Like you always say, we are all connected in some way." She can't help but point out that I sure seem sad for someone who claims to have had such a great time in Miami. I quickly put on a fake smile. "I have a lot on my mind right now, that's all," I tell her.

To be truthful, though, the only thing I have on my mind is Sonny. I know it should be Alejandro. But try telling that to my heart. This whole situation I have gotten myself into is so fucked up. In my craziest of thoughts I even consider calling his offices, telling them who I am and asking how he is doing. Maybe I could even try to get a message to him. But who am I kidding here? I can't do that. They probably wouldn't even talk to me. I don't know what to do. What I do know is that I feel like an outsider right now. Not knowing anything is practically killing me.

It's time for me to shut out everything from my mind. I just want to sleep. Pulling on a t-shirt with my panties seems odd after sleeping nude all week with Alejandro, with nothing but his arms wrapped around me.

As I climb into bed, my cell phones rings. Grabbing it I silently pray it's Sonny. As I check the screen though I see it's Alejandro. I stare at the phone for a few seconds debating. Should I answer? I swipe my finger across the screen and accept the call.

"Buenas noches, Alejandro."

"Buenas noches, mi bella reina preciosa."

"I was just getting in to bed."

"Good. Then I'll be the last thing on your mind as you drift off to sleep."

"You don't give up do you?" I say in a joking voice.

"Like I told you before Victoria. I go after what I want and I want you. Here in Miami, in my bed with my arms wrapped around you."

His last comment has me blushing and I can feel the heat flush in my cheeks. "I just need time Alejandro. Please? Can you give me that?" I ask in a pleading voice.

"Take all the time you need. I'm not going anywhere. I'll be waiting. When you close your eyes tonight think about this past week. Think about the nights I spent making love to you. Think about how it felt going to sleep wrapped my arms."

With an exasperated sigh I say, "Okay. Okay. No wonder you own the world's largest Latin recording company. Who would ever tell you no? I do miss you. Sweet dreams Alejandro."

"Good night, Victoria," pausing he adds before hanging up, "I'll be dreaming of you."

Fuck! Fuck! Fuck! I absentmindedly say out loud. I have never felt as out of control of my life than I do at this very moment. This is not me. This is not who I am. Since Blake's death I've had everything under control. I was focused and knew what I wanted. I *wanted* my career. I *wanted* to be number one. Now my heart is telling me it needs more.

My life has taken a 180 degree turn over the past months. I shut myself off from allowing a man in my life and now I find myself with two men-two very different men. Alejandro wants me to open my heart to him. He wants me to be a part of his life. He could be my everything. Sonny wants nothing more than to share my bed. I have become a slave to his touch. To a married man's touch. I feel like I'm drowning when I'm with him and yet I feel so alive. I know the dreams I had in Miami were trying to tell me something. How can I entertain the idea of moving to Miami when I'm not sure where my relationship with Sonny stands. Relationship? *Really?* I don't even know what to call it. I need to figure things out before I go insane. I need to hear from Sonny; to know he is going to be okay. I need to know where I stand in his life.

My heart has been torn in half. It's like fate is playing a cruel joke on me. Two very different men each hold a half in their hand. I need to stop thinking about how stupid I was to allow both of these men into my life and worry more about how to let one go. I can't continue to have both in my life. It's so wrong. I know this isn't some kind of fairytale, but I want my happy ending. I want a life filled with breathless moments.

There is no stopping the pain that has flooded my heart. I can ignore it all I want, but I know exactly what it is. There is no denying it and I owe no one an explanation, after all, you can't change what the heart wants. I'm just not sure I'll survive this one. It wasn't meant to turn out this way. I deserve to love again.

It will take every trick in the book for me to try and get some sleep tonight.

I know in the morning the reality will be there waiting for me as it always is. Mornings are always the hardest.

The end of book one.

1. Addicted Enrique Iglesias

2. Conga Gloria Estefan & Miami Sound Machine

3. Dance Again Jennifer Lopez featuring Pitbull

4. Esto Es Vída Draco Rosa

5. First Love Jennifer Lopez

6. The Heart Wants What It Wants Selena Gomez

7. Limbo Daddy Yankee

8. La Bomba Ricky Martin

9. Magalenha Sergio Mendes

10. Paraíso Prometido Draco Rosa

11. Bon, Bon Pitbull

12. You've Got the Love Florence + The Machine

13. What Now Rihanna

14. P'ra Ti" by To' Semedo

15. Slave to Love Bryan Ferry

16. Mágico Mika Mendes

17. Precious Annie Lennox

18. Hip Hip Chin Chin Club des Belugas

19. Hold On, We're Going Home Drake

20. Make Me Like You Gwen Stefani

ACKNOWLEDGEMENTS

Thank you for reading Steps of the Heart First Dance. I hope you enjoyed the first book in the series. I have said this from the beginning I am not an author. I am a story teller. Thank you for letting me share my story with you.

There are so many people I need to thank for coming along on this crazy journey with me. To my husband Sig who has been my biggest support, I love you. I remember the day I lost three hours of writing and even though he knew nothing about the clouds he was sure my iPad had saved my work some where in the clouds. Thank you for the trip to Miami so I could do book research and for supporting me every step of this journey. Thank you for loving me unconditionally and always believing I could finish this.

To my friends at work who were there from the beginning. Patti, Chandra, Randy, Ashley, Victoria, Ann, Astrid, Liz, Joanie,

Genka, Louise, and Stacy. There are so many I'm sure I have forgotten someone. Thank you for listening to my crazy story ideas and helping me come up with character names. Genka thank you for answering all my dance questions. Patti H. thank you for never once telling me to shut the fuck up because you were tired of hearing about my book. Randy R., thank you my sweet friend for going to see Draco with me and always being such a great support. Stacy F. I am so thankful you were with me that day I needed support the most. Thank you for the hugs. Without all you I would have given up. I love you all!

Thank you to my beta readers Allison and Sue. Allison you really went over and above the call of duty for me!

Scott and Stevie B. thank you for being you! Stevie B. thank you for helping me come up with a title for the book and the series. Scott thank you for the beautiful promotional video for Steps of the Heart. Thank you both for your support and hilarious promotion videos for my cover reveal event.

To my amazing and beautiful sisters Debbie and Pam thank you for reading the first rough drafts of Steps of the Heart. Thank you for your kind, supportive words and for begging me for more chapters. I love you both.

To my mentor and friend Al Daltrey, I remember the day I received an email from you thanking me for my review of your first book Testing the Submissive. I am so very thankful for that introduction. You Mr. Daltrey are the true definition of a mentor. Thank you for answering my countless, stupid email questions and always offering advice and encouragement.

To my sweet friend Tiffany Huegele thank you for understanding and bringing my vision to reality for the cover of Steps of the Heart First Dance. You nailed it. It's gorgeous.

Thank you Alexandria Sure for believing in me and featuring me in your first book Before Him Comes Me. I will be forever grateful for your kindness.

To my dear friend Laura thank you for everything! I know Steps of the Heart is a part of you! I love you!

A very special thank you to Maria Martinez. Maria, you were an angel sent to me. Without you I would have walked away. Thank you for teaching me how to become a better writer. I will always remember our first phone conversation. I had to learn to trust you and dig deep to give you what you wanted. Thank you for pushing me, believing in me and loving my story.

Thank you to everyone on Facebook that has helped with promoting the book by sharing teasers and the cover. Big shout out to Mandy S., Britt G., Serena W., Diane H. You girls rock!

As you know Steps of the Heart is a series. The good news is the second book in the series Next Dance is already written. I still have a lot of editing to do so I am hoping to release in about 6 months. While you are waiting don't forget to listen to some really great music and get off your ass and dance!

Thank you and I love you all!

AUTHOR

Di Anne is originally from Wheeling, West Virginia and now lives in the central Florida area with her husband Sig and their chihuahua Lola. She could always be found at gatherings and parties telling the stories and sharing memories amongst her family and friends. After meeting a romance author at work one day, she discovered she had a story to tell and took the author's advice to write it! Di Anne tried the suggested method and immediately walked away from it. Then two months later she opened her iPad and using the Notes app (without a keyboard) started writing. Once she started writing she couldn't stop the story from flowing.

Two years ago, when she started on this writing journey, she walked away from watching television and made big changes in her life. She opened her mind and her heart and music became her motivation and muse.

Di Anne's day job is in the retail beauty industry... so she's a bit of a diva and has a true love for makeup and skincare. But her guilty pleasure, aside from makeup and music, is high heels. You might say she's addicted to them and has acquired quite a collection. When Di Anne's not writing you will find her on her beautiful patio sporting a set headphones, listening to music and dreaming up a new story idea.

Facebook Di Anne Sandvik

Twitter @DiAnneSandvik

Instagram dianne1978

Introducing new Author Stacy Fischer

Iron Will

Chapter One

It was your typical Monday morning for Rowan Walker. She was faintly aware of the crisp aroma of her favorite Kona coffee already brewing in the kitchen just as her alarm sounded with "Come and Get Your Love". She reluctantly drug herself out of bed, poured a cup of coffee fit for the gods and threw on her gym clothes with just enough time to make it to the new gym in town.

They say what doesn't kill you makes you stronger, well Rowan decided to make this a literal statement. One month after being left at the altar by who she thought was her forever and always she came to realize that she had lost who she was and was willing to try anything to get her back. Determined to purge all the memories from past loves and heartache she decided to sign up for a personal trainer and take out her new found aggressions through sweat and self-inflicted physical pain.

"Welcome to the Iron Will." A tall blonde with a body as if it had been carved from stone greeted her with a smile.

"Hi, I'm here to meet with Alex. It's my first training session with her."

"I'm sorry but do you mean Alex Cooper?" She pulled up a clipboard with all of the gyms appointments for the day, followed her finger down the line to Alex's column and asks, "Are you Rowan Walker?"

"That's me," is all that escaped my mouth before I found myself fumbling for breath at the mere site of perfection rounding the corner and heading directly towards us. He was 6'4" with dark brown hair styled with a classic crooner cut, five o'clock shadow with eyes as blue as the Caribbean ocean two full sleeves of tattoo's and a build reminiscent of Thor.

"Rowan? Alex, nice to meet you."

She was too busy imagining this statue of a man passionately pinning her against the wall to register that this man, the only man to ever make her pussy throb simply by looking at her was the Alex she was there to meet.

"Alex...you're Alex Cooper. Of course you're Alex fucking Cooper!"

"Excuse me?"

"I'm sorry, it's just when I signed up for these sessions I naturally assumed I was signing up with a female trainer not the Rock."

As he stared me down like I was the crazy lady in the park I couldn't help but find myself falling into a fantasy world in my head. I promptly pulled myself back to reality and apologized to Alex for being so brash then decided to jump in head first.

"All right, so where do we begin?"

"Why don't you tell me a little about your current fitness routine."

"Well, it's pretty much nonexistent unless you count curling beers."

"Okay so we are starting from scratch, got it. Follow me."

I trailed closely behind Alex staring at his perfectly chiseled Adonis like ass so intensely that I could paint you a picture from mere memory if I had to. We walked down the long hallway leading into the main gym. The hallway was painted a deep burgundy with the Iron Will logo painted in black and white with a bright yellow accent. There were pictures lining the halls practically from floor to ceiling of all the top names in the world figure competition circuit, most of which have trained alongside the gyms owners. The smell of sweat mixed with iron and rubber flooring lingered in the air so thick it hugged me tighter than any body builder ever could. As we reached the large opening leading into the gym I felt my nerves begin to kick in. It was starting to hit me that this beautiful man was going to be working very closely with me for as long as it took to wipe away all memory of Bryson Taylor and the broken shell of a woman he threw out like yesterday's trash.

If you're not begging for rest you're not training your best. This was painted down the length of Alex's office door.

"Go ahead and have a seat Rowan."

His office was exactly what you would imagine for a personal trainer. A large mirror directly in front of his desk, ideal for admiring his perfect physique. Two arm chairs for potential clients to make themselves right at home while discussing their options and signing on the dotted line, a rather large glass top desk with a MacBook Pro off to the left hand corner and finished off with several framed pictures of himself in Iron Man competitions across the country.

I felt very out of my element, but I kept my composure while Alex investigated further what my physical goals were.

"Rowan, tell me what is it that you're looking to achieve with us here at the Iron Will?"

I was quickly learning that Alex was all business.

After seeing the intensity within the gym's walls I wanted to scream FUCK IF I KNOW! But I thought about it for a moment. "Simply put Alex, I'm hoping to find myself again. I want to push myself to my limit and sculpt my inner badass."

He took a minute to finalize my contract, hit print and that was it… I was signing away my body to be at his command for at least the foreseeable future.

"Rowan, let's hit the ground running. Today we are just going to see where your physical ability lies so that I can customize a routine for you."

Weighted box squats, burpees, kettlebell swings and step ups. It's like he is speaking a foreign language to me but I'm trying to take it all in and focus on developing a proper form rather than rushing through each motion in a race towards the finish line. After what seemed like an eternity with this man my body felt as if it were on the brink of collapse. Dripping in sweat and aching more than I would have thought humanly possible, Alex said the sexiest sentence any man had ever said to me.

"Great job today Rowan. Your first sessions under your belt."

I had never been happier then right at that moment as this torture session came to a close. Now I just had to figure out how to move as I attempted to make my way to the gyms main entrance.

"Make sure you follow the dietary plan I gave you and drink your water, complete at least 45 minutes of cardio each day that we are not training. I'll see you in two days for your next session, sound good?"

Shaking my head in agreement I paused for a minute pondering if this pain was worth it and realized that physical pain was all that I felt. It was the first time since being left at the altar that I wasn't feeling sorry for my recently shattered heart. I could focus on nothing more than how badly my body hurt and I found myself looking forward to my next sculpting session as Alex called it.

If putting my body through this premeditated hell was what it took to not feel heartache then I was not only looking forward to my next run in with Alex, I was in love with the idea of exercise and the entire weight training lifestyle.

Bring it on Mr. Cooper!